T0268724

Last to Leave the Room

Also by Caitlin Starling

The Death of Jane Lawrence
The Luminous Dead
Yellow Jessamine

Last to Leave the Room

A NOVEL

CAITLIN STARLING

ST. MARTIN'S PRESS
NEW YORK

First published in the United States by St. Martin's Press, an imprint of St. Martin's Publishing Group

LAST TO LEAVE THE ROOM. Copyright © 2023 by Caitlin Starling. All rights reserved. Printed in the United States of America. For information, address St. Martin's Publishing Group, 120 Broadway, New York, NY 10271.

www.stmartins.com

Design by James Sinclair

The Library of Congress Cataloging-in-Publication Data is available upon request.

ISBN 978-1-250-28261-3 (hardcover)
ISBN 978-1-250-28262-0 (ebook)

eISBN 9781250282620

Our books may be purchased in bulk for promotional, educational, or business use. Please contact your local bookseller or the Macmillan Corporate and Premium Sales Department at 1-800-221-7945, extension 5442, or by email at MacmillanSpecialMarkets@macmillan.com.

First Edition: 2023

10 9 8 7 6 5 4 3 2 1

For James

I'm afraid.

Are you? Or are you excited?
This is only stage fright, Dr. Rivers. Activation of the sympathetic
nervous system in anticipation of a crucial performance.
You chose this. You called to me, and I answered.
And now we have to finish our work.
Are you ready?

Yes.

Don't hesitate.
It will be harder if you hesitate.

The City

Chapter One

Dr. Tamsin Rivers stands in the abyss.

The absence of light and sound has a weight all its own, separate from the gravity that, along with the sound of her blood and breath, are the only reminders that she has a body. She is standing on a catwalk, suspended in the center of a geodesic dome far below the city of San Siroco. Its walls are several body lengths thick, and the sensors it houses are silent, giving off no telltale hum of electricity. Even the air is tasteless, scentless. She keeps one hand always on the guideline, the only way back to the door she entered through.

This space is a cathedral of the mind. A monument to science. Her flawed human body vibrates with the deprivation of its senses, unable to perceive the immensity around her, and after twenty minutes, a red light beside the single door will switch on, to remind her to turn back. Without the light, some people never come out. Left to their own devices, it's entirely possible that they'd sit here until they starved.

Tamsin has never felt at risk of losing herself. Her thoughts remain coherent. The panic never comes for her, nor the dissolution; only a quiet, invigorating hum. Here, away from emails and funding requests and board meetings, in the heart of her research, she knows exactly who she is.

There's data flowing through the chamber, invisible and constant. Test messages sent across the city, traveling along a network of chambers just like this one. Cut out all the noise, and the message comes through, fast and crisp and clear. Stronger than any cell signal, faster than any satellite, bouncing between technological mirrors that can only exist here, in the deep quiet. If it works, she's going to revolutionize the world. She's going to be lauded as the fucking genius that she is.

And it *does* work.

Just a little longer to prove out all the particulars. A few more months, maybe a year or two, and her name will enter history. Dr. Tamsin Rivers, bringer of a new age.

The air shifts, wobbling in her ears, her lungs. The change startles her. She turns and sees a sliver of light grow and expand. Not the call-back light, but the glow of the entryway silhouetting a figure.

The dome swallows all sound, even her footsteps as she retreats back toward the rest of the lab. Yvette Olsen, one of her researchers, isn't looking at her, her attention fixed on the tablet she's holding. Her expression is grim.

The door to the chamber shuts behind them.

"Well?" Tamsin asks, eyes adjusting once more to the light.

"There's been an incident, at the boundary," Yvette says. "We officially have a problem."

A few more months, maybe a year or two, and her name will enter history.

Unless everything falls apart first.

"The city is sinking."

Tamsin's voice rolls out across the conference room. She is pristine, her scarlet curls perfectly defined and gleaming down her back, her dress precisely tailored, her makeup impeccable. Her audience, made up of most of Myrica Dynamic's C-suite executives and many of the other R&D section heads, watches her carefully, rigid in their seats. Murmurs ripple through the room, but they're soft. Respectful and cautious.

She taps the clicker in her hand. Behind her, the dark screen comes to life, showing a wire-frame model of the city. It stretches well aboveground in the downtown core and plunges below the surface in a warren-path of subway tunnels.

Another tap. The map lights up at three different points along the tunnels. "The first reports came from three different engineering teams monitoring the subway expansion project. Survey equipment at each site began showing a regular, consistent decrease in altitude. After ruling out sampling errors, mechanical defects, and algorithmic GPS drift, we went hunting."

The altitude drops are minor, and there have been no fissures in the earth, no delays to the construction work underway. But while the subway project isn't officially hers, her research is the reason Myrica Dynamics bought and privatized the crumbling network of infrastructure below the city. It's her the engineers come to, because anything that impacts the subways impacts her. It's a lot easier to build unsanctioned labs that far down with a plausible reason to have teams working on subterranean maintenance and the desperate thankfulness of the city's government helping them not look too closely.

So if there's going to be a problem, she needs to be seen dealing with it. She has to lead the charge. It's the only way she can ensure her research continues in the meantime.

On the screen, the unremarkable green lines sketching out the city turn to orange in a jagged ring, tracing the rough outline of the consolidated metropolitan area. The image shifts down, but at this scale, it's not so much visible as subconsciously unsettling.

"By taking measurements at sites across the city, we have been able to determine that the subsidence is happening in nearly every neighborhood of San Siroco." Not the suburbs, though. On a whim, they'd checked population-density maps, and that had *almost* fit the pattern. But after months of looking, they've found no direct mathematical correlation with the boundary, nor any other explanation for the sudden stop.

It's almost as if the subsidence simply ends beyond what Tamsin thinks of as San Siroco proper, ignoring every objectively measurable variable.

Confirmation bias, she's sure.

"The geological traits the sites have in common are superficial at best, with nothing directly putting them at risk of subsidence. Only a handful are connected to the subway system. And over the last two months of observation, all have subsided at a rate of twenty-seven millimeters per month. Consistently."

That gets a reaction.

Several different low conversations spring up across the darkened room. At the far end of the conference table, Mx. Woodfield, dressed in her usual sharp black suit, watches Tamsin. Not the screen behind her, not the burgeoning tumult around them both. The muscles between Tamsin's shoulders tighten; there's going to be an unavoidable discussion after this, about her withholding of this information. For all the freedom she's been granted working for Myrica, there are limits.

She's crossed one.

Tamsin does not wait out the chatter; if she tried, she might be standing there for hours. Instead, she lifts one pale hand, advances the presentation once more. She makes herself relax and ignore Woodfield.

The wire-frame begins to sink again, this time noticeably.

Everybody in the room falls silent, staring.

"I don't think I have to tell you that this degree of subsidence is unprecedented. Its consistency across such a wide area is deeply concerning, as is its independence from the ongoing construction efforts. Our best theory is that it's some formerly undiscovered geological process, with no currently suspected cause, perhaps a micro-plate subduction event."

Their best theory is also highly unlikely, and everybody in this room knows why it's a closed-door meeting: they have to rule out Myrica Dynamics's involvement first, before anybody else can start asking questions. Basic damage control, the same instinct that made her start investigating after the first unsettling reports.

Luckily, the precise nature of her team's experiments in the deep labs is strictly confidential. Nobody in this room, aside from Mx. Woodfield, has any real reason to ask if the labs might be connected; their physical construction was completed almost a year ago, well ahead of these issues, and their exact locations and numbers are proprietary.

And they aren't connected.

Probably.

She pushes the thought aside, as she has repeatedly over the last several weeks. Red, blinking indicators come to life along the grid. First one, then ten, and then an eruption, elegant and terrible. "Regardless of its origin, unless steps are taken to anticipate and mitigate its effects, we have to assume that we'll be seeing disruptions in everything from fiber-optic and water lines to road integrity within the next six months. In fact, as of this morning, we have our first confirmed incident."

This time, the response is an explosion, voices no longer kept low. Tamsin glances at Mx. Woodfield, then to Mr. Klein, the head of Myrica Dynamics's public relations department; their reactions are going to influence whatever she does next most directly. Woodfield is, as usual, inscrutable. Klein is less so; his face has gone blotchy beneath his fashionable beard, and his hands grip his pen tightly. They must itch for his phone, but those were all collected at the door.

There aren't any mentions of the subsidence on social media yet; she had her team check. And the last thing they need is for any inkling of this to leak before they have a plan.

"We've verified reports of a water-main break in the Sunnyside neighborhood, at the edge of the subsidence zone," she says over the din. "There's no visible sinkhole at this time, but we are confident the crack in the pipe was caused by strain due to the phenomenon. Now, that section of the water and sewage system is in a very poor state of repair; we don't think it's likely that there will be a repeat in the immediate future. But it's coming."

Evelyn Herrera, the head of legal, sits forward, face grim. "Who, exactly, is working on this?"

"My team is intending to stay the course for as long as we're of help, given our access to subterranean facilities. However, we are not geologists." People quiet down; Myrica Dynamics doesn't *have* any geologists. "We will need additional capacity to both gather data and liaison with whatever experts we decide to pull in."

Legal looks unhappy. Public relations looks apoplectic. "Do we know if anything like this is happening elsewhere?" Klein demands. "Is San Francisco seeing the same sinking?"

"Unknown at this time. We haven't reached out, for obvious reasons."

That earns a satisfied nod from legal. Tamsin knows how to keep containment.

"Nothing discussed here can leave this room," she says. "Not without authorization and clearance from Ms. Herrera's office. If you think your teams can help, or you have questions, contact her or me."

(It's a power move, and not a subtle one, but it's also reasonable; that buys her some leeway, even if Herrera shoots her a warning look for deputizing her without prior discussion. Tamsin ignores it.)

"I want to see the raw data," one of the other R&D heads says. "Will that be made available?"

"Of course," Tamsin says. The discussion devolves into further logistics after that, with everybody jockeying for position, feeling out just how screwed they are. Nobody looks more interested, or excited, than anyone else, which means nobody's going to play the hero in an attempt to get publication credit on their newly discovered disaster.

This is what she likes about the private sector. People here focus on what needs to get done. They're cutthroat in a different way.

Ten minutes before the scheduled end of the meeting, Mx. Woodfield stands, smooths out the line of her suit, and steps out of the room, gloved hand at one ear. No doubt reporting in to Mr. Thomas, Myrica Dynamics's owner and Tamsin's official manager. He doesn't do much managing, but he uses Woodfield as his eyes and ears.

He's the reason she was hired, the reason she's been able to pursue her research as far as she has. He's the one who will ultimately decide if she can continue or not.

His opinion is the only one that matters. She wishes he'd been here in person; she wishes she knew what Woodfield was telling him. Her chest buzzes with unresolved nerves. She boxes them up and tucks them away, focusing on the discussion instead.

Finally, the only other person left in the room is her assistant, Cara Vigneault. Tamsin takes a seat at the conference table, shifting aside barely touched mugs of coffee. Cara sets down a glass thermos of steeping green tea and a small silicon pod containing two aspirin.

"That went well," Cara says.

"As well as it could have," Tamsin concedes. She swallows the aspirin dry and watches the soft drift of color as the tea leaves give up their caffeine.

"Klein's going to have a field day figuring out how to sell this to the city," Cara says, flipping the thermos once the tea has steeped enough. Off comes the top compartment with the spent leaves. "What should I do when he comes asking for more details on the project?"

"Assure him it's not related and still confidential." She's more worried about legal on that front, but they won't approach her directly. Woodfield's oversight ensures that, one of the many benefits of their arrangement. "And offer me up as a public face, if he needs it." It's not her first choice. She doesn't want to be on nightly news shows for anything but her communications technology. But out of the people on her team, she's highest ranked and best suited to walking the tightrope necessary to protect herself—and therefore Myrica Dynamics—from any scrutiny. She has the attractive face, the facility with lying, the ability to be political. "At the very least, say I'll come to any meetings with the city."

If they're lucky (if Klein is good, and he is), the city will be desperate for their help, the way they were desperate for Myrica Dynamics to buy the subway system from them and renovate it "*for the public good.*" But there's always the chance that, as a private company, Myrica will be shut out.

But then again, if they get territorial, they'll never get their shit together long enough to figure out what's actually going on. Leave it to San Siroco to get so scared they hamstring themselves.

Cara is typing on her tablet. Tamsin watches her for a moment, unscrewing the thermos and taking a sip of the tea. It goes down sour and too hot. By the time Cara looks up again, Tamsin has pushed it aside. She nods at the darkening sky. "Go home. I'll text you if I need anything. Nothing left here."

Thirty seconds later, Tamsin is blessedly alone. She lets her head fall against the leather seat back. Another few minutes and then the elevators will be empty, and she can head home without smoothing any more ruffled feathers. Take out that box with her worries about Mr. Thomas and Woodfield once she's gotten herself a drink. Looking sidelong at her phone, she swipes over to her car-service app.

A text alert drops from the top of her screen.

> From: Lachlan Woodfield
> Perigee. Two drinks.

She was wrong. It's going to be a long night.

Chapter Two

Perigee is a slick little speakeasy tucked deep in the business district, a few miles from Myrica Dynamics's campus. At this time of night, traffic is heavy, and walking might have been faster, but Tamsin takes advantage of the delay to apply fresh lipstick and gently tease her hair into something more appropriate for the venue. Appearances are important after all.

A summons from Lachlan Woodfield holds as much weight as a court order, with much swifter censure if she takes it in contempt. She is not precisely a dog on a leash, but obedience is still her best option. A show of humility, followed by acting as she always does: like she deserves to be here, like she knows the rules.

Her lips are curling ever so faintly, a predator's smile, as she passes into the air-conditioned cool of an eighty-story high-rise.

There are no signs, but Tamsin makes her way unerringly to the bank of elevators. She presses the button farthest to the left, which calls only one car. That car feeds all of the businesses in the tower, but it also is the only one that goes down.

As the car begins its descent, five flights into the earth, she reflects on the very real possibility that this office building will soon be having some startling foundation problems.

Anybody else might have been too frightened to step in the car in the wake of that evening's announcements, but she knows there's time. Her own labs aren't showing any stress yet, and they're nestled far deeper underground than this little gem. It's the sewer systems that are going to feel the pinch next, according to the projections, and that's still a few weeks off.

The elevator comes to a stop.

The bar is more Tamsin's style than Lachlan's, and more Mr. Thomas's than either: deep teal wallpaper and gilded fixtures, a hammered-copper bar and a surfeit of glass and mood lighting. There's a brief moment where Tamsin half expects to see the CEO in the flesh, but when she spots Lachlan, she's alone.

On balance, it's probably better that way.

Lachlan Woodfield is a tall, broad woman with either a taste or a dress-code requirement for tailored black suits and shiny leather brogues, which set off her dark, slicked-back hair and her gold-kissed skin to great effect. She's sitting in their usual booth, small and private, and she's still got her gloves on as she idly turns her rocks glass. Condensation beads on her leather-clad fingers.

Her eyes have been on Tamsin since the elevator opened, as always.

Two drinks does not mean that Lachlan desires her company, of course. It means Tamsin has earned a dressing down for bypassing Lachlan and Mr. Thomas, springing the problem on them at the same time as everybody else. Whatever Mr. Thomas's opinion on the matter, his feedback is going to be more involved than *Here's your funding, enjoy.*

She steels herself. Two drinks, and whatever it is will be over.

The bar seating is full, as are most of the tables. Tamsin makes her way to their booth, not staring back at Lachlan but not looking away, either. This is always the most awkward part. It's a long walk.

And then she's there, slipping into her seat and setting her purse off to one side of the table.

"Mx. Woodfield," Tamsin says, and the greeting loosens her limbs with an imagined hydraulic hiss. Their game is now once more in the active phase, and she knows how to play. They've worked together now for eight years. At times, they go months between meetings. It depends on Tamsin's current mandate from Mr. Thomas, her general willingness to play by the rules set out for her, and likely the demands of whomever else Lachlan's been assigned to . . . manage.

(Tamsin has never been able to figure out who those people might be.)

"Dr. Rivers," Lachlan replies, reaching across to take Tamsin's purse and set it in the curve of the bench seat, between them both. It's courteous on the surface, but it's really a reminder of how easily Lachlan can cross her boundaries and how little Tamsin can do about it.

Manage is the best term she can think of for what Lachlan does, but it's management in the sense of a sheepdog to its flock, not business administration. Lachlan is, above all else, somebody who fixes problems by any means necessary. Tamsin is at risk, always, of becoming that problem. She has a great deal of freedom, a great deal of funding, and a great deal of access to proprietary corporate data. The job plays to her strengths. Back in her academic days, she bypassed the softer sciences to avoid having to comport or edit herself for internal ethical-review boards. Not all of what she's asked to do, or wants to do, is strictly advisable or legal.

And that means that for all that she's a jewel in the crown of Myrica's research department, she's also a liability—and she's ambitious. The risk of her straying to a competitor or spilling secrets for a profit is high.

Among other things, Lachlan is in her life to make sure she doesn't. It's a fair arrangement.

"And what have you ordered me?" Tamsin asks, crossing her legs, the tip of her shoe very close to Lachlan's knee.

They don't touch.

This is as much a power play as dragging Herrera into a gatekeeping role in the new emergency project, but Lachlan's answer will also say a great deal about the mood Mr. Thomas is in.

"A Negroni," Lachlan says, leaning back against the booth, one arm along the top of the cushion. It's not the most aggressive maneuver; it's a drink Lachlan knows Tamsin likes, something Tamsin has ordered for herself in the past, but it is one that lends itself to slow sipping. A shorter leash, to keep Tamsin's attention.

"I apologize for what must have seemed like an end run around proper protocol," Tamsin says. The room is designed to dampen sound, but it's still polite to keep things vague. She drops her gaze to the table for no more than a breath. "But in this case, I wanted to start the conversation with a path to a solution instead of an ambiguous problem."

Lachlan takes a sip of her drink. "You certainly have everybody's attention."

"I'll be sending over a report of what we know to you in the morning." It will be a very different report than the one she's making available to the team, and Lachlan inclines her head in understanding.

The waiter drops off Tamsin's drink along with a variety dish of olives.

Tamsin considers, but doesn't order, the fig appetizer; she doesn't remember the last time she ate, but she doesn't want to encourage interruptions, either.

Besides, she likes olives. She eats three.

When they're alone again, Lachlan says, "We're concerned that by creating a larger investigatory body for the problem, we may run into containment issues."

"Either we expand the scope or somebody else does it for us," Tamsin says. "This way, we guide the discussion. On the off chance there's a connection, we're already there on the ground."

"Does that mean you haven't ruled out some causative link with your labs?" Lachlan's voice goes a degree colder. It's not an intimidation tactic as much as it is analytical. It still makes Tamsin uneasy. The report is going to cover this exact issue, and yet she still feels pointedly exposed, being asked directly.

Tamsin eats another olive, then sits back and cradles her drink. "You can't prove a negative, Mx. Woodfield."

Lachlan taps two fingers against the table, then knocks back a good third of her drink. She sucks her teeth after, as if searching for patience in her enamel. "Please, Dr. Rivers," she says at last. "This is not a time to be your iconoclastic self. I need straight answers, as you get them, not a miraculous presentation once you have all the grit cleaned away."

Tamsin glances to one of the windows made of a thick, transparent material that isn't entirely glass and can withstand the crush of earth against the walls. Recessed lights illuminate the dirt and rock beyond. "And you'll get them. In the report tomorrow, properly encrypted. Trust me that I'm doing the necessary work."

A click as Lachlan sets down her glass. "I want to hear you say it."

And that's new. That's *galling*. Tamsin bites back a snarl and takes a too-large gulp of her own cocktail, then sets it on the table between them so hard it nearly cracks the glass.

Calm. Focus. Lachlan is not the enemy. She isn't a friend, either, but they ultimately need one another.

In another life, they might even have wanted one another.

"The onset of the issue postdates the beginning of our experiments by a wide margin," she says quietly, picking her words with care. All the drilling finished up a year ago. All the construction was completed four months after. For eight months, they've been testing and calibrating and trying to work out exactly how the new technology functions and what *else* it can do, but the first few millimeters of loss were only measured two and a half months ago. "However, preliminary analysis does show a correlation between the beginning of our active testing cycles and the likely start of the subsidence. It's not a direct one-to-one, but it's statistically significant." She lets that hang in the air between them, sipping languidly at her Negroni once more. "The lack of discernible underlying geologic process is . . . concerning, but we also have no theories as to how data transfer might account for any of what we're seeing. While the timing overlaps, the locations don't, and there's no known mechanism."

Her handler is entirely focused on her, making her feel trapped by the booth at her back. It isn't easy to admit to fault, even knowing this is the safest person she can tell. "There's a good chance we won't need to disclose the existence of the labs," Tamsin says. "I would like to formally request that we continue to run our experiments. We're getting very close to the next phase of testing, and there is still a real possibility that the relationship we're seeing emerge is not causative. We may even be able to better monitor the problem from our vantage point."

Lachlan's expression is grim as she spears an olive on a toothpick, pale wood contrasting sharply against her gloves. "You have provisional permission to continue, on the condition that you report in on a regular basis. Full transparency, Dr. Rivers."

"Of course."

That has always been the deal: Mr. Thomas receives an accurate accounting of her work, no matter the circumstances, and she doesn't have to scrounge for grant money. It's a fair enough trade, and he has yet to hold any failures or missteps against her.

"You'll be given every resource necessary. You will be given a leadership role in determining Myrica Dynamics's response, as public or private as you'd prefer it to be."

Inside, Tamsin thrills at that. Outside, she quirks one manicured brow. "Surprising."

"The subway lines breaking will cost a lot of money, Dr. Rivers."

And a lot of good will goes unspoken.

Myrica bought the crumbling money pit of San Siroco's public-transit system to allow Tamsin to do her research, but in doing so, they also positioned themselves as a company dedicated to the public good. If anybody connects Myrica's actions to any of the impending disaster, it's not just Tamsin who will go down for it.

They're going to walk this fucking tightrope together.

"Anything else?" Tamsin asks, finishing her drink. One down.

Lachlan mirrors her, then meets her gaze placidly. She gestures for the waiter. He arrives quickly.

"I'll have another old-fashioned," Lachlan says.

For her second drink, she's being given a choice. It's a small concession. A show of approval, if not trust. "Classic daiquiri," she says. Simple, comforting, entirely the opposite of Lachlan's choice, and quickly drinkable.

The waiter leaves.

"If the two projects begin to conflict," Lachlan says, "you are to immediately prioritize the subsidence. How crucial are the underground labs to the actual functioning of the project? Beyond the research. Day to day."

"Essential," Tamsin replies. "The communications protocol requires the shielding provided by the node depth."

"It can't be replicated aboveground now that you've had eight months to test? We can't build something to spec?"

"No." The labs take advantage of the quiet of the deep earth, the lack of particle interference, the vast and empty dense space. It goes beyond the shielding possible with feet of concrete, and it's the only way to have messages mirror instantaneously between rooms miles and miles apart, bypassing the limitations of satellites and fiber-optic cables and cell towers.

She refuses to give up on it, not when the invention of that technology will immortalize her name.

"Then you need to prepare an exit strategy," Lachlan says. "The moment there is any indication that causation is likely, the whole project ends."

Her chest tightens.

"Mx. Woodfield—"

"Nonnegotiable." She has the gall to look apologetic.

Tamsin feels sick.

Her daiquiri arrives.

"Is there anything else I need to know?" Lachlan prompts when she doesn't reach for it.

Tamsin doesn't flinch. She takes her glass, sips, sets it aside. "No," she lies. "You said I'll have the resources I need to cover all angles on this?"

"Of course."

"Approval to work off-site?"

Lachlan's brows rise. "Depends. How far off-site?"

"Just from home. Away from office politics, as needed." It's not her usual mode; she prefers to have an iron grip on her personnel as well as her experiments. But it's a reasonable request. Lachlan would need to have a very good reason to deny her. "If you want my full attention, that's the best way to get it. A few days a week where I can focus on the data only."

"Consider it done."

The nausea hasn't let up, but it gentles now. She can do this. She *will* do this. "I'll figure out the causative factors. We're far from running out of options." She smiles and holds out her coupe, clinks it gently against Lachlan's glass. "I promise."

Lachlan's knee shifts and brushes the spike of Tamsin's heel.

"Good."

Chapter Three

Tamsin leaves Perigee half an hour later and calls a ride home.

The town car winds through San Siroco. Traffic pulses around it in a steady flow, then trickles out block by block, turn by turn. The night is dark through the tinted windows, but she drinks in every detail just for the stimulation. The distraction. She can still hear Lachlan's voice echoing in the back of her skull, a counterpoint to the headache that's making its way back.

Is there anything else I need to know?

Lying to Lachlan is dangerous, and Tamsin doesn't enjoy doing it. She's a confident liar, but she has no real sense of the scope of Lachlan's oversight of her, and every lie is a gamble at a high-stakes table. It's easier to be honest, and in return, Lachlan has never punished her for that honesty.

But sometimes lying is necessary.

The car begins to slow, then pulls to a smooth stop outside of Tamsin's house. She exits the car without a word to the driver, heels clicking on the manicured path, through the professionally landscaped garden, up to the smooth white facade of her house.

She taps out the lock code on the front door, resisting the urge to look over her shoulder. It's entirely possible that Lachlan has a tracker on her phone; it's impossible for her to have access to Tamsin's home security system.

Her cat, Penrose, is waiting for her just inside the door. He rubs up against her shins, oblivious to her anxiety. She exchanges her heels for house shoes, letting the routine of the night get beneath her skin and start to unwind the knots there. Organic raw food goes down on the floor for

Penrose, and she dumps a pre-portioned cup of fruit and vegetables into the blender with probiotic yogurt and churns up her own dinner.

Five minutes to make, five minutes to swallow down. Pre-batched smoothies and meal kits and soy-based meal replacements are the life-blood of the tech industry, convenient and delivered on subscription plan, and it all comes with a nice discount thanks to working for Myrica. The strain from the day starts to fall off of her as it settles in her belly. She's home. Away from the lab, the board room, Lachlan.

How strange, to yearn to be here so much when for so long, it's only been a place to sleep, a monument to her life's success that she hardly utilizes.

And now she's bought herself an excuse to stay here a few days a week, unobserved, freely granted. Some of that time will have to be given over to the subsidence project, of course; she'll have to put in the hours, emails, virtual meetings, and reports. But that will still leave her at least all of her commute time and likely a few more hours besides that she can carefully carve out.

Her blood fizzes with the thought, popping, tugging at her veins like the iron in it is calling to a magnet. Urging her into the hallway.

Because while the city is sinking, Tamsin's basement is sinking faster.

Where every other site in San Siroco measures a three-millimeter-per-week decrease, the instruments Tamsin has set up in her own home indicate three *centimeters*. Just like all the other sites spread across the city, the rate of subsidence is even and the area it affects seemingly precisely limited. Tamsin's basement is sinking, but not in a way that impacts the structural integrity of her home. It might be fairer to say that the walls of her basement are stretching, their measurements shifting but their structure remaining consistent.

Unfortunately, that's physically impossible.

She has not logged any of her research with her team. She keeps her observations on the encrypted partition of her personal computer. Until she knows the cause, until she knows what makes her house so different, she doesn't want anybody else to know that her basement is now fifteen centimeters deeper than it used to be.

If anybody else ever learns of it, they might draw connections. Start to wonder if maybe Tamsin is tied not just to the solution, but the cause.

If *Lachlan* finds out, Tamsin's research will be shut down immediately. She'll be judged unfit to continue it.

That cannot happen.

She's installed two locks on her basement door. One is electronic, like the one on the front door, though it's disconnected from the house network, instead linked to a firewalled setup originating within the basement proper. The second is purely mechanical. Neither is easy to crack, and just one should have been enough to quell her nerves.

But better to be thorough.

Tamsin slips through the door and locks it behind her. The stairs are steeper than they once were, each tread now just a hair under a centimeter farther apart, and she takes them carefully. The brain doesn't do well with subtle changes; she'd tripped and nearly fallen last week, anticipating a step where one wasn't quite present anymore. The stairs have no banister, a concession to modern architectural style.

If she adds a railing herself, will that distort, too? Or is whatever is happening here limited to the architecture that existed at the start?

An experiment for another day, perhaps.

The basement lights used to be warm and soft, but two days after she first noticed the shift, when she became certain that her observations weren't just the result of an overstimulated, exhausted mind primed to see subsidence in everything, she switched them out to five-thousand-lumen bulbs and added several standing lamps. There are no shadows left now, save for beneath the workstation she's set up along the right-hand wall.

Everything is laid bare as she documents. The measurements she takes along the stairs and each wall confirm the steady progression has continued in her absence. The floor remains level. There are no cracks, no fissures, no points of stress.

This morning, her basement ended 2.585 meters belowground. Now it is 2.587.

She photographs everything, all her markers and test points along the walls, and checks her instrumentation. The experiments her lab is carrying out at the subway sites are replicated here in miniature, to the extent she's been able to filch the equipment without anybody noticing. An older-model seismograph shows no changes. Air-composition tests show the same atmosphere, no trace of any perception-altering chemicals or off-gassing from stressed building materials.

Her signal tests show no bleed-through from the node labs across the city.

By the time she's done, it's after midnight. The light has not changed. She knows, distantly, that she's tired, but she lingers anyway. She looks at the white walls with their careful markers, at the stairs that will eventually grow difficult to climb, at the utilitarian furniture.

Tamsin has never had strong feelings about her house before. All that's mattered is its privacy, its adherence to certain standards of quality and aesthetic pleasure, its ability to impress her few visitors and to allow her to rest and recharge between stints in the lab. The basement itself went unused, useless.

Now it's the most important thing in her life, outstripping even the deep darkness of the node labs. It's the greatest question of her career.

If she can't unravel the cause of the subsidence, if she can't find a way to stop it, she's going to lose everything.

Chapter Four

She doesn't take advantage of the work-from-home allowance immediately. There's some additional setup to do on the tech side, for one thing, and for another, it looks better if there's no abrupt transition right after her bombshell announcement.

Legal pulls her into a meeting first thing the next morning, and between them and PR, she barely has time to check her emails, let alone make the progress Lachlan is after. Still, she gets the confidential analysis off to Mr. Thomas and tries not to get nervy and irritable when she has to stay late that day, and the next, putting out fires.

On the third day, she bypasses the office and goes straight to one of the node labs.

She hires a ride to a nondescript office building two miles north of the city center. She doesn't use the standard ride-share services, instead paying extra to ensure she always receives a higher class of car, of discretion, of service. The driver of this car opens the door for her, and she steps out, shouldering her purse, and turns left. She takes the nearby stairs down below the street.

The subway stop is freshly renovated and in active use, recently reopened to the public. When the train pulls in, precisely on time, its brakes no longer screech and squeal. Passengers cross a clean and comfortable platform to board the climate-controlled car. The train pulls away again.

Much better than a couple years ago; then, the only passengers had been those who had no other choice, and the trains ran on a consistently inconsistent delay. Half the lines had been down at any given time. The whole system was a mess.

Myrica Dynamics's influence is undeniable.

Yvette meets her at the unmarked maintenance door with a lab coat and hard hat ready. Tamsin gears up, then boards the cart waiting for them. The third node lab is nearly a mile straight down; the drive will take a little north of fifteen minutes.

Two minutes in, her phone loses signal.

There's no visible change to the passages, even though she knows that they've descended, in total, roughly a thousand feet. Where her stairs are undeniably steep now, this incline feels just like she remembers it.

"Does it bother you?" she asks at minute five, somewhat to her own surprise.

Yvette seems similarly startled. They accelerate just a little more, until she eases her foot back to where it was on the pedal. "Does what bother me?"

"Being underground," Tamsin says.

Yvette's hands shift on the wheel. "There are no signs of structural instability," she says.

"That's not what I asked."

She shouldn't have asked anything. Why *did* she ask? It doesn't bother her, even though it should. Maybe that's it; maybe she's trying to recalibrate her own perceptions, remind herself of what a normal person would feel right now. Would feel walking into their basement to find it distorting, not knowing what the long-term impact will be.

"I don't know," Yvette says after a long, uncomfortable silence. She darts a wary glance at Tamsin. "I used to mind, when we first started down here. Now it's the same as working on a basement floor, just with a longer commute. It's so familiar that it's hard to remember what's happening sometimes. I can't *see* it, you know?"

Tamsin thinks of her basement, of the expanding steps, of nearly falling. She can't see it happening, either, but she can feel it.

"When I'm looking at the numbers, though . . . yeah. Sometimes it bothers me."

The lab consists of two main spaces. There is, of course, the node chamber itself. Its scale is hard to comprehend; even when it was being built, it was only ever visible from the inside, and there was nothing to compare it to but itself. Now, with no construction lighting and added acoustic dampening, it could be the size of a closet or of an aircraft hangar.

The rest of the lab, a much smaller proportion, is a series of workrooms, simple boxes filled with desks and computers, the latter hooked up to fiber-optic shielded internet specially run down this deep during construction. The walls are studded with fake windows, glowing rectangles of daylight-equivalent light, all soft focus as if seen through gauzy curtains. Nothing points to how deep they are. There are no portholes out into the sedimentary layers like at Perigee.

There aren't many other amenities. Food is tightly controlled down here; the HVAC system can only handle so much, and pungent odors have a tendency to linger. The only exception to that is coffee, but Tamsin has brought her own. She takes her thermos into the conference room, where the lab staff are waiting for her along with several other team members appearing by video chat. All conversation stops when she enters. Maybe half of the people there look right at her, the rest all finding something more interesting in their notes.

"Right," she says, taking her seat. "Let's get started, then."

Yvette clears her throat. "Phase two is almost complete," she says. "Preliminary data analysis shows everything is in line with our last round of projections. We should be ready to move on to phase three by the beginning of next month, barring anything unexpected."

A pointed silence follows on that. *Anything unexpected* now ranges from computer crashes to city-wide disaster. Or project cancellation. Nobody here knows what Lachlan told her the other day, but it's not hard to guess that their work is currently in the crosshairs.

And phase three is an escalation, a graduation from sending basic text chains to transmitting larger data packages. Images, this time, at medium resolution. It feels riskier, like baiting a bear. Superstitious anxiety makes her want to slow this down, stall out phase three until they have the subsidence sorted, but she can think of no mechanism that would make a few extra megabytes of data traveling through the earth cause the subsidence to accelerate.

If anything, it's binary. Either they transmit, or they don't. Either the city keeps sinking, or it stops.

"Has there been any change to our guidance?" asks one of the newer additions to the team. "Do they want us to hit pause?"

"No," Tamsin says. "We are to continue on with our primary research in addition to the subsidence investigation." Rustling papers, shifting bodies. "We're going to be pulling more hours for the foreseeable future," she confirms, "but Myrica Dynamics is pleased with our progress and with our attentiveness to the emerging issues.

"Speaking of, what are our latest measurements showing?"

The next fifteen minutes are full of predictable updates. Depths are still falling across the city. Soil is stable. No signs of any changes outside of the city limits, and no actual damage to any parts of the subway system.

"Still no changes in the rate of descent," Satya Chaudhari, leader of the second node lab team, summarizes. "And we've confirmed the chambers are still sinking as well."

Confirmations roll out from the representatives of the other node labs on the video link.

"So if there's an origin point, it's still lower than the nodes," Tamsin says.

"Or the surface is the origin point," Yvette says. "Things descending from the surface, instead of something below us giving way and causing a gap."

Silence falls over the table at that. They all know it's impossible for something to sink when nothing below it is disappearing or compressing. Geology does not work that way. *Physics* does not work that way.

Tamsin thinks about how only her basement has distorted; the ground floor of her house is as it always has been.

She has proof of the impossible right below where she sleeps.

Of course, there's a glaring hole in their methodology. Their measurements still reference depth only. Tamsin taps a few notes on her tablet, then looks up at the screen. "Dr. Torrence, do you have anything to add from your recent testing?"

Isaac Torrence works in her central lab, on projects only partially connected to the node network. He's young, only two years out of his PhD, with clean-cut good looks and a confident speaking voice. He looks up to her like a mentor, eager to grab on to her coattails and ride them to fame and glory. The problem is he's clumsy about it, and his fingers are liable to leave stains.

It was easy enough to suggest a new avenue of investigation to him, in order to plug the gap without raising any questions about where Tamsin had gotten the idea from.

It also serves as a validation tool. A test of how important what's happening in her basement is to the rest of the mystery.

"We've moved a few crystalline-growth matrices into some of the node labs and two R&D labs that happen to be underground. Our hope was to identify microtremors based on growth disruption. We haven't seen any indication of seismic activity, but they are showing a . . . distortion."

This is it. Tamsin sits forward before she can stop herself. "Please be more specific, Dr. Torrence."

He looks uncomfortable in the face of Tamsin's pronounced curiosity. "This is highly preliminary," he says. "We only have one week of data; there could still be measurement errors."

"Dr. Torrence."

"Compared to surface-and-above control groups, the matrices are stretching, Dr. Rivers. Like taffy, but with no discernible structural defects. They're simply measuring longer than they did previously."

Just like her basement. Tamsin's exhale is tremulous. The link remains, growing more undeniable by the day. But now that the information is in the team's hands, they can start looking for a solution.

"Thank you, Dr. Torrence," she says. "Please keep us apprised of any further developments. In the meantime, I want us to set up rapid-sampling length measurements on various substrates in the node labs. We'll want multiple reference points at each location in order to look for any signs of variation."

"Stretching makes no sense," says Dr. Chaudhari. "Particularly not without stability impacts. Are we certain—"

"It's worth measuring," Tamsin says, interrupting her smoothly. "But given its unprecedented nature, I do want this data and this testing initiative kept under lock and key. That way, if it proves to be an error, we don't end up with pie on our face." She offers up a smile, reassurance to a group growing even more anxious. "Is there anything else?"

The meeting lasts another ten minutes, more because of reluctance to go back into a world that seems newly incomprehensible than for any substantive reason. As they close out, she asks Dr. Torrence to remain a few minutes longer. Yvette casts her a curious look as she files out with the rest.

When the door is firmly shut, Tamsin gets up and approaches where the camera stares down at her with an unobtrusive, unblinking eye. "I'd like you to be at the meeting with the city on Thursday," she says.

Dr. Torrence flushes. "I appreciate your vote of confidence, Dr. Rivers, but—"

"Your involvement will be beneficial to your career," she says. "It will position you as part of the rising tide of researchers within Myrica Dynamics. You have a strong handle on what we do know so far and novel ideas of how to test what we're witnessing. That's what the city leadership needs to see right now." Her voice has grown warm, and a little conspiratorial. She can see, in real time, the effect of her flattery. Torrence glances over his shoulder, as if to make sure he's alone, then ducks his head with a small, pleased smile.

It's almost irritating. It's certainly a sign of poor character that he's swallowing all of this so readily.

"You'll present the details of what we know already. You'll be the representative of the work we're doing."

"But," he says, smile sagging, "without the growth-matrix data, I don't have anything to present that's my own work. And as you pointed out, we can't share that yet."

"Which is why you're going to lie."

Silence.

"You're going to tell them about the growth matrices. But instead of referring to stretching, I recommend you go with your initial seismic-disruption hypothesis. Microtremors are much more palatable than impossible distortions. And," she says, because Torrence has his mouth open as if to speak instead of gawp, "if we can get this problem contained and fixed promptly, the exact mechanism isn't going to matter to the people in charge. Do you understand me?"

It's petty, but Tamsin has learned, over the years, that pettiness is sometimes clever. Dr. Torrence isn't competition yet, but given another decade, he could be. He looks good in front of a camera, he's smart, he's willing to think outside the box. He's not prone to political maneuvering, but that's something that can be learned. Most importantly, he's *ambi-*

tious. He's not like Yvette Olsen or Satya Chaudhari, whose aspirations fit their roles; he's going to get root-bound someday, itching for expansion.

He's not going to get it, here or at a competitor.

"Yes, Dr. Rivers," he says. "I understand."

Tamsin cuts the connection.

After the meeting, Tamsin spends the remainder of her day in the lab. She pores over readouts, oversees the implementation of the new measuring apparatuses, and tries not to think too much about her basement.

When she can no longer focus, when the words are swimming before her eyes and she can't write another email, she packs up her things.

And then she stops off in the node chamber.

They can only get good data when the chamber is entirely empty, but their tests run near continuously; a twenty-minute stint of Tamsin visiting the chamber, appropriately flagged, gives them confounded data that can still be played with for side projects. She lets Yvette know she's going in, then makes her way through the series of doors between the habitable space of the lab and the yawning vault of the chamber.

By the time she passes through the final door, she feels her breathing more than she hears it. Her fingers close around the guideline as she steps out into the dark, shoeless, flat-footed. It's such a contrast to the brilliant light of her basement, and yet there's some element that feels the same. Essential. The isolation, maybe, or the questions that hang on every atomic particle in the air.

Give me an answer, she entreats the dark. *What are we missing?*

It's the same question she asks the basement. But where she means it to be desperate, she finds herself asking from the stance of a curious child. *I don't understand,* she wants to say. *I can't see how it all fits together.* Data flowing through the dark, mirrors upon mirrors. A room in her house, unremarkable, barely used. Is it happening anywhere else? Or is it only her?

How can *she* be the link?

Her thoughts drift there, on the black, and she loses track of where her limbs are, of whether her eyes are open or closed. Her heartbeat is loud inside her skull. There must be something she's overlooking, some element of her work, some connection between home and node. Or maybe there's no connection to the node at all. Maybe all her covering her own ass is right. There's no mechanism at all, just bad luck and coincidence. Maybe it's not her fault.

A red light turns on, outlining the catwalk and equipment in dim shadows. She startles, gripping the guideline tighter. She's never seen that light come on before, never had to be herded back to the world at large.

It's been a long day. She turns back. Her answer will not be found in epiphanies. It will be found in the work that's gotten her this far already.

Penrose greets her at the door. Tamsin spares a thought for the masses who seem to think only dogs care about the comings and goings of their owners, but she has always had a cat, all her life, and every one of them has known her footsteps. Penrose hates the click of her heels but is waiting all the same, sprawled across the hardwood as Tamsin steps out of her shoes and sets them aside.

The night unfolds like every other night this week. Food, tended to and then forgotten. Some token resistance to going downstairs, an attempt at focusing on emails and alerts. And then, inevitably, she's unlocking the basement door and padding down the steps into the brilliant light.

But tonight, something's different.

She knows before she's halfway down. The steps are farther apart, but on their usual schedule. The markers on the walls have spread. And there is something different, something out of place.

Her heart quickens as she descends the last few steps. Her hands clench into fists, helpless fists, fists that won't do her any good at all, but she needs to hold on to *something*.

Across from her, on the other side of the single basement room that she has measured and inventoried and paced over and over again, is something that wasn't there last night or the night before.

Across from her is a door.

The Door

Chapter Five

The door is thirty-six inches wide by eighty inches tall. It is made of a fine-grain wood painted white, and its hinges and knob look like standard brass. It is surrounded by a frame that is painted to match the trim in her basement. It is exactly like every other door in her house, entirely unremarkable, except for two things:

It did not exist twelve hours ago, and it will not open.

It's not locked. There's no keyhole, no sliver of mortise in the jamb, and the knob doesn't even have the telltale pinprick of a pop-lock on the other side. When Tamsin tries to turn the knob, it moves smoothly, evenly. She can feel the subtle motion of a mechanism when she does it. But the door resolutely does not move, doesn't even waver in its frame.

Tamsin doesn't sleep that night. She barely even leaves the basement, certain that each time she does, she'll return and the door will be gone. But it remains every time, as if it's *just* a door, as if it's always been there.

She documents everything. She photographs, measures, videos her attempts to open the door. She double-checks the stairs, the walls; their sinking has not accelerated. The door is not emerging as if uncovered by the lowering floor, but stands whole and entire.

There's no gap along the bottom, though. No movement of air from whatever is beyond it. Likewise, it sits in its frame exactly. There's no weather stripping, no obvious insulation, just precise manufacturing.

(Manufacturing? This wasn't made by anybody's hands or machines. She tries to check the seams, curious if the door and frame are actually all one piece, nonfunctional, only *representative* of a door, but gets nowhere. The gaps are too tight for any of the tools she has on hand.)

When she's exhausted every inventory she can think of, she sits down leadenly and simply stares.

This is no longer an issue of degree. Her basement isn't *just* distorting faster than the rest of the city, isn't *just* flouting the laws of physics at an accelerated rate. A door appearing from nothing is impossible. A door appearing from nothing is inexplicable. There's no way she can slip experimental designs in front of members of her team to test what's happening here.

She's not sure what would be worse: this being the only unprecedented door or more of them starting to appear all over San Siroco.

Tamsin covers her face with her hands, groaning. There's one option, and one option only: she needs to shut down the node experiments. It doesn't matter how much that galls her. The pain at losing her future, the undeniable recognition of her genius, the esteem and accolades and money—it's worth next to nothing if the debut of her work comes bundled with this . . . this . . . *horror* seems like too great a word, but what else can she call it? This redefinition of not just a scientific understanding of the world, but the common, direct experience of it. There are careers to be built off of discovering a new seismic process. The same can't be said for triggering some B-movie-style door-based apocalypse.

A derisive laugh slides out of her. Even putting it in those terms makes her feel like she's losing her mind. A door out of nowhere?

Poor Tamsin Rivers, finally cracking under the pressure of her ambition. It's the simplest answer, really. How does she know she *isn't* just losing her mind? Put somebody under intense stress, exposed to sensory deprivation and new technologies . . . even if the door is real, even if all her measurements and records tonight are verifiable, it might just be that she's somehow forgotten the door always existed.

She can check that, of course. She's sure she has photos somewhere from the inspection she had done before buying the place. But if she can't trust her own perceptions, if her brain is busy editing and recontextualizing everything she looks at, if the delusion of the appearance of a mysterious door, the harbinger of the fall of her career, is so deeply rooted . . .

She needs outside verification, and she can't ever allow that.

"Fuck," she whispers, then makes herself leave the basement.

It's just before dawn, but she pours herself a measure of vodka anyway, curling up on her couch. The cushion is stiff beneath her, almost factory-fresh, and she appreciates the rigidity. The inhospitable support. She refuses to even orient her body toward the hallway. The vodka goes down fast and searing, an analgesic against the unfamiliar panic making her heart race.

Lachlan needs to know. She can't hide this. She shouldn't have from the beginning. In hindsight, the accelerated sinking of her basement wasn't *that* damning. It had felt pointed, a direct accusation against her, but that was just paranoid anthropomorphizing of a problem. The worst that could have happened was Lachlan pulling her from the project, shutting it down. She could have come back from that, with time. Now that distance is exactly what she needs.

But she also needs an explanation. An explanation that doesn't have Lachlan packing her up and carting her off. What happens when an asset like Tamsin Rivers, with all the dirt she knows and all the things she's done, is no longer useful? Is unreliable? Is certifiable?

She wouldn't be the first person connected to Myrica that quietly disappeared, never to be heard from again.

That thought turns the burn of the vodka to an icy chill.

Lachlan Woodfield is dangerous. It's not just the slick suits and the black gloves; there's something in the way she carries herself, a comfort in her own skin, an alertness. It's not gratuitous. She doesn't sit in on meetings to intimidate. But Tamsin is certain she has some sort of military background. She isn't management; she's there to fix problems.

Still, part of the deal is that Tamsin is honest with Lachlan. There are other ways to make problems go away. And the smaller the problem is, the smaller the intervention necessary.

She pours herself another drink and drains it just as quickly. Her gaze drops to her phone. When she reaches for it, her hand shakes, but she makes herself unlock it. She stares at the home screen, mouth unaccountably dry. She almost fills her glass a third time, but that would involve looking away, and she's certain that if she does, she won't go through with this. Likewise if she navigates to her email and sends off a note saying she's working from home today.

Lachlan has never seen her basement. Lachlan doesn't know there was never a door. Maybe—maybe she can just have her over, show her the documentation of the stretching. Apologize for the withholding, but god, that won't look good, either.

Can she get away with saying she's only just noticed? Clean up everything first, claim she never goes down there and had no idea, that she went down on a whim?

The phone screen changes.

Incoming call: Lachlan Woodfield

She nearly drops it. It's not even six in the morning; how does Lachlan know she's awake? She looks over to the windows, but the curtains are drawn. The lights are out. There's no way Lachlan could know and no reason to call this early.

An emergency?

More doors?

She doesn't want to answer, could just claim she slept through it. That's what a normal person would be doing. But maybe Lachlan knows she's an early riser. Maybe not answering will earn more of Lachlan's attention, not less. She clutches her phone tightly, torn, terrified, hating being put in this position.

Tamsin hits Accept.

"Good morning, Mx. Woodfield," she says, the vodka burning low in her belly, damning.

"Dr. Rivers," Lachlan says. She sounds exactly like she always does. "You're up early." It's impossible for Tamsin to tell if Lachlan is surprised to find her awake or is calling *because* she's awake.

She tries to remind herself that Lachlan has never actually threatened her. Isn't threatening her now, either. (Yet.)

Still, she lies reflexively. "My cat occasionally has opinions about appropriate working hours."

She could have just said, *I've been working through the night.* She's done it before, in the lab even. But then Lachlan might ask about what specific work, and Tamsin could say, *I've found something strange,* and Lachlan could come over.

It's the best option she has, but despite all her arguing with herself, the fact remains: she does not want Lachlan in her house. She can't make herself ask for it. The words scald her throat, and she grits her teeth.

"The details for tomorrow's meeting with the city have been finalized,"

Lachlan says. "Mr. Thomas and Mr. Klein agreed that, for now, our best move is to not include any of our local competitors."

"This could have been an email," Tamsin points out, then grimaces. The vodka and the lack of sleep have her tongue loosened. Just not in the right direction.

Lachlan doesn't respond. It could have been an email, and the phone call only makes sense if Lachlan knew she was awake.

How *could* she know?

"I'd like you to reconsider your refusal to lead the meeting instead of Klein," Lachlan says finally. "You have the training and the confidence." She leaves unspoken, *You've never shied away from the chance to be in the spotlight.*

And she hasn't, but she knows how to sell it. "I'd prefer not to be so directly associated with a crisis," Tamsin says simply. "Even in the role of hero. There's too much risk if anything goes the slightest bit wrong." It's more than that, of course; she can't handle getting up in front of that room, knowing that something is wrong with her, specifically. There's no way for anybody else to guess the truth, but it feels like a mark emblazoned on her forehead. *The woman with the sinking basement, the woman with a door she can't remember and can't open.* It's basic risk mitigation. If she can't get herself to tell Lachlan everything *now*, this is the least she can do. For her career, for her company.

"But you'll be in attendance?"

"Of course. And I've asked Isaac Torrence to step in for the technical presentation."

There's a soft sound that might be a laugh from the other end of the line. "I see. A sacrificial lamb."

"That's entirely up to him," Tamsin says. She wishes she could smile. She wishes she couldn't feel the liquor stealing into her limbs, catching up with her all at once. "He'll do what he needs to."

"Very well. I'll see you tomorrow, then." A pause. "Get some sleep, Dr. Rivers."

Lachlan hangs up.

Tamsin grabs the vodka bottle before she can think better of it and sloshes another, heavier pour into her glass.

Chapter Six

Tamsin tries to sleep off the vodka, restless and overheated.

The sunlight that manages to get through the blinds keeps pulling her awake, hour after hour, until finally, around lunchtime, she gives up. She showers, dresses, and heads downstairs with every intention of going into the office.

First, though, she makes a large mug of coffee and goes over the night (morning) before, starting with the phone call.

Lachlan clearly has some way of knowing her movements, but that could be as simple as knowing how Tamsin usually behaves and extrapolating. It could also be something considerably more sinister, but either way, Lachlan doesn't know about the door. Can't. She wouldn't be as calm as she is if she had any idea of what Tamsin was hiding.

Setting that aside, what does *Tamsin* know? She has a project that appears to be, but still may *not* be, causing demonstrable, measurable change to the city that may (or may not) be destructive, but which will eventually become noticeable even to people who aren't looking for the distortions. She has a basement that is undergoing the same changes but faster, despite nothing connecting it to the project but the fact that her name is on the mortgage. And she has a door that appeared through some mechanism either supernatural or delusional.

She knows herself. Hallucinating doors out of paranoid guilt doesn't fit her. What she needs is time, and more data, in order to understand.

So why not just delay phase three?

Just. It's not so hard, functionally, but it hurts to type out the emails. Every word is torn from her fingertips. A delay is not abandonment. A delay is not defeat. But it is acknowledgment that there is no other path forward but to redirect. She can't run everything in parallel.

Just a little longer until her breakthrough. Just a little more grinding. She can do this.

She ignores the weight of the basement tugging at her feet.

After she sends off her decree, there's a whole host of other emails waiting for her that need immediate responses. She tries to set up shop in the upstairs room that was designed to be her home office, but finds it uncomfortable, poorly laid out, more style than substance. When she'd first moved in, she'd had the room decorated instead of just ordering copies of the furniture she uses in her lab, knowing she'd rarely use it. Pointless; nobody has ever seen it, so why render it unusable?

She settles in at the dining room table with her laptop instead and orders delivery for lunch, reviewing the final agenda for the next afternoon's meeting, putting out fires, and then getting sidetracked by the newest results from Torrence's experiments. By the time she registers the alert on her phone saying her meal's been delivered, it's been sitting on her doorstep for the past hour, and it's half past three.

She doesn't have an appetite, but she eats the sandwich anyway, distracted by the numbers she's running through her statistical program. They don't tell her anything new and should be easy to set aside, but they have a hold on her. They're tea leaves, but tea leaves she can have another set of eyes review to make sure what she's seeing and calculating and inferring is all reasonable. Reassurance, of a kind she normally wouldn't need, but now feels is crucial. Her only bulwark against the fear that any of this might all be in her head.

At any rate, she can do it as well from home as from the lab, and it's already getting close to the end of the workday. No sense in dragging herself downtown only to come home in a few hours.

Penrose, already confused by her morning nap, gets increasingly agitated as the afternoon wears on. He must be used to her absences and feel that his space is invaded. Or maybe it's the opposite, that he's delighted by her company but doesn't know how to handle it. Either way, he races through the dining room on more than one occasion and keeps bumping at her knees. When she gets up to use the bathroom in the hall, he follows, and on her way back to the dining room, he sits down in front of the basement door.

She glances at it, then at him. "No," she tells him, nudging him away with her toe. "Not for you."

He looks up at her, pupils wide, and refuses to move.

She hasn't gone downstairs again, not since she fled in the small hours of the morning. She doesn't *want* to go back down. She knows last night happened; she checked her call log when she woke up, and Lachlan's number was still there, beside *5:32 a.m.* But if she doesn't look, she can keep thinking that the door has always been there, and she'd just been loopy from lack of sleep. Or that the door was never there at all, and she'd been half dreaming.

Either one of those would be fine, really.

There are measurements to collect, though. The way she's shut off the basement from the rest of her home network means she can't pull them without going downstairs. She can't even check her records from the days and weeks behind her, can't verify *anything*.

She pushes Penrose farther from the door, keys in the code, unlocks the mechanical lock, and climbs down into the brilliant light.

The door is still there.

She does go to sleep at a reasonable time that night. It takes willpower and some Benadryl, but she's in bed by eleven, out by midnight. When she wakes up, she bargains with herself over breakfast (a meal-replacement shake); the meeting with the city isn't until two, and traffic is at its worst right now. Yesterday, a shipment of digital survey markers had come in; she can set them up on the basement stair treads to better map their divergence in real time, then head into the office. It's a reasonable step to take, she tells herself, even as she's unlocking the basement door.

When she looks at her phone next, it's past twelve. There are two missed calls and a stack of pending emails. She's gone down the rabbit hole of articles on materials distortion under sonic stress on the off chance it might explain the stretching.

The door, which she tried to open again a little bit ago, stands unchanged.

She chalks up the missed calls and lack of alerts for her emails to poor cell service—although she couldn't say it's ever been an issue before. (But she's never spent this much time in her basement before, either.) Except she gets Wi-Fi in the basement, and it should've pushed through.

Well, she was busy.

There isn't time to linger on her unease at the lapse in any case. She shuts down her workstation and abandons the basement, pausing only to lock it tight before hurrying upstairs. There's barely any time to dress. She swaps out her loungewear (had she really gone down this morning without throwing real clothing on?) for a black knit dress and sheer hose and adds a small astrolabe pendant on a fine gold chain. Glancing in the mirror, all she sees is *mess*. Her curls are getting a little fuzzy on the margins, obviously in need of a keratin treatment, and she looks unpleasantly tired. Klein will not be happy, but it's nothing makeup can't take the edge off.

She'll have to do it in the car.

She summons the ride service, then puts down an early dinner for Penrose, redolent of pureed chicken liver. It makes her stomach flip, and she realizes she's forgotten lunch at the same time her phone pings that her car is out front.

Fuck it. She grabs another shake from the fridge, shoving it into her purse. Phone, cosmetics, polished heels. That's everything she needs; Klein will have the rest.

Tamsin stops with her hand on the doorknob.

Really, she doesn't need to be there.

She curses herself for having Cara volunteer her. She's not going to be the face of this, and it's going to be a shit show. She's not even there to look pretty; she's there because she's territorial and a control freak, but she doesn't *need* to be. Not on this one. She doesn't need to watch in real time as everybody gets their first taste of the disaster she's maybe causing.

The app pings. She has five minutes to get in the car.

Her chest buzzes with searing, desperate flies, all seeking to explode out from between her ribs. She needs to go in, at the very least. She can apologize her way out of the meeting, head to the lab instead. (Lachlan's going to know. Lachlan's going to see her missing and is going to have questions.)

(Lachlan wanting her there is just a power play. She doesn't have to rise to the occasion.)

Tamsin stares at her hand, wills it to turn the knob.

And then she's out in the early-autumn heat, the midday sun warming her face, and she has the door locked and is climbing into the sleek town car. They slide into the pulse of the city, and after a moment, Tamsin can't remember why she hesitated.

Tamsin sits near, but not at, the head of the conference table. Lachlan is seated by the far end, as usual, and off to the side. Her suit is less severe than usual, and she's kept her hands (gloved, as always) clasped in her lap, the better to not draw attention. She almost looks like she belongs.

Tamsin is fairly certain that she's the only one in the room who can feel the relentless weight of Lachlan's attention on her, the subtle, ongoing evaluation. Or maybe that's only Tamsin worrying; maybe it's only the common variety of Lachlan's observation.

The rest of the table is filled by representatives of various city departments, their aides, and one professor from the local university. It's hard to judge who looks most horrified. Klein has been leading the presentation for the last fifteen minutes. The room is deathly silent, save for his voice, measured and calm.

She's almost relaxed when he reaches the end of his section of the presentation.

"Esteemed guests, we have a problem," he says, voice still steady. "And Myrica Dynamics is here to help."

Shocked silence follows, and Tamsin wonders if that's better or worse than an eruption of confused outrage. Klein did an admirable job of walking the line between alarmism and confident support, but he made sure to lean on the risks to infrastructure even harder than Tamsin did in her initial presentation. They're all awash in images of sewage-line ruptures and gas-main leaks.

It was a smart choice to leave building collapses off the list.

Next on the agenda is Dr. Torrence's orientation of their audience to the so-far identified mechanics and proof of the situation. Klein had suggested they wait until their audience asked, but Tamsin recommended he take the lead. She watches Dr. Torrence fuss with his slideshow.

Her lips curve. *This* is definitely worth getting out of the house for.

The room doesn't want to know more about the sampling methods at the various measurement sites. Only half the audience is looking at him;

the rest are making notes. (On paper; Myrica's lawyers had insisted on all laptops and cell phones being handed over before anybody entered the room, again. Nobody wants a panic after all.)

His intro patter is a modified, shortened version of her own on Monday. He's even using the same graphics, something Klein turned down and Tamsin didn't recommend. The green and orange lines are too stark and complex, and when he pages forward to his next slide, the change is jarring.

"Disruptions in the crystal-growth matrices we use in our R&D labs indicate the presence of microtremors," Dr. Torrence is saying. His gaze flicks to the screen, where a figure demonstrates how the discontinuity translates to a more familiar (and entirely fictitious) seismographic readout. His jaw tenses, and he shifts his weight.

He is a passable liar, but not a confident one. It's clearly consuming all his attention; it distracts him from the growing tension in the room.

"These microtremors may be causing widespread settling in the soil across the city, allowing compaction that would take decades to occur in the normal course of events," he continues, looking back at his audience, pointedly avoiding the edge of the room Tamsin is in. Sweat is starting to break out along his hairline. Tamsin rolls one ankle, idly, and focuses on the deputy mayor, who is growing ever more visibly agitated.

San Siroco's budget has been floundering for years, and the mayor herself is absent, leaving her deputy trapped, watching an impending disaster with no way to get the news out. His knuckles are white where he grips his coffee mug, and as Tamsin watches, his expression shifts from irritation, to a flash of panic, to utter rageful disdain.

"Nobody cares about your *product development*," he snaps finally, rising to his feet.

Dr. Torrence's carefully rehearsed speech sputters out. He even takes a small step back. "Sorry—I—that is, the evidence—"

Oh, Torrence.

If anybody at that table thinks about Dr. Torrence again, they'll only remember their irritation and his uncertainty. And if he tries to tell any of them what the growth matrices *actually* look like, they'll assume he's just scrabbling for attention.

Whether or not Dr. Torrence ever figures out Tamsin knew exactly what was going to happen to him won't matter. How would he prove it?

The little win is a bright spot in her day and makes up, however briefly, for the strain of performing where Lachlan can still see her.

"You've made your point," the deputy mayor continues, waving a hand. "Cede the floor and let somebody present *solutions*."

"Mr. Wilkes," Klein says, "our recommendations are derived from the evidence Dr. Torrence is so thoroughly laying out for us."

Wilkes's face remains flushed. "I don't need to know *why*, I need to know *what*. And how much this is going to cost us."

"Myrica Dynamics is committed to assisting San Siroco in this unprecedented time," Tamsin cuts in. She didn't mean to and probably shouldn't have; Klein throws her a quelling look. But while Torrence's hobbling is satisfying, she doesn't want it to disrupt the rest of the meeting. "Just as with our recent public-transit initiative. I'm sure Mr. Klein would be happy to walk you through the resources we have to put at your disposal."

"And your team has ruled out that same *recent public-transit initiative* as a cause?" asks the head of the city water bureau. Her tone is polite; the implication of her words is clear. "With all of the expansions and renovations to the lines . . ."

This, at least, is something that they have a wealth of evidence disproving.

"The subsidence has been measured at enough sample sites to show no correlation between recent subway activity or, in fact, subway *presence*, and the extent or existence of localized sinking," Tamsin replies, smile sharp on her face.

"Of course, we have engaged an independent engineering firm to review not only our plans but our implementation," Klein cuts in. "Just in case. This is too important a situation to let arrogance obfuscate reality."

"We have a number of avenues we will be pursuing in the coming weeks," Tamsin adds, "both to discover more about the cause of the subsidence and, in the meantime, to prevent the more disastrous effects. To that end, you can all expect further contact from our research teams and leadership in the coming days." It's another difficult line to walk, between self-effacing simpering and demonstrating the confidence needed to keep this room under control. But nobody pushes. Maybe it's best she's here after all. "Now, I can walk us through the basics, but I suspect we're all feeling . . . shaken."

A smattering of nervous laughter. Klein dips his head with a chagrined smile, and Tamsin settles back in her seat.

"When Myrica contracted with the local and state transportation departments to take over the municipal transit system," she continues, "we did it to give back to this city that has so graciously made itself a home for us. It was always designed to be a charitable offering." The PR bump had been unprecedented, even when the local newspaper found out about the strong tax advantages and kickbacks from the city that Myrica Dynamics got in return for its *selfless* bailout. "This is no different. We're here to do the right thing. This is an opportunity, for all of us. And though the risks are great, we stand ready to protect and improve the great city of San Siroco."

There's no applause. Tamsin doesn't expect any. But she can feel the tension beginning to ratchet down as measured, less panicked conversations spring up along the length of the table. *Good.* Her intervention succeeded, then.

"As I'm sure you can all understand," Klein says before it becomes too loud, "we would ask that news of our findings is not spread immediately. Myrica Dynamics will work with city officials and the geology department of the University of San Siroco to develop informative, clear, and, most importantly, non-alarmist messaging for us all to use going forward."

Nods, all around. NDAs have already been signed, of course. Eventually, it will leak, or somebody else will independently notice the sinking, but everything indicates they still have at least two weeks before then, possibly more.

It will have to be enough.

Chapter Seven

Tamsin makes it home a little after ten. To Tamsin's relief, Lachlan had left the conference room without a word and hadn't sent any drinks invitations, but Torrence had needed some amount of coddling, and Klein had been nearly vibrating with nervous energy. She took them both out to dinner as a thank-you for handling the majority of the meeting. That way, they'd remember her with relief and not their frustration at how she'd put the both of them in the line of fire.

She picked the restaurant from the usual set that she uses for this sort of thing and never visits otherwise. The conversation had been intolerable, but the food and drinks had been good. Klein had spent a good deal of time comforting Torrence, which was fascinating to watch because Klein had at least as good a sense of how much that had torpedoed his local career as Tamsin did. Tamsin had offered platitudes occasionally and made her way through three glasses of wine before she realized she needed to pace herself. Lachlan texted just after their entrees arrived, a simple *Mr. Thomas thanks you for your involvement.*

No acknowledgment of the phase-three delay. In fact, any mention of the delay has been conspicuously absent since yesterday morning, but Lachlan must know. It's on Tamsin's mind the entire ride back to her house and is still bothering her as she wobbles out of her heels in the foyer. She's just tipsy enough to think asking Lachlan directly might be a good idea. She's not sure if she's worried that Lachlan can see through the delay, or, worse, that she wants the approval that comes with performing correctly for her handler.

The latter option sobers her up a bit. It's humiliating, particularly because it's actually possible.

No, she's not going to text Lachlan.

Penrose sits halfway up the stairs, regarding her with his tail lashing slowly across the carpet.

"Bedtime, huh?"

He blinks slowly.

For all the variance in her schedule, all the late nights in the lab, fundraising dinners, working weekends, they still have this nightly ritual; Penrose all but herds her to bed when he's decided she needs to sleep. He's often right, too. So she follows him upstairs, strips down, wipes off her makeup, curls up in the dark. Penrose nestles down in the crook behind her knees, and Tamsin is asleep within minutes.

Around her, the house is silent.

It's nearing three when Penrose leaves the bed. Tamsin shifts, wakes just a hair, the way she always does, and finds herself gazing at the bedroom door. It's open, just the way she left it. The hallway beyond is black.

Her mind is soft-edged and quiet as her legs slip from beneath the covers. She stands and walks, naked, out into the void.

The bedroom has an en suite, but she ignores that door and goes to the guest bath down the hall. She thinks she hears Penrose digging in his litter box, but the room is empty when she gets there. She relieves herself and rubs at her face, not sure why she's awake, not sure if she even really is. But when Tamsin dreams, she dreams of her old university campus. She dreams of wide-open plains. Her mind relitigates old challenges, reaches back for old versions of herself.

She never dreams of her house.

She looks in the mirror and doesn't recognize herself.

Red hair, blue eyes, the faint beginnings of crow's-feet—all things that should be familiar but are utterly alien. She reaches out and half expects to not touch glass at all, only air, or water, or thick syrup, but the surface of the mirror is cold and smooth, just as it has always been.

Is it a window, then?

But her reflection touches the glass just where she touches it.

She never played those sleepover games as a child, never chanted *Bloody Mary* into a nighttime mirror and scared herself, but she's only human. She's always carried a healthy fear of gazing into bathroom mirrors at night, if only because of the off chance of *something else* lurking behind her. And yet now, here, she looks. She measures. She inspects. She waits for something to happen, remembering reading about strange-face illusion in college. In a darkened room, faced with a mirror, the brain malfunctions. Even waking, the brain sees its walking cradle melt, distort, rotate, or else be replaced entirely. It no longer recognizes itself.

Nothing changes. It's only the familiar-unfamiliar lines of her own face staring back at her.

Maybe that means she's dreaming after all.

That would explain the tug at her sternum, firmer now, almost painful. She rubs at her chest, steps away from the bathroom sink, and stumbles back toward her bedroom. But there are stairs below her feet. She doesn't want to go downstairs, does she? But oh, she does, she *does*, the longing filling her like a wellspring, soaking into her brain and heart and lungs, pulling her down.

If this is a dream, surely there's no harm. And if it's not, she could check her instruments. See if the walls of her basement have grown another millimeter. Look for cracks up along the ceiling that she'll never find.

But the house is dark. It is massive. Her ribs hurt, and her head hurts, and this is foolish. She needs to wake up.

She cannot make it back to her bed, but she can crawl beneath the living room coffee table. She can shelter there, put her hands over her ears, press her forehead to the rug. If she closes her eyes, if she falls asleep in the dream, maybe she'll wake up.

She closes her eyes.

She goes to sleep.

She is awake.

The room is so bright, nearly without feature, and at first, she can't understand where she is, what she's looking at. It's frigid water thrown over her, making her gasp and pull in on herself, chest heaving. But bit by bit, she understands.

She is standing in her basement, naked in the piercing, cold light of too many lamps. Her hands ache. Her fingers are wrapped around the knob of the door. She jerks away, as if burned, and falls back two panicked steps, three.

She's running upstairs before she can stop herself.

* * *

It's less upsetting once the sun is up and she's on her way into the lab. With a little distance, it's easier to contextualize. It's not the first time she's sleepwalked, although it's been decades. Add in the stress of the last few weeks, and the wine, and it's not all that strange. (Undoing the locks, though? Getting the key? Remembering the code?) And is it really all that different from waking up thinking of theorems, jumbled and half imagined?

(Yes. But what, exactly, can she do about it?)

She's heading down into the subway station that leads to node lab one when her phone buzzes with a message

> From: Lachlan.
> Phase three postponed-did you find something?

Finally some acknowledgment, though she's unsure why Lachlan has waited two days to comment. Had she really just . . . not noticed? It's both frustrating and a bit of a relief. Lachlan can't be watching her as closely as she'd feared in the wake of that early morning phone call. A commuter shoulder-checks Tamsin as she pauses on the stairs, and she glares after them before descending to the platform proper. She has just enough signal to reply.

> From: Tamsin
> Abundance of caution.

She gets no response, but she also shoves her phone into her purse and passes through the maintenance door, then down into the tunnels. She doesn't need the distraction.

Unfortunately, her day is all distractions. Management issues, emails from the mayor's office, Klein sending her half a dozen pieces of messaging to review and give feedback on. She handles all of it with a simmering baseline of annoyance. And then, even when she has time to review the reports from each node lab on the last week's rounds of testing, she finds her thoughts tugged back to the subsidence data. When she starts parsing through *that*, she drifts into wondering about her basement.

She didn't get this far by being flighty, and she goes and shuts her office door in case it's the intermittent chatter in the workrooms beyond that is keeping her from settling in. Then she turns off her email. She has enough of a data set to work from; she doesn't need new information urgently.

There's nothing unexpected, once she's run what's become their standard statistical assay on the new numbers. It's a very consistent mystery, their sinking city. Nothing seems to impact it. Not local geology, not density of human construction. It's almost as if it's a measurement error, some skewing of a sensor, but each site is sampled with their own tools, monitored for calibration issues.

But she can't let the thought go, sitting forward in her seat, scrolling through the data again. Maybe *measurement error* is the wrong way to characterize it. *Observational effect* seems closer. Though they aren't observing the whole of the city at once. It's not a one-to-one cause and effect. But maybe observing does produce the result observed; maybe if nothing had been measuring depth at the construction sites, not only would they have not noticed for months or years, maybe there would have been nothing to notice.

If she hadn't been going down to her basement, maybe the door would never have appeared.

And *if* the door is real, and appeared exactly as she believes it did, then maybe she's looking at this all wrong.

Maybe she should be looking for an opportunity instead. Science isn't only what can already be explained, or even imagined. Every so often, something comes along and shakes up all their foundations. Her communications work is proof of that. The subsidence is a real phenomenon. The door, likewise.

There has to be an explanation. If she can find *that*, then it tames the beast. It's not proof of her instability or her unsuitability to lead this project. It's another breakthrough discovery.

Of course, she'd need to consider how to publicize it very carefully. She doesn't need to be looked at the same way Stanton Friedman was when he transitioned from his nuclear work to joining the fringe lecture circuit on UFOs. And she doesn't want to make her basement, her home, a circus. But if she can figure out how and why the door appeared, maybe she can replicate it elsewhere. And if it can be replicated, then it can be dissected, and it can be *useful*.

Maybe the node research being slowed down won't matter so much after all. Maybe she's approaching an even larger discovery. There's no evidence that the appearance of the door has accelerated any of the subsidence, either in her basement or in the city at large. She checked. The floor didn't suddenly drop to make room for the door; its depth has continued its precise descent.

But the door exists, all the same.

"—Rivers?"

Tamsin flinches, then looks up and behind her to where Jordan Cherry, lead researcher at this lab, is peering into her office with a concerned expression.

"Sorry," Tamsin says, then wonders why she apologized. She never apologizes. "Was running down a train of thought. You were saying?"

Cherry hesitates before speaking, and Tamsin wonders how long they've been standing there, trying to get her attention. "A few of us are going out for dinner," they say. "Would you like to come with us?"

At least they sound like themself, not . . . concerned. The question is bad enough, grating and intrusive. It probably started out as the usual attempt to get her engagement and approval, but now it feels entirely like pity. Somebody must have noticed that she didn't break for lunch. Again.

"No," she says and glances at her monitor. It's asleep. But Cherry said *dinner*, not happy hour, not drinks, so it's late enough. "I'm going to wrap up here. Is there anything needing approval?"

"No, Dr. Rivers." Cherry looks relieved at her lack of interest, and Tamsin tries not to overthink it. They can all just chalk this up to the strange times they're living in.

Cherry's turned back to the hallway when Tamsin, gathering up her purse and waking up her computer to lock it properly, says, "I'll be working remotely for the next several days."

They glance back, brow furrowed. "If there's an emergency, will you be available to come in?"

"Of course," she says.

They nod and leave her to join the rest of the lab. She can hear voices in the distance. They all sound happy.

Chapter Eight

Her house *feels* different when she returns that evening. There's an anticipatory hush in the air, replacing its usual empty stillness. It's her own hyperfocus, she knows, but it still makes the skin between her shoulders prickle and crawl as she locks the front door behind her and goes through the ritual of shedding shoes, putting down food for Penrose, feeding herself.

She doesn't even try to resist the siren call of the basement door. As soon as she's swallowed the last mouthful of tonight's hurried meal, she's keying in the code and heading down the steps. The impossible door waits for her, not looming as it had seemed to this morning, but complacent and unawares. In moving from threat to opportunity, it's become something akin to prey.

Tamsin does make herself start with her usual daily inventory of the space. It's far easier to focus on than anything at work that day and feels like changing into loungewear, a full-body relief she didn't even know she was craving. She takes her measurements and writes out some of her new theory of observational effect, along with a few other stray thoughts. On the screen, it looks laughably impossible, but she doesn't let that discourage her this time. She can't afford to artificially narrow her thinking; her instruments and the limitations of a human brain will already provide more than enough challenge.

It's nearly midnight when she finishes up and turns, at last, to the door. There are so many things she wants to do that she isn't entirely certain where to start. Her head aches, distantly, and she knows she's exhausted. Last night's sleep wasn't restful, and if she starts now, she may make some error or miss something crucial. Still, she's reluctant as she goes up to bed for the night. It's a small miracle her sleep is unbroken once she is finally able to drift off.

In the morning, she showers, dresses, even eats a full breakfast before going downstairs. The chaos of the last few days clearly hasn't been doing her any favors, making her scattered and irritable, prone to missing things and jumping to conclusions, and the antidote is order, not avoidance. Maybe resuming her old cardio routine, going for evening runs to clear her mind when she can fit them in. She sets an alarm to remind herself to eat lunch. She'll work this like she's on deadline; in a sense, it's even true. Figuring out how the door fits into everything might be crucial, but she'll have to slot the work in around everything else. Better to maximize the time she has right now.

She gets to work.

She starts by remeasuring the door. Only once that's done does she look at her original notes to compare. There have been no distortions to the door itself. It's staying firmly anchored to the floor, at exactly the proportions it arrived in, while the wall above it stretches to keep up with the general sinking. She adds a few markers around the frame, curious if the wall will continue distorting evenly along its length, as it has been, or if the presence of the door will create a zone of stability. Does the wall change along the sides of the frame or only above it?

From there, she repeats her attempts to open the door. Everything is the same there, too. The knob turns, she can hear a mechanism at work, and yet she can't pull or push the door open with any amount of force. There are still no gaps for her to feel air move through or to slip something between door and floor or jamb.

But when she puts her ear to the wood, she can hear—*something*. It's not recognizable, is barely perceptible, and reminds her, more than anything else, of the absence of sound in the node chambers. Of course, that absence can only be experienced from the inside, not from the other side of a door.

Her fingers itch to open it.

She writes up her findings in exhaustive detail, then she pads upstairs in search of her toolbox.

It's stuffed in a disused closet, and the only reason it's free of dust is because Tamsin hires a cleaner once a month to (with supervision) go over the entirety of the house. She has a set of fine-detail tools upstairs in her office that she uses occasionally on pieces of misbehaving tech, but she's not a particularly handy or crafty person, generally speaking, and she knows when to hire out home repairs.

Back downstairs, she eyes the hinges, with their entirely average screws. This isn't something she can hire out.

She hesitates before getting out the screwdriver, though. If she removes the hinges, and the door does open, what then? Is she prepared to see what's on the other side of the door? Or is she rushing ahead foolishly? There are other things to do. Hardness and materials tests, to confirm her conclusions about the door's composition. Passing a camera through to the other side through a gap or small hole.

Well. One screw does not an open door make. She fits the screwdriver to the lowest one and turns.

It doesn't move. She wiggles the screwdriver one way, then the other, to no avail. The other screw on the hinge is the same. They certainly *look* like screws, and there's even a fine gap between screw head and plate, but they are fixed entirely in place. The ones securing the knob, likewise. Her frustration grows, and the screwdriver slips, gouging into the wood beside the knob.

And then, a moment later, there's no mark. No line in the paint. Tamsin frowns and scrapes the screwdriver against the door again. It bites in, peels, and she sees the mark.

And then she blinks, and it's gone again.

She scrambles to her feet. She stares at the door.

Everything in her screams to get an axe, a hammer, *something*, and bust through the wood to the other side in some undeniable, incontrovertible way. The door is only wood. She can see it; she *felt* it. But she stands frozen.

No. She needs to document this. She needs to proceed carefully.

The alarm on her phone goes off.

She needs to eat something.

That afternoon, she trains a camera on the surface of the door. She gathers a variety of implements. A knife, the screwdriver, a drill, a hammer.

"Unexpected property first discovered via accidental application of a screwdriver to the door," she says, replicating it. She half expects, now that the camera is rolling, for the mark to persist. But as before, even after she scrapes up a thin curl of paint, the door appears untouched.

She sets the screwdriver down and takes up the knife instead.

"Test one," she says. "Cutting force."

The knife bites into the paint. Catches on the wood and doesn't want to move. She draws it down, steadily, watching the line it produces.

She pulls the knife away. The mark is gone.

The drill is the same, with the added discovery that regardless of which bit she uses, the drill never seems to pierce through to the other side, nor meet any resistance. The hammer splinters the wood, *dents the knob*. And yet when she sets the hammer down again, the door is still the same as it ever was.

She stops the camera. She replays the footage up in her living room, where the walls have not changed since she bought the place. Again, she half expects the camera to reflect a different reality than her eyes witnessed. For it to show a door growing battered and scarred where all she could see was white paint. But there, captured in data, is the door, marked and then untouched, over and over again.

When she loads the files onto her laptop and tries to slow the footage down, she thinks she sees a flicker of—something. Movement of some kind, following each injury she does to the wood. But there are too many gaps between frames.

A better camera, then.

And not just that; she's reaching the limits of what the equipment she has on hand can do. She has too many questions she needs answers to. They multiply relentlessly the longer she looks, tearing her in too many directions at once, leaving her hungry. One of the labs has a scanning electron microscope specifically designed for in situ mechanical testing. Requisitioning it may raise questions, but without it, she's going to hit a wall.

If nobody's using it, perhaps she can just have it sent to her central lab, and from there . . . borrow it.

She writes the requisition order and sends it in to Cara to route.

* * *

On Sunday, Tamsin makes herself log into her work laptop. There are emails for her, of course, and new data packages. She doesn't care about any of them, and they can all wait until Monday, but Tamsin almost always logs a few hours on weekends, and technically she's responsible for any emergency. Tamsin is fairly certain Lachlan can view her work email—and possibly her private one—at will, and between that and the log Tamsin's ID badge creates whenever she goes to one of the research sites, Lachlan can derive a great deal about Tamsin's work habits.

It usually doesn't matter. Tamsin works because she wants to work. But Lachlan's constant presence this last week hovers in the back of her brain, and Tamsin tries to log time. There's not enough to do down in the basement. There's more than enough to do up here.

She's back downstairs before the morning is out, more alarms set to keep her on task.

Lachlan doesn't call.

Tamsin is used to working long hours underground. She's familiar with the way the lack of windows and the constant light levels can distort her sense of time. Everything is brightly lit and unchanging, and no matter how long she stares at the door or the stairs, she can't perceive the sinking herself.

It's not worth trying.

It'll be a day or more before she can go fetch the equipment she needs, which leaves her with little to do after her usual measurements are collected. But as she looks at the door and the marks she's made around it, she decides to expand on the method. First, she draws on the door itself, a few short lines. They remain, even after she looks away. On the other three walls, she carefully measures out squares, then fills them with dense, regular patterns, the better to test how evenly the distortion spreads.

Her art supplies are limited: a few Sharpies that soon run dry and pens that gouge into the wall. She strokes her thumb over the gouge, tongue between her teeth, curious as to what it will do.

When she takes her thumb away, the gouge is gone, just like at the door.

There's no way of knowing if the walls were resilient like this before the door appeared. She could kick herself for not testing them. But that is the nature of an evolving phenomenon; her own knowledge of it can only grow as it develops, and there will always be things she misses.

That frustration drives her upstairs once more. The auto-feeder she uses to make sure Penrose gets the bulk of his meals on schedule ran hours ago; her alarms never went off, or maybe she dismissed them. The cat avoids her as she puts down his supplementary wet food now, tops up his water bowl.

She goes to sleep dissatisfied.

On Monday, she wakes feeling like she hasn't slept at all.

She drags herself out of bed and to the bathroom, where her reflection gazes back at her with deeper bags under its eyes than she's seen since three years ago, the last time she was the primary author on a grant proposal, when one of Myrica Dynamics's other projects needed the validation and cachet of external support for their research, not just Myrica's dark-money funding. Her whole body seems to protest as she strips and climbs into the shower, and the hot water is a relief. She tips her head back, reaches for the shampoo. But when she goes to lather up her hair, she hisses in pain and jerks her hands away.

Her fingertips, beneath the suds, are red and raw.

One of her manicured nails is torn.

She stares and tries to think of when she might have scalded or scraped her hands and comes up empty. They were fine when she went to sleep. They are not fine now. She rubs shampoo into her hair with the palms of her hands only and rushes through the rest of her shower.

The soft cotton of her towel is too much, and she grits her teeth as she dries off. She can't properly finger-comb or twist her curls and has to settle for detangling and braiding—and even that is torture. By the time she's dressed, her eyes burn with tears and her jaw aches from how hard she's clenching it.

She takes two ibuprofen and heads downstairs.

The timed feeder has already filled Penrose's kibble bowl, but he meets her in the hallway anyway, golden eyes fixed on her, ready for his morning serving of wet food. She walks past him, and after a moment, he follows.

"Breakfast can wait," Tamsin says. "Just a few minutes, buddy."

The door to the basement is properly closed and locked. When she'd woken up in the basement Friday, it had been hanging open; her sleepwalking brain hadn't thought to close it behind her. Her stomach churns, and she wonders if she should be feeling relief.

She's not sure what she's feeling.

Her fingers ache as she types in the code, as she turns the key. Penrose gives a frustrated little meow, then pads off. Tamsin makes her careful way downstairs.

The door is still there, with its ink marks from the night before intact.

There is a faint darkening along one edge, just above the knob.

Tamsin approaches, slowly, on an angled path that takes her to her workstation first. Her heartbeat grows loud in her ears. She grabs the camera, then continues her oblique path, as if walking straight up to it would be dangerous.

The thought is ridiculous. She just sleepwalked again. An issue for a doctor, not—not—

She's close enough to see her blood clearly now, a rust-brown stain, uneven and stark against the white paint. Her fingers throb. She lifts the camera and takes photo after photo. She doesn't stop, staring at the screen as each shot shows the same thing, over and over again.

It's only the faint tap of Penrose's paws on the stairs that makes her turn away at last.

"No, buddy. Upstairs," she says, and she sounds breathless. *Is* breathless. Her face is hot and her throat is tight, as if she's been hyperventilating. Tamsin swallows it all down, staring after Penrose's retreating tail as he obediently leaves the room behind.

She's been in the house for too long. That's it. That's all. She needs to go upstairs, feed the cat, go in to work. Monday, it's Monday; she hasn't left the house in over fifty hours. It's not healthy.

Penrose rubs up against her ankle. She jumps, cursing. Hadn't he been up in the hall not fifteen seconds ago? She certainly hadn't seen him come down again.

It must have been a shadow up top.

"I said *upstairs*," she says, dumping the camera back on her desk and heading for the stairs at last. Penrose follows, tawny coat rippling in the bright lights.

Chapter Nine

The farther the town car travels from Tamsin's house, the larger the city feels.

San Siroco is smaller than San Francisco and was founded more recently, with more room for modern urban planning. Even in bad traffic, it takes less than an hour and a half to traverse. The roads are well maintained, the buildings familiar. She's lived here for close on two decades; she *knows* this city.

It feels bigger than it used to.

The canyons between the downtown skyscrapers are deep and dark, and she is small, out of scale, cowering. It takes effort not to hunch her shoulders, draw up her knees. Her pulse kicks up without her consent.

The cocoon of the car doesn't provide enough of a barrier. It's a kind of mental lag; the team calls it *lab fever*. They've all experienced it, especially those working in the node labs. The mind gets used to its surroundings. Right now her anxiety is a consequence of staying in her house, in her basement, for too long, a neurological reflex from not looking farther away than twenty meters. It's happened before, after long weeks under deadline. During grad school, when she sometimes didn't leave the lab, even to sleep, while an experiment was running.

It will go away. She just needs to exercise some mental hygiene. Getting out of the house is the first step. Looking at faraway items is the second.

She fixes her attention on her phone instead. She gave the door her entire weekend, barring her half-hearted attempt to log time for Lachlan's sake on Sunday morning. Nobody else took the weekend off; there's a host of reports to review, fires to put out. She types out emails, catches up on the news.

No mention of the subsidence yet. No breathless stories about cracked foundations or rising groundwater (but of course there aren't; the extent of the sinking is not that bad yet, nowhere but at her house, and even there, there's no crisis). No alarms raised by anonymous sources, no outwardly well-meaning slips by the city.

A weekend is only that: two days, and under two millimeters of change. The door didn't give her the breakthroughs she wanted, but it will. She just has to keep working at it when she can afford to.

The car passes out the other side of the city core. They're maybe ten minutes from Myrica Dynamics's campus, and the lower profile of the buildings shows too much sky. She's trying to ignore how her breathing is too fast, too thin, when her phone rings.

Lachlan's name glows on the screen.

She answers, voice as calm as she can make it.

"Mx. Woodfield."

"Dr. Rivers. Are you on your way into the office?"

"Yes. I'll be there in a few minutes."

"Good." There's a note of approval in her voice. It's the sort of approval reserved for children. "I was beginning to worry. It's not like you to take a weekend off."

Lachlan calling attention to it is a threat, and a demand, and a reminder that even with permission to work from home, there are appearances to maintain. A few emails on Sunday morning don't count.

Tamsin flips through an arsenal of lies.

"I decided isolation would improve my perspective," she says finally, though no more than two seconds have passed in silence. "My work, by necessity, takes place partially within my own skull."

"And did your theory pan out?"

Tamsin thinks of the door in her basement and feels a tug between her ribs, as if being pulled back to it. "It's still in progress. Does Mr. Thomas have any new concerns?"

"No."

"Then you shouldn't, either. If that will be all?"

The other end of the line is silent except for a faint whisper that might be Lachlan's breathing. It feels strangely intimate, like Lachlan is just beside her.

It can't be long before Lachlan speaks again, but it feels like a small eternity.

"Take care, Dr. Rivers. I would hate to have to get used to your replacement."

Tamsin's hand goes slack on the phone for just a moment, because that *should* sound like a threat.

It doesn't. It just sounds like . . .

Concern.

She swallows. "Stop worrying," she says, more tersely than she means to, and hangs up.

Tamsin stands in the lobby of the main Myrica complex, looking at the bank of elevator doors. Her lab is near the top of the building, on the sixteenth floor. Climbing up the stairs would be ridiculous, particularly in the heels she's wearing, but she's seriously considering it. The elevator boxes are glass on one side, giving a view out across the campus and to the city beyond as they rise. The promise of that view makes her uneasy.

And something about going up that fast, that high—

More hangover from the weekend. She stabs the call button, boards the elevator, and scans her badge. The elevator's mechanism is smooth; just like with the subsidence, she can't feel the change in action.

She keeps her gaze fixed on the climbing floor numbers, back to the window.

The elevator lets out onto a short entry hall. The lab is the only thing on this level, and the receiving area is only there for privacy. It's familiar enough to help ratchet down the tension thrumming through her body, and when she catches her reflection in the gleaming material of the main door, it looks right. Her makeup is flawless, and her braid hides how frizzy her hair looks, how dull. Even her broken fingernail has been filed down enough to look fine at a glance. The raw tips of her fingers are powdered over and not quite so sensitive, now that she's appropriately medicated.

She enters the lab, thinking everything might be okay after all.

Cara, her assistant, is waiting for her. Her expression isn't a frown but might as well be. "Good morning, Dr. Rivers. Can I get you a coffee?" She hesitates a moment, then adds quietly, "Or something else? You look pale."

Pale. A pale creature crawling up out of a hole. "Coffee will be fine," she says, ignoring the rest. Cara leaves. Broad windows span the wall, and Tamsin catches a glimpse of the city. The space below is too big, too hungry, too open. She flinches away.

Not so okay after all. Not yet.

"Got lab fever?" Isaac Torrence asks.

Tamsin hides a grimace. He's right, but it's infuriating coming from his mouth. At any rate, it's part of why she arranged for the central lab to have views like this, to counteract how much they're all prone to burying themselves. It will fix itself if she can just get through her day.

Torrence is looking at her closely now.

"Spent all weekend in the node labs," Tamsin says, not sure why she's lying, even as she does it. "Try working underground during an unprecedented seismological event and see how *you* feel."

"I think I'd feel relieved to see the sky again," he says. God, he doesn't even have the decency to sound judgmental or suspicious—just concerned. Everybody, so concerned, as if they can see that something is wrong with her.

Lachlan didn't even need to see her. She could hear it.

"Dr. Rivers with an attack of nerves," a lab tech (*Octavian Valdez*, her mind supplies after a moment's lag) says cheerfully. "Another unprecedented seismological event for the records."

Tamsin looks at him incredulously. Torrence pales somewhat, and she catches a flash of movement, him motioning for Valdez to shut up. Valdez immediately looks embarrassed. "Sorry," he says. "I didn't mean—"

"It's fine," she says. It's not.

She goes into her office. It has more windows, but she pulls the blinds down and then it's mostly okay. No glass into the rest of the lab, everything the way she prefers it, and a lab coat tailored to her is waiting, armor for the day. She's just pulled it on when somebody knocks on the door.

"Come in," she says, expecting Cara, but it's Torrence. He moves to close the door behind him.

"Leave it open," she says. Whatever he wants to talk about, she wants it to be over quickly.

He has her coffee. She tamps down the brief flare of anger at Cara—not irritation, outright *anger*—for allowing that and accepts the thermos. It's made perfectly, at least, so Cara only outsourced the delivery.

"I wanted to apologize for Valdez," Torrence says, voice pitched not to carry through the cracked door. "Everybody's dealing with the stress differently, but that's no excuse for what he said."

Her anger leaps to Torrence, lightning to a rod. She sits down in her chair, crossing her legs, expression blank. "I can handle a poorly thought-out joke, Dr. Torrence," she says. She wants to add *Stop groveling, it doesn't become you*, but this doesn't feel like groveling. Or rather, not *just* groveling. He's using the situation to set himself up to be positively regarded after this whole mess is over, the colleague who provided the support nobody else would give to his superior during a trying time, but she knows what pure self-interest looks like (she's even played this role before, years ago), and this isn't it.

He actually cares. The concern is real, and she hates him for it, more strongly than she was bothered by Cara or unsettled by Lachlan.

It's in every inch of him as he shifts his weight uneasily. "Setting the joke aside," he says, "I wanted to offer to take on more work. I may not be well suited for the government-interfacing role they're asking of you, but you know my qualifications. I can handle some of the top-level analysis for you. Take a few things off your plate."

She almost wishes this was a blatant grab for credit, an embarrassingly transparent coup.

It's not.

Is this because she coddled him at that dinner on Thursday? Does he think they're friends now? "I am managing perfectly fine," she says. No *thank you for your concern*, no *I appreciate the offer*.

He looks at her.

"With all due respect," he says, "I don't think you are. You've been out of the office repeatedly, you've seemed distracted, your latest report had several errors." Tamsin's face heats at the damning litany. "Under the circumstances, I don't think you should be doing this alone, and—"

"You're fired," she snaps.

Torrence's brow crumples. "I—what?"

"Get the fuck out of my lab." She enunciates every word carefully.

"Dr. Rivers—"

She stands, holding eye contact. He shuts up, panic and confusion flitting over his face, then twisting into affront. Anger. *Good*, she thinks. *Good*.

"I lied for you," he whispers.

"They didn't care about your lie."

"I could go to the city. I could tell them exactly what you told me. Tell them about how you had us falsify the data, hide the distortions." His voice is shaking. He's not really going to do that, at least not immediately, and more importantly, he still doesn't get it. He doesn't understand that the lie doesn't matter, that it never mattered.

But part of her mind is shrieking now, telling her to walk this back. This isn't the long game; she'd meant for him to keep trusting her, to let her continue to hamstring his career until there was no way for him to wiggle out of it. Him storming off in a crisis—she's probably done enough, but maybe not.

There's no walking this back, though.

She smiles. It is not kind. "Research evolves, Torrence. And preliminary results are sometimes adjusted to manage expectations with the understanding that they'll be firmed up, corrected, in time. Of course, you can do what you want. I'd just suggest you keep in mind how much you'll need a favorable reference from Myrica on your job hunt."

Torrence stares at her for another tense few seconds, then spins on his heel and flees. She follows him as far as the door to her office and watches, coffee in hand, as he bypasses his desk entirely except to grab his phone and shed his lab coat. The front door closes silently after him.

"Have Dr. Torrence's desk cleaned out by lunchtime," she says to Cara, who's staring after him.

It's like lancing a boil, she thinks, rolling her shoulders, feeling herself settle back into her skin. A momentary flare and then relief, and the possibility of healing. She ignores the small voice that whispers that she's made a mistake, that she shouldn't have exploded. She's better than that, but it was necessary. Her colleagues know to defer to her, to stay out of her way. She's never resorted to raised voices and direct derision, not to this level.

But then again, she's never been under this much *pressure*.

"Yes, Dr. Rivers," Cara says. She's not worried anymore; she looks plastic instead. Maybe this will serve as a reminder to everybody to not overly involve themselves in her life.

"Have we received any updates?" Tamsin asks.

Valdez blows out a shaky exhale. "Just a write-up from the university team. I've added it to the server."

"What's the upshot?"

"That they have no idea what they're looking at, either."

Tamsin sips from her coffee, then nods. "Well, we expected that," she says, and Valdez smiles weakly. He's a good man, all things considered. Good at getting on with the work, at least. Much better at it than Torrence. "Progress on intervention tests?"

Valdez pulls up images and statistics onto a screen, and Tamsin settles in.

The day drags on with no real solutions ventured. Just before noon, Cara takes Torrence's things down to the lobby for him. When she returns, she's juggling several boxes—the equipment Tamsin requisitioned. Cara takes it all into one of the currently unused conference rooms and bustles in and out over the next few hours, grabbing the last items.

By mid-afternoon, it's all there, packed neatly for her. Cara lets her know it's ready and doesn't ask any questions. Tamsin goes to look over the bulk of it, considering. It'll be conspicuous if she leaves with all of it; she'll want a handcart. Better to take it a bit at a time, but the thought of coming into her office towering over the city, with her lab on eggshells around her, day after day, makes her skin crawl.

She gets the handcart.

Chapter Ten

That night, Tamsin tries to take her time with dinner. She pulls out a meal kit: kale and squash salad with pickled cherries. The pre-cut squash needs to be roasted, the cherries soaked in vinegar and sugar. The instructions are simple and direct, and her fingertips barely ache anymore, but as she works, the strain of the day refuses to shed off of her. She leans against the counter, hands on the edge, head down between her shoulders, while the squash cooks.

Too much. Today was too much.

Two weeks ago, it would have been normal.

She's out of control, unrecognizable to herself. She blew it with Torrence today, and even before that, everything had been *wrong*. The sleepwalking was bad enough, but she has to be honest with herself. What happened in the car was just shy of agoraphobia. Diagnosable, pathological. She can blame it on hyperfocus and being belowground all she wants, but that doesn't make it okay.

She needs to get herself together. She needs to focus on the world outside, on a city she has no real attachment to beyond familiarity, on a job that feels ill-fitting for the first time in years. Still, ill-fitting or not, she's given up so much for this life. Some of it has been easy: few relationships, no family, no hobbies. But she's made sacrifices, too, bypassed other opportunities, left academia behind, burned bridges to get to where she is. She *chose* this life. The door's important, the basement is important, but if she can't balance it all, they have to drop off first.

Lachlan's voice echoes through her. *Take care.*

Tamsin's fingers tighten on the counter. The timer dings. She finishes the salad and takes it to her barely used dining room. She eats each bite mechanically.

Penrose hops up onto the table, and she doesn't have the energy to shoo him away.

He settles down close enough to her plate that he could touch a paw to it, then rolls halfway onto his side and gazes at her. She frowns at him, reaching out and running a hand over his sleek head.

He purrs.

Tamsin rubs a knuckle over his chin, and he pushes into it. He doesn't nip, doesn't roll away to his other side. Penrose is an affectionate cat, but not like this.

"Are you feeling okay?" she asks, stroking along his belly. He goes limp with pleasure. He doesn't squirm closer or get up to reposition himself.

It feels ridiculous to take him to a vet for being calm and *friendly*, but after five years of cohabitating, Tamsin knows something is wrong.

Her appetite deadened, she dumps the rest of her salad. She thinks about getting a shower, packing up for the night, getting some rest.

She goes down to the basement instead.

There's equipment to set up, after all. Work to be done. She can't do anything about Penrose right now, and rest doesn't produce results. In the morning, she'll schedule an appointment for Penrose and go into the lab.

For now she'll start with hardness tests.

They're inconclusive.

No, scratch that; the tests *conclusively* show that the door is made of wood. Entirely average wood. They're only inconclusive about how the wood can heal itself and why she never sees it in progress. That only increases the hunger inside of her, the frustration that the door refuses to behave as she knows it should, the need to find an explanation. She turns to the new camera, fussing with the settings, training it on the door. Her first few attempts at scraping the door for the camera to capture are clumsy, her wrist dropping too low and obscuring the image, or the gouge she's using not cutting deep enough. But finally, she gets a clear shot.

She slows it down, the way she couldn't with the old camera, and watches the material of the door . . . flow. It fills the channel left behind, smoothing over any damage, as if it's a fluid that can ignore the tug of gravity. And when Tamsin repositions the camera so that it can see her as well, a tricky angle where the gouges and one of her eyes are all visible at once, she can see that the flow only happens the moment she blinks.

It knows when she's watching.

Observational effect.

She recoils from the camera and the door, as if burned. She paces, but she doesn't climb the steps. She just walks, back and forth, back and forth, chewing at her thumbnail. Her skin protests; her fingertips begin to throb again.

Eventually, she moves the camera far enough back to fit the whole door in the frame. She sets it up to run all night alongside the original rig. *It doesn't matter,* her hindbrain whispers; the door doesn't seem to care if the camera is on it, only if her eyes are on it. And even if she could stay up all night, it can change in the space of a blink.

All the same, Tamsin drops into a chair and stares. She stares until her eyes burn, until her head swims. And then she covers her face with her hands and tries not to laugh.

Tries harder not to cry.

She must be dozing when she hears the turning of a doorknob. The sound is unreal, distant and too close all at once, and Tamsin sits up straight, blinking rapidly, lips parted. Fear rises in fits and starts, and she twists in her seat, looking up at the stairs. But the door up there is static. Not even the shudder of Penrose leaning against it, or the slight movement that accompanies the HVAC system coming to life, shifting air pressure in the hall.

A latch gives. Hinges sigh. Tamsin turns to the far end of the basement.

She sees herself, stepping through the door.

You're dreaming, she tells herself. If she looks away, she'll see the notes she's written on the walls are gibberish. It's a repeat of the dream of her bathroom, of staring at herself in the mirror. It's just the same, the strange feeling of looking at a reflection that isn't a reflection. But there's so much light, nearly blinding, no dim shadows and obscured landmarks to warp her perception.

There's only herself, red hair gleaming in the lamplight, frizzed at the edges by a long day, in the same dress, the same heels, the same necklace.

Slowly, Tamsin rises to her feet. They're of a height, her reflection and her, but they don't move in sync except to stare at one another. Her body feels heavy, numb, anesthetized. There's no room in her for a reaction to the impossible.

Look behind it, a distant part of her mind whispers, and with great effort, Tamsin tears her gaze away and tries to catch a glimpse of what exists through the door.

Her reflection closes it behind her before Tamsin can make out anything in the shadows.

The writing on the walls is legible. Coherent. Her reflection smiles, a soft and gentle thing.

"Hello," it says.

Tamsin does not scream, but only because her throat has closed tight. Her breath is a thin, high whine, and she reaches out one trembling hand.

The impossible thing in front of her looks down at that hand, head tilted, lips slightly parted. There's something almost childlike in its expression. Curious and sweet. Tamsin's eyes flick across every feature, finding nothing she does not recognize and yet nothing that feels right, either.

Wake up, she demands of herself. *Wake up.* She closes her eyes, wills herself to sleep and wake again.

Warm, slender fingers close around her wrist. The scream leaves Tamsin's throat, and she jerks away, eyes wide now, stumbling back, then falling.

The thing blinks down at her, shocked. "Did I frighten you?" it asks, and it's her voice, *her* voice, but not the one she hears when she speaks. It's the one out of recordings. Her voice as others hear it.

But she has never sounded so gentle.

"I'm fine," Tamsin says, but her chest hurts, and her breath is hard to catch and keep. She is shaking, all through her body, and she's awake. She knows she's awake.

She can't be awake.

Tamsin makes herself stand, clutching at the worktable for balance. An avalanche of questions jockey for position in her mind, on her tongue.

The one that falls out is, "Who are you?"

What, she wants to correct. *What, what are you?*

The thing opens its mouth, then hesitates. It looks down at its own hands, runs them over the tail of its braid, draped over one shoulder. It takes in its clothing, its pale skin, its body.

It looks back at her.

"I don't know," it says. "Aren't I you?"

Tamsin swallows around the tight lump in her throat. She edges around the thing, toward the stairs. "No," she says. "No, you're not."

"Oh," it says.

She reaches the stairs.

"Wait here," Tamsin says.

"Okay." It smiles again, and it looks so easy.

Tamsin climbs the stairs backward, unwilling to take her eyes off of it until, at last, she's through the door. The thing doesn't move to follow her. It sits down on the floor, cross-legged. It waits.

She shuts the door tight, activating every lock with furious, trembling hands.

The Double

Chapter Eleven

Lachlan Woodfield's name glows in the midnight dark.

Tamsin sits at her dining room table, alone. She stares down at her phone, hands clawing against her scalp. Her braid hangs half-undone, hair tangling under her clenching fingertips. She's shaking again, has been shaking since she got out of the basement and hasn't stopped once. There's a sweating gin and tonic at her elbow. She hasn't taken a single sip.

It was stupid, locking the thing downstairs. Her laptop is down there. All her equipment is down there. The damn *door* is down there, and who knows what else might come through it. Can the thing open it at will? It must be able to. Anything else . . .

What? Doesn't make sense?

None of this makes sense.

Maybe, when she unlocks the basement, the thing will be gone. Left, or never existed at all. The unhinged imaginings of an overwrought mind. It didn't work with the door, but she wants to believe now. Needs to.

But if it's still there, she needs a plan.

Lachlan would come if she called. She can see it clearly: Lachlan on her doorstep, black gloves in place, as always. Lachlan, gun in hand, ready as Tamsin unlocks the basement. Or maybe she'd use a knife; a gunshot would wake the neighbors, and Lachlan is nothing if not mindful about appearances. About *management*.

Lachlan can fix this.

Myrica Dynamics will spread that thing wearing her face out in a lab somewhere. And she'll be right there with them, cutting into its flesh. She doesn't have the medical training, but she'd insist. She needs to know what's inside, needs to see that it's nothing like her, that it can't be real.

Blade parts flesh, reveals undifferentiated tissue inside, no sign of liver, of heart, of lungs. Not like cutting into herself at all, really, as long as they get the right answer.

(Maybe they won't. Maybe the thing bleeds when sliced up. Maybe it has a brain.)

No, that's not the right option, the safe option. Calling Lachlan means revealing all that she's been hiding and would put her into an even more precarious position. It would put that spotlight incontrovertibly on *her*. Who's to say she wouldn't end up on a table right next to that thing?

She can't call Lachlan.

But she doesn't know what to do instead.

Aren't I you?

Tamsin gathers her hair up into a simple, pragmatic bun and takes a deep breath. First things first, she supposes. She has to prove—to herself, at the very least—that the thing in the basement isn't her.

Before Tamsin ventures back down into the basement, she fortifies herself with strong coffee. She gathers a few items: a tablet she hasn't used in a few years, her phone, fresh clothing. She eyes one of the meal-replacement shakes in her fridge, wondering if the subject will need to eat, then closes the door; better for it to make its needs known than for Tamsin to assume them. Otherwise, she might skew her data and come away with the wrong conclusions.

She pauses at the door. Her stomach twists. If it *does* need to eat, and she just keeps the door closed for a few days, that thing will starve. Will transmute into a harmless, inanimate corpse. Easier to manage, to hide.

But that doesn't get her answers. She needs to go down there, and she needs to know what she's dealing with. She keys in the code, flips the lock.

The thing waits for her in the center of the room.

It sits right where Tamsin left it, though in a different position, as if it'd gotten uncomfortable. And when it sees Tamsin, a smile blooms across its familiar-unfamiliar features. Tamsin wants to run. She closes the door instead, listens for the lock engaging.

"You came back," it says.

Tamsin shudders. That voice—it's almost unbearable, so similar to her own but from the wrong vantage. She makes her way down the stairs, taking each step with care. She really needs to add the safety railing soon.

The bundle of supplies goes on the worktable, save for her phone, which she has recording audio in her pocket. She goes to the cameras and reorients the first, simpler one to be trained on the thing wearing her face. She never turns her back on it.

Tamsin keeps the camera between them, but though it would be far easier to watch through the display, she looks directly at the not-her.

It looks back, sitting with its legs straight out in front of it on the cold floor. *Childlike*, she thinks again. So far from her own mannerisms that it turns her stomach.

"Do you have a name?" Tamsin asks. She expects confusion again; it's not so far away from *Who are you?* But this time, the thing doesn't hesitate.

"Dr. Tamsin Rivers," it says.

Tamsin flinches.

It tilts its head, brows drawing together. "Did I say something wrong?"

Tamsin looks at the laptop, but it's exactly where she left it. Is her name written anywhere else? She doesn't think it is. Her head hurts.

When you look away, does it change again? Like the door?

Her eyes snap back to the thing. It still looks like her. It's still sitting on the floor, in her clothes, with the wrong expression.

"How do you know that name?" she demands.

"How do you know yours?"

Her anger demands that she shut this down, that she maintain firm boundaries, but she won't get useful answers that way. This thing either doesn't understand the question or is trying to explain. "I was taught it a long time ago. By my parents," she says. The memory of carefully printing her name on large, lined paper surfaces in her mind, unseen for decades thanks to the lack of children in her orbit. Tamsin wets her lips. "Did somebody teach you that name?"

The thing is uncertain again. It frowns, then makes to stand.

Tamsin allows it, though she tenses.

"I don't remember," it says. "Maybe?"

"It's not your name," Tamsin snaps before she can stop herself, before she even registers that the burning resistance that sparks up in her is jealousy. This isn't objective. She needs to note what she's been told, listen to the thing's logic, not *argue*. She knows that, but she doesn't stop talking. "However you know it, it's not yours."

That name belongs to her.

The thing's frown deepens. It wraps its arms around its chest. It's such a strange, vulnerable motion, another crumb of horror. "Then what is my name?" it asks, and its blue eyes are wide as it looks to her.

For guidance?

Tamsin's hands form tight fists at her side. She doesn't want this responsibility. She wants, more than anything, to send this thing away, forget it ever existed. But it is here, and just like the basement, just like the door, she can't walk away. It's getting more and more imperative that she keep her attention right here, right now. That she figure out why this is happening *to her*.

What name fits an unnerving . . . doppelgänger?

It's tempting to give it a meaningless name. Something that simply isn't *Tamsin*, something more in line with *Jane Doe*. But naming a thing describes it, and the thing before her, captured by the camera, has a few undeniably salient characteristics.

"Prime," she decides finally. Written out Tamsin', in mathematical or chemical notation. "It means a copy," she says and watches the thing's face for a response. She sees only curiosity, no opposition, no argument. "A copy, but transformed, somehow, or rotated, or located at a different place along a molecule."

The *how* isn't clear yet, but it will be. And it reinforces the fact that Tamsin herself is the original pattern. $Tamsin^0$.

"Prime," the thing repeats. Its limbs relax, anxiety replaced by a visible calm. "I like it. Thank you."

Aboveground, it's morning. In the basement, the light remains unchanging. So far, over the last several hours of study, Tamsin has found no structural difference between them. They are precisely the same height. Their hair is the same texture, the same length, the same shade of red, showing an identical recent lack of attention. Their irises are the same color, and Tamsin suspects (fears) that if she were to take photos, the patterning would be exactly the same as well.

Prime changed into its new set of clothes without protest (or any hint of shame, stripping without hesitation) around two a.m. The yoga pants and an older sweater are things that Tamsin rarely wears. It's a token attempt to make them look distinct. It works enough to ease the nausea in her gut.

Makes it easier to look at Prime as she slides the tablet over to it.

Prime looks at it with the same curiosity it seems to have for everything.

"Can you read what it says?" Tamsin asks when Prime makes no move to touch anything.

"California Psychological Inventory," Prime replies with no hesitation. "What is it?"

"A series of questions to help me understand you," Tamsin says. She reaches over, though the closer her hand gets to Prime, the more she has to fight a growing tremor. "Read each question, then all the answer choices. Pick the one you think sounds most like you." She taps an option to demonstrate. "When you're finished with each page, touch the next button. Does that make sense?"

Prime nods. It takes the tablet, finally, and pulls it close. Its posture is wholly unlike Tamsin's, cradling the object carefully, tapping with the slightest brush of fingers.

"I don't understand what some of these questions are asking," Prime ventures after a moment.

"Go with your gut," Tamsin replies.

Anything else might bias the thing across from her. It frowns, then begins tapping at the screen again.

On her laptop, Tamsin fills out the same personality test. She answers questions between long periods of watching Prime. Prime finishes first, and Tamsin moves it on to the next test in the series. When Tamsin completes her own, she pulls up Prime's results.

They do not match.

Unsurprisingly, Tamsin scores much more strongly in dominance, independence, and intellectual efficiency. Prime, by contrast, scores high in flexibility and tolerance. They are closest together in self-acceptance, of all things, followed closely by self-control.

And Prime easily outstrips her in empathy, which unsettles her. Prime has made no reference to other people; how can it be empathetic if it exists in isolation?

"Prime," she says, not a question, and Prime's head comes up immediately.

"Yes?"

"What's on the other side of the door?"

Prime frowns. "That door?" it asks, gesturing to the stairs. "I don't know. I haven't gone through it. But you have."

Tamsin's lips thin in irritation. "No," she says, "the door you arrived through. *That* door." She jerks her chin at it, positioned behind Prime, right where Tamsin can keep an eye on it. The camera is set behind her shoulder, capturing them all together.

Prime looks surprised, twisting in its seat to look.

"I don't remember," it says after a long moment. With a glance back at Tamsin, it rises to its bare feet and approaches the door, wringing its hands together.

Tamsin observes, pulse loud in her ears.

Prime comes at it from an angle, much as Tamsin has done before, as if wary and untrusting. When it reaches out a hand toward the knob, that hand shakes. Prime hesitates, looks back once more.

"Do you want me to open it?" it asks.

Yes. She wants to say *yes.* The cameras are rolling, and Prime has already opened the door once, even if it was from the other side.

But she's not ready. Not prepared, if another Prime should step out. Not equipped for whatever new questions lie beyond that door. There are already too many moving parts to keep track of.

"No," she says reluctantly. "No, not right now."

Anxiety visibly leeches from Prime's shoulders. It lingers another moment at the door, then returns to the table and sits down across from Tamsin. It reaches for the tablet, then looks to her for guidance.

Tamsin exhales slowly, then nods. "Keep going," she says. "We have a lot of tests to get through."

Prime bends its head back to the personality inventories and other cognitive tests.

Tamsin puts in an order for a baby monitor, nanny cams, some hardware, and another electronic lock system for same-day delivery.

Chapter Twelve

By the time the supplies arrive, Tamsin has confirmed a number of things about her doppelgänger:

Its reading level is equivalent to her own and is limited to languages that Tamsin knows (and to her ability level in each).

It has a working understanding of calculus and linear algebra, again equivalent to her own. Theoretical physics as well, or at least the amount they've covered. Tamsin has, so far, stayed away from the specifics that underpin the node experiments. That feels too intimate to test. Too risky.

They differ on most measures of personality.

They weigh the same, have the same measurements.

Prime's face and thumbprint can both unlock her phone.

When she goes upstairs to feed herself and retrieve the boxes stacked on her doorstep, she takes her phone and encrypted laptop with her, just to be safe. She locks both locks behind her. She also spends a long time staring into her fridge. Prime has yet to ask for food or water, but it looks distinctly uncomfortable now. The constant light can't be helping, either, if it has the same need for sleep Tamsin does. And if it has a digestive system at all—

Well. All the more reason to keep working.

She takes the boxes upstairs, to her bedroom.

The windows in the en suite are the hardest to secure. They take well over half an hour, which is ridiculous, given how small they are, but Tamsin is not willing to take chances. The baby monitor she puts into the ceiling vent, and she toggles off the zone climate control for the room. She empties all the drawers, removes everything from the bathroom and her bedroom. Not just potential weapons; anything and everything that is not bolted to the walls, save for the bed. She takes the sheets and pillows, too.

All of her things go into the guest bedroom, the guest bathroom. She hasn't been in either room in maybe an entire year (save for, perhaps, her dreamlike wanderings), leaving it up to her monthly cleaning service to air out the linens. The dresser has room for most of her clothing, but the closet is small, and everything feels cramped and wrong. It's not going to be comfortable, but she wants Prime's space to be as self-contained as possible, which means the main bedroom and the en suite bath. Penrose watches from on top of the dresser, unnerved and fidgety. This is the easiest answer to any number of logistical problems and has the added benefit of separating Prime from the door in the basement, but she knows what it looks like.

It looks like ceding ground.

It looks like building a prison cell.

The cameras are easily secreted into the windowsills and other nooks and crannies, and the lock installs easily in the door. She sets it up to work only from the hall. And then, when she's certain that the room is ready, she goes down to the basement.

"Come here," she says from halfway down the stairs. Prime is reading over the notes penned onto the wall.

"Stretching isn't sinking," Prime says. It's swaying on its feet.

"I know," Tamsin says, impatient. "Prime, come here."

"If the basement were sinking, the house would be, too."

"The floor is sinking. The rest isn't. *Prime*."

Prime, at last, leaves the writing and approaches the stairs. Its eyes are bright, almost fevered. It peers up at Tamsin. It mounts the first step. "Do you know why it's happening?"

"No," Tamsin says. Her mouth is dry. "Do you?"

Prime frowns at her, then shakes its head. "It doesn't make sense," it says and climbs another step. A third. On the fourth, it stumbles, feet catching on the too-tall riser. For half a second, Tamsin sees her own image falling, snapping its neck on impact.

Her chest lurches, as if she's the one about to die. She catches Prime and hauls it close.

It's the most physical contact they've had, and Tamsin recoils immediately. The copy of her body is too warm, too vulnerable, and she hates it with a burning passion. She grabs Prime by the wrist and leads it up the remaining stairs with harsh tugs whenever Prime hesitates.

She really needs to install that railing.

Prime tries to stop at the threshold into the house proper, staring and blinking against the dimmer interior, but Tamsin leads it down the hall, to the next flight of steps. From the kitchen, Penrose watches them, tail flicking.

"Where are we going?" Prime asks, stumbling behind Tamsin.

"To your new room," Tamsin says. "It will be more comfortable."

Prime's quiet after that, until Tamsin ushers it into the bedroom. It's still unsettling, seeing the space so bare, seeing *herself* as an outside observer in a familiar area, and she wonders if she's making a mistake. If she's losing her mind after all.

But Prime is looking around in wonder, and when it turns to Tamsin, there is joy on its face. "For me?" it asks.

Tamsin nods. "And the bathroom is through that door."

Prime glances over. Its face goes still for a moment, then the joy becomes shocked desperation. It trembles. "I—I need—"

"Go ahead," Tamsin says.

It makes for the bathroom. Tamsin locks the door and heads back downstairs.

With Prime's containment squared away, Tamsin turns her attention back to the question of figuring out what Prime *is*.

All appearances indicate that the thing is human, but its provenance makes that seem, in a word, unlikely. She has yet to do a detailed physical examination beyond size and shape. That will require more physical contact between them, which she's dreading, She doesn't want firsthand knowledge of how their skin feels the same. How their breathing might sync up, or their heart rates. Not to mention, she lacks even basic first-aid training.

And she doesn't have the supplies.

The latter can be remedied, at least.

Some of what she's after, she'll order from a medical-supply store, but the rest is going to take a little time and a lot of administrative know-how. She ignores all the unread emails in her inbox and instead opens a new one, addresses it to her assistant.

Cara, need you to track down a few pieces of equipment ASAP; see if you can borrow them from other departments, but keep my name out of it for now. Project-related, confidential.

-Compound microscope, 100x capability, slides, etc. Ability to capture images/video required

-Robot sample arm, with table mount-an older model is fine, I think R&D should still have a few decommissioned models from the demos two years ago

-Ultrasound machine, portable

TR

Email sent, she sits at her dining room table, closing her eyes. She's been up since yesterday morning, and it's almost four in the afternoon. Her head aches, her sense of balance softly tilts when she closes her eyes, her ribs are sore. She needs sleep. She needs to log some hours on the subsidence question. She needs a lot of things she isn't going to get.

But she can at least clean herself up a little.

The guest bathroom is lacking compared to what she's used to, the showerhead not quite as nice, the towels stiffer from lack of use, and everything is still jumbled, the chaos of the recently moved. But the water is hot enough to be blissful, and she's tired enough to not care about the rest. She's fresh out of the guest shower when her phone rings.

Tucking a towel tightly around her chest, she scoops up the phone. Her mood sours when she sees Cara's name, but she hits *Accept Call.*

"I hope you're calling to tell me when to pick everything up," she says by way of greeting.

"I've got everything but the ultrasound squared away, Dr. Rivers," Cara confirms quickly. "But I needed more information on that one and thought you wouldn't want me to pry via email. What output do you need?"

"Imaging," Tamsin says.

"So one of the machines they use to test welding integrity—that won't work?"

"No, I need—" She cuts off, closing her eyes a moment. When she opens them again, her reflection gazes back at her, mocking. *You need a medical one, and that's going to raise too many questions.* But her chances of getting one on her own are minuscule.

It's an easier ask than a human-grade X-ray machine, at least. And maybe what Cara's offering will work, if she gets creative. Still, the learning curve on a medical ultrasound is going to be steep enough. Figuring out how to translate a paper readout of fracture depth on a model that isn't designed to process living tissue . . .

"Dr. Rivers?"

Tamsin shakes herself. "I need one with a visual display, like they use in medical offices. Is that going to be a problem?"

Cara doesn't respond at first. Tamsin hopes it's because she's running some kind of search.

"How is any of this related to the project?" she asks.

Shame ripples below Tamsin's skin, followed by a white-hot anger not so dissimilar from what she'd felt when she fired Torrence. But she needs to control that; she can't lash out at everybody who questions her.

"That isn't your concern," Tamsin says. Her voice sounds almost calm.

"I can keep your name out of it, but if I associate it to the project, it will raise questions. Mx. Woodfield has been by twice in the last week—"

"I'm investigating a novel line of inquiry." Tamsin rubs at her temple. The last thing she needs is Lachlan having proof she's doing something . . . nonstandard. Her absence today will do enough damage. "I don't know that it's going to pan out. I would prefer that Mx. Woodfield not be aware until there is something to make her aware *of.* You said you have everything else squared away?"

"On personal favors, Dr. Rivers."

"Good. Keep it that way. Don't log it anywhere." It occurs to her that she should reassure Cara that if anybody catches on and complains, Tamsin will shield her.

She doesn't. She can't, if it comes to that. The research has to come first.

"Of course, Dr. Rivers. I'll let you know in the morning when you can come pick them up."

Bring them to my house is on the tip of her tongue. She stops herself just in time. No, better that she go in to pick them up, just like she did everything else.

Too many questions otherwise.

She decides against bringing Prime any food, but does bring a water bottle when she returns. Dehydration is a relentless killer, and it may take longer than a few days for Prime to decide to ask (or conceive of asking) for a drink; after all, it only seemed to occur to Prime that it needed to use the restroom when it encountered the concept.

(Or maybe she's imagining that. Assigning more meaning than Prime's behavior warrants.)

At any rate, there's water in the bathroom and no way to control Prime's access to it. Prime very well may already have had some on its own, spoiling any conceivable experimental results. Therefore, Tamsin will provide water, but no food.

She doesn't knock, just deactivates the lock and lets herself into the cell. Prime is curled up in the center of the mattress, sound asleep. It doesn't stir as Tamsin sets out her other supplies: nitrile gloves, a thermometer, a blood-pressure cuff, a cup of ice, a cup of steaming water, and a long, sharp pin. All supplies she had on hand already.

It doesn't stir as Tamsin draws closer, peering down at her copy.

Prime sleeps soundly, still dressed in the clothing Tamsin offered, with no tension pinching its brows. If it dreams, they are quiet dreams. Soft dreams. The sight makes Tamsin long for the guest bed.

She should be sleeping, too. Her head swims a little. It wouldn't hurt, would it, to just take everything and go away? Wait a few hours? Put her head down, forget everything for just a little bit . . .

Prime makes a soft noise, then opens its startlingly blue eyes. Tamsin stares down at it, at its relaxed body language, its trusting gaze. Nausea rises in her throat. Does *she* look like that?

No. She never looks that guileless.

Prime stares up at her. It doesn't react as if startled to find Tamsin watching it sleep. Something about that calm blankness makes Tamsin furious, and she goes over to get the first of her tools.

"Sit on the edge of the mattress," Tamsin says.

Prime, as always, obeys. *Why?* Tamsin scowls as she tugs on a pair of gloves, then scoops up the thermometer. She makes herself approach the bed, refuses to let herself shy away or hesitate. "Open your mouth. I'm going to put this under your tongue."

No resistance to that, either. Nor to the blood-pressure cuff after. The readings are normal, and in the range of Tamsin's own. Prime's are both a little lower, but it's only just woken up.

Every test points to Prime being human, but that still feels wrong. It feels—threatening. Tamsin puts the emotion aside to study later, once she's gotten a chance to rest.

She busies herself instead with the cups. The one has stopped steaming, but the water inside is still painfully hot. The other's ice has begun to melt, but still burns to the touch. She crouches in front of Prime, and Prime looks down at her.

"Close your eyes and give me your right hand."

Its gaze tracks past her, down to where the cups rest. It opens its mouth, perhaps to ask a question.

Then it looks back at Tamsin and closes its eyes. Holds out its hand.

Tamsin takes Prime firmly by the wrist and with her other hand picks up the first cup. She presses Prime's fingers to the ice inside. It makes a shocked noise, hand twitching. "Cold," it says, without being prompted. "Ice?"

"Yes." Tamsin swaps out the cup, submerges Prime's cold-reddened fingers into the hot water. This time, Prime's entire body jerks.

"Hot!"

Tamsin makes a mental note that Prime not only immediately recognized and named the sensations, but has the same response as most humans would. She only slowly releases Prime's hand, though, and when Prime pulls it free, the skin is flushed and scalded.

Of course it feels discomfort, she thinks, but—is that truly a given? Does it actually feel discomfort, or is it only playacting out the response Tamsin expects? More observational effect at work?

Unclear. But she can't very well set up a double-blind experiment, even without an internal review board to justify the ethics of this to, and there's one last test she wants to perform, one last piece of data she needs for now.

She gets up, dumps the cups out in the bathroom sink. And then she retrieves the needle, hiding it in the curve of her palm.

Prime is wary as Tamsin returns to the bed, as she sits beside it.

"Give me your hand again. Left this time."

Prime hesitates. It's learning, perhaps, not to trust so readily.

She wonders why it ever trusted Tamsin at all; Tamsin wouldn't have.

"Your hand," Tamsin repeats, making her voice softer this time.

Prime finally offers up its left hand. Tamsin takes it gently. She slips the needle from where she secreted it away, a subtle movement that Prime doesn't seem to catch.

The needle touches the soft underside of Prime's wrist.

"Stay still, Prime," Tamsin warns as Prime stiffens beside her. She pushes the needle harder into Prime's skin. It dimples, and Prime tries to shift away despite the warning, but Tamsin's grip on its arm tightens.

"That hurts," Prime says, voice wavering.

"Can you describe the pain?" Tamsin asks, glancing up at Prime's face. Its brows are drawn tight together, its lips pursed. It's anticipating more pain, clearly, and trying to figure out what Tamsin means to do.

But still, it cooperates. "Sharp?" it ventures. "Small, but growing."

Tamsin pushes harder. The needle breaks the skin. Prime yelps and tries to pull away again. Tamsin bares her teeth but loosens her fingers. The pin comes free, and blood wells to the surface.

Red. Entirely average red blood.

Tamsin lifts the pin, considering the smeared metal. What she wouldn't give to run tests on Prime's blood—but she has no ready access to a discreet-enough phlebotomy lab. It's too far outside her research area, and if the results come back unusual, it will be difficult to shut down any potentially resulting inquiry.

She sets aside the pin. Prime has retreated across the room, cradling its arm to its chest, eyeing Tamsin warily. Tamsin feels nauseated again, more strongly this time, and can't determine if it's because she can't stand seeing the pathetic echo of herself that is Prime or because *she* made Prime cringe away and cower.

"I didn't like that," Prime says. "Why did you do that?"

"To understand you a little better," Tamsin says, standing.

She leaves Prime huddled in the corner.

Chapter Thirteen

From: Lachlan
Drift, 8 pm. Two drinks.

Tamsin swears and tosses her phone on the kitchen counter. She doesn't have the time for this, or the stamina; she still hasn't slept. And moreover, she has no desire to leave the house. Drift is a glitzy rooftop bar, expensive and the perfect place to be seen, all things Tamsin is usually more than happy to partake in—but not now. She doesn't want to see and be seen. She doesn't want to feel the wind in her hair and see the entire city stretched out below her.

And Lachlan telling her to go to Drift means there's a problem. A problem like her disappearing from the lab again, she's sure. She thinks she told Cara she'd be working from home today, but it's distinctly possible she never actually did.

It's fine, though. She'll get her makeup on, give Penrose his dinner, head out. She's done more than a few social events she's hated every second of. Two drinks will make for a three-hour trip out, give or take, and she'll be back home before midnight. It will be fine.

Except she can't leave Prime alone, not even in the cell she's built for it. The nanny cams and baby monitor feed to her phone, but if something happens—if Prime *tries something*—there will be no way for her to get home fast enough. If anything brings suspicion to her house, or if Prime gets out, Tamsin is fucked. And even if nothing happens, Lachlan will be able to tell her attention is elsewhere.

Her phone pings again. She grabs it.

From: Lachlan
Dr. Rivers, please confirm.

That's new. Lachlan is worried. Or (*and?*) Lachlan doesn't trust her anymore.

She double-checks that the first text is recent, that she didn't miss it in the shake-up of Prime's appearance, but only five minutes have elapsed between the two. She chews at her lip, staring down at her phone. She can't leave, and she can't put Lachlan off.

From: Tamsin
Can't make it to Drift. Come over.

Tamsin stares at herself in the guest-room mirror. She's made herself a little more presentable, changed into a long-sleeved, jade-colored sweater and black slacks; not something she'd wear out, but something that conveys respect for Lachlan making the trip. Her hair is officially a disaster zone, but she doesn't have the time for a proper detangle and condition, so she's thrown it back into a frizzed chignon. She considers covering up the dark circles under her eyes as well, but decides to leave them visible. Illness and exhaustion are better excuses than anything else she can come up with.

She's stalling, though. There's only half an hour before Lachlan arrives, and there's one last thing to do.

She goes to the locked bedroom door. Keys in the code. Knocks, this time, before entering.

Prime is awake. It eyes Tamsin with the wariness that it had when Tamsin left it huddled in the corner. It's moved back to the bed, but it's sitting with its knees clutched to its chest. The wrist with the pinprick is exposed, as if Prime has been looking at it.

She regrets that pinprick. It was poorly done and, more importantly, poorly timed. She needs Prime to listen to her now. To continue to obey her.

"I'm having a guest over," Tamsin says. "You may be able to hear us talking. Can I trust you to be quiet until my guest has left?"

Prime cants its head to one side. "Why?"

"Because she thinks I live alone," Tamsin says, wondering if she's making a mistake. But regardless of how Prime feels about her, she trusts it to follow a request more than she trusts Prime to intuit a need to be quiet or to restrain its curiosity absent any direction. "It will confuse and upset her if she hears another person in the house. She may become angry. When she's angry, she causes pain."

An exaggeration, but only in that Tamsin has never been on the receiving end of that particular brand of fury. Prime rubs at its wrist. "I'll be quiet," it says.

"Good." She hesitates, then adds, "Thank you."

Prime's expression brightens somewhat. Tamsin's discomfort twists and grows.

It tucks a stray bit of hair behind one ear, and that gesture, more than any other, is upsettingly familiar. Alienating. Tamsin has the oddest feeling that she's looking at herself, and that the *she* who is doing the looking is—not her. Is more akin to a camera with nerves than a person.

"Can I have something to eat?" Prime asks. "I'm hungry."

No. The answer is reflexive but doesn't leave her mouth. She's gotten the answer she was after by withholding food: Prime can get hungry and knows what eating is without needing to be shown. Prime bleeds red. Prime is alive, and Tamsin therefore has a responsibility, doesn't she? She wouldn't gain anything by starving the thing.

And the thought of her own reflection dwindling to skin and bones—

It doesn't matter. None of it matters. All that *does* matter is that Lachlan is coming, and the more Tamsin pacifies Prime, the more likely it is that Prime will stay quiet.

"Yes, of course," Tamsin says. "I'll be right back."

She locks the door behind her and, in a distracted haze, descends to the kitchen. She needs to eat, too. She hasn't, not since lunch. She could cook something for the both of them, see if Prime has the same likes and dislikes she does.

But a glance at the oven clock says there's no time for that. Maybe in the morning. For now she grabs two meal-replacement bottles and takes them both upstairs.

Prime has uncurled from the bed and is looking out the window from between the slats of the blinds when Tamsin reenters the room. "Come away from there," Tamsin snaps.

Prime pulls away as if stung. "Did I do something wrong?"

"Somebody might see you. Come here, I brought food." She holds out one of the bottles, and Prime edges closer. It looks at the meal, then up at Tamsin.

"This is food?" it asks.

"It's nutritionally complete," Tamsin says. She gestures with the bottle, and Prime takes it. Then she makes a show of shaking her own, opening the cap. She takes a sip. "It's functional."

It tastes vaguely like chocolate. It's . . . fine.

Prime shakes its bottle, opens it in the same fashion, brings it to its nose. "I don't think I like this," it says.

"It's what we're having. It'll make you feel better." Tamsin takes a larger swig, then heads for the door. "I'll see you in the morning. Remember, be quiet tonight."

"Alright," Prime says. Tamsin leaves it taking a hesitant sip of its dinner, locking the door behind her.

It's seven fifty-five by the time she's finished her own. Lachlan isn't far. Her heart kicks up in her chest. She feels lightheaded, but that might only be the lack of sleep.

She slams a caffeine shot just in case, then goes to her liquor cabinet to fetch a nice bottle of bourbon and a few other ingredients. It's the only way she can think to prepare.

Lachlan Woodfield has been in her house once before. She is not, in any way, the bodyguard of the CEO of Myrica. But when Mr. Thomas came by for a dinner, a little over two years ago, to discuss the final timeline for the node-lab construction, Lachlan had attended as his shadow. That night had been a small affair, with only a few other guests, and though all the cooking had been done by caterers earlier in the day, Tamsin had been the one to serve everything. A flawless performance, the appearance of domestic mastery.

Every detail had been planned within the finest tolerance. Every minute had gone according to that plan. It was the only way she'd gotten through the night. She isn't a natural hostess.

And Tamsin doesn't have a plan now.

The knock comes at one minute after eight. Tamsin freezes where she's setting out a bowl of furikake rice crackers.

She's got the lighting on its preset entertaining profile. The caffeine is bubbling along her nerves. She's as put together as she's going to be.

She goes to get the door.

Lachlan wears one of her usual suits, though Tamsin doesn't recognize the subtle black-on-black pattern. It might be new. Her hair is slicked back, and her hands are, as always, gloved. She is broad and steady, and for a moment, Tamsin wonders what it would be like to fall into her. If Lachlan would bother to catch her or just watch her stumble.

"You look unwell, Dr. Rivers," Lachlan says, and she sounds more irritated than concerned.

"Come in," Tamsin says.

Lachlan follows her to the living room and takes a seat on the couch, leaving Tamsin with the chair across from her, the coffee table in between them. Tamsin measures a bit of sugar into each glasses, drips bitters on top from a small, dark bottle. Pours them both two fingers of whiskey and adds one thin slice of dried blood orange to each drink. Ice comes from the nearby ice dish.

Old-fashioneds are almost always Lachlan's drink of choice; she's glad she still has the ingredients on hand from that first dinner. Mx. Woodfield knows exactly what Tamsin is doing, playing to her preferences in an attempt to charm her, and takes the glass anyway.

"You fired Isaac Torrence," Lachlan says without preamble. She punctuates it with a sip from her glass before setting it aside. Acceptably made, then.

Tamsin sits back and crosses her legs. "I did."

"And then did not log any follow-up paperwork."

"I wasn't aware there was a deadline on that."

"Don't bullshit me, Dr. Rivers." Lachlan's voice is steady and cool. She leans forward, elbows braced on her splayed knees, gloved hands folded. "You know exactly how closely you're being watched. You know how much pressure you're under. And you know the risks of cutting a member of your team loose after humiliating him publicly and then ignoring the follow-up work to ensure he doesn't retaliate." Her palms press together. Her gloves creak. "Please tell me why I just covered for you, again."

Tamsin bristles. Lachlan's right; she shouldn't have fired Torrence in the first place, and she should have made damn sure her ass was covered by the correct paperwork after. That she didn't is embarrassing, but she papers over the feeling, lifting her chin.

"He's not going to cause trouble. Even if he went to the mayor and explained about the distortion, he'll sound insane, or he'll just be telling her something she's going to find out in a week or two when the water and sewage department starts reporting their pipes visibly distending." She rubs at the short stump of her ruined nail. "I also didn't ask you to step in."

"Is that because you just assumed I'd do it, or because you've stopped caring about consequences?"

Tamsin bites the tip of her tongue, then takes a drink. "Neither," she says. Her throat feels raw as she says it. Her ribs feel raw. Everything feels oversensitive, and she thinks of Prime's fingers in the scalding water. "I wasn't thinking."

Lachlan tips her chin up, as if to say *obviously*. "Not thinking for the same reason you weren't in the lab today and haven't been answering emails? Not thinking for the same reason you look like . . ." A gesture with her glass, at Tamsin's entirety. "Not thinking for the same reason you invited me *here*? Dr. Rivers, you don't entertain at home. And you certainly don't invite *me* to your house."

In fact, a week ago Tamsin had been desperately trying to avoid exactly this scenario.

"I haven't been sleeping well," she confesses. And somehow, the confession makes her straighten up, not recoil away. It's easier than being evasive. And it is something she can defend. It is, for once, not a lie.

She can give little pieces of herself and still hold on to the whole.

Lachlan takes the scrap she's been offered, sitting back against the couch cushions. "Do you want me to get you a prescription for some sleep aids?"

"Not the problem," Tamsin says. Her glass is getting low. Lachlan's, too. *Two drinks.* "The work is—engaging. But in a way that makes it hard to put away when the day is done."

"And now is not the time to enforce a better work-life balance."

Tamsin inclines her head. "I don't think my presence in the labs is helpful, at the moment. I can do the majority of my work from here, where I have fewer interruptions and am less at risk of . . ." She tilts the glass, watches the slice of blood orange twirl lazily in the remaining bourbon. "Reacting without forethought to lower-priority personnel issues."

Lachlan's mouth quirks up on one side. She finishes her drink, setting the glass between them. The tension cracking and whipping between them shifts in tenor, gains an added layer of amusement, of familiarity. They click into place, playacting the right *sort* of danger, of opposition. Lachlan's unyielding resolve is an old friend, of sorts. It provides her something to orient from.

She can do this.

Lachlan sets her glass aside, and Tamsin moves to refresh her drink. For a moment, they are almost close enough to touch.

"When we poached you from the ivory tower," Lachlan says, voice low and just the slightest bit rough, hazel eyes fixed on Tamsin's hands, "you seemed too good to be true. The glittering prodigy, aiming for the top of the theoretical-physics hierarchy but willing to be wooed by industry for a better paycheck and louder PR trumpeting your successes. Too many talents, no preoccupation with academic admiration, no family to distract you, presence and social skills not only serviceable but enviable, and an incredible ability to be both brilliant and able to stay on task. I suppose it was only time until we found a project that would turn even you into a rude little recluse."

Tamsin laughs, adding sugar and bitters to the glass. "Careful," she says, reaching for the bourbon. "You're starting to sound fond."

Lachlan doesn't reply, but her gaze remains on Tamsin, warm and heavy.

The room feels a little closer. The lowered lighting is intimate, and for a moment, they are the only two people in the world.

Tamsin pours the bourbon and holds out Lachlan's glass.

Lachlan takes it, and their fingers do not touch.

"I meant what I said the other day," Lachlan says finally, after she takes a long and thoughtful draw from the glass. "Adjusting to your replacement is not high on my list of desires. But whatever is going on in your head needs to find its way into meetings. Memos. *Something.* Stop clearing your calendar. Start putting in appearances. When I said you could work remotely, this is not what I meant."

Another swallow. Tamsin barely sips at her own. Her heart is pounding again, and she doesn't think it's the caffeine, or the lack of sleep. Lachlan has destabilized her as quickly as she'd found her footing again.

Tamsin sets her glass down, and Lachlan reaches out, touches gloved fingers lightly against the back of her hand. Tamsin looks up, and Lachlan is now gazing directly at her.

"Don't make me tell you again," she says, and the intimacy of it is barbed now, sharpened to a cutting edge.

Fondness will not stop Lachlan from fixing a problem.

Tamsin's throat bobs. "Understood."

Lachlan doesn't smile. She just throws back the rest of her drink and sets it aside. Her hand only leaves Tamsin's when she stands and twitches her jacket and trousers back into line.

Tamsin rises and walks her to the door.

"Thank you," she says as Lachlan steps out onto the front stoop, "for agreeing to come here."

Lachlan doesn't respond, gaze flicking across Tamsin once more, as if taking a final measure, looking for a final fracture point. And then her attention goes a little behind Tamsin. Tamsin tries not to tense. Tries to convince herself that she would have heard if Prime had gotten out. It's just the two of them.

"I didn't realize you'd gotten a second cat," Lachlan says finally, looking down at Tamsin once more. "Good night, Dr. Rivers."

The world is very quiet. Lachlan Woodfield turns on her heel and slides her hands into her pockets, striding away toward where her car is parked. Tamsin grips the edge of the door tightly, then makes herself close it at a reasonable pace.

She looks behind her.

Penrose sits in the hall a few feet away.

And Penrose also sits on the stairs.

Chapter Fourteen

It takes half an hour to get both Penroses contained. They are both sleek, and fast, and recalcitrant. The first one she catches purrs as she hauls him over to his carrier, and she thinks he might not be the original. But the second seems just as alien.

By the time she's locking the other cage, a live trap she got when there was a stray coming around her backyard a year ago, she's laughing. It's unhinged, choked, and helpless, and she can barely breathe through it.

Her eyes are burning. Her head is swimming. She wants to throw up.

She staggers up to her feet. The used glasses are still on the living room table with their blood orange rinds reossifying along the bottoms. The lights are still on low. It doesn't matter. Tamsin grabs the handles of each carrier, and from inside, both cats protest as they're hoisted up into the air, their tiny prisons tilting wildly as Tamsin mounts the stairs.

Down the hall, to the locked door, the keypad, and then the door is open, and Tamsin has to focus so that she doesn't throw either cat into the room. She sets each one down with as much care as she can manage.

Prime is standing in between Tamsin and the bed and goes to its knees, peering into the carriers.

"What the fuck is happening?" Tamsin demands, unsure of what else to say.

"You'll have to be more specific," Prime replies, glancing up at her.

"There's only supposed to be *one* cat."

One of the Penroses lets out a low moan of irritation. The other rustles in his carrier.

"And there is only supposed to be one of you," Prime says slowly.

Tamsin can see Prime's mind working and she hates it. The entire world has finally spun out of her control, and her only chance of setting it back to rights is to *think*, but she can't even do that. Only her double can, this thing that shouldn't exist, this thing that must be a direct threat to her.

She grabs hold of one of Prime's wrists. Prime flinches.

"Come with me," she says.

Prime doesn't fight, but it is tense as it stands and follows her, stumbling, out of the bedroom. It casts wary glances back over its shoulder. "Shouldn't we let them out—?"

"After."

"After what?"

Tamsin doesn't respond, navigating down the stairs and to the basement door. "Close your eyes," she demands, and Prime only stares in response, shoulders hunched forward, body language the same as a dog who has learned it will be kicked.

She makes herself gentle, breathing slower. "Just for a moment. Please."

Please feels false on her tongue, but Prime closes its eyes.

Tamsin keys in the code and unlocks the basement. "You can look now," she says, before tugging Prime down the stairs.

The basement is exactly as they left it that morning. It's been barely more than twelve hours, and the light down here remains unchanging. Prime is rigid beneath her hand, following only because it's being dragged.

That reluctance nearly makes Tamsin's mouth water with the need to understand, to crack Prime open. What is it afraid is going to happen?

Tamsin comes to a stop in front of the cameras and jerks her chin toward the door.

"Open it," she says.

Prime shakes its head, its refusal much more marked this time than when it first appeared. It flexes the hand Tamsin is keeping captive. The wrist is the one Tamsin drew blood from; she can feel the tiny pinprick scab.

"Do you think that's a good idea?" Prime asks. Its voice trembles.

It isn't. Tamsin can think of so many ways it could go wrong. But there are two Penroses, and two *hers*, and if Prime came out of this door, so did the duplicate cat.

She wants to toss them both back through to where they came from, then bolt the door shut. Fill in the whole basement. Erase the entire mess from existence.

"I think that at this point," she says, "it's essential."

Prime doesn't move. Tamsin tears her gaze from the door, where it's come to rest as if magnetized, and whatever Prime sees on her face, it makes it flinch again, drawing back to the farthest extent their arms allow. Tamsin hangs on tight and waits. She can threaten, and cajole, and force, but Prime is obedient in all things.

It doesn't take long.

"Okay," it says. "Okay, I'll do it."

She waits until Prime eases closer again, the line of its shoulders slackening as it takes a few steps in the direction of the door. Only then does she let go, watching Prime, arms crossing over her chest as much to intimidate Prime as to soothe herself. Her heart pounds as Prime moves across the room. Its hand reaches out. It trembles, as before. A few yards separate Prime and the door, and then a few feet, and then a few inches.

Prime falters.

It's almost like watching magnets repelling one another; Prime's hand swings to one side, and then Prime is turning, too, to face Tamsin again. "This is dangerous," it says. "You don't know what's on the other side."

"Do you?" Tamsin asks.

Prime looks distraught. "You know I don't."

Tamsin hums low in her throat and approaches, herding Prime closer to the door. "I know you told me you don't. That doesn't mean you told me the truth. Do you know what's on the other side, Prime?"

Prime takes a step back. And another. But then its posture firms up unexpectedly. "No," it says and glances, as if helpless to resist, back at the door once again.

It's impossible to tell if Prime is frustrated or scared. It looks like both at once. But the fear, the fear is *fascinating*. The fear is learned, but not from Tamsin. Prime didn't want to open the door that morning, and it certainly doesn't want to open it now. *Why?* echoes loud on loop through her skull, and her hunger for an answer grows teeth.

"If you don't know," Tamsin says, "you should open it and find out."

Prime has no argument against that.

"Please," Prime whispers. Tamsin ignores it and takes Prime by the shoulder, pushing it around to face the door.

"Give me a reason, backed by evidence, why you shouldn't do this."

"I don't know."

"The only thing that should be beyond that door is dirt," Tamsin pushes. "Are you afraid of dirt?"

"I don't *know!*"

"Open the door, Prime."

Beneath her touch, Prime has gone from trembling to all-out shaking. Tamsin thinks she'll have to grab its hand, put it on the knob herself. But Prime is obedient. Prime reaches out, even as its chest heaves with repressed sobs, and grasps the knob.

Prime's fingers tense and clutch. Its wrist moves. The knob rotates.

The door does not open.

"Pull," Tamsin says, low and fervent.

"I am," Prime whispers, and Tamsin can feel the flex of muscles in its shoulder, the resistance of the door.

"Pull harder, then," she demands. It takes everything she has not to place her hand over Prime's and help.

Prime's shoulders tense, its body trembles, and she leans away from the door. The door doesn't open, despite all of Prime's weight desperately trying to retreat from it.

Tamsin lets go of Prime.

"It's not going to open," Tamsin concedes, reaching out and touching the seam where the door meets the doorframe. Her fingers pass over her own dried blood.

Prime lets go with a cry and retreats haphazardly from the door. Its hip collides with the desk, and then its shoulders hit the back wall, and it sinks down to the ground, hyperventilating, clutching its hand to its chest as if it's been scalded again.

Tamsin turns away from the door entirely.

"I'm sorry," Prime is gasping. "I'm sorry, I'm sorry, I'm sorry, please— please—"

Tamsin approaches, hands up. "It's alright, Prime," she says, words unfamiliar in her mouth, clumsy. She doesn't mean them, but it's not the sort of lie she's practiced with. "It's okay."

Prime begins to cry.

Tamsin goes to her knees before she can think better of it, resting one hand on Prime's ankle. Prime twitches. Seeing herself cower after the sensory experiments that afternoon was strange; seeing herself break down is so much worse. She waits for the disgust to rise up and overpower the guilt the way it has before, disgust at seeing a mockery of herself display this much vulnerability, this much weakness. But this time, all she can think is *This is wrong.*

The door won't open. Prime is trapped here.

Fuck.

"Come on, let's get you to bed," she says as coaxingly as she can. "No more experiments today."

Prime is reluctant.

But it obeys.

Chapter Fifteen

Tamsin stays up into the early hours of the morning, watching Prime sleep via the cameras installed in the main bedroom. Prime moves, occasionally, but never leaves the bed, never seems to open its eyes. It's the picture of repose, and Tamsin has to resist the urge to go to it, touch it, measure it again and again. She wants—no, *needs*—to find where it ends and she begins. Needs to divine if what she's done to it is wrong, fundamentally. It shouldn't feel wrong. It should feel necessary.

And yet the shame hasn't left her. It curls around the base of her throat, digging into the notch of her collarbone. Prime cowering, Prime weeping, Prime cornered. The images repeat, again and again.

Maybe that's why, when morning comes and she drags herself out of bed, she goes and unlocks the bedroom door. She doesn't open it, but leaves the keypad unarmed. She stares at it for a long time, giving herself the opportunity to change her mind.

This isn't permanent, though. This is an experiment. What will Prime do, if it can move around the house? What will it choose for itself?

There's no indication that Prime is awake, so Tamsin goes and showers. Her head is pounding, and her hair is still a tangled mess. She makes herself take the time to fix it, but it'll take a fresh keratin treatment to get it up to snuff again; luckily, her standing appointment is only a week or so away. When she at last dresses and exits the bathroom, both Penroses sit in the hallway.

Prime has let them out, then.

She stares at them, considering recaging them as soft sounds coming from downstairs filter into her awareness. The air is warm with the scent of cooking.

It smells like—

Shrimp?

Tamsin leaves the cats and makes her way down and into the kitchen, regret warring with curiosity. Prime stands at the stove, and yes, there are shrimp frying in the pan in front of it. To the right, a larger pot bubbles away. The liquid inside is a brilliant red.

Prime shouldn't know how to work the stove, let alone cook a meal, even if the meal resembles no breakfast Tamsin has ever seen. It certainly shouldn't have stumbled onto *prepare food* as its first action upon finding its prison door unlocked. Why isn't it exploring? Why isn't it sitting and waiting to see if Tamsin is testing it again?

"Good morning," Prime says. Its voice does have an edge to it, a wariness, but it's no worse than an awkward morning-after, which Tamsin supposes this is. It slides the cooked shrimp onto a plate. "This should be done soon."

"What are you doing?" Tamsin asks. Prime visibly relaxes when there's no note of censure in Tamsin's voice.

"Cooking," Prime replies. It doesn't simper or ask if that's okay. *Interesting*, after its pleading the night before. The cooking itself could serve as an attempt at appeasement, of course. Proving utility to try to avoid another unpleasant test, or in some misguided attempt to head off another traumatic attempt at the door. Or maybe it's simpler than that; that Prime recognized its own hunger, then worried that Tamsin's hunger might have consequences.

Prime scored highly not only on empathy, but also flexibility and tolerance. Maybe that's at work here: a pathological generosity of spirit, willing to forgive and forget so easily. What that says about the door, and about the reason for Prime's existence, Tamsin can't say yet. It feels slippery and uncomfortable. But she also wants to trust that generosity. Wants to trust that this is just what it looks like: a houseguest making breakfast because it's morning and it's time to eat.

The problem is that trusting Prime means trusting something that walked through an impossible door in her basement. It also means trusting something that looks like *her*, and Tamsin knows better than that.

It doesn't stop her stomach from rumbling.

"Was I supposed to stay in my room?" Prime asks. It's turned away from the stove now. "The door was unlocked."

"I wanted to see what you would do," Tamsin says, both a reassurance and a reminder that Tamsin had only promised that the experiments were over for the day before. Prime understands, if its briefly blank expression is anything to go by.

She waits for it to ask about last night, to apologize or demand an apology of its own. It does neither, turning back to the stove.

There's discarded meal-kit packaging on the breakfast bar, and Tamsin goes to it. She picks up the cardboard. *Spanish shrimp soup with potatoes, peas, and paprika.* Emphatically not breakfast food, and the seafood smell and the tang of tomatoes is just this side of nauseating. She'd picked it for the tidy list of tags printed helpfully along the side: paleo, carb-conscious, dairy-free, soy-free. But the chances of getting to it in a timely manner had been low, and—

She flips the packaging over and sags with relief when she sees it was part of the delivery two days ago. Should be more than fine.

Just not breakfast.

"How did you select this one?" she asks Prime, who is frowning at the pot of soup, the burner finally off.

"It's food," Prime says, casting her a confused glance. "We eat food when we're hungry. And the stuff that comes in the bottle is *not* food."

Strong opinion, Tamsin thinks. *That's new.*

Prime tries a few drawers. "I need a . . . ." Its hand works in the air beside its hip as it thinks. "A large spoon. For serving the soup."

"A ladle."

Its frown is replaced by another broad grin, too chipper, too earnest. Entirely wrong on its face, *Tamsin's* face. Tamsin wants to wipe it away. "A ladle! Yes. Thank you. Where is it?"

Tamsin isn't even sure she has one, but she indicates the drawer it would live in if she did. It does, in fact, exist, and Prime returns to the stove, filling two bowls with the soup as if it has done this a hundred times.

It's fascinating, in its way. Just like, underneath the horror, it was fascinating to watch her complete mathematics problems. A new data point, one that confirms that letting Prime occasionally have the freedom to interact with the house is only going to illuminate its nature more. She'll just have to be thoughtful about when and how she allows it.

"Do you know what breakfast means?" Tamsin asks.

"A morning meal," Prime replies, now sliding shrimp from the plate where they've been resting onto the top of the soup.

"How do you know that?"

"I just do. Like I know everything else."

Except what's through the door, Tamsin thinks, frustration from the night before poking its head out for just a moment. But that's not where to push. Not now, anyway.

"Like you know how to cook."

"There were instructions on the packaging," Prime replies, *garnishing* the soup with finely chopped chives, which Tamsin is fairly certain were not included in the kit. Prime brings both bowls over to the breakfast bar, then goes back to get spoons. "We've already established that I can read."

"But the instructions don't cover how to work a stove," Tamsin says. "Or the best way to hold a knife. You have a level of procedural knowledge that exceeds your ability to understand instructions, just like with mathematics."

Prime tastes the soup and hums in satisfaction, or maybe answer. It eats another spoonful.

"Could you have done this yesterday?"

"I don't know," Prime says. "I didn't have the chance to test it until now."

It's a very clinical answer. Tamsin isn't sure if Prime is mocking her or not; the specter of the night before hangs heavily over them both. The fact that Prime could even conceive of sarcasm is unsettling. Very . . . human. Very pointed. Tamsin swirls her spoon through the soup, ravenously hungry and yet unsure if she can stomach it. "This is a terrible choice for breakfast," she says.

Prime tilts her head to one side. "I don't understand. It tastes good."

"You don't make something like this for breakfast. I barely even *eat* breakfast, but breakfast is . . . is . . ." She pushes a shrimp into the tomato broth, frowning. "Eggs. Toast. Oatmeal, maybe."

"Breakfast is culturally determined," Prime says, and Tamsin is unsure if she's being corrected or agreed with. "And this is what you had. What would you have made instead?"

"Probably another shake."

Prime scowls. "That isn't food," it repeats.

"It's nutritionally complete. It's convenient."

"It's disgusting."

Tamsin can't entirely argue with Prime and doesn't volunteer the fact that an exclusive diet of shakes tends to screw with her digestive system. Still, Prime's opinion raises its own questions.

"So you care about how things taste?"

"Of course. Don't you?"

Tamsin opens her mouth, then shuts it again. She looks down at her soup. Stirs it once more, then finally takes a bite.

It's very good. The potato she got in her spoonful is just soft enough. And when she fishes out a shrimp, the flesh snaps between her teeth, not overcooked in the slightest.

Prime is a better cook than she is. The thought is—destabilizing. Out of their short list of differences, this is the first one that suggests Prime has the potential to exceed the original.

And as for the others, they don't seem as prominent this morning as they did even twelve hours ago. Prime argued in favor of cooking over drinking a meal shake, yes, but it is still patient and seemingly focused on Tamsin's comfort, inventing a task Tamsin didn't request but Prime intuited the need for. That very intuiting, though, makes it appear more a person and less an uncomfortable echo of Tamsin herself. It has its own preferences, has drawn its own conclusions.

It's getting very hard to still think of Prime as an *it*.

"Last night," Prime says, and Tamsin's head jerks up. "Your guest. Who was she?"

Tamsin considers lying. There's no reason for Prime to know details about her life, and every reason to keep it in the dark. But then Tamsin looks at the logistics, at having a prisoner in her bedroom, and a sinking basement, and Lachlan breathing down her neck. It's unsustainable. She needs to re-evaluate which risk is the greatest, and right now, at this exact moment, it's not Prime.

"My minder," she says, and feels like she's lost something.

"Like you're mine?"

Tamsin's smile is thin. "Something like that. She's been keeping an eye on me for years. Making sure I perform up to expectations. Making sure I remember what stakes I'm playing for."

"And what are those stakes?"

"Prestige. Money. Comfort." Tamsin shakes herself, returning to her soup. "Right now I'm supposed to be figuring out why the city is sinking."

"Like the basement?"

"That's a potentially unrelated phenomenon." Her gaze flicks over Prime. "As are you."

The door. The Penroses. All of it possibly extraneous, probably not.

"Potentially unrelated, potentially related," Prime echoes.

Tamsin finds herself nodding, then twitches, as if she's bitten down on tinfoil. Just then, Prime had sounded almost exactly like Tamsin. Not just in voice, but in tone, in attitude.

(She tries not to think about how it had sounded as it begged for mercy.)

Tamsin shifts in her seat, taking another bite of soup to allow herself a moment to recover. "She was here because I've been too distracted," she says once she's swallowed.

"She doesn't know about your potentially unrelated phenomena."

"No, and I intend to keep it that way until it becomes directly relevant."

Prime sets down its spoon. Its bowl is empty. "Can I help?"

Tamsin wants to say yes. The urge takes her by surprise, and she sets her spoon down, though she's only managed half her bowl. She looks at Prime, at the clever light in its eyes, at the way it's leaning forward in its seat, intrigued and eager.

"No," Tamsin makes herself say. "Not when you're potentially connected. It would—muddy the waters. And not after last night."

Prime's shoulders droop.

Tamsin has the absurd impulse to cover Prime's hand with hers.

Chapter Sixteen

After breakfast, Tamsin locks Prime back in its room.

It's a temporary measure. This first experiment was a success; Prime is self-managing, and the opportunity to interact with a less restricted environment is producing faster results than Tamsin's own experimental design is. But Tamsin doesn't want to worry about it while working today.

Prime, for its part, goes without protest. It does ask for a change of clothing, though, and some bedding, and Tamsin provides both, along with toiletries and a few books. From beyond the locked bedroom door, Tamsin can hear the shower turn on.

No more waiting for instruction and permission.

Was it just time passing that allowed Prime to change like this, or was it something Tamsin did? Some fallout from the night before, maybe, or even a response to being given a modicum of freedom? It's impossible to tell. Maybe just proximity prompted the change. The longer Prime has to observe Tamsin, the more it seems to *become* like her.

Tamsin tries not to think about that as she settles in to work. Pointedly doesn't check the camera feeds. The more she looks, the more questions Prime raises, the more uneasy Tamsin grows with her observant little mirror. Her inbox is swamped, and she buries herself in the muck of it, wading through pointless ccs and invitations to meetings she's already missed, flagging actual inquiries to handle next. She makes it about half an hour before she finds herself wondering if Prime could handle admin work like this. If it could be trusted with an unlimited portal to the outside world.

No. The answer is *no*.

It's another hour from there before she's gotten the rest of her emails sorted. The equipment she asked for is waiting for pickup. She's told Cara to set up calls with the deputy mayor and a few other attendees from last week's meeting, and she's accepted a (blessedly virtual) meeting invite from the University of San Siroco's geology department for the afternoon. Next up is parsing through the updated data, but Tamsin sets her laptop aside and gets up to stretch.

She's washing out the cocktail glasses from the night before when Penrose—the sweeter one, probably the new one if Prime's temperament is any clue—hops up on the counter beside her and flops onto his side, gazing at her and purring loudly.

"All forgiven, then?" she asks. The cats have been avoiding her all morning, no doubt in retaliation for penning them up so abruptly. She thinks of Prime, so ready to move on from the night before, as she dries one hand and strokes Penrose's fur. "Shall I call you Penrose Prime?" she asks him.

He rolls onto his back.

"You're not supposed to be on the counter," she adds.

He shimmies into a brighter patch of sunlight.

Lunch is handed off through the bedroom door, but that night, they sit down to dinner together. Delivery, this time. Thai food, two items, and Tamsin lets Prime pick which one it wants. It agonizes for several minutes, then takes the green curry.

"Why did you pick that one?" she asks, taking the box of noodles.

It eats the way Tamsin would, scooping out a spoonful of rice and then dipping it into the curry. "I wanted it less," Prime says after a few bites. "Which means the pad kee mao is your favorite, right?"

Tamsin looks down at her dinner, appetite souring. "Correct," she says.

"Did I do something wrong?" Prime has paused, spoon halfway to its mouth.

Prime having the capacity to anticipate her desires based on their similarities, and to adjust its own behavior to utilize that knowledge, is both predictable and horrible. She'd only wanted to test if they had the same preferences for food, between two menu items she's happy to eat, and instead, Prime has generously put Tamsin in front of itself, while making it very clear that it *knows* Tamsin.

"No," Tamsin says, but Prime must be able to tell that's a lie.

They finish dinner in silence. Prime puts itself away for the night; Tamsin only has to double-check the lock.

She sits up past midnight, drinking vodka slowly, watching Prime sleep on the camera feed and wondering what the fuck she's going to do.

The next day, Tamsin works from home again. She considers going in to the lab, but now more than ever, she can't stand the thought of Prime being left alone. Most of her instinctive rejection of the idea comes down to a lack of control, but some, enough to be upsetting, is fear that something could happen *to Prime*. That Prime could get hurt, or fall ill, or simply be . . . gone when Tamsin comes home.

Not that Prime could be discovered, that it could expose Tamsin.

The absurdity of that fear is almost enough to drive her out of the house to prove it's not an issue, but she stays set up in the dining room, unable to take the risk. She checks in with the various lab groups, talks to legal for half an hour, and generally hates every second of it. She hasn't been down to the basement since she forced Prime to try the door. When she thinks about the altercation, her shame overrides the constant background hum of curiosity, of anxiety. Even as her mind is tugged downward, it's also pulled *up*, wondering what Prime is doing, wondering if it's changed overnight again.

Her phone pings. She glances over; the baby-monitor app is reporting more noise than usual. She taps the screen, and Prime's voice filters in.

"—sin, would you like me to make lunch?"

Tamsin frowns.

This is the first time the monitor has picked up speech or anything above the rustling of Prime moving around. She hasn't told Prime about the microphone, but Prime is speaking at a reasonable volume. It isn't shouting through the door.

Ignore it. This may be Prime testing a theory. No need to confirm or deny.

But really, what does it matter? Lunch is lunch. Prime can cook. Tamsin is tired, and frustrated, and could stand to talk to somebody whom she doesn't have to lie to quite as extensively.

She taps the screen again to swap to two-way mode.

"I'll let you out in a bit," she says.

The microphone captures some rustling, and when Prime speaks again, its voice is clearer. "So that's where it is," it says, and it sounds pleased.

Tamsin turns off two-way mode and gets back to work.

Prime makes another meal kit for them, this time turkey-and-apple patties with a beet salad and cucumber salsa. It asks for Tamsin's approval of its choice and then works quietly, humming to itself. Tamsin makes an idle note; it's no song she recognizes, but it *is* a song. It has rhythm and structure and an end point.

It is achingly human.

Prime has chosen a new outfit today. It's still made of old discards, but this time it has picked something less soft loungewear and more clothing for going out. A high-necked sweater and wide-legged slacks. Its hair is still damp from a shower and hangs unrestrained down its back, curls finger-twisted into loose definition. Somehow, the scarlet mass of it doesn't get in the way as Prime grates the apple. Its hands move confidently.

Tamsin watches, chin propped on one fist. The meal kit is one of the last in the fridge. The next week's shipment will come in another few days.

Which means they need groceries.

She could, of course, just order what she needs and have it delivered by midafternoon. It's what she usually does; grocery shopping in person is time-consuming without any real benefit. But as she watches Prime cook, she thinks of how Prime's demeanor has become so unremarkably normal. If a stranger were to meet it, Tamsin doubts they'd notice anything amiss. Not at first, at any rate.

It's a terrible idea. It puts Prime at risk (of getting lost, of getting hurt, of not coming home), and isn't necessary in the slightest, but it has a certain appeal. Tamsin doesn't have the time and inclination to go out herself, and Prime has proven its obedience over and over again. A trip out and back will tell Tamsin a great deal about exactly how independently Prime is capable of functioning.

And there's a chance, however small, that Prime won't be able to leave at all; if the accelerated stretching is specific to her house, maybe Prime is, too. Maybe it's a localized phenomenon.

Which means there's only one question Tamsin needs to answer:

Do you trust it?

After last night's dinner, and the glimpse into how complex Prime's mind clearly is, she would have said no, she doesn't, she can't. But at the same time, Prime had acted in *her* interest. There's been no indication at any point that Prime has anything other than her well-being at heart, potentially even to the detriment of itself. After all, it had tried to open the door for her, despite the severe distress it had caused.

So yes. Tamsin does trust it—enough for this. Perhaps she can't understand it, but she can put it to use, surely.

"Do you still want to help?" she asks.

Prime has its hands sunk into ground meat. It looks over its shoulder at Tamsin, hesitantly hopeful. "Yes."

"How do you feel about going to the store?"

It doesn't feel like ceding ground this time. It feels like relief. One less thing to concern herself with, if Prime proves itself. There's still a chance it won't come back if she lets it leave the house. But she thinks the odds are low, and there are ways she can guard against that.

Prime considers, turning to look out the window. Tamsin is sitting far enough back and to the side that nobody looking in would see the both of them at the same time. She watches Prime, the subtle flexing of its jaw, the way its hands flatten out in the bowl of meat.

"You'd trust me to do that?" Prime asks at last.

"Yes," Tamsin says without hesitating.

Prime ducks its head, but Tamsin can still see it biting at its lip even as it smiles. It's a genuine smile, too. Tamsin relaxes a little more. "I can go to the store. Will—will anybody recognize me?"

Tamsin snorts. "Unlikely. I mostly get things delivered." She sits back, propping herself against the wall, balancing on her stool. Another experiment is brewing in her skull, and she discards the list she was beginning to think up. "I want to see what you think we need."

"A test?"

"An encouragement," Tamsin says, instead of *yes*. "You seem to pick up skills as needed. So: here's a need."

Prime hums, slowly resuming work. It forms patties and lays them into a hot pan. Tamsin watches a moment longer, then gets up and retreats to the dining room, where her laptop waits. She fusses with the settings on a program she hasn't used in a few months now.

Half an hour later, Prime brings out two plates. It doesn't formally set the table, though it does go back for cutlery and glasses of water. Tamsin puts her laptop aside.

Lunch, just like yesterday's breakfast, tastes wonderful. Nothing is burned or undercooked. Prime keeps glancing at the laptop but doesn't ask about Tamsin's research.

A few bites in, Tamsin gets up and fetches her keys and a slim wallet. Taking her seat again, she pushes them across the table to Prime.

"You'll need this to get back in the house," she says, tapping the key. The ring it's on has an unobtrusive GPS tracker designed for finding lost objects. "And this," her hand moves to the wallet, "is to pay for the food. Do you know how to use a credit card?"

Prime purses its lips but flips the wallet open, sliding the one card inside free. Tamsin's main wallet is still in her purse; this is a card she rarely uses, kept just for its credit history, with a low limit and an alert set up to tell her when it's used. Prime holds it carefully, rotating it this way and that. Its eyes flick back and forth, as if it's memorizing it.

"I think so," it says finally. "Or at least, I can figure it out. But I do need to pay?"

Tamsin huffs a laugh. "I guess you don't *technically* have to, but I would prefer you don't get arrested for shoplifting."

Prime slides the card back into the wallet. "Food is not free."

"No. Welcome to capitalism." It's fascinating, what Prime knows and what it doesn't. The distinction seems to fall out along procedural versus cultural lines. Prime can perform tasks, but the *why*, the nuance, doesn't always accompany them. But it's a quick study, as always, and it tucks the wallet and keys into a pocket.

"Where is the store?"

"About a fifteen-minute walk away." Tamsin pulls up the address on her phone, then holds the screen up for Prime to see the directions. Prime stares for maybe thirty seconds, then nods. Tamsin taps again, and a picture of the storefront comes up. "Think you can find it and then come back?"

"It doesn't look too hard."

"You'll have to cross a few streets. Use crosswalks. Pay attention to the traffic lights." Tamsin quirks a brow. "If it's too much, come back. I don't want you getting hurt."

She doesn't want Prime ending up in a hospital somewhere.

Prime absently rubs at its wrist. There's no mark there that Tamsin can see, not anymore, but its fingertips are still a little pink.

The moment Prime is out the door, Tamsin returns to her laptop. On it, a blinking green indicator shows Prime's path down the block. With every step farther away, Tamsin half expects the indicator to stop moving, for Prime to evaporate. Instead, Tamsin watches it follow unerringly the map Tamsin had shown Prime over lunch. Prime's memory appears impeccable, like Tamsin's own.

And Prime is real, even outside the confines of this house.

It was a wild theory, but having it disproven still leaves Tamsin adrift. The implications are staggering. Prime is not a figment of her imagination and can interact with the world at large. Prime is alive, in every way that matters.

She watches the GPS tracker a moment longer, then forces herself to minimize the window and return to scanning through reams of data.

A few new types of information have been added this morning; strain monitors on roads and important utilities at the city border, where the distortion effect stops abruptly, where that first water main broke a week ago. No more disasters yet, but they're coming. Asphalt cracks under differential tension, and the topsoil's slow shifting will impact storm runoff the next time there's a substantial rain. The moment either of those things becomes obvious is the moment Klein's office is on the phone with the deputy mayor directly to coordinate messaging rollout. But so far, all signs point to that still being several weeks, if not a month or more, away.

Everything else shows the exact same inexorable progress. It's irritating. Infuriating. At least her basement has evolved. At least her basement keeps giving her *new* things to deal with, even if the answers are just as slow in coming.

An alert buzzes her phone. Prime's used the credit card, and at the correct shop. Tamsin manages a small smile, then flips the phone facedown and looks back at her screen.

And that's when she spots it.

There is a slight discrepancy between the sinking measured at the three original sites and at an additional point, recently added out of an abundance of caution. Nobody but her and a few other individuals have access to the readings of the real-time submeter GPS information broadcasting from the basement of the main Myrica office building.

It has dropped two millimeters *less* than any other site, the opposite of her own basement in miniature.

Tamsin stares at the reading, then leans back in her seat. She thinks about the stretching of her basement and how she doesn't know what happens where her basement ends and the surrounding soil begins. Does it mesh evenly, somehow distributing the strain? Is there some kind of supernatural easing that goes on? Her water still works, her electricity, and that all routes through the ground. But on a broader scale, if there are more locations like her basement, localized spots that stretch faster or slower than those around them, then the effect would potentially be—

Chaos.

Broken water mains within the city proper, snapped fiber-optic lines, roads splitting, sinkholes opening. Every worst-case scenario she had originally promised the city government and their competitors was not a present and immediate risk is all back on the table and could potentially happen anywhere, not just at the city limits. The city center is a dense network of interacting utilities and architectural interventions; changes there will have far graver consequences than any in the suburbs.

She's in the middle of drafting a memo to her immediate team concerning newly observed behavior in the subsidence phenomenon, carefully assembled to communicate urgency without indicating the need to panic and without revealing the actual data she has just yet, when Prime returns. Tamsin almost doesn't notice the door opening. She only looks up when Prime sets the keys and wallet down by her hand along with a to-go cup of coffee.

Tamsin missed that purchase.

Chastisement rises to Tamsin's lips, buoyed up by shock. Since when has Prime known about coffee shops? Or was it just a lucky guess?

"Find something?" Prime asks, nodding at the laptop and the haphazard, still disorganized notes glowing on the screen alongside the draft memo. Embarrassment overtakes the shock, obliterates worries about coffee shops.

"Yes," Tamsin says, lowering the laptop lid, even though it's too late. She's not annoyed with *Prime* now, but herself; she should have better information control after all this time. This isn't the first confidential project she's worked on. She takes the coffee, sips it. It's perfect. Exactly to her taste. "Can you handle putting the groceries away?"

"Of course." Prime puts the receipt down next to her cup. "Here. So you can see how I did."

Tamsin slides her phone over the folded paper. She nods, and Prime disappears into the kitchen.

The memo comes together, and she fires it off into the ether to the people who need to see it. She calls a meeting for the next day. Cara will handle scheduling as replies come in. In the meantime, she needs to arrange for a few more tests.

She considers leaving the house herself, heading to the Myrica campus. If there's distortion of any kind, it might be within the building, just like her basement. She should be the first to see it. But this isn't something she intends to keep secret, and she'd be of limited use. What she needs is somebody who can set up the required equipment, get folks working on the necessary experiments. What she needs is . . .

Isaac Torrence.

That's not happening, of course, thanks to her ill-advised outburst. Whom to send instead? Her first thought is of Yvette; she's good with people and could pull together a team easily. But even with phase three of the experiments paused, the deep labs can't be left short-staffed, not now.

Ah. Octavian Valdez. Poor comedic timing, but he'd pulled himself together admirably in the wake of her fuck-up. She pulls up his CV. He's been on the team half as long as Torrence, but he has the skills. He also has the benefit of being on-site.

She pulls out her phone, dials the central lab number.

"Valdez," she says when he picks up, "I've got a new job for you."

Chapter Seventeen

Prime cooks dinner without being asked. It has the run of the house again; Tamsin was too distracted to shut it away in the bedroom after the groceries were unpacked, and by the time she realized the lapse, it seemed pointless to pursue. She's still working at the dining room table when Prime enters with steaming plates of—

"Pancakes?"

"Breakfast for dinner, to balance out dinner for breakfast," Prime says.

Tamsin almost asks how Prime figured out pancakes are breakfast before remembering that breakfast food has a whole labeled aisle at the store.

She shuts the laptop and pulls her plate closer. Prime sits down across from her and watches, with unnerving focus, as Tamsin takes her first bite.

"It's good," she says after she swallows. "Did you use the instructions on the box?"

"With a few alterations." Prime smiles, then begins to eat as well. Its eyes slide over to the laptop periodically, the way they had over lunch. Tamsin tries to imagine being in its shoes, having all the same drive and curiosity and being denied access not only to the mystery of her own existence, but also to the quandary that's occupying all of her caretaker's time. It would be infuriating, of course, no matter if she agreed that her involvement might skew the data.

She could tell Prime. She doesn't have to go into detail. She can just say she's found another place that might be behaving the same way as the basement. Or she can ask theoretical questions. *What do you think would happen if . . . ?* Prime already knows about the stretching, has already shown curiosity about what it might mean. Surely that wouldn't cause any problems.

She cuts her pancakes into smaller and smaller bits. She's not sure if she's working up courage or wearing her objections down. But Prime is quite capable and is the only person whom Tamsin can actually talk to about everything, no filters, no editing.

"We found another site of anomalous stretching," she says finally.

Prime leans in, intrigued.

From there, it's surprisingly easy. They swap theories. They debate. Tamsin comes alive in a way she hasn't in years, engaged and eager and luxuriating in having a conversational partner who can keep up.

"But the extra matter has to be coming from *somewhere*," Tamsin says, leaning forward.

"Why do you assume there's extra matter?" Prime replies, mirroring her, fingers tapping lightly on the table.

"Because I haven't found a structural limit to the stretching. There are no fracture points, not here and not at any other site. And then there's the door. When damaged, it repairs itself. It conserves itself, somehow. Adds to itself, really. I can remove material, but when unobserved, the material . . . exists again."

"When unobserved?"

Tamsin grins, exhilarated, because for the first time, she doesn't have to tell herself that she's losing her mind. "Whenever I look away, or blink."

Prime twists in its seat, looking toward the basement door with fascination.

They sit at the table for hours, conversation taking them from the basement out into the city and back. It feels like her own thoughts written into reality, but Prime responds, occasionally, in ways Tamsin could not have predicted. She's *more* than the externalization of Tamsin's thought processes.

She.

At some point, Prime transforms from a thing to a person in Tamsin's mind. She barely notices when it happens; it's only obvious in hindsight, when the pancakes are gone and they're cradling mugs of tea Prime has made for them. She feels momentary regret over it, then moves forward. It was a fiction of dubious utility anyway.

"What if," Prime says after a moment's lull, "whatever allows the stretching is a form of self-replication. Like cellular reproduction."

"But everything tests as just wood and drywall," Tamsin counters. "And there's no input. No raw materials."

"Then maybe it comes from whatever's beyond the door," Prime suggests. "Something that pushes to the surface. Have you taken core samples of the walls?"

Not yet, but the idea is brilliant. With the microscope Cara is getting for her, she'll be in a perfect place to analyze them. Tamsin reaches for her phone to make a note, and it buzzes with a new email just as she grabs it.

She takes a peek, then drags her laptop back over. "First report is in," she says, and Prime nods, getting up and going into the kitchen without having to be asked. Tamsin almost regrets it.

Valdez's report doesn't mention any distorted rooms. It's possible he's obfuscating, but Tamsin doubts it. It's a relief and supports her decision not to go in person.

The report does confirm what that single data point suggested; Myrica is sinking a little bit slower than the rest of the city is. The *why* is still unclear, but Valdez has gotten permission from Mr. Thomas (via Lachlan) to run sonic tests in the basement of the building overnight, to try to ascertain the geology beneath the building and to set up surface trackers to see if it's having any impact on the surrounding area aboveground. By morning, Tamsin hopes they'll have something—interesting.

After a moment's consideration, Tamsin sends an email to Yvette and asks her to look into doing the same at the node labs. Just in case. They have initial data from the construction phase of both the subway tunnels and the labs to compare to; the tunnels have been checked again since the subsidence began, but they haven't started in on the labs yet due to confidentiality considerations and concerns about the geological tests influencing their experiments. But with phase two wrapping up, there won't be any data left to skew.

While Tamsin works, Prime handles the dishes, and Tamsin wonders, idly, if this is what it's like to be married. It has its advantages, to be sure, even if she's never felt the impulse to be so vulnerable to another person, so yoked to their needs and desires. The few brief relationships she'd had in her school days had never been this domestic; she'd kept things casual, carefully scheduled dates and no blurring into indulgent weekends. She'd had too much work to do and too little interest in really getting to know the other person.

The sink shuts off. Tamsin tabs over to check for new data sources; she's expanded the range of what she's willing to sort through manually. Footsteps approach, and then Prime's hand settles lightly on her shoulder.

Tamsin nearly jumps out of her skin. They haven't touched since the basement. Prime hasn't initiated since the moment they met.

It's not as upsetting this time, though, past the initial surprise. More comforting. Self-soothing, almost.

"It's late," Prime says. "You're going to have a long day tomorrow; you should sleep."

Tamsin gets her startle reflex back under control and shrugs her off. "I still have work to do." She shuts the laptop anyway.

"It will be there in the morning."

"There will be *more* of it in the morning." Irritated, she gets up and goes into the hallway but not toward the bedrooms. Instead, she goes to the basement door and lays a hand on the wood. "I haven't been down there in almost two days. I need to see if anything's changed," she says, and glances over her shoulder.

Something flickers in Prime's expression. The memory of their last trip down? Falling apart on the basement floor?

"I can look," Prime says.

Tamsin's brows go up. "No," she says. "You can't." Talking over the city's subsidence is different from letting Prime down in the basement unsupervised. And beyond that, Tamsin isn't convinced Prime will be emotionally capable of managing herself down there. What will happen the next time she's confronted with the door?

It doesn't matter. Tamsin doesn't just need to take measurements, she *wants* to go back into the basement. Not looking at it feels like giving it an opportunity to change again. Not looking at it feels like an abandonment of her own safety.

Prime looks as if she wants to argue, but she doesn't. Instead, she nods and retreats a step. "I'll—go upstairs, then. Don't stay up too late."

Tamsin waits until she can hear Prime's footsteps above her in the upstairs hall before she keys in the code. Really, she should have escorted

Prime up, locked the bedroom door behind her. But she can do that on her way to bed.

Bright light spills through the door. The stairs tower below her.

She takes each step with care.

It's the longest she's gone without looking at the basement since she first discovered the distortion, but recording her measurements takes the same time as always. She's done before the hour is up. There's no reason for her to remain, and Prime is right; she needs to sleep. And yet there's a sort of peace that settles over her down here that makes her want to stay just a minute longer.

The world is quiet. There is a cathedral-like quality to the air. Maybe it's just the height of the ceiling, but it's similar to how she feels in the node chamber.

Cara's scheduled a virtual meeting for ten in the morning. Just the core team. It will reignite their research, take the project up to a fever pitch. It will, no doubt, satisfy Lachlan that she's as engaged with the subsidence issue as she needs to be. And a part of her hungers for it, for every new scrap of data she'll be given, every new phenomenon that has been confirmed externally that she can write up and display to the world one day.

But when she thinks of the fallout—the new plans, the PR wrangling, the pressure to save a city she barely cares about, not on a personal level— all she wants is to stay right where she is.

She approaches the impossible door, after too long spent delaying and fiddling with the cameras. Its surface is smooth and cool, and just like before, just like with her and with Prime, the knob turns but does nothing. She leans against it, forehead pressed to the wood. She has none of Prime's fear or revulsion; instead, all she feels is a curious longing. Like the door itself is calling to her.

She listens and hears nothing.

No susurration of water, no shifting of soil. Not even the creak and groan of her house adjusting to the descent of the ground, the supportive strut of her distorted basement. Everything is silent, that all-encompassing *nothing* that she's only ever heard in the node chambers before. If she could open the door, she's certain that's what she would find: an expanse of absence, no guideline before her, nothing to keep her from being swallowed but her own sense of self, the knowledge of where she begins. Where she ends.

Did Prime come from somewhere like that? Somewhere that obliterated where she started and stopped, lost in the abyss? Or is she made out of that nothingness and only putting on what she sees in Tamsin every time their eyes meet, their bodies touch?

If Tamsin ever opens the door, if she steps out into that vast black, will there be a light that blinks on twenty minutes later to call her home?

Would it bring her back here?

Her thoughts drift far from her, ranging across the brilliant emptiness. When she registers how vague and drowsy she's become, she pulls away, turns back to the basement at large. The lights are so bright, and she squints her eyes, making her way to the steps. It's time for bed.

The stairs are impossibly high. She has to drag herself up each one. They are white and flawless, so smooth she struggles to grip them.

One. Two. Three. She pauses, panting for breath, considering resting her head down for just a minute.

Behind her there's a soft click.

She glances over her shoulder. The door is open, just a little, maybe two inches wide. Beyond it is the abyss, exactly as she pictured it, exactly as she remembers it. It spills from the doorway like a substance, not an absence. It washes over the basement floor, lapping at the table legs, covering her notes. The lights cannot pierce it and are swallowed in turn.

The line of the dark rises.

Tamsin jerks away from it as it encroaches on the step her feet rest on. She scrambles up, her hands aching. She doesn't remember clawing at the door to open it, only testing the knob, but her fingers are raw and bloody. The door is open, and the choice to step through it has been stolen from her. There is only nothing, nothing, *nothing*—

The door above her opens.

Prime stands there. Or no, no, it's not Prime. Prime is gentle and kind. Prime does not wear sharp, towering heels.

Dr. Rivers stands at the top of the stairs, arms crossed, entirely unimpressed.

And her, climbing up the stairs . . . who is she?

She looks down at the tread she's clinging to. The step is so polished that she can see her reflection. Red hair. Blue eyes, with shadows beneath them. The reflection is only that, not a window, not the surface of the water.

Below her, the nothingness has reached the top of her desk.

She makes herself climb another step. When she looks forward, up, she can't see the black. It's the last few brilliant lights, still enough to illuminate the space, and herself, styled in clean lines, entirely in control.

She wants it. God, she wants it so much, that control.

She extends her hand, and Dr. Rivers takes it, hauls her up the last few steps and onto her feet. They regard each other, and she sways forward, helpless.

"You have to finish your work," Dr. Rivers tells her. Hands close around her shoulders, turn her to face the void below. The abyss runs in rivulets up the stairs, against gravity, as if seeking higher ground. "You need to close the door. Are you ready?"

Dr. Rivers's voice curls in her ear, low and sinuous, and she nods.

The hands slide to her back.

They push.

She falls.

Tamsin wakes up in the living room, curled tight below the coffee table. Her lungs heave and seize, and she drags herself along the rug, gasping for air.

From here, she can't see the door to the basement. She staggers up to her feet, half tumbles toward the hall. The lights are out, and through the windows there is only night and the orange sodium glow of street lamps.

The basement door hangs open.

There's only pitch-black inside.

Tamsin swears and comes to the threshold, staring down into the dark. The cameras—are they still running? They need to still be running. But in the dark, they'll see nothing at all. No matter what happens, all they might capture is sound, and there had been no sound in her dream, not until she'd spoken.

She flinches and looks over her shoulder, heart in her throat, almost expecting to see herself standing there, ready to shove her down. But she's alone.

Just a dream. Dreams are not reality. Probably the power is just out.

She takes a deep breath, then shoves her hand past the basement entrance. Her fingers find the light switch. It's flipped down.

When she turns it on, brilliant white light floods the room, spills up the stairs, illuminates the hall. Everything below is as she left it. The door at the bottom of the stairs is closed.

Behind her, her shadow stretches to the ceiling.

Tamsin locks the basement door. She makes her way up to the bedrooms. She stands in front of Prime's room, looking down at the keypad. It's not armed.

She locks it and goes to bed.

Chapter Eighteen

Tamsin sleeps until after eight, far later than she usually would. She's groggy as she pulls herself from the guest bed, and even once she's showered and dressed, she's still sluggish. Coffee will help, but the meeting is sooner than she would've liked. Her hair is dull and frizzing; she braids it back, counting on iffy webcam resolution to obscure the worst of it. Last night's dream still clings to her like a shroud, wound tight but gossamer thin around her throat.

She stands in front of Prime's room for a long time, not exactly warring with herself, but unable to make herself reach out. It was only a dream, but the lingering emotional resonance of it *feels* real. The yawning abyss behind the door, the betrayal, the confusion between herself and Prime. Likely only some outgrowth of her own lingering guilt for forcing Prime to attempt opening the door to the point of tears, but maybe . . . maybe . . . should she check the cameras first? Confirm Prime is even in there?

Her phone buzzes in her pocket; the meeting is in an hour. She needs breakfast. Caffeine. To stop jumping at shadows.

She keys in the code to disarm the door.

Prime is awake and dressed, nose buried in a book on quantum entanglement. Tamsin doesn't remember lending it to her. She must have grabbed it on her way up to bed the night before. Tamsin stares at her, looking for some sign of whether her dream last night was a reflection of Prime's vulnerability or her own.

"Good morning," Prime says once she's finished reading whatever line she's on, oblivious or choosing not to mind Tamsin's staring. Her finger marks her spot in the book. "Were you up late?"

"Later than I should have been," Tamsin says. Nothing in Prime's body language screams *danger* to Tamsin, and she scrubs a hand over her jaw. "Make some coffee?"

Prime nods, setting the book aside and getting up. "Your meeting is soon, isn't it?"

"In an hour."

Prime smooths down her shirt but doesn't move toward the door. "Can I listen in?" she asks instead.

Just like last night, offering to take the measurements in the basement.

Tamsin looks at Prime again, more closely this time. Her clothing is still several years old, and leans more toward leisure-wear than work appropriate, but she's styled it well. She's a recognizable echo of a competent researcher, of *Tamsin*, refusing to be shut out of something she is more than qualified to handle. It unsettles her, but it's just another step on the same trajectory Prime has been on, mirroring more and more of Tamsin's traits, her mannerisms, her interests.

You're just going to tell her anyway, Tamsin thinks bleakly. She is not one to turn down resources, and Prime, regardless of whatever else she is, was perfectly helpful over dinner last night. She can't tell if she'd be more of a fool for utilizing or ignoring that.

"Yes," she says.

A smile spreads over Prime's face, not as boundless and earnest as it might have been a day or two ago. "Thank you," she says and leads the way to the kitchen.

Tamsin wonders if she's making a mistake the whole way down.

By ten, they've both eaten breakfast, and Tamsin is nursing her second cup of coffee at one end of the dining room table. While Prime finished tidying the kitchen, she'd gone over the preliminary results from Valdez and Yvette one last time, and there's something there. Their information is patchy still, and rushed, but both are teetering on the edge of a breakthrough.

Different breakthroughs.

Her skin buzzes with anticipation as she flips through the results. Prime reenters the room and takes a seat at the far end of the table, enough distance between them that the laptop's microphone won't pick up the soft glide of her pen over her notepad. For a moment, their eyes meet, and Prime must mirror her body language: leaning forward, alert, *hungry.*

The meeting invite blinks on Tamsin's screen. She clicks Join.

Video squares come to life, showing the subset of her team she's invited for this meeting. Octavian Valdez, Yvette Olsen, Aidan Davis, Satya Chaudhari, Jordan Cherry. Cara, taking notes.

In the corner is Lachlan's name, video and microphone off.

When are you coming to get the equipment? Cara privately messages her as everybody settles in.

Busy, Tamsin types back, gaze flicking up and over the screen to where Prime is sitting. It's tempting to send Prime in her place, but—no. Cara knows her well enough to be able to spot the difference. Tamsin hesitates a moment, then sends, *Can you have a courier service bring it by? Charge it to my personal card.*

There's a slight flicker in Cara's expression that might be confusion, but she replies, *I'll have it there by this evening.*

"Good morning, everyone," Tamsin says, closing the chat window. "I'm sure you've all read my memo regarding the differential sinking at the Myrica campus?"

Nods all around. One or two faces look strained.

"I had Mr. Valdez run some baseline tests on the ground below the campus last night. Based on his preliminary findings, I also asked Dr. Olsen to expand the suite of testing being performed at Deep Node Three. Dr. Olsen, please walk us through what you found last night."

Yvette is one of the tense ones, but she nods and shares her screen. A three-dimensional mock-up of the lab and surrounding environment, including the nearby subway line and the tunnel connecting the lab to it, fills Tamsin's screen.

An amorphous shape below the lab turns red.

"There's no other way to say this," Yvette says. "We found a suggestion of a pocket of . . . *spongiform* soil below the node lab, perhaps two-thirds of a kilometer down."

The team is too professional to start whispering, but Tamsin hears pencils working, keys tapping.

Yvette plunges on ahead. She pulls up a side-by-side comparison of two readouts, annotated with arrows. "It's hard to get a clear look at it, given the distance. We weren't sure we were even looking at anything unique until we compared it to scans taken during and immediately after construction."

"But it's new," Tamsin says.

"It's new," Yvette confirms. "And we've had no indication of the change on our seismographs or other constant-tracking instruments."

"So this could be happening anywhere," Valdez says, pushing his glasses up with one hand to pinch at the bridge of his nose. "And we won't know where to look for it."

"The node lab isn't sinking any faster or slower than any other point of measurement," Yvette says.

"No, but spongiform implies pockets of space," Tamsin says, tapping a finger on the case of her laptop. "And pockets of space are unstable, under so much weight. Depending on what the . . . supporting lattice is formed of, it could compress or outright collapse in on itself at any time, leading to an abrupt decrease in support below the lab."

Yvette nods, chewing her lip.

"Of course, it could also work in the opposite way," Tamsin says. "That whatever is forming the lattice is stronger than the existing soil. Is there any indication that the formation of these bubbles might be what's causing the extra support below the Myrica building, Valdez?"

"If anything," he says, "the ground below the building is becoming *more* dense, which, I know, doesn't make sense."

But it does match what Tamsin has seen in her basement, which is both a relief and deeply intriguing. The walls are not becoming more porous. The drywall is standard hardness and density, just as it always has been—there's just more *of* it.

Perhaps, when she takes the core samples, she can see if the walls are getting thinner to compensate for their added height.

"Please walk us through your findings," Tamsin says when she realizes Valdez hasn't continued.

He chews at his lip but does take over from Yvette, pulling up a more haphazard display of data.

"Unlike with Deep Node Three, we don't have previous scans to compare the tests we ran last night and this morning to," he says. "And we also haven't found anything as obviously strange as the low-density pocket Dr. Olsen's team has spotted. But we have confirmed Dr. River's initial observation that the campus is sinking at a demonstrably slower rate than the surrounding city, using survey equipment to resample measurements taken during various construction projects in and around campus over the last five years. The lowest point on campus is still lower than it was when it was built, but not low *enough*."

"And?" Tamsin prods.

"Well, we got lucky—we found an inclusion of probably a metal of some kind that's visible on our scans, and it appears to be deep down enough that it's being affected by whatever is going on," Valdez says. "But its behavior is . . . confusing?"

He pulls up a series of screen captures annotated with depth. In them, the inclusion appears to rise, if only by a few millimeters. Above the inclusion, the lowest point of the Myrica building shows no change in altitude. The distance in between looks normal, none of the gaps from Yvette's figures.

"Of course, this is only over a less-than-twelve-hour period. We're absolutely within the range of sampling error. I'm hoping that's what this is, because otherwise, it looks like the ground below the Myrica campus, but above the metal, is, uh . . ."

"Compressing," Tamsin says softly. Pushing up, toward the surface. If that's true, there's only two things that can happen as the pressure from below increases:

Either the lower floors of the building start to collapse up into themselves, pipes narrowing to uselessness, walls potentially buckling . . . or the whole building eventually starts to rise.

Yvette has gone entirely white. Jordan Cherry looks like they might throw up.

"That's not possible," Aidan Davis, their materials specialist, says.

"Neither is the spontaneous loss of matter that would be necessary to create a spongiform area of soil," Tamsin says. She should be horrified, like the others. She *should* be terrified for what this means for the city and for their entire understanding of the world. Instead, that giddy fizzing along her skin crackles into something greater, something all-consuming. This is new, maybe integral to their understanding, and she has a whole host of ideas of novel things to test in her basement the moment she has the time.

She'll make the time.

"We need to figure out what's going on, and quickly," she adds. Label it, test it, write it up. Make their names on it. "This, more than the gross subsidence, has the potential to cause chaos in the coming weeks. The surface isn't going to stay stable for much longer, and if Mr. Valdez's observations are right, compression's going to break pipes a lot faster than stretching is going to screw up the water pressure. We need to figure out how bad things are likely to get and when. And how to predict *where*." She mimes the appropriate level of concern, pursing her lips as she tries not to look at Prime, whose eyes she can feel fixed on her face. But even as the plans are flowing out of her, her thoughts keep coming back to the house, not the city. "Let's pull Nikkya Keiling, get her on this. If she doesn't have the tools to model it, she'll know somebody who does."

She's met with silence. Blank, confused stares from almost everybody on the call. Valdez is new; he likely doesn't know whom she's talking about, but everybody else should.

Their lack of response derails her. She looks at each window in turn, including Lachlan's. No answers appear.

"Is something wrong?" she asks, irritated enough that it comes out with an edge of patronizing drawl.

"Nikkya Keiling?" Cherry asks, brow furrowing.

"Yes, obviously," Tamsin bites out. "She's the perfect fit."

"She hasn't worked with us for years. And . . . she hates you," Cherry says, each word delivered carefully, as if to someone's senile aunt.

Tamsin scowls. "Why would she hate me?"

"I . . . Is that a serious question, Doctor?"

She sees heads down, hears furious typing, but nothing pops up in the chat, except a private note from Cara asking, *Are you feeling alright, Dr. Rivers?* Lachlan's camera remains off, but suddenly she can feel the empty square trained on her, the predator lurking in the brush.

Something is wrong. "Remind me," she says reluctantly. "It's—been a long week."

"Well, aside from her working for our main competitor now, you also took her spot as keynote speaker at the Wasatch conference two years ago, after raising doubts about her co-authorship on the Titchmarsh paper. It's what made her cut ties with us." Cherry shifts uncomfortably in their chair.

Tamsin can't remember the Wasatch conference.

That can't be right. Tamsin wouldn't have forgotten something like that, not all of it, not a speech and a conference and the assassination of a competitor's career—and yet there's no trace of Wasatch in her brain, no flicker of recognition. But she's been under a lot of stress lately, and really—how is she supposed to remember *every* foot she's ever stepped on to get where she is?

It's a long list.

The way they're all still staring at her is infuriating. After Torrence, everybody is walking on eggshells around her. Singling her out for special treatment. But strain has a real impact on the human mind, and she's not the only one who's suffering. Yvette looks like she hasn't slept in a week. Maybe Cherry is the one misremembering, mixing up two different events. It's as least as likely as Tamsin forgetting.

"Right," she says, swallowing around the anger tightening her throat. Arguing would be pointless and would only further convince the team that there's something to be worried about. Better to move on. "Of course. But she remains a strong option. Perhaps, if we pass the invitation on through a different channel—"

"I don't trust her with the data," Dr. Chaudhari says. "Sorry, but there's got to be some grad student at the university who can do the work just as well and won't fight an NDA. Until we know what this is, we should keep it under our control."

Tamsin waves a hand, dismissive and sharp. "Fine. Track our person down, then. But I want this underway by tomorrow morning, including a sampling plan of where else we should be looking for these . . . anomalies."

Murmured assent fills the dining room. Conversations break off, who will take care of what. Tamsin's heart begins to slow back to its usual rhythm, and she chances a glance up at Prime.

Prime offers her a smile.

When Tamsin looks back at her screen, Lachlan has dropped from the call.

Chapter Nineteen

As promised, a courier service arrives just before dinner. Tamsin has Prime go up to the bedroom while she lets the two men carry the boxes into the house. After they've gone, she sits in the living room, looking at the equipment she's unpacked and shoved unceremoniously into the corner. Prime comes down the stairs quietly and takes up a perch on the couch arm beside her.

"What do you plan on testing?" Prime asks.

"You," Tamsin says.

She expects a flinch or some other echo of Prime cowering in the basement. She has reassurances at the ready, but Prime remains calm. "Our similarities?"

"Maybe. Eventually. But first, I need to know what you are."

That piques Prime's interest. "Aren't I just like you?"

Yes, Tamsin almost says. But no matter how much in sync they can be with one another, no matter how much Tamsin now appreciates Prime's presence much of the time, there's still a boundary. A boundary she can't allow herself to ignore.

"You look human. You act human. But you walked out of an impossible door in my basement. A door you can no longer open. I don't know what you are, beneath your skin."

"You know I bleed."

Tamsin shrugs.

Prime levers herself off the couch and goes over to the equipment. "Do you know how to use any of this?" she asks, running her hand along the molded plastic of the ultrasound cart.

"To some extent. I'll need to do some reading."

"Will you let me help, or will that *muddy the waters* too much?"

The echo of the other morning is pointed. Not mean, but . . . not kind, either. Very much like how Tamsin would have said it.

She considers. "Learning to operate the tools shouldn't conflict with what we'll be testing with them," she says slowly. "I can handle the microscope. And I'll handle everything to do with the mechanical arm. But the ultrasound machine . . ."

Was both a risk and, possibly, overambitious. Prime has a point, even if she's not entirely aware of it. Tamsin gets up and retrieves her tablet. She unlocks its internet access. "I'll find resources for you," Tamsin says. "It will be a good test of your . . ."

"Plasticity?" Prime offers.

"Your ability to learn something I don't know," Tamsin rephrases.

Prime smiles, and when Tamsin finishes loading the tablet and locks it back down, Prime takes it with poorly masked delight.

The specialty medical supplies Tamsin ordered a few days back arrive Saturday morning. Tamsin sets up the robot arm in her disused office. The desk is barely strong enough to support it, but the tubs of water she adds help balance the load. To each tub, she adds a heater with a programmable thermostat, and she wires them together to a Raspberry Pi she has lying around from a project several years gone. Some simple programming and setting up the arm itself, and she has a rudimentary PCR machine.

The microscope is entirely standard, though well featured, given the brief requirements she'd outlined for Cara.

Drawing blood has the steepest learning curve.

She works through the day, ignoring the occasional buzz from her phone as emails come in from her team. They have enough work to keep them occupied for the weekend. Her curiosity over Valdez and Yvette's findings has soured in the wake of the meeting; this is just as important and far more satisfying than working for a team that second-guesses her. At any rate, Lachlan will no doubt call her if there's an actual issue.

Lachlan doesn't call.

That evening, they put what Tamsin has set up to use, running every test they can think of. By the next morning, they know Prime is human, indisputably. Her blood looks just like Tamsin's, no matter what they do to it. Electrophoresis tests run on their DNA shows identical banding. They are, as far as Tamsin can tell, the same biological entity.

Prime is not so squeamish about the needles anymore.

Sunday evening, Prime suggests they try the ultrasound machine.

They make a workstation in the living room. Along with the machine itself, Tamsin sets up her laptop and pairs it with the wide expanse of television screen she rarely uses. She leaves it connected to the internet; chances are good they'll need to look up references as they go, along with the resources Prime's been using to learn how to work the machine.

Tamsin reflects, not for the first time, that if she'd been relying only on herself, she would likely never have gotten around to actually figuring any of this out. Cara would have been suspicious for nothing. But Prime has the time and the aptitude. She's confident as she rolls up her sleeve, squirts a dollop of conductive gel onto her inner arm, and presses the ultrasound wand to it.

On the display, Tamsin can see a slice of gray. It's spongy, and it swings dizzily as Prime adjusts the wand and gets her bearings. The gray grows brighter and resolves into an oblong shape. Prime eyes it appraisingly.

"Can you hold this?" she asks.

Tamsin reaches over and takes the wand from Prime, holding it as steady as she can while Prime taps at the machine, taking measurements and screenshots. When she's done, she gently eases the wand from Tamsin's hand, sets it aside, and wipes her arm clean.

"Test run," Prime says, reaching past her for the laptop. She brings up an image and compares what she's scanned to it. "Here, that's the median nerve," she says, pointing to the pale lozenge.

"Have you been practicing?" Tamsin asks, stunned at how quickly Prime has oriented herself. But then again, Tamsin has always been a quick study, too.

"Just reading," Prime says. "And the extremities are easier. Fewer things to look at."

"You're intending to do the entire scan yourself, though?"

"How else? You haven't had time to learn."

"Show me how to key the measurements and capture images, at least," Tamsin says.

Prime, after a moment's hesitation, agrees.

They do one more test run, now with Tamsin at the cart, clicking and capturing and trying futilely to catch up to Prime. The leg, this time, with Prime shucking her lounge pants and seeking out the femoral artery, the sciatic nerve. Prime gets disoriented once or twice, but she recovers quickly.

Once they've fallen into a rhythm, Prime strips down to her underwear and stretches out on the couch. Carefully, methodically, she runs the probe over each of her limbs and then her abdomen. It takes her a fair amount of time to get her bearings over her liver, over half an hour of pushing and pulling at the wand, frowning at the screen, and batting Tamsin's hands away to adjust the contrast and color of what she's looking at.

Tamsin lets her, taken by surprise at her assertiveness.

In the end, everything is where they expect to find it. Two kidneys, one liver, a uterus, a stomach. Prime goes down the list, capturing everything. Later, when Prime has wiped the goo from her skin and redressed, when they sit together at the dining table and go over the readouts, Prime proclaims that everything is within the normal range, and Tamsin, keeping up with perhaps eighty percent of what Prime is pointing out, can't find any errors in her logic.

"Now you," Prime says.

Tamsin frowns. "What about me?"

"We should repeat the scan on you, now that we know what we're looking at. It should go faster. And then we'll have confirmation that we're the same."

Tamsin opens her mouth to protest, but what would she say? That they should just assume she's identical? That because Prime looks as expected, that means she must be patterned specifically off of Tamsin? She's never had surgery, so everything should be exactly where it is in Prime, but there's no way of knowing if they don't look. And if they don't look, the scan only serves to tell them that Prime is physiologically human, just like all the other tests have indicated.

That's only half of the puzzle.

"Fine. Now?"

It's getting late, but Prime nods. "Dinner can wait," she says.

"Shake?"

Prime fixes Tamsin with a steady, unimpressed look. Tamsin snorts. "Right. Not food. Let's get on with it, then."

Tamsin goes up to the bathroom to strip to her underwear. She fumbles with the closures on her top, embarrassment making her clumsy. Embarrassment? At what? Prime knows exactly what she looks like under her clothing, knows the location of every freckle, can see it whenever she wants to just by looking in a mirror. And yet it's like removing armor that has been keeping her safe all this time.

She shoves the feeling aside and pulls on her bathrobe. Back down in the living room, she only hesitates a moment before dropping that, too. Prime won't care. The blinds are down. Nobody else will know. She stretches out on the couch and offers up her arm.

The gel is cold. Prime slides the wand over her skin with a constant, even pressure. Up one arm, down the other. Along her legs, pressing into her thighs. Tamsin is reminded not of medical appointments, but of children's games. Playing doctor. Lying stretched out on somebody's parents' couch, letting them poke and prod her, and then switching places. A little thrill going through her as she pushed her hands against another girl's skin, as she felt the warmth, the life. A larger thrill going through her when she pinched and pet and made the other girl squirm, half in irritation, half in adoration.

She'd considered, briefly, going into medicine. She would have made an excellent surgeon. She thinks she might have specialized in neurosurgery, but she remembers, vaguely, reading some editorial where a neurosurgeon complained that these days, most operations he had to perform had nothing to do with the brain. It was all spinal work. A downgrade, both in terms of payoff and satisfaction, entirely out of the surgeon's control.

"Anything strange?" she asks, realizing she's lost track of what Prime is doing. The wand is on her belly, and there's no gel farther up, so her mind couldn't have wandered that much.

Prime is frowning at the screen.

"Hm," is all she says.

Tamsin moves to sit up, but Prime reaches back, pushes against her sternum. "Stay still," Prime says, not a frustrated demand but a distracted expectation. Tamsin almost shoves her away, but it's a pointless thing to argue over. Prime sweeps the probe up and to the right. Over her liver, Tamsin thinks.

The screen looks wrong.

Maybe it's just the orientation, but Prime makes a considering sound, takes measurements. She's not acting like she's lost. She squeezes more cold gel onto Tamsin's abdomen, and Tamsin tries not to shiver. Every inch of her is sticky, the gel clumping the faint hair on her arms together, slicking her thighs. Her pulse thunders in her ears.

"What is it?" Tamsin asks.

"I need more data," Prime says.

The probe dances across her skin again. Tamsin recognizes a few of the landmarks. Intestines, she thinks. Kidneys, one and then the other. More measurements are taken. She should've been the one to learn how to do this; relying on Prime to interpret the results was a mistake. She must be missing something, and she has no idea what it could be. Bile rises at the back of her throat, and she stares a burning hole into the screen, willing it to make sense.

On the monitor, the color-coded rush of blood and the chaos of opening and closing valves that is her heart appears. Its rhythm is fast, but looks like Prime's had. She stares at the screen, willing herself to calm down.

But then Tamsin registers that the probe is over her right breast.

"Prime," she says, and her voice is shaking. "Tell me what you're seeing."

"Everything is healthy," Prime says. "Or at least, looks like mine. Except . . ." She pulls the probe down one last time, down the left side of her body. At last, what Tamsin thinks is the liver appears on the screen.

It's supposed to be on the other side.

"Your organs are arranged in the mirror image of standard anatomy. Of my anatomy."

Tamsin tears her gaze away from the screen to Prime, who sounds curious, not concerned. She looks down at Tamsin now with hunger in her eyes. Slowly, not looking away, Prime lifts the probe from Tamsin's belly.

"Have they always been like that?" Prime asks.

Tamsin doesn't know.

With a snarl, Tamsin scrambles off the couch. She doesn't retrieve the bathrobe, too focused on getting away, getting upstairs. Getting the fucking gel off her skin. It's making her flesh feel as if it doesn't fit right, as if she's not *built* right. Her heart pounds on the wrong side of her chest with every step she climbs.

Prime doesn't follow her.

Autopilot takes her not to the guest bathroom, but to the en suite. She turns on the water, strips out of her underwear, and freezes, staring at herself in the mirror.

In the mirror, all her organs are exactly where they should be.

But only in the mirror.

She's wrong. Wrong, wrong, wrong, *wrong*. Pieces fitted together haphazardly, stacked up out of order, pressing on each other with slick, insistent error. All her blood vessels, running opposite to how they're supposed to, the beat of her heart proving out the path over and over. She can feel her pulse pounding in her skull, and it makes her stomach lurch. Her stomach, twisted to the wrong side.

She forces herself into the shower, hair still braided. It will be a nightmare to untangle later. She doesn't care. All she cares about is scrubbing the gel off her skin and mapping out the planes of her body. They're familiar. She's lived inside of them for almost forty years. But when she tries to think back to if she always looked like this, if her freckles and moles were always in the same arrangement, she isn't sure.

What if it's like Keiling? What if Cherry was right, and she did forget an entire keynote address, an entire falling out, an entire sabotage? What if there are other things she's forgetting about herself? How long? How *long* has she been like this? It feels impossible, that she could have known but forgotten, but then again, it feels impossible that she'd forget an entire conference.

It's different. There have been so many conferences. So many papers. So many strategic moves to get herself where she needed to be. She was bound to forget some of them.

Her hand settles over where her heart should be. She lets out a shuddering breath, steaming water cascading from her nose, her breasts. She would have known if something so fundamental was wrong with her. Wouldn't she? Wouldn't it have been caught on some routine physical?

There are only two options: One, that it has always been like this, and she's forgotten. Two, that something in her has changed.

How. *How* could she have changed? The thought makes her want to peel her skin off, dig into the meat of herself and reset the error. Did it start with that dream, the night after the PR meeting? She'd stared at herself in a darkened mirror, but it hadn't felt like a mirror. It had felt like a window.

And in the basement, in front of the door, she'd dreamed of being Prime.

But they were both just dreams. Dreams didn't change biology. Dreams didn't change *reality*. (But in reality, walls don't stretch and bedrock doesn't cavitate, either.)

Tamsin shuts off the water, leaning heavily against the tiled wall. She's crying; she must have started once the water hit her face. She swipes at her tears, then steps forward, presses her flesh against the tile. It leeches heat from her. Pulls emotions with it. Her body drips dry while she stands there, her mat of hair the only thing still damp by the time she steps out of the shower.

The towel is only for modesty. Prime is waiting for her in the bedroom, sitting primly on the edge of the mattress.

"It's called *situs inversus*," Prime says. "It's a rare but well-documented condition. It causes no complications when, like in your case, it's complete. It's usually only discovered during surgery."

"I've never had surgery," Tamsin says.

"Then it's probably been there since birth," Prime replies.

Perfect.

That's the answer Tamsin wanted.

Chapter Twenty

Sleepless nights are getting too familiar.

Tamsin sits in the living room. Prime is asleep, her door left unlocked. They'd sat up together after Tamsin's shower, after Tamsin had donned a set of soft sleep clothes Prime had handed to her. As the last of the adrenaline had faded from Tamsin's system, leaving her drowsy and numb, they'd talked. About Myrica, about Tamsin's career, about the coming week. At some point, Prime had coaxed her into lying down and had settled in beside her.

But where Prime had gone to sleep, Tamsin had stayed resolutely awake. In the dark, she'd cataloged Prime's every feature again. She'd rested a hand gently over Prime's chest and felt her heart beat in the right place.

And then she'd slipped out of the room and come down here.

She's moved one of the chairs so that she can see the door to the basement as she nurses a glass of vodka. It's locked; she checked. Whatever is down there can't get out.

But whatever is down there, she can't see.

There's a chance that nothing is wrong, beyond what she already knows. A sinking city, a distorting basement, a strange door: all undeniable. But the rest? Perhaps the memory lapse was normal. Perhaps her body has always held within it a unique configuration of parts.

But she'd be a fool to keep ignoring the basement the way she has been. There's a reason this is all happening to her, and she needs to find it before it can get any worse.

In the morning, Tamsin hands Prime the tablet, loaded down with the most relevant reports and data sets.

Prime's eyes skim over the file listing. "The subsidence question."

"Yes. Think of it as a start-up guide. Everything you need to know to be able to work on it."

Prime looks up at Tamsin sharply. They're sitting at the dining room table, with breakfast (a frittata meal kit accompanied by fresh fruit) and steaming cups of coffee in front of them. "I can have this?"

Tamsin nods. "I want you to help."

I need you to help.

Last night, by the time she'd finally returned to the guest room and tried to steal a few hours of sleep, she'd already decided. Things can't continue as they have. Lachlan needs answers. The city needs answers. The basement might *have* those answers, but she can't keep dashing between it and the world outside. She got lucky last week, but it's more likely that she's going to miss things than discover them if she keeps this up.

There are two fronts to this war.

There are two of her.

She sets the baby monitor, retrieved from Prime's room while she made breakfast, on the table between them. It had been right where Tamsin had left it, in the vent, which was all the more surprising because she knows Prime knew exactly where it was. "I'm going to be spending more time in the basement," Tamsin says. "If you need anything, this pushes to my phone."

It might have been simpler to just leave the basement door unlocked while she works, but she wants as few interruptions as possible. No Prime bringing her coffee, no visits because she's grown bored. And if Prime is like her, she'll appreciate it, too.

"You're sure about this?" Prime asks even as she takes the monitor.

"You won't have access to my laptop," Tamsin says. "I'll still need to handle emails and meetings. But this will be a better use of my time. You're more than capable of parsing through what's coming in, and I'll be more likely to learn something that can help if I'm studying an active distortion site. We can reconvene at meals." She tilts her head to one side. "Unless *you* don't think you're capable?"

Prime's mouth firms into a hard line. "I am."

Tamsin manages not to smile, pleased that Prime responds to manipulation just like anybody else.

"Then get to work. I'll see you in a few hours."

* * *

It's easy to unlock the basement. She experiences no hesitation, no uncertainty, not even an echo of the feeling of somebody just behind her, ready to push. Instead, it feels like coming into the lab after a long weekend away, and really, isn't that exactly the case?

She slips inside, into the cool, calm embrace of the room, and picks her way down the dangerously steep steps. The lights are still on.

The first thing she does when she reaches the bottom is finally put in the order for the safety railing that she's been holding off on. That done, she does her circuit of measurements and data entry. The rhythm of it is soothing.

The basement keeps getting larger, but it is a self-contained world.

She finds work to do, the way she knew she would. She drills holes in the drywall until she hits the cement behind it. The holes close back over themselves, but the bit of the drill produces slender cores that she can measure. She sets them aside to look at under the microscope and run further tests on, then turns to the door. She takes samples there, too, though only from the surface, curling gouges of wood and paint.

She checks the camera logs next, running through at full speed in reverse. An entire weekend of nothingness, save for a barely perceptible creep as the markings on the wall spread to keep up with the distortion. She'll need to double back to analyze the exact movement of the walls around the door; she adds it to the list.

And then the cameras are dark as she hits the time stamp of when she woke up beneath the living room table, her flipping of the light switch reversed. She slows the replay. The simpler camera shows nothing, but on the newer camera, there's . . . something.

It's completely unidentifiable, no matter how much she slows it down or fusses with contrast and brightness settings. There's just not enough light. There's no light, and yet she could swear there's a flicker of a darker black, just for a moment, a perfectly vertical line, right where the door must be. It doesn't come through on any screenshots, but it's *there*.

It's probably just an artifact.

And yet . . . she stares at it, worrying at her lower lip, stopping just short of petting the screen, seeking to feel what she can't truly see.

Her phone pings with an alert from the baby monitor. Tamsin sits back and checks the time. *Lunch.* She nearly opens up the two-way function to tell Prime she's going to be a bit longer, but she should check emails, confirm nobody's trying to get ahold of her. And has it really been five hours already?

She goes upstairs.

Prime summarizes everything she understands so far over a quick meal of pasta and what Tamsin realizes, belatedly, is jarred sauce. Much simpler than Prime usually goes in for. They both must be getting caught up in the work.

Tamsin tells her nothing about the camera footage. Once her bowl is empty, and she's confident Prime has a grasp on the existing research, she makes a quick review of her emails, sends off a few replies, and then returns to her makeshift lab.

She'll put in a few more hours tonight, after dinner, to keep her bearings on the day-to-day.

It's clearly too easy to lose track of time in the basement, even more so as she fusses with the camera footage, so she sets up alerts on her phone. By the time she allows herself to go back further than the maybe-movement in the darkness, the half-hour timer has gone off twice. It goes off again as she watches herself appear on the screen, moving in reverse toward the door. It's hard to say if it's more unsettling because of watching time flow backward or because she knows she's sleepwalking.

Then she settles against the door. This part, Tamsin remembers. She watches herself stand there for what the time stamps say is hours. *Hours.* There's no obvious moment where she shifts from sleeping to awake. There's only the moment where she comes to the door in the first place and before that, her coming in and out of shot as she takes her measurements.

She stops the film, then lets it play again, straight through, this time moving forward.

It's a little after her four-thirty alarm when her phone pings, and she reaches over for it without looking, tapping the button to hear whatever the baby monitor is picking up. The last two times, it was Prime washing their lunch dishes and then an inquiry as to what she'd like for dinner.

This time, she can still hear Prime's voice, but it's softer, and—

"Can I come in?"

Lachlan Woodfield.

She doesn't, thankfully, sound angry. Polite, perhaps. Tamsin fumbles with her computer and finally manages to hit Pause on the replay, then snatches up her phone. There's no video functionality, but she can picture this all too well. Lachlan at the door, and Prime, dressed down from what Lachlan is used to seeing, standing uncertainly before her.

Why didn't she ever move the nanny cams downstairs after Prime was no longer confined to the bedroom? But no, she could never have anticipated something like this, could she? "Why did you answer the door?" she begs the silent air around her.

She checks frantically for some earlier alert that she missed, Prime trying to get her attention, but there's nothing.

"This is an unexpected visit," Prime is saying. She *almost* sounds like Tamsin, but not quite. There's hesitance there; Tamsin would just be angry. Is angry.

(Is terrified.)

"We need to talk," Lachlan says. "Can I come in?" Her tone has shifted. It's not a request anymore.

Prime, luckily, seems to understand. "Of course." Shuffling, and the sound of the front door closing.

Tamsin eyes the stairs. She has no idea where the baby monitor is sitting right now or if Prime has any chance of concealing it. If they move to another room, Tamsin will lose track of them; the basement door muffles sound completely, so there's no chance of eavesdropping that way. But if they go to the living room, maybe she can—

The living room still has the ultrasound machine in it.

Tamsin's knuckles go white from clutching the phone. Footsteps keep coming from its speakers. Prime has the monitor. Tamsin stays where she is and sags with relief when she hears the sound of the dining room chairs scraping over the floor.

"Would you like something to drink?"

"No," Lachlan says. "Please, sit down, Dr. Rivers."

Prime doesn't reply—not audibly, at least. There's no telling if she's sitting or not. Tamsin can barely see the brilliant room around her, she's so focused on trying to picture the two of them. Trying to predict everything that could go wrong.

"Sit down," Lachlan repeats. Her patience is wearing thin.

"I wasn't expecting you today," Prime says. Her voice is too hesitant. Unsure. Lachlan will pounce on that weakness.

"I should have come Friday, but I was detained." A pause, then: "I'm not going to ask again. Sit."

Tamsin flinches. Prime is more confident, more assertive than she once was, but she is not Tamsin. She's a terrible mimic. Lachlan clearly can already tell something is not right, and once Prime sits down and the exchange begins in full—

"Give me a moment to go change?" Prime asks. "I feel . . . underdressed."

Lachlan's reply is lost, but Tamsin can imagine the monosyllabic grunt of acceptance. It must be, because she can hear Prime moving now. The closing of a door.

Thank *fuck*.

"Tamsin?"

She jabs the two-way button. "What the hell were you thinking, letting her in?"

A pause. Then, "I was thinking about how dangerous you made her sound. I didn't want to keep her waiting when she knocked. I'm upstairs. If you can leave the basement quietly, I can come down the steps just enough to make it sound right."

It's a clever ruse, and Tamsin tries not to get distracted by how quickly Prime came up with it and how reflexively Prime thought to lead Lachlan away from the living room. It's clever, and clever is what she needs right now.

"I can do that."

There's the sound of dresser drawers moving. Prime must be in the guest room. Lachlan won't be able to hear that from the dining room, but the attempt at verisimilitude makes her calm down a little more.

"Are you ready?" Prime asks after a minute of soft rustling.

Tamsin looks down at her clothing, straightens a hem. She tries to remember how Prime is wearing her hair today. A braid, Tamsin thinks. Like hers.

"Yes," Tamsin says.

"I won't be able to give you a signal."

"I'll listen for you on the stairs," Tamsin assures her and then toggles off the two-way in the app, puts her phone on mute, and slides it into her pocket.

She creeps to the top of the basement steps, undoes the locks from the inside as quietly as she can, and eases the door open.

Prime's footsteps are barely audible at first. Tamsin slips through the door as they grow a little louder. She eases it closed behind her. Prime's footsteps fade off, and Tamsin strides toward the dining room, grateful that she doesn't wear heels in the house; there's no telltale click suddenly ringing through the hall.

But the dining room is empty.

For a moment, Tamsin stares at the table. Two chairs are still pulled out, evidence that Lachlan *was* here. She looks back the way she came, out to the hall. Did Lachlan follow Prime? But no, those footsteps on the stairs had been coming down. And Lachlan wasn't waiting near the basement door.

That leaves the kitchen and the living room.

Her heart lodges in her throat. She moves to the living room and there's Lachlan, standing there with her hands in her pockets, frowning at the ultrasound machine.

"Mx. Woodfield," Tamsin says and hopes she sounds more chastising than upset.

Lachlan glances back over her shoulder. "Playing doctor?" she asks, lifting her chin at the cart. "Not a cheap piece of equipment. It had better not be Myrica property."

Tamsin doesn't flinch, but it's a near thing.

"It is," she says. "Borrowed, but not what I was after. Cara misunderstood my request. I wanted an industrial ultrasound, but I suppose it's an understandable mistake. I'm sending it back tomorrow."

Prime, thankfully, took the time to wipe the machine down at some point, unplug it, and return it, more or less, to its out-of-the-box condition. It looks unused. Tamsin hopes it's enough.

"You didn't requisition it through normal channels." *I would have known* goes unspoken. (Which means Lachlan must know about the camera. The scanning electron microscope. She's said nothing, though, which must be a good thing. Right?)

"It was ahead of the discovery of the spongiform zone below the node lab," Tamsin says, barely restraining the way her voice wants to shake. "I had a hunch. Intended to test things on my own to see if it was a *useful* hunch. I didn't want to take it out of one of my own labs, so I had Cara find another one."

"Hm." Lachlan doesn't sound convinced, but she does, at last, turn away from the machine and toward Tamsin.

"Obviously," Tamsin continues, "I won't have need of the industrial model now, either. All normal channels from here on out."

She's protesting too much.

Lachlan approaches at something like a casual stroll, and Tamsin breaks. She takes a step back. Lachlan doesn't falter, doesn't slow until there's only a foot between them, at most. She's several inches taller than Tamsin, broader, and better practiced in using her bulk to intimidate rather than her mind.

She's using it now.

"You weren't in the lab today."

"No, I was working remotely," she says, too fast. "As we discussed."

"Working implies being active."

She sets her jaw. "I was working offline with the data. Reviewing reports. Not everything comes with mouse clicks and emails." She straightens a little more. "You were at Friday's meeting. You know we're making progress."

"Yes, I was at that meeting." Lachlan's upper lip peels back from her teeth for just a moment, and it's the only warning Tamsin gets before Lachlan's gloved hand is below her jaw, tilting her chin up. Tamsin's breath hitches. Lachlan doesn't—Lachlan never—"I got to see your memory lapse over Keiling. And I gave you the weekend to get yourself back together, but I have to admit, I am now officially concerned, Dr. Rivers."

"Don't *touch* me," Tamsin says, jerking away and turning toward the dining room. Before she can make it more than a few steps, though, Lachlan grabs her wrist and tugs sharply. Tamsin stumbles, and Lachlan's arm closes across her abdomen, crushingly hard and unyielding, Tamsin's back pressed flush against her chest.

"I think," Lachlan murmurs in her ear, "you've been forgetting for a long time. Forgetting how precarious your position is. Forgetting what the nature of our relationship is."

"*Lachlan—*" Her given name slips out, unbidden in Tamsin's rising panic, to no effect.

"You aren't going to talk your way out of this, Dr. Rivers. You are going to listen to me, and you are going to follow directions." Lachlan's other hand tangles in her hair, the leather catching roughly against her scalp. She tugs, and Tamsin's head falls to the side. She's shaking, her knees barely holding her weight.

Behind her, Lachlan is steady.

"Something," Lachlan says, "is wrong. I don't know what it is yet, and maybe you don't know what it is, either. But you are not acting like yourself. So here's what's going to happen: You are going to inform your team that the deep node labs are closed until I tell you otherwise. Not just no phase three, but no work at all. I want them empty. They are all going to move into the central office and shift their focus entirely to the subsidence problem."

"But—"

"You are going to make an appointment with your physician as well as a psychiatrist. I will send you a list of practitioners who are Myrica-approved, given the unique nature of the circumstances. You will see them as soon as they have availability. If you do not make those appointments yourself, I will make them for you. If you do not *go* to those appointments, I will take you to them myself. Do you understand?"

"Yes," Tamsin bites out. It's fine. She can do all of those things. Especially with Prime at home to work the data, she can balance all of this. The loss of the deep nodes is going to result in a pointless loss of data, and it stings, but it's only temporary. She's going to make sure it's only temporary.

And then she'll get the all clear. The doctors will say she's fine. Lachlan will back off again.

(Or they won't. She won't.)

"Until that time, I'll allow you to continue working from home; you're clearly not fit for travel or long hours in the lab. But this is under the condition that you do *work*, Dr. Rivers, when you are able to. We are also going to speak on the phone each night, and if I ask you to meet me elsewhere, you will do so without complaint. You will continue to include me on all meetings that you take, and you will copy me on all written communications. If I see any indication that your memory is continuing to degrade, or that your behavior is becoming more erratic, I will step in. Do you understand?"

"It's not going to get worse," Tamsin says. "It was a one-time thing. Stress from the project—"

Lachlan's hand shifts in her hair in answer. Tugs at the roots. Tamsin bares her teeth at the far wall.

"I understand," she says.

"Good." Her hand gentles. It strokes against her scalp, then retreats entirely. The arm around her waist loosens; in its absence, her own flesh feels too hot. "I am here to help you achieve your goals, Dr. Rivers. Myrica Dynamics's goals. Trust me, and everything will be fine."

Tamsin bites down a laugh, pulling away and straightening her dress. She does not turn to look at Lachlan. "You can go now," she says. Her voice trembles too much for it to be a command.

Lachlan takes it as she intends, though, in one brief show of consideration. But when she reaches the hallway, she pauses, looking in the direction of the basement door.

Don't, Tamsin thinks desperately.

And, as if she hears, Lachlan keeps walking. To the front door. Out of the house.

Tamsin doesn't move from the living room, even after she's long gone.

Chapter Twenty-One

Tamsin stands very still in the center of her living room and feels the ground sinking below her feet. Her scalp gives phantom aches where Lachlan's fingers pulled. Her waist burns like it's been branded.

The house around her is silent.

A week ago, she'd have dragged her outrage around her like a mantle, spitting fury at Lachlan daring to treat her like that, to touch her, to threaten her. But then she looks at the ultrasound machine and thinks of the locks on the basement door, the sleepwalking and the mistake of firing Torrence and the memory lapse, and wonders if Lachlan has a point.

Maybe she can't solve this on her own. Maybe whatever's wrong is already so far out of her control that she's delusional to even try.

She paces, and Prime does not appear. She could call out. She could get her phone out of her pocket and activate the two-way mic. She could just go upstairs. But every single option feels like giving in, in some way, and so she just waits.

And waits.

And wonders what Prime is doing right now. What Prime is thinking. What Prime wants.

Because while Prime's explanation makes sense, that she answered the door because she was taken by surprise and worried by the repercussions of delaying, it doesn't *feel* right. And Prime is capable, to some extent, of deception. She knew not to take Lachlan to the living room. She knew to go upstairs and allow Tamsin to swap places with her. She even had a plan to do it. She's clever. Clever, like Tamsin is.

Did Prime let Lachlan in on purpose?

To what end?

Again and again, she finds herself stopped in front of the basement door. She doesn't mean to keep coming back; half the time, she intends to go upstairs. But then her mind wanders, or her feet wander, and then she's back, staring at the latch, thinking of how she'd looked in the camera footage, dreaming against the door. Thinking of her nightmare, of one of them at the top of the stairs pushing the other down into the dark.

You have to finish your work. Are you ready?

She hasn't locked it yet, she realizes on the fifth return.

Just a normal mistake. Equivalent to walking into a room and forgetting why she'd come. It happens constantly, to everybody, and it means nothing.

But her hand is shaking as she rearms the door. Her throat is tight. There is something wrong with her, and if Lachlan can tell, then it's not subtle, not anymore.

If a doctor looks at her, what will they find? She can't really believe that they'll just send her on her merry way, can she? She flattens a hand over her abdomen. What else inside of her is jumbled out of place?

She hasn't been cautious enough. Letting Prime move freely about the house was a mistake. Giving her access to the subsidence data this morning is proof that Tamsin is losing touch with reality. She's been getting worse ever since Prime arrived, and just because Prime scores a particular way on a personality inventory, just because she soothed Tamsin the night before when she was desperate, doesn't mean she can be trusted.

It doesn't matter that Prime is human (by every metric Tamsin can measure), that Prime is as smart as she is, that Prime clearly dislikes pain and has preferences and opinions and is in every way a *person*. Prime also came through a door in her basement that doesn't obey the laws of reality, and what was Tamsin thinking, allowing Prime to touch her? To take over the heavy lifting of her job? To be in a position where she could ever speak to Lachlan?

What if she'd crept down here while Tamsin paced and slipped into the basement? Tamsin is sure she would have noticed, but *what if, what if, what if . . . ?*

What if Prime turned the lights out on Friday? The cameras can't see the stairs.

Something changed in the dark.

Tamsin is in the kitchen now. She doesn't remember entering. She stares at the knife block and wonders, for the first time in days, what she really gains by keeping Prime alive.

She pulls out a chef's knife, heavy and sharp and rarely used. It fits poorly in her hand, and she has to bite down a hysterical laugh. Her, with a knife. Does she really think she can do this? The pin was one thing, the door, but a sharp edge, the parting of flesh, a *body* left behind—

And what is all of that against her own safety? Her own sanity?

In the hall, both Penroses are watching her, curled tight together by the front door. Their eyes gleam as she approaches the staircase, as she takes the first step, then the second. The pitch feels wrong beneath her feet, too tall, like the stairs in the basement at the beginning of the distortion. She staggers, nearly trips, and catches herself on the railing, chest heaving. She stares down at the steps below her.

The risers look taller. Are they taller? Her vision is so narrow now, her heart pounding so fast.

There have been no distortions above the surface of the earth. She repeats that to herself, over and over again, until she believes it. Until, when she tests the next step, it's exactly where she expects to find it.

She can do this.

One step, and then another. She forces herself up them, arms shaking, knees unsteady, knife held carefully in case of another stumble. Up and up, there seem like so many *more* of them now, until she's at the top, breathing heavily, looking right to where the bedroom door should be. Where Prime should be.

The hall curves off to the left instead.

Tamsin presses the heels of her hands to her eyes, biting down a frustrated, terrified growl, an animal sound for an animal panic. She backs up until she hits the nearest wall, entirely solid, cool and familiar. Real. The world fights her, or maybe her brain does, overstimulated and overstressed.

Or maybe she's asleep right now. Maybe this whole afternoon has been a nightmare. Maybe Lachlan didn't stop by the house, didn't threaten her so sweetly, voice pouring into her ear like caustic honey. Her dreams have been unwieldy and wild ever since the door appeared.

But when she fumbles her phone from her pocket, she can read the time: 5:17 in the afternoon. It unlocks, and all the apps are what she remembers, all the words sensible and legible.

She's not dreaming.

She's standing in her upstairs hallway, yards away from her bedroom, hyperventilating and clutching her phone and a knife, and something is very, very wrong with her. Something is very, very wrong with *Prime*.

Lachlan. She needs Lachlan. She can't be trusted to do this on her own. But she can no longer call Lachlan; the lingering ache of her arm across Tamsin's belly is testament to that.

Nobody can fix this but herself. She knows what she has to do, because in the end, it all comes down to one question:

Would Tamsin trust herself, if the scenario was reversed?

No.

No, she wouldn't.

Tamsin would be looking for a way to take advantage of the situation. She'd be eager to get the upper hand, to flip the power dynamic between them, if she found herself the half-imprisoned one.

It's so clear, then, for one terrible, nauseating moment: Prime could have faked the personality test results. Prime could have steered Tamsin to the decisions she needs her to make. Prime could have been acting this whole time. Tamsin is a good liar; Prime might be even better.

She clutches the knife more tightly.

This can't be allowed to continue.

When she opens her eyes again, the hallway is more or less exactly as she expects it. The walls seem to shudder, yes, and the ground feels uneven, but she can orient herself again. Her feet move without conscious intent, until, at last, she's standing in front of the bedroom with its keypad lock. Prime must be inside. She'll unlock the door, and she'll—she'll—

Do *what*, exactly? Creep into Prime's room? Lunge forward like a horror-movie slasher? She's never tried to kill anybody before. Could she even do it? Maybe if Prime was asleep, but it's the middle of the day, and when she tries to picture it, the knife sliding between familiar ribs, blue eyes flying open, wild and startled and betrayed, so much like her own, she falters.

Tears overtake her then, useless tears, and she can't stop them. No matter how much she tries to ground herself, to manage her breathing, nothing works, and she drops her phone and the knife and clutches at her face, her shoulders, trying desperately to hang on. *Pull yourself together,* she demands. It evaporates into nothing.

"Tamsin?"

Prime's voice, *her* voice, from behind her. Prime wasn't ever in the bedroom. She shudders, bending double. "No," she says to herself, to the world. "*No.*"

Footsteps, and then Prime's beside her, on the floor with her, cradling her in her arms. Tamsin can smell her shampoo. Their shampoo.

"Don't touch me," Tamsin snaps. It's louder now than when she begged the same of Lachlan. (Because it was begging, wasn't it? And it still is.)

Prime lets her go.

Tamsin almost reaches for her anyway.

"Did Lachlan hurt you?" Prime asks, low and fervent, and that only summons up another wave of frustrated tears, because it's exactly the sort of thing a rational, caring person would say.

"No. Yes. It—it doesn't matter. I need you to go back into your room." Needs Prime to be where she thought she was. Then maybe she can have a second chance, but god, she's failed already, hasn't she?

"I don't want to leave you like this," Prime says. "You seem ill."

Something is very, very wrong. You're not acting like yourself. Memory lapses and emotional outbursts.

"Go back into your room," she repeats. "Please."

Prime gets to her feet. Tamsin fixates on the thin, fine fabric of her socks as Prime steps around her to the bedroom door, opening it. It's not locked, of course. "Come in with me?" she asks on the threshold. "I really don't think you should be alone."

Tamsin shakes her head. "I'll be fine," she whispers. It sounds pathetic. Devastated. The worst lie Tamsin has ever told. She stops looking at Prime, back down at her phone and the—

And nothing. It's just her phone on the floor.

Her gasping breaths falter, then catch entirely, as she realizes Prime hasn't mentioned the knife.

Did Tamsin actually take it from the kitchen? If she went back downstairs, would it still be in the block? It must be. It must be, Prime would've said something otherwise, or been afraid, or—or—

She never had the knife.

The realization spills over her, cool water against a fever. Of course she never had the knife. What would she have done with it?

"What happened down there?" Prime asks when Tamsin doesn't move.

Her scalp aches where Lachlan had fisted her hair. This is all Lachlan's fault. Lachlan's visit has put her in this spiral, desperate to *fix* this, and she'd seen the knife, and she'd—it doesn't matter. Doesn't matter that she'd been so out of her head with fear that she'd forgotten the layout of her own house. What matters is Prime didn't do this to her. Prime hasn't done anything.

"Lachlan has instituted a rigorous . . . oversight program," Tamsin says finally.

Prime's eyes widen. "She'll be coming by more often?"

"Not unless I give her cause," Tamsin says, desperate to reassure her. They both need that reassurance; Lachlan is dangerous. "But I need to call her, every night. Need to come when called."

"She thinks she can't trust you?"

"She thinks I'm sick." Tamsin feels sick. Prime says she looks sick. Maybe they're right, maybe she needs rest, and care, and nothing else. "She threatened me. A strange approach to caring about somebody."

"Is it?" Prime asks.

Tamsin flushes. She can remember the feeling of the pin pushing below Prime's skin, the color of the blood that welled up after. Prime, forced against the basement door, then crying on the ground. She'd done that, and yet Prime still believes Tamsin cares.

She stares at where she thought she'd put the knife.

"And after she left?" Prime pushes.

"What?" She lifts her head.

"What happened after she left?"

"I . . ."

I temporarily lost my mind. It already feels distant, foggy and unreal. Impossible. It slips through her fingers as she tries to grasp it.

"I came up here," Tamsin says slowly. "And it was just . . . too much. It's too much."

"What is?"

"All of it." A laugh cracks out of her. "Balancing it all. Trying to figure out what it all *means*. Hiding it from everybody, hiding you," she says, then adds, in a rush, "I've—I've been sleepwalking. Sometimes I don't know when I'm asleep."

"You're awake right now," Prime says.

"Maybe I shouldn't be."

Prime comes to her then, holds out a hand. "You should lie down," Prime says. "Let me go make dinner. I'll wake you up when it's ready. Okay?"

Tamsin nods and lets herself be helped to her feet and into the bedroom. It's shadowed and cool, and the bed is inviting. She could rest for just a few minutes; that would be okay. She hasn't been sleeping well, and it's making everything that much harder to manage.

Prime walks her to the bed and stays until Tamsin is curled up on her side. Prime did change her clothing, she notices, while Lachlan was waiting. She's wearing newer clothes of Tamsin's, plaid slacks and a wine-colored sweater.

It looks good on her.

Chapter Twenty-Two

Dinner is pork with a glossy, red sauce that tastes like wine and mustard, served alongside a potato gratin. It's richer than anything Tamsin has had in weeks, and as it settles in her gut, it feeds the heavy languor in her limbs. Across from her, Prime smiles and pushes a glass of Chablis her way.

Her nap had been free of dreams. She'd woken not to Prime fetching her, but to the buzz of her phone, which Prime must have put on the nightstand while she slept.

> From: Lachlan
> No need to call tonight. How are you feeling?

She'd stared at the text for a long time. No answer felt appropriate. She didn't want Lachlan to know what had happened after she'd left, and more than that, she couldn't have articulated the blurred, muted blend still souring her gut. All she'd wanted was to close her eyes again. Put her head down. Leave herself behind for a little bit longer.

But she had to say something. And as long as she got it mostly right, she'd get the help she needed. Lachlan's interest would wane, and the danger would pass. And whatever convolutions of her overworked mind had left her overwhelmed in the hallway, it would all be better soon.

> From: Tamsin
> I took the rest of the day off. Catching up on sleep.

> From: Lachlan
> Good.

* * *

The next morning, Tamsin sends the emails to shut down the node labs and redistribute duties. She feels no pain, only numbness. She expects it will hurt later, but for now it's like paring the bruise out of an apple.

It's just one less thing to worry about. Her world contracts a little more. Maybe that should concern her, but simpler is better. Simpler lets her focus on what's important.

"Are you going downstairs?" Prime asks, sitting down next to her with fresh coffee. They had shakes for breakfast today, and Tamsin sips at her mug, washing the pseudo-chocolate flavor away.

"No," she says. "I have to handle emails. Put in face time." She can sense Lachlan's presence, like a living thing, just behind them both, and can almost hear the creaking of her gloves. Feel a hand on her shoulder, keeping her in her chair.

And getting back to work has always helped before. It's centered her. Refocused her. That it keeps Lachlan at arm's length is just a very important bonus.

After all, if Lachlan runs out of patience, if she is no longer willing to manage Tamsin for *Tamsin's* benefit as well as the company's, then what happens to Prime? On the off chance Lachlan doesn't find her, she'd be trapped by their shared face, nowhere to go.

If Tamsin goes missing, Prime has to go missing, too. If she goes down, they go down together. It's clarifying, that realization.

"I can do some of that for you," Prime says, pulling her away from her darker thoughts. "At least on the admin side. If you want."

Tamsin looks over at her, startled. "No," she says, "you can't. You don't have the history with everybody. I'd need to supervise." It's a noble impulse, offering, but surely Prime can see the problem? If the team was distressed over the Keiling slip (and Lachlan's visit confirms it *was* a slip), how much worse would Prime's lack of familiarity be? There's a limit to how much she can do.

(Should do. Tamsin has a responsibility.)

Prime takes it in stride, at least. She cups her own mug in her hands, the same way Tamsin holds hers. "At the very least, block out some time for the basement," she says. "If Lachlan is looking for progress, that's where you're going to make it. Right?"

Yes, that's right. Tamsin nods. "An hour can't hurt," she concedes. "Here and there." She opens up her calendar, looking for spots she can mark as dedicated work time. It's not unusual for her to do that; she's never liked being interrupted. Each block she drops into her schedule feels like a band loosening around her chest. This is not unsalvageable.

The doorbell rings, and the band ratchets back down, so hard she's not sure she can breathe.

Lachlan.

"Do you want me to get that?" Prime asks.

"Absolutely not. Stay here," Tamsin says, getting to her feet. She can feel herself trembling, but she doesn't want Prime anywhere in the potential line of fire. The urge to pretend nobody is home is high, but she keeps walking. She tries not to cringe as she unlocks the front door, as she pulls it open, as she faces Lachlan and—

There's no visitor waiting for her, just a long, heavy package. Relief makes her lightheaded for a moment, or maybe that's just how bright the sun is. It's the safety railing she ordered for the basement.

Her first work block isn't for another fifteen minutes, but that's close enough. "Shut down my computer, please," Tamsin calls into the house, locking the front door. Her muscles strain as she pulls the box down the hall to the basement entrance.

Prime peeks out from the dining room. She's helped herself to Tamsin's closet again, and by comparison, Tamsin feels underdressed. She's in loungewear, her day not fully started yet, but Prime wears a tailored dress with no wrinkles or creases in it. Her hair is neatly combed and bundled into a chignon, while Tamsin's hangs in a matted, disorganized ponytail down her back.

The contrast is striking. Prime looks more like Tamsin than Tamsin has in days.

"All closed down. Do you need help with that?"

Tamsin looks at Prime, then toward the basement. It's a risk. She still doesn't want Prime down there, near the door or interacting with the experiments. *That* needs to remain solely Tamsin's purview, for the sake of any results.

But the railing is a two-person job.

"Yes. Yes, come here," Tamsin says, and together, they maneuver the rail into the basement, unpack it, lay it out. Tamsin fetches tools. They add brackets and a few support struts to the outside of the steps, then bolt the metal into place. It barely reaches the full length of the stairs.

"Will it stretch as the stairs grow?" Prime asks as she repacks the toolbox.

"Unclear," Tamsin replies, gazing at the length of metal with a warm glow of pleasure in her belly. It's good to be back in the basement. Prime was right to suggest it. It gives her more of a sense of control than wrangling proposals, and control is what she needs right now. It cuts through the last of that lidocaine numbness handily. "It'll be another experiment."

Prime looks around them, to the notes, the power tools, the samples laid out on the table for eventual analysis. Tamsin has the immediate impulse to hide it all. To get in between Prime and her work.

"Does the phenomenon impact the cameras?" Prime asks.

Tamsin opens her mouth to demand she leave it and go back upstairs, but then she realizes she has no idea. Another variable she never thought to account for. She goes over to the newer camera. "The door heals whether the camera is rolling or not," she says after a moment's silent consideration.

"That's not what I meant." Prime shrugs. "Just, if everything in this room distorts—the walls, the stairs, maybe the railing—what's to keep it from impacting equipment?"

"The door is stable. The table, so far, too." Except now the idea is burrowing into her gray matter, and she doesn't want to let it go. "But . . . the other night, I turned the lights off," Tamsin says, because it's easier than saying, *I sleepwalked upstairs, and somehow, the lights went out.* "The cameras kept rolling. One of them captured something."

Something moving in the dark. A faint ache starts up at the base of her skull, and she reaches back to knead at the muscle.

Prime's eyes are wide, almost startled, and she looks between the cameras and the door.

"They were oriented like that?" she asks.

Tamsin nods. "But whatever it was, it barely resolved. I've gone over it so many times. It might just be a glitch. Graphical artifact. If you're right about the distortion, that might be what it is."

She thinks of the deep node labs and how their sensors pick up data only in the darkness, with everything else shut out. Her basement isn't deep enough for that, but maybe some kind of meaningless interference, radiation noise . . .

"Does the camera have thermal imaging?" Prime bends to peer more closely. Tamsin's headache grows. "You could let it run overnight, that way. Lights out, door locked. If it repeats—"

"This doesn't have anything to do with the subsidence," Tamsin interrupts. Prime straightens up abruptly, as if burned, and Tamsin is almost as surprised. The objection was reflexive, almost subconscious. It's so *easy* to slide when Prime is being helpful, to forget to set boundaries—but she needs to stick to her methodology. Prime doesn't interact with the basement. Prime only works on the bigger picture. Will only ever work on the bigger picture.

"It might," Prime says, wary but sharp-edged. "You don't know that."

"I shouldn't even be telling you this," Tamsin continues, shaking her head. "The railing's up. Go back upstairs, Prime. There's data sets I can give you, if you want to dig your hands into something useful."

Prime's expression shutters, turns conciliatory. "I'm just trying to be helpful. Maybe together we can figure this out more quickly."

"You can't be down here," Tamsin says. "I can't have you influencing . . . all of this."

That gets a cold glare out of Prime, sudden and unfamiliar. "For all that you worry about my impact on your experimental outcomes, you were more than willing to throw me at the door on a whim. Or are you claiming that had any scientific rigor?"

The words are venomous. Caustic. It's the first time she's seen Prime get *angry*, and it's like looking in a mirror. Pointed, incisive, precisely aimed. Prime is right. That's the worst thing.

She's right.

"This isn't for you," Tamsin snaps, unwilling to concede. This is hers. Her basement. Her double. Her door, her lunacy, her—

It's happening again.

Last night is happening all over again: the spiraling panic, the nonsensical paranoia, the vicious overreaction. She needs to get herself under control. She cuts herself off and rubs at her temples, taking a few deep, slow breaths. Fighting over this gets them nowhere.

"I need you to focus on the city," she says finally. "There's no way, even together, that we solve this problem fast enough that we don't need to play by Lachlan's rules. I'll take your hypothesis into consideration. But this needs to stay separate. Understood?"

Prime nods. The anger in her is gone too, and she looks almost . . . ashamed.

"Let's go upstairs," Tamsin says and leads the way. Prime follows, obedient, and god, but she needs that. She needs to be reminded that, for all Prime is like her, there is still that crucial difference. Tamsin leads, and Prime follows.

Chapter Twenty-Three

The sun sets golden through the windows. Tamsin curls up on the living room couch and stares at her phone.

She owes Lachlan a call.

With any luck, it will be perfunctory. A quick exchange of greetings, a reassurance that she's feeling a little better, and Lachlan, perhaps, giving her a brief recapitulation of her lecture from the day before. She's been good after all. Bolted to her laptop for most of the afternoon, after the argument with Prime, working away and only taking one more basement break, even though she would have preferred to take shelter down there all day long.

But Lachlan's contact info glows up at her accusingly. The last two times she found herself here, she'd been at a crossroads. She could have told Lachlan about the door. Could have told her about Prime, right from the very beginning. If she'd just told her back then, how differently would this have turned out?

She would have taken you away, Tamsin tells herself, the exact reason why she didn't make those calls. *She wouldn't have helped you.*

Unless, of course, being taken away was exactly what she'd needed.

Her thumb ghosts over the touch screen, her breathing speeding up, growing ragged and audible. She fights down the response even as she teeters on a knife's edge; on the one side, a rejection of being *minded*, carefully monitored, treated like a child. On the other, the tantalizing opportunity to no longer be responsible for any of this.

She feels both. Wants both. It makes no sense. She simultaneously wants to be rescued and to be left alone to keep digging.

She stabs the Call button.

It rings twice. "Dr. Rivers," Lachlan greets.

"Mx. Woodfield." Her voice is admirably even. "This is my daily check-in."

"Timely. I appreciate it." There's no hint of a smile in Lachlan's tone. "How was your day?"

It's an oddly domestic question. Out of place for them. She can't tell if it's genuine fondness or proprietary derision. Both options make her want to hang up. Both options make it impossible to tell the truth: *I split time between the research you know about and the thing I've been lying about.*

"Productive," she settles on instead. "Dr. Chaudhari found our modeling candidate, and preliminary mock-ups look promising. Mr. Valdez has suggested a resin-injection method of shoring up any more spongiform sections like the one Dr. Olsen discovered, though I'm not sure the mechanics are entirely feasible."

Lachlan hums in approval. It's forward momentum, even if it all feels clumsy and haphazard. "Have you had any more symptoms?"

Her throat closes up.

Say something. Anything. Tell Lachlan about the breakdown last night. About the basement. About Prime.

But the impulse dries up as quickly as it sprang forth. Those are *hers.* Lachlan won't understand any of them, will only drag her out and hurt her and take from her. She's already taken the deep nodes.

"Would I remember them if I did?" Tamsin says instead, voice brittle.

Lachlan doesn't dignify that with a direct response. "As you apparently haven't had the time yet, I've taken the liberty of scheduling those initial appointments for you," she says instead. "One less thing for you to worry about. The first is on Friday. Full physical examination. Psychiatrist is on Monday. I'll send you the calendar invites."

Tamsin bristles. *You wanted this,* she reminds herself. *You wanted to not have a choice.* But it's one thing to idly daydream and another for Lachlan to once more ignore her autonomy.

Sure, she still hasn't so much as opened the email with Lachlan's list of doctors, but she would have. In the morning.

"Of course," Tamsin says after too long of a pause. "Will you be escorting me?"

"Not unless you think I need to. Do I need to escort you, Dr. Rivers?"

"That won't be necessary." She can manage. She doesn't know what she'd do if Lachlan was standing in that exam room, watching over how they poked and prodded her.

God, what would Lachlan do if she found out that Tamsin's anatomy is . . . wrong?

What will the *doctor* do?

Normal variation. Prime had been emphatic that it was normal variation, and Tamsin trusts her.

"There has been a small incident, however," Lachlan adds, as if it's an afterthought. Tamsin stiffens, clutching her phone a little tighter. "Your warning about the water department proved prescient, though they spotted a drop in water pressure first, not the dilation of the supply pipes that's causing it."

Tamsin closes her eyes, swearing softly.

"Dr. Torrence hasn't popped back up, has he?"

"No. I told you that he was handled." Lachlan's voice grows chilled.

"I know," she reassures Lachlan hastily. "Not a memory lapse. Just . . . they don't have any reason to think that we lied. Do they?"

"The mayor has certainly raised the possibility."

That's bad. They need the mayor's trust and buy-in, and they absolutely need her to not go sniffing around for anything *else* Myrica Dynamics might be hiding.

"Shouldn't Klein's team have gotten in front of this?" she asks.

"Yes, and they're working overtime on a correction as we speak. This isn't a failure of your team, Dr. Rivers." A brief flare of relief sweeps through her, then evaporates as Lachlan adds, "But I do need your participation. There's a luncheon tomorrow. Mr. Thomas, the mayor, a few other department heads. You're going to attend."

If I ask you to meet me elsewhere, you do so without complaint.

"Me?" she asks all the same, hoping she misheard. It's far from the first time she's had to wine and dine people for the company's sake, although it's usually investors. It's just with how she's been lately—with how busy she is—with how much issue Lachlan's taken with her comportment—

"Yes. Is that going to be a problem, Dr. Rivers?"

"No problem," Tamsin says.

And it won't be. A luncheon isn't hard. A waste of time, perhaps, just a song and dance to smooth some ruffled feathers, but if she plays it right, she'll be the woman who can deliver the hard news and make it into an opportunity.

Besides, it won't be just her on the sacrificial altar. The other department heads will soak up some of the blame, and Mr. Thomas will be careful not to throw her under the bus. She's still an asset, and if Lachlan intended to end her career, this isn't the way she'd do it.

Anyway, a short trip downtown, an overpriced salad, maybe a glass of wine . . . she could use the break. Could stand to get out of the house, remember why she's doing all of this.

It's a reasonable ask. That it feels miserable and unappealing doesn't matter. It'll prove to Lachlan that she has this under control. They'll both be happier for it, after.

"The invite should be in your email now," Lachlan says.

She checks, putting her phone on speaker. "Received," she says, accepting the invite along with the doctors' visits. They overlap with basement work blocks, and she deletes those, reluctantly. "Is that everything?"

"No. Thanks to the shake-up with the water department, we've elected to move forward with a go-live date," Lachlan says. "A week from today."

That makes Tamsin sit bolt upright. "A week."

"Yes. You'll be getting a packet from Klein by tomorrow morning, outlining your responsibilities and deliverables."

She'll have to shift focus entirely to prepare. Between the luncheon and the doctors' appointments, which take up large chunks of Friday and Monday, she's not going to have much time. She can feel the basement slipping away through her fingers. They clench tight in reflex, capturing, covetous.

She can't let it go.

But Prime can't do this for her. There's only Tamsin, worn down and so obviously a mess that Lachlan is forcing her through hoop after hoop.

"I don't—I can't—" she says, scratching at the back of one of her hands anxiously. "The doctors aren't going to have time to . . . fix me."

"I'm confident you can present yourself appropriately," Lachlan says. "Get yourself cleaned up, back to your usual standards. Is that going to be a problem?"

She saw herself in the mirror this morning. Bloodshot eyes, dull and tangled hair, unkempt nails. A hunted, haunted look. And she knows what she *should* look like because she has spent years perfecting her image, and Prime embodies it to the last inch.

Tamsin has makeup. She has practice. But no, Lachlan shouldn't be confident, because—because—

"Lachlan," she says softly, and her given name feels as wrong in her mouth as it did the day before, too intimate, too large. "I . . ." Her gaze darts around the room, trying to find the courage to just confess already, to explain that not only is Lachlan correct, that something is wrong, but that it's so much worse than what Lachlan thinks.

Prime stands in the doorway to the dining room, watching her, brow pinched.

If you tell, they'll hurt her, too.

"Dr. Rivers?"

She looks back down at her phone. "I can do this," she makes herself say. "When have I ever failed you?"

Lachlan's breath whispers over the line. "I'll see you on Tuesday," she says. (Not the luncheon. Not the doctors' appointments. A little bit of breathing room to get herself back together.) "Take care of yourself."

A rustling as Lachlan shifts, and Tamsin finds herself wondering where the other woman is. At home? What sort of home would somebody like Lachlan even keep? Something as sterile as Tamsin's or with more life in it?

How much does Tamsin intrude upon her comfort?

Does Lachlan care about comfort?

It doesn't matter. It doesn't *matter*. What matters is getting things back on track, making Lachlan care less. "I'll call again tomorrow," Tamsin says.

She hangs up before Lachlan can respond.

"What happens on Tuesday?" Prime asks as Tamsin pushes herself up off the couch. She's shaking enough that she has to take it slowly.

"Press conference," Tamsin says. "We're finally going to tell the city it's fucked."

Prime frowns. "Before we have a plan?"

"There's no time anymore. Word is starting to spread. We need to get ahead of it, make sure there isn't a panic. If we act like we've got this handled, it buys us time to actually handle it." Tamsin glances behind Prime and sees the table laid out with dinner and wine. She doesn't remember the sound of Prime cooking and isn't sure if the living room is just far enough away or if she was oblivious. Had Lachlan heard?

No. She would've asked about the noise.

"I have to go out tomorrow," Tamsin says as Prime takes them in for dinner. "Around noon." It will be the first time Prime has been left alone in the house, and Tamsin eyes the warm grain salad on her plate as she runs over options. Locking Prime in her room seems pointlessly punitive now, but it would, technically, be safer.

"How long will you be out? I could go to the store," Prime says, taking a sip of her wine.

Tamsin shakes her head. "No need. There's a kit delivery scheduled. I'll only be two, maybe three hours at most."

Prime sets her glass down. "You can just say that I need to spend the time in my room," she says without heat.

Tamsin still looks away, guiltily. "Does it bother you?"

"Yes and no. I can see why you do it." Prime takes a bite of dinner, still without any obvious rancor. "And if you leave work for me to do, it won't make much of a difference if I'm upstairs or in the living room. But it's not necessary."

"And it's potentially dangerous," Tamsin admits. "If there were a fire. Or if the basement suddenly gave way."

Prime lifts a brow but doesn't say anything.

"I won't lock you in," Tamsin says into her wineglass and drinks half of it at once.

Prime smiles, like she can't help it, childlike and relieved. "Thank you," she says, then, "Are you finished with work for the day?"

Tamsin takes a more moderate sip of wine. "I never got around to looking at those samples under the microscope," she says after a moment's thought. "And I still have to do today's measurements. But then yes, I think so. Why?"

Prime shrugs. "I want to know more about the lab nodes," she says. "I know you've written them off as uninvolved, with no clear mechanism of action for the subsidence, but maybe there's something you've overlooked, since you're buried so deeply in them."

It's something they haven't discussed, but Prime has clearly overheard enough from various calls and meetings to know there's *something* there.

"And," she adds, "part of me wants to know what you work on when there isn't a crisis."

A crisis. Prime's very presence counts as one, no matter how comfortable they get with one another. Tamsin takes a bite of her dinner to keep herself from laughing at the thought and considers.

"I can walk you through it," she agrees once she's feeling steady again. "It's my best work, honestly."

Later, when the dishes are cleared and the wine is finished, and Prime is busy cleaning up in the kitchen, Tamsin peels herself away from the easy conversation. The basement calls to her, and it's so much simpler, not having to leave the door locked anymore, or even closed.

She makes her way downstairs, gripping the railing, grateful that the builders put one in. The stairs would be murder otherwise.

Chapter Twenty-Four

Wednesday morning is a trial.

The litter boxes need full emptying, thanks to having to pull double duty. She has two meetings, each of which runs long, neither of which she cares about. Prime doesn't make breakfast, and the shake Tamsin chugs down sits leaden in her stomach. She has no time to check the basement, and when Prime asks if she'd like coffee, Tamsin is not kind telling her to leave her alone.

Work fights her. Nobody is happy about the lab closures or the swiftly impending press conference. Everybody seems to want something from her, and by eleven, she's only handled half her urgent emails.

The work of Olsen's team, at least, has helped the main lab identify a new pocket of the spongiform geology, this time shallow enough that sampling is reasonable as well as a test run of the resin injection. She checks on the permit requests, all with expedite fees. She makes sure Olsen has everything she needs to move her team to the central above-ground lab.

A video call request from her assistant intrudes on her screen.

Tamsin eyes it, then hits Refuse and gets out of her chair. She dials Cara on her phone instead and starts to pace.

Cara picks up in two rings. "Good morning, Dr. Rivers."

"What do you need?"

Cara is too professional, and too used to Tamsin's moods, to comment on her tone. "It's been a few days since our last check-in," she says evenly. "I wanted to touch base."

"Nothing's changed," Tamsin says. The irony makes her pause beside the dining table, biting down a huff of bleak amusement. "I'll call if I need something."

She's moving to hang up when Cara says, "James Dunford wants a private meeting."

Tamsin pauses. Brings the phone back to her ear.

"Private as in . . ."

"Just you."

Tamsin drums her fingers on the tabletop. Penrose (the friendlier version, she thinks) takes it as an invitation, hopping up and nudging against her hand. She pushes him away. "I take it the request came to you directly?"

"By phone, from his executive assistant, yes."

An interesting approach, for the COO of FlexEast, Myrica Dynamics's main competitor, to set up a clandestine meeting. Any other time, Tamsin would have assumed it was the lead-in to an attempt to poach her. But now she has to assume they've spotted the subsidence as well. "They're concerned," she ventures.

"Not my place to say, Dr. Rivers."

No, it isn't. But the refusal to engage is grating, and Tamsin snaps, "I'm *telling* you to say."

Bristling silence. Tamsin regrets not having accepted the video call. She wants to see Cara's face. "Then I'd say," Cara replies at last, "that you're probably right."

It's a dodge.

"Fine. Set up the meeting." Penrose flops down on the table, and she shoves him across the smooth surface. He drops to the ground with an irritated flick of his tail, then saunters off toward the living room. "Next Wednesday," she adds, watching him go. "Or later. I'm busy for the rest of the week. And expect him to cancel or reschedule as soon as the news goes live."

"Yes, Dr. Rivers. I can see the appointments Mx. Woodfield set up on your calendar."

Insult piled on insult. Tamsin massages her temples. "Is Mx. Woodfield causing any problems? Asking questions about the equipment?"

"No," Cara says. Her tone is as brittle as Tamsin's now. Wary. "Should I expect that?"

"Maybe. I'll handle it," Tamsin says.

She shouldn't have mentioned it. It only draws more attention to how erratic Tamsin's days now appear, how at the whim of Lachlan. But she can't take it back; she can only move forward. "The equipment can be returned," she says, recalling her hurried assurances to Lachlan the other day. "I'll have it ready for pickup tomorrow."

"Of course; I'll set it up." The sound of typing. "Oh. And you missed your standing appointment with your salon Monday," Cara adds. "I've rescheduled it for next Thursday."

"I need it to be sooner," Tamsin says. Her heart seizes, falls; she's been going to that salon every eight weeks for years now, to keep her curls perfectly managed, and being *busy* has never made her forget. And now, on the eve of the press conference, she can hear Lachlan's demands echoing in her skull: *Get yourself cleaned up.* "Can you set it for after my lunch?"

"I'm afraid they didn't have any other openings."

"Call them back," Tamsin snaps. "Or find another salon."

"Of course," Cara replies tightly. "Have a good rest of your day, Dr. Rivers."

Cara hangs up. Tamsin's phone buzzes, a calendar alert glowing on the screen.

Lunch. Downtown. In forty-five minutes. God, but she doesn't want to deal with this right now. It's not hard, though: schedule the car, freshen up a little before she heads out. Make sure she looks pristine. Maybe if she straightens her hair, it will hide the neglect. Her purse is sitting in the entryway, ready to go, as it has been for days.

It's just a hoop to jump through, a brief lunch, and then she can come straight back here. She's even under *orders* to come back here: Lachlan has agreed that nobody should see her until things are stable again. She doesn't have to go to the lab. Out, back, and if it wraps up a bit early, she might even have time to pop downstairs, if she plays her cards right.

No time for a hair appointment. Grudgingly, she sends Cara a message to just make it happen before Tuesday. She gets a read receipt but no other acknowledgment.

Setting her phone aside, she climbs the stairs; it's like walking against the surf. She applies concealer, lipstick; her hand trembles as she inks her lash line. But her reflection is fine, she's *fine.* Some finger combing, some hair oil, a claw clip, and her hair looks acceptable. Acceptable enough.

She goes back down. She grabs her phone again. She calls herself a ride.
Five minutes.

Her front door stands just as it always has. She's gone through it hundreds of times. Probably thousands, at this point. But she hasn't left the house now in over a week, and it feels wrong to break that seal.

Wrong? The thought makes no sense. She pushes it aside, then realizes she should tell Prime she's going, but she's not sure where Prime is. Eyeing the front door warily, she turns into the kitchen instead. It's empty.

Outside the kitchen window, the day is bright, and she can see a wedge of sky, brilliant and cloudless and open. It's a nice day. She can almost feel the sun on her skin. Feel the soft purr of the town car beneath her feet. Her stomach twists.

Her phone pings. Her ride is a minute out. The app pulls back to show the route, miles into the city, into traffic, away from home.

Her stomach flips one final time. She vomits into the sink, praying that once her stomach is empty, her nerves will be gone as well, but when it's all over, she can only sag to the floor, panting for breath.

It takes all her effort to splay out instead of curling into a ball, but the cool tile on her cheek helps. Being low to the ground helps. Her fingers are still wrapped tightly around her phone, and she hangs on. The case creaks slightly within her grip.

"Tamsin?"

Prime is in the kitchen doorway, staring down at her in horror, and Tamsin can't help her low, helpless moan. A panic attack. She's having a fucking panic attack at the thought of leaving the house.

One of the cats slinks in around Prime's ankles and sprawls on the floor a few feet from Tamsin. Not close enough to touch, but close enough to observe.

"Are you alright?" Prime takes a few steps toward her, then hesitates. "You look ill."

"Need to go out," Tamsin gasps. In her hand, her phone vibrates. "Ride's here. But I can't—I can't—"

There's no rational reason for her to be this worked up, this *afraid.* There's no specific fear bearing down on her, no consequence of going outside that is eating at her, but the thought of leaving the house fills her with a cold, unrelenting dread. Like the day she'd fired Torrence, how she'd all but cowered in the back of the car on the way into the lab, but amplified a hundredfold.

"There's something wrong with me," she whispers.

Prime crouches beside her. "It's okay," she says. "That's what the doctor is for. Friday, right?"

Tamsin nods.

"And today is a social performance? Putting the mayor at ease?"

Another nod. She feels so weak. Her head is spinning.

"Then I'll go for you," Prime says. "I'll listen, let the other department heads take the lead. And if attention falls on me, we've been over everything. Last night, and before—I know enough about the sinking and what you want to keep hidden. Don't I?"

It's a stunningly simple solution. Prime is all made up already; was she planning to go out? It doesn't matter. What matters is that Prime could take her place.

Except Mr. Thomas knows her. The department heads all know her. Tamsin shakes her head. "You can't go. Somebody will figure out something's wrong."

"Who? Lachlan couldn't tell the difference," Prime reminds her. Her voice is so soothing, so calm, and Tamsin wants so desperately to believe her.

Her phone buzzes in her hand; the car is on a countdown now.

"How will you get home?" Tamsin asks, holding the phone to her chest, feeling her resolve give way.

Prime's gaze flicks to the phone, but she doesn't ask for it. "How would you?"

"I'd order a ride."

"Can you schedule one in advance?"

Tamsin nods.

"Then schedule one for an hour and a half after the lunch starts. If it wraps up early, I'll occupy myself." Prime smiles. "This doesn't have to be hard. Let me make it easier for you."

Tamsin hesitates, but only for the length of one shaky, surrendering breath. "It's a good idea," she says softly. "Thank you. But you have to go now."

Prime tucks a strand of hair behind Tamsin's ear before standing. Tamsin, still huddled on the kitchen floor, watches her go.

When the door closes, and the car pulls away, Tamsin schedules the return ride before she can forget. Then she rests her forehead against the cool tile and tries to get her pulse back under control.

Chapter Twenty-Five

Tamsin cleans out the sink and stays off her work laptop all afternoon, the better to maintain the illusion that she's out at lunch. Her phone is also powered down, just in case. It's probably paranoia, but Lachlan always seems to know when she leaves the house. It's possible that location tracking is quietly running in the background.

All the while, she tries to figure out what the fuck just happened.

It's been just over a week since she last went into the lab. That's longer than seems reasonable, in hindsight, but nine days of being inside shouldn't result in a panic attack so intense she throws up and then cowers on the floor at just the *idea* of going outside. She didn't even make it out the front door. Sure, yes, last Monday the city had felt . . . too big, and she remembers having to distract herself with her phone the entire ride into campus, but that had been explainable. She's felt like that before, a few times, when she's gotten buried in her research. Even Valdez had understood it.

This, though?

She sits herself down in the kitchen and makes herself look out the window (from the floor, because part of her worries that Lachlan has eyes on the house, might see her inside and become suspicious). Occasionally, the sight of the sky makes her stomach lurch, but for the most part, it's unremarkable. It's only when she thinks about personally going outside that anything even remotely like fear rises up in her, and then it only feels like an echo, a hangover.

By the time the front lock disengages, Tamsin has concluded that today must have been a fluke. Aftereffects of her first panic attack the other day. Over-sensitization of neural pathways she's rarely used and has no coping mechanisms developed for. Yet. That can be rectified.

Soft thuds from the hall as Prime takes off her heels. A meow from one of the Penroses.

"Tamsin?"

"In here." She doesn't look away from the slash of sky, hands fussing with her hair idly, picking apart knots and causing even more frizz in the process. Prime's footsteps are soft behind her. *Prime.* She's spent this whole time agonizing over herself, with barely a thought paid to how Prime was faring out in the world, or what might go wrong, or what she's missing.

But what could she have done, if she had? Nothing. Absolutely nothing. The helplessness that provokes is unbearable for the moment she allows herself to dwell on it. Her subconscious must have known and accepted that, and turned to the proximal issues.

"The lunch was uneventful," Prime says from behind and above her, by way of greeting. "The mayor postured a little but accepted the timeline we gave her, as well as the argument that leading with *Everything is stretching and we don't know why* would have been a nonstarter."

"That's good." Tamsin tips her head back. Prime looks immaculate. Not exhausted, not overwhelmed. "Anything else I need to know?"

"Mostly that the other department heads were happy to dominate the conversation but even happier that you're still the actual lead on the investigation."

"They get all the career-advancing attention and name-making, none of the actual risk."

Prime smiles. "Exactly." Her hand brushes against the top of Tamsin's head. It's patronizing, like petting a cat.

Penrose slinks around Prime's legs and sits next to Tamsin, purring softly. Tamsin decides not to pull away. It's not worth it. It's nice, even, if she lets it be.

"How are you feeling?" Prime asks, hand falling back to her side.

"Ready to try again," Tamsin says. She gets to her feet, grimacing at how stiff her legs are. A glance at the oven clock shows she's been down there on the floor for at least two hours. She moves into the hall, the better to hide that there are two of them, just in case.

"Try what?" Prime asks, following.

"Going outside. Whatever happened today, it's not happening again."
She means to sound firm, determined, but it comes out nervous. She eyes
the door warily and is rewarded with a warning flutter in her chest.

Absolutely not.

Penrose follows them from the kitchen, rubbing his cheek along her
calf. His teeth scrape against her skin lightly. *He* hasn't been outside more
than five times since she bought him. If faced with an open door, he avoids
it. It hasn't seemed to harm him any.

But Penrose doesn't have to stand up at a press conference in six days.

Tamsin fires up her phone, checking for missed calls, emails. None
of the former, a few of the latter. A new salon appointment, ahead of the
press conference. Nothing from Lachlan. *Good.*

"What do you need from the store?" she asks. "The trip's short. A good
test run."

Prime frowns at her. "I can give you a list," she says slowly. "But maybe
you should start with something smaller. Proof of concept. Your reaction
this morning was intense."

"It won't happen again," Tamsin says, pulling up her notes app. "There's
no precedent for anything like it. No reason for it to repeat."

"You don't know that yet." Prime reaches out, covers Tamsin's wrist
with her hand. "Set a timer. Five minutes. Check the front yard, and if
you're feeling good after that, *then* go to the store. I'll have the list ready
when you are."

Tamsin clenches her jaw, then nods. It's reasonable. Entirely reasonable.

She cues up the timer and is reaching for the door when she hesitates
again. Going outside does have real risks, risks she's not being cogni-
zant of.

"Can we swap clothing?" Tamsin asks, turning from the door.

Prime blinks. "We can," she agrees. "Would that make you feel safer?"

Her voice is curious, not empathetic. It's as if she's observing an experiment. (She is, isn't she?) It's far preferable to concern, and Tamsin nods.
"It's a reasonable precaution. We don't know if Lachlan is watching. Or
somebody else who just saw you come in, who will notice you've suddenly
done a costume change."

Prime doesn't ask if that's really likely, and it's impossible to tell if it's because she's humoring Tamsin or takes Tamsin at her word about the danger Lachlan poses. Instead, she goes to the guest bathroom, then holds out a hand. "Come on. It'll be more efficient this way."

Tamsin joins her, though it's a tight fit. Her back to Prime, she strips down, then holds out a hand behind her to take Prime's clothing. She can feel Prime, though they rarely touch. Her warmth, the static electricity of her skin. To her surprise, it's more comforting than uncomfortable, though she doesn't relish being half naked in front of anybody, her own mirror image included.

When Prime's clothing (*her* clothing, this is Tamsin's clothing—she shouldn't think of it as Prime's) is in place, Tamsin feels somehow . . . armored. The sweater's collar chafes gently against the front of her throat, and she feels steadier than she did five minutes ago. Just the barest guard over the sliver of nerves that touching the front door had given her.

It makes no sense; once Prime pulls on Tamsin's clothing in turn and they step back into the hall, she looks just as put together as she did before. It isn't like all the past days where Tamsin has never made it out of her loungewear. But it still works, maybe just thanks to a placebo effect, and Prime is watching, expectant. It's enough to get over whatever minor anticipatory hurdle remains. She starts the five-minute timer on her phone, slips it into her pocket, and opens the front door.

Tamsin steps outside.

It's just a habit, her hermitage, not pathology. She reminds herself of that as the sun falls unobstructed on her skin. She isn't going to panic. She isn't going to collapse. She is going to be fine.

She isn't fine.

The terror swells, the world sprawling out around her in its thousands of miles, its vaulted atmosphere, the light pulse of traffic on her residential street. It's all falling away from itself, or collapsing in, or both, she can't tell. She sways, clutching at the doorframe behind her.

In her pocket, her phone counts down, too slowly.

Five minutes. She can do five minutes. She's not on her knees yet, hasn't vomited on her stoop. She forces herself away from the door, down the step, into the garden. The landscaping company is coming soon. For now it's scraggly, and all she can see are the tangled weeds, the unkempt rise and fall of native plants she's never cared for but look good for an audience. Bees hum around her and the sound drills into her skull.

It takes everything in her not to curl in on herself or dash back into the house. She only avoids it by refusing to look up or out; anything more than ten feet away is too much. Her gaze fixes instead on the rosemary plant just beside her door, ornamental and studded with the filmy evidence of bugs.

She flinches when a car passes by.

Lab fever. This is just lab fever. Too much time inside, focused on her work, not enough time looking out windows. She's been here before.

(It's never been this bad before.)

The human brain acclimates quickly to new circumstances and behaves strangely under stress. Paranoia is common during periods of duress. The solution is exposure.

Every justification feels hollow. Feels like she's papering over the real problem, a deep and unrelenting wrongness, a blaring alarm screaming that she needs to get back inside. That she needs to take shelter in the basement, where there are no windows at all.

The timer goes off. She fumbles for her phone with heavy, clumsy fingers, already hurrying back to the house. She's inside by the time she silences it, door slammed shut behind her, shoulders pressed to it as she gasps for air.

"We're ordering delivery," Prime says.

The anxiety is no better by Friday.

She knows what it is now, the vibrato of her nerves that makes every minor inconvenience a calamity, that acidifies her blood and makes her whole self feel precarious. It's simple anticipation of disaster. She's tried the front yard three times now, most recently after the courier company had picked up the ultrasound and other equipment yesterday evening. Each time, the panic crashed over her the moment she stepped outside, regardless of time of day, of weather, of the size of her goals. She made it a little longer each time by sheer force of will, but the last time was still only fifteen minutes.

And it took her half an hour to recover.

The doctor's appointment this afternoon will be hell. She lets herself acknowledge that as she logs out of her laptop and heads upstairs to change.

She'd allowed herself the comfort of soft things for the morning, but now it's time to gird herself.

Before she can get to the guest bedroom, though, she spots Prime through the open guest bathroom door. Her hair, conditioned and glossy, is tucked into a neat chignon at the nape of her neck, and she's dressed in one of Tamsin's favorite work dresses.

"What are you doing?" Tamsin asks, bypassing the bedroom.

Prime looks up at her via the mirror, eyes bright, as she fastens on a bracelet. "Getting ready to go out."

"I don't want us both out at the same time."

Prime frowns a little, turning to face her. "I thought you'd be staying in."

Tamsin's frown echoes hers. It's not like Prime to forget things. "I have that doctor's appointment."

"I know. I'm handling it for you."

The blood drains from Tamsin's face, even as her chest eases at the mere idea of not going out. "We didn't discuss that," she says.

"Not directly, no," Prime confirms.

Tamsin looks away, jaw quivering with unnamable emotion. (Relief? Fear? Confusion? No, bigger than all of those, more amorphous, more all-consuming.) "It's . . . kind of you, to offer. But you can't do this for me. This isn't like a lunch."

"No, it isn't," Prime agrees. When Tamsin looks at her again, Prime is still primping. Applying lipstick now. Her hand is steady, and when she's done, she adds, "This is more important. So far, it's only the situs inversus that distinguishes us, but we're not medically trained. There could be other differences. And if there are, you're the one who we know diverges from the norm."

Tamsin is caught on *we're not medically trained*. She isn't, of course, but Prime isn't trained in anything. It's an odd phrase to apply to herself. Technically factual, and yet—and yet—

And then the rest of Prime's argument settles in. "You said it's a rare but understood condition," she says, warily. "With no knock-on effects."

"It is. But I thought you'd appreciate the privacy. That's why you never sent my blood out to a lab, right? You were afraid they'd find something strange about me. I'm only returning that care." Prime turns to her and gently cups Tamsin's cheek. Tamsin flinches away, baring her teeth. "If you want to go, I won't stop you. But I thought you would like to keep some of this to yourself."

She's only being kind.

"If I don't go, they won't be able to figure out what's wrong with me," Tamsin says.

"Do you want them to?" Prime asks.

Tamsin's frown intensifies. "Yes," she says, because she's supposed to. *Yes*, she thinks, and then, *maybe?* She wants to be better. But does she want this . . . this . . . breakdown in her medical history? The onset has been so sudden, so rapid, and she can't give any details about what has been going on in her life. What if they assume it's a psychiatric crisis? What if they declare she should be in in-patient care? Lachlan won't stop them.

She'd be trapped. Picked apart to pieces. Her heart clenches, pulse spiking.

It's just a physical, she reminds herself. This time. But the psychiatric evaluation is only a few days away. And then, if Prime goes today, and Tamsin goes the next time, there might be discrepancies.

Which means she needs to go today. She needs to go every time. And she needs to lie.

Or.

Or.

Prime goes every time and doesn't need to lie at all. She's human. She's stable, more stable than Tamsin feels. They can keep up their quiet regimen of exposing Tamsin to the outdoors, and Prime can tell the doctors just enough to get the guidance they'll need to figure out the rest.

Prime is watching her with endless patience. She is as clever as Tamsin is. In under two weeks, she's caught up to Tamsin not only in knowledge, but in planning, anticipation, drive.

They might as well be indistinguishable.

"You should go," Tamsin says. "I don't want them intruding." She's never wanted anybody intruding. Not houseguests, not Lachlan, and certainly not doctors.

She can feel nitrile-clad hands on her. Thermometers, speculums, scalpels. Every tiny indignity combined with the risk of being found out, of the doctor wanting to know more, wanting to dig deeper.

Her face burns with disgust and anger, but Prime is right there, smiling at her. Another option. Another way out.

"We'll figure it out together," Prime says and turns back to the mirror to finish applying her face.

Chapter Twenty-Six

Tamsin does not give Prime her phone.

It's silly, since Tamsin just turns it off the moment Prime is in the town car, like she did on Wednesday, but too much of her life exists on it. Prime's face can unlock it. The real world is already at Prime's fingertips as she rides to the physician's office, but Tamsin's digital footprint is the one thing beyond the basement Tamsin can still keep for herself.

She turns the inert phone over and over again in her hands. Her laptop sits closed on the dining room table. She has no way of tracking Prime's movements, no way of listening in on what she tells the doctors. When Prime comes home, she'll only have Prime's word to rely on.

It will be enough. It has to be enough. Either she's right that she can trust Prime, or Tamsin is already screwed.

She sets her phone down and gets up, stretching. She still needs to shower, and there's work to be done in the basement. She wants to go over the camera footage again. She hasn't had the opportunity to order a thermal-imaging camera, but there's a night-mode setting on the newer one that picks up near-infrared. If she can rig an emitter from what she has in the house, it might be able to pick up on something new.

The day spools out before her, uninterrupted now by meetings and press-conference prep and the certainty that Lachlan is monitoring her activity, ensuring she's jumping high enough. It's almost as if she's a ghost; nobody will know what she does during this time, and nobody will care, because to all appearances, she's somewhere else.

Why didn't she think of this sooner? The relief is absolutely narcotic.

She wanders to the living room, trying to remember what she used to do on days off. Back when she allowed herself days off. It's been so long that she hardly remembers. Nail appointments and salon visits, of course, and she hasn't gone to either of those in some time. She used to go for runs, too, and read for pleasure, though she feels as if she doesn't recognize half the titles on her carefully curated bookshelves. Did she really just buy these to look nice?

A thud and scuffle intrude on her daydreaming.

The two Penroses are tussling in the hall. One gives a low growl, and Tamsin frowns, trying to discern if the tussle is actually a fight. When she takes a step toward them, they leap apart. One races for the bedrooms upstairs. The other slinks off toward the kitchen.

She's never had more than one cat at a time. She has no idea if this is normal.

Luckily, she doesn't need to figure out *everything* on her own. She retrieves her phone from the dining room table and goes to unlock it.

Strange. Her phone is off.

It must have run out of battery; did she not plug it in overnight? But when Tamsin takes it into the kitchen and plugs it in, it acts like it's off, not drained. Experimentally, she powers it up.

It's at eighty-three percent battery.

Something itches at the back of her brain, but before she can root it out, her phone begins to buzz. *Lachlan Woodfield* blooms onto her screen. Her pulse quickens, memories of being in Lachlan's arms washing over her. The way those gloved hands had felt in her hair.

She swipes Accept.

"Dr. Rivers," Lachlan greets. She does not sound pleased.

"Lachlan," she replies. "Is something wrong?"

"Would you care to tell me why your phone is showing as being at your home, even though your appointment is scheduled to begin in ten minutes?"

You suspected it was being tracked, she reminds herself.

You turned it off to avoid this, and then forgot about it, she realizes a moment later, and her throat tightens in sudden panic.

"Dr. Rivers?" Lachlan prompts.

No answer is more suspicious than a haphazard answer. Lachlan is too attuned to her. Tamsin forces herself to speak around an adrenaline stricture.

"I'm on my tablet right now. Wi-Fi calling." The tablet is one of the few older-model items she still has lying around. She's fairly confident it doesn't have location tracking capabilities. Nothing that Lachlan could co-opt. "My phone's been having issues. I decided do a backup and reinstall the OS, and I left it at home to complete."

"Your phone was deactivated until a few minutes ago, then came back online," Lachlan says, unimpressed.

Tamsin doesn't flinch. "It must have just finished reinstalling."

Lachlan is silent.

"I'm in the waiting room. If you don't believe me, call the doctor's office. I'm sure they'll be happy to confirm."

She hopes Prime is on time. She hopes Lachlan doesn't call her bluff.

"Please stay on the line," Lachlan says and puts her on hold.

Tamsin wanders to the dining room in a daze, sitting down heavily at the table. She runs her hand over her closed laptop. It's the first undeniable memory lapse she's had since . . . Keiling? No, there was something else, something that happened after Lachlan's house call. But she was so distraught, so overwhelmed—better to chalk that up to the obliterating effects of the panic attack, whatever it was.

She pulls up the notes app on her phone and jots down the issue with the tracking, though.

The quality of sound from her speaker changes. Lachlan is back. "The front-desk staff confirm that they can see you," she says without preamble. The cold venom in her voice has drained away; now she just sounds tired. "They do say you don't appear to be on a call, however."

Prime's hair is in a bun, but not pulled back tight from her face. "Bluetooth earbud," she says, this lie slipping much more easily from her lips. Lachlan is unlikely to call the office back, let alone run both simultaneously to ask after mouth movement. Besides . . . "How else would I be talking to you right now?"

"Hm."

Tamsin checks the time; still two minutes until the appointment, and it will, almost certainly, start late. She can't duck out yet.

"While I have you," Lachlan says. "I want to set up another time for us to meet. Outside of your house, if you would. Tonight, at Perigee."

Tonight, unless it's substantially far into the evening, may not give Prime enough time to get home, up to date, and sent back out. It would probably have to be Tamsin, and she—

No, she can't go. Not even to see Lachlan again.

(*Not even to see*—she doesn't *want* to see Lachlan. What if Lachlan notices something is wrong?)

"Not tonight," Tamsin says. "In case they start me on something, or any of the tests run long. Tomorrow? It has been a long time, you're right, and I've been wanting to try the new fall menu."

Lachlan is quiet for a few seconds, then agrees, "Tomorrow. Four. I'll see you then."

Crisis averted. Tamsin eases back in her chair, then checks the time again. Realistically, there's more time to kill, but she's not sure how else to extend this.

"They're calling me back," Tamsin says. "I have to go."

"Good luck, Dr. Rivers," Lachlan says and hangs up.

Tamsin goes to add the event to her calendar. The app prompts her to copy the details over from their last outing four months ago.

The appointment is not a short one.

Lachlan had blocked out three hours on her calendar—one of the last things Tamsin notes before putting her phone aside. Three hours, plus transit time, until Prime returns. Longer if the appointment runs over and Prime misses her scheduled pickup.

If Prime misses that . . . Tamsin will have no way of knowing.

It's not her responsibility. Prime is clever; she'll figure it out.

And what is her responsibility right now? No work. No phone calls. The press conference, perhaps, but the most she can do to prepare is to try going outside for a little longer today. Too risky before Prime gets home. No, she has time. Protected, contiguous, glorious time.

She should go rest. Take care of herself. That's what Prime is buying for her, more than *time* alone: privacy to get better without interference.

But she's not tired.

She goes down to the basement and takes food and water with her.

* * *

On the camera playback, Tamsin leans against the door for hours.

There's no change the whole way through, but she keeps it playing anyway. Her research showed no reliable way to build an infrared emitter of the type she needs, so she's put in an order for a thermal camera; she'll resume the darkness testing when it arrives in a few days. Until then, the cameras are just company, the footage oddly comforting. Maybe because it shows her in a moment she almost remembers.

Tamsin's notes cover the walls. They go beyond the sinking—there's very little left to be discovered about that. It is happening at a consistent rate, and it does not thin the walls as it happens. It is happening, and Tamsin has run out of ways to find out *why*. But that's inspiring, not galling. To be in the basement is to be immersed, to be curious again, like a child.

She gives herself over to it gladly.

The day stretches out, unmeasured.

Prime returns eventually. The basement door is unlocked, and Prime appears on the stairs. "Clean bill of health," she announces. Tamsin barely looks up from where she's running a series of analyses on some of the node-chamber data sets she'd taken three months ago and hadn't had a chance to get back around to, plotted against more recent ones.

"You have drinks with Lachlan tomorrow," she says. "The bar is called Perigee. Did you have any trouble getting home?"

"I called a cab," Prime says, picking her way down the stairs. "We finished early and I didn't feel like waiting." Prime drifts to one of the walls, peering up at her fresh notations. "Do you really think that drinks with Lachlan is a good idea? The department heads are one thing, but her . . ."

"She suggested it. And she'll be suspicious if I cancel."

"Tell her you're on bed rest," Prime says more firmly. "When did you talk to her?"

"While you were in the waiting room at the doctor." Tamsin sighs and pushes back from her computer. "I wasn't thinking. Turned the phone back on. She called immediately to ask why I wasn't where I was supposed to be."

"That's concerning."

"Not unexpected." Tamsin shrugs. "But bed rest—you said they gave you a clean bill of health. And Lachlan will almost certainly get ahold of the records from today. I can't—"

"Clean bill of health in general. In specific, they agreed that it sounded like I was fatigued. They advised taking it easy until the psychiatric appointment."

"That might be enough, then," Tamsin concedes. "Especially if she wants me fresh and functional for the press conference. But surely you could manage drinks?"

"Drinks, yes. With Lachlan Woodfield? You told me to be wary of her, Tamsin. And you have a long history together, a history I don't know."

"I could tell you," Tamsin says. It's a problem easily fixed, and telling would be like draining an abscess. Not having to be the only one holding the leash on all her wariness, her fear, her longing for things to be different. "The projects we've worked on. How involved she's been. It varies. This is the most she's ever intervened, you know. Before this, we were— cordial. I performed, she observed, she helped grease the wheels when it was in Myrica's interests. We never touched."

She reaches for details, crystalline moments, and realizes that she can't recall any. Forgettable. They were all forgettable, except for the impression they left. "She's dangerous," Tamsin adds softly. "She was just never dangerous to *me* before. I liked knowing that."

Prime watches her closely, then shakes her head. "That's not going to be enough," she says. "Not for something face-to-face. But we could start smaller—I could take over the evening check-ins? You could listen in. Correct me if I behave . . . noticeably."

That's reasonable. And yet Tamsin hesitates, unsure. Knowing how Lachlan feels, sorting out what she might be suspicious of . . . that's not something it's safe to delegate, is it? Prime's original point still stands.

"I'm not sure," she says. "Maybe. I should try to go to Perigee, though. Oh, but it's . . . it's underground." She runs her tongue along her teeth. "Last time I was there, the subsidence hadn't impacted it yet; if Lachlan's suggesting it, it's probably still fine."

But wait, that can't be right. The last time she was there was four months ago. Well before the sinking started. Of course it hadn't been impacted; why would she remember that? She frowns, looking down at her phone's lockscreen.

Prime taps the wall, then turns to face her fully. "You should be resting," she says. "Especially if you want to try going out."

That's also reasonable, but unacceptable. "This *is* rest," she says. "Play, almost. I've put aside the matter of the subsidence for now. I'm just . . . exploring."

It's hard to articulate, and Tamsin hopes that she and Prime are similar enough at the core that Prime will understand. Fear twinges at the base of her spine. If Prime doesn't understand, if Prime herds her up to bed—

"Alright," Prime says. "I suppose stopping you would be cruel." Her expression softens. "You seem happier."

And she is. She feels good. Like a great weight has been taken off her shoulders. Tamsin smiles, then retrieves her phone. "I'll cancel the drinks meeting altogether," she says. "Log you into my work laptop for the evening. Do you think you can handle emails and analysis?"

"Of course," Prime says. And she looks happy, too.

Lachlan accepts her apology. They don't reschedule.

Tamsin gets back to work.

The basement waits for her. The door stands forgotten on the far wall. There are twenty-five steps between the hallway and the basement floor, and each one requires careful traversal. She has a hundred new ideas. Innovations, opportunities. So what if Lachlan has pulled the plug on the communications project? So what if it winds up not being a temporary, emergency measure? Even with the deep node labs taken from her, she still has a roaring font she can draw from.

It's been years since she's felt like this. Or perhaps she's *never* felt like this. It's the best flow she's ever been in, the most stimulating debate. She barely remembers to feed herself. Dragging herself up the stairs feels like an impossibility. But Prime is there for her, making sure she eats the food that lays abandoned on her desk, urging her to come up and wash at least once a day.

And then they sit together in the living room, and they discuss her ideas, and Prime's findings on the subsidence problem. Prime writes up two memos that weekend, Tamsin watching over her shoulder: a theory of how to predict new pockets of distortion, and a preliminary explanation of the mechanism at work.

It's good work, as good as Tamsin's.

Prime helps Tamsin prepare for the press conference, too, when Tamsin can stand to think about it. Tamsin rehearses what she's meant to say, and Prime gives notes. Prime completes the mock-ups and sound bites that the PR department has assigned her, and Tamsin signs off on every piece. Each day, Tamsin goes and stands in the front yard.

She never makes it longer than fifteen minutes, but each time, Prime tells her they'll just try again.

And in the evenings, she's still the one to talk to Lachlan. Prime sits nearby and listens in. Their conversations are short. Polite. Lachlan asks if she's been sleeping better, and Tamsin says yes.

She has always been an excellent liar.

Chapter Twenty-Seven

Tamsin's phone buzzes. Cara. *Meeting starting*, it says, along with two calendar reminders.

It's Monday morning.

Tamsin doesn't know how long she's been awake, but it's long enough that her eyes are burning. The thermal camera arrived yesterday, and her only break since she got it set up was a half-hour period where she left the basement, turned off the lights after her, and managed a shower. That was three hours ago, she's fairly certain, and she hasn't had time to review the footage yet, even though she's been back in the basement for about an hour and a half.

Her chest aches, another sure sign she hasn't slept recently. But she's dressed, at least, in something approaching workwear. Nothing objectionable, though perhaps already a bit wrinkled for a morning call. It will have to do.

She does still have responsibilities, even if they chafe. Prime can only handle so much for her.

Her work laptop is upstairs, and so is coffee, but she doesn't have the time. Her personal laptop is technically set up for the appropriate VPN access, so she switches out of the section she's partitioned and encrypted for her basement research and loads up the main segment. She's calling into the meeting less than a minute later.

"Sorry for the delay, everybody," she says. "Got a bit caught up."

If there was chatter before her arrival, there isn't any now. An array of faces peer back at her. Some she recognizes, others are strangers.

"Where are you calling from?" Valdez asks.

Tamsin glances over her shoulder at the white walls covered in inked observations and calculations. It's a very bright room, and on camera, she's a bit overexposed. It's hard to make out the substance of her notes. "My basement," she says.

The stairs are not in view, and neither is the door. She maybe should have made the trek upstairs, but—there really wasn't time. And it's fine. It's fine.

This is so much easier.

"Any updates overnight?" she asks.

At first, nobody speaks, but then Aiden Davis jumps in, bringing everybody up to speed on applying Tamsin's—*Prime's*—new predictive approach to the modeling efforts. According to a researcher named Jordan Cherry, samples are finally being taken and should be in the lab by the afternoon. Cherry speaks like they know each other, addressing her with an irritating amount of familiarity.

Tamsin doesn't recognize them in the slightest.

She doesn't shut down that familiarity, though; it's not worth it, not when the first instance of a within-city infrastructure break was reported overnight, albeit in an area with preexisting seismological concerns. The partial collapse of an old parking garage. Nobody was injured. For now the news is saying it's just a tragic accident, but they all know the noose is tightening. Tomorrow, their findings go public. There's so much to go over.

"I know we're operating under a tight time limit," she assures them as the meeting wraps up, "but we're making strong progress. Thank you, everybody. I'll talk to you after tomorrow's press conference."

Video blocks blink out as people leave the room. A red notification bubble hovers over the chat toggle.

Cherry has sent her a message.

Are you feeling okay?

She closes the call without answering.

Myrica Dynamics's records say Cherry has been working in her department for at least three years. There are photos of them together on the internet, at press conferences and donor events. She clicks through each one with growing horror. Tamsin *knew* them. Tamsin has forgotten them. This goes beyond forgetting the nature of her connection to Nikkya Keiling last week. Have there been other lapses? How often? How close to one another? She should start a list, the better to keep track of these memory gaps.

She opens her notes app.

There's a list already started. *Forgot the need to keep phone powered down while Prime was acting in my stead.* That's it. For a moment, it lightens the load, but then she looks at the time stamp (three days ago), and realizes there's another explanation.

Forgot existence of list of memory gaps, she types.

Forgot Jordan Cherry.

She tries to think back further.

Forgot salon appointment. Forgot relationship history with Nikkya Keiling.

"Prime?" she calls, heart thudding in her chest as she stares at the list. "Prime!"

No answer. She gets up on unsteady legs and mounts the stairs. Her thighs burn from the effort. Upstairs, the hall seems to yawn away in both directions, and she shakes her head fiercely to clear it. When she looks again, everything is normal.

That's happened before, too, but only during a panic attack. She's not that far gone right now. And the panic attacks and the forgetting aren't related, are they? Except—except there was *something,* that afternoon. She'd had something in her hand, hadn't she? And then when she'd looked, it had been gone.

Her head aches. She rubs at the bridge of her nose.

"Prime?" she calls again, and again, there's no response. She fumbles with her phone, opens up the camera feed from the bedroom that she hasn't looked at in—how long? It's felt pointless ever since she started letting Prime move freely around the house. The app loads, but the feeds are offline.

No cameras detected.

She's frowning at the words, wondering if they've somehow gotten disconnected from the Wi-Fi, when a calendar reminder drops from the top of the screen.

Psychiatric appointment, 10:30 a.m. Today. Prime is already gone.

Did Prime tell her she was going out? Tamsin doesn't even remember making the appointment but, of course, Lachlan made it, according to the calendar details. The thought of Lachlan makes her reach for the power button, but she hesitates.

The list. She needs to update the list. She thumbs over to Settings and turns on airplane mode, shuts down Bluetooth connectivity. She's not sure if that alone is enough, but it will have to be.

Noting down what she's forgotten only once she realizes it's gone isn't enough. She needs to set up alerts, reminders. She needs to write down the narrative of what's happened to her, just in case. The basement, and Prime's arrival, and her apparently accelerating decline. There's a narrative in process on her laptop, but it's too hard to update in the moment, and if she's right—

If she's right, she's forgetting things frequently.

She sags against the wall, thumbs flying as she taps out everything she remembers, everything she can think of. She uses code as best she can, then stops when she realizes she could potentially forget the code entirely. Panic nips at her heels, but she stomps on it; there's no time for panic, only action.

A knife.

She'd had a knife, that afternoon last week. She can remember the weight of it, and Prime's bedroom in front of her. The details are hazy, but she knows the knife had been there, up until it hadn't been.

Prime's never mentioned the knife.

What happened?

Tamsin keeps typing.

When she reaches the end, at last, it's been over an hour. Her body hurts. Her eyes burn. She stares down at the scroll of text she's made and wishes she could at least encrypt it.

But then she might forget how to access it.

Groaning, she powers the phone off and slips it into her pocket. She takes a few stumbling steps toward the kitchen, her legs heavy and half asleep. Water, calories, and then sleep. It won't fix this, but it'll at least help her headache, and she needs to keep her strength up.

She's at the entrance to the kitchen when she hears a soft trill behind her. Turning, she sees Penrose sitting on the steps.

One Penrose.

The two cats don't spend all their time together, just as Tamsin and Prime don't. But they're often both within eyeshot at any given moment, and as Tamsin turns in a circle, she doesn't see the other one. The world tilts, just a little.

The panic begins to wriggle again beneath her heel.

She scoops the cat up in her arms, and he doesn't protest. She has a carrier, she knows, but she can't remember where she put it. That might be just normal forgetfulness, or it might be this swallowing, all-consuming *thing*.

She forces away the thought.

She needs more data.

Penrose allows himself to be carried through the house. First the ground floor, then up, into every bedroom, every closet. He doesn't purr. He waits her out, then begins to squirm when her grip tightens, when her breathing quickens.

Back in the first-floor hallway, she lets him down.

There is only one Penrose.

"Tamsin?"

Prime stands in the entryway, back from the psychiatrist's office.

It's entirely possible—likely, even—that the other Penrose slipped out the front door with her. Or any of the times Tamsin has tried to wait out her agoraphobia. He's never done it before, but there's a reason he's chipped and vaccinated; accidents happen. Erratic behavior happens.

And yet . . .

"One of the cats is gone," she says.

She doesn't know which one.

Her hands curl into fists at her sides, as if they can clutch on to reality, to the world as it was an hour ago. A day ago. A week ago.

Prime frowns. She's holding a small bag. Her hair gleams, professionally treated. "Are you sure?"

"Yes. No. I don't—"

Prime can't help her. Or she could, but there's too much to catch her up on, and Tamsin's gaze has already drifted back to the basement door.

There were two cats. There are two of them.

Tamsin knows where Prime came from.

Prime calls her name as she all but runs for the basement. The stairs are treacherous, and she nearly trips as she pelts down them, grasping the railing. The lights are blinding, and there is nowhere for a cat to hide. The room is empty.

The door is solid and untouchable, save for the ink and blood still stubbornly clinging to its impossible surface. She grabs the doorknob, twists, heaves. She pulls with all her weight, and the door doesn't move, but she remembers Prime walking out of it. She remembers—what, a dream?—where the door opened, and blackness spilled out.

She's certain the missing Penrose left not through the front door, but through *this*.

Prime is on the stairs now, saying something. Tamsin doesn't care. That door is going to open. She's going to figure out how it works even if it kills her. The need builds up behind her clenched teeth, perfuses her chest and belly with a burning fire, blots out everything else in the world that she no longer has time for.

The door is going to open today.

She retrieves the drill she used to core out the walls. She loads her largest drill bit. Prime's heels click on the steps as she eases her way down.

"What are you doing?" she presses. "Tamsin, talk to me."

"Experimenting," she snaps and strides to the door. She looks it up and down, considering her plan of attack. She could try to drill out the knob itself; that's probably the best way to get rid of the lock mechanism. But she won't have much time, only as long as she can keep her eyes on it, and wood is softer than metal.

She pushes the bit against the door, just below the knob. The motor whines to life.

"Tamsin!"

The drill bites into the wood, and she hauls on the trigger. Sawdust and splinters fling out in all directions, some brushing over her cheeks, many landing in her hair. She keeps her eyes open wide, refusing to blink.

The world around her contracts. Tunnels. It's like she's being dragged from the door, and she holds on, pushing forward, *forward*, surely the door can't go on forever, surely it can't heal itself as long as she doesn't look aw—

Her shaking hands slip. The drill jerks sideways. There is a sharp *crack*, and then pain, searing pain, and her face is wet, and her eyes close reflexively. The world is brilliant light even through the lids.

When she tries to look again, one of her eyes sees nothing but red.

And the other one sees that the door is untouched.

Chapter Twenty-Eight

Tamsin is numb. Shock is a useful analgesic. The only painkillers she'd had on hand stronger than ibuprofen were two Vicodins left over from a dental procedure a few years past.

She's taken one. Prime won't let her have the other yet. But she did give Tamsin a tiny white pill. *Valium*, she'd said. *From the show I put on for the psychiatrist.*

It's starting to kick in, but she's still shaking.

"Ambulance," Tamsin says, not for the first time. She's been repeating it since Prime dragged her, screaming, from the basement. "Professionals."

"No," Prime says, irritated, no longer patient. She has Tamsin seated in the dining room, one of the bright basement lamps hauled up to better show off the damage Tamsin has done to herself. The light hurts, even with the wad of gauze she's holding gingerly against her face, even with the pain medication. Her head is pounding.

They've already managed to irrigate it, get most of the shrapnel and sawdust out. But some of the broken drill bit is lodged in the eye itself. Her left—she can feel the metal spike every time she tries to look somewhere other than straight ahead, every time she blinks. She can't close her eyelids. The light always gets through.

The press conference is in less than twenty-four hours.

Her breathing hitches, panic breaking through the numbness as she sees it in full, bloody color: standing at the podium, incoherent, her eye a pit of shredded meat, everybody watching.

"Tamsin."

Tamsin snaps back into her body, from psychic pain to physical agony, and she whimpers, even as she focuses as best she can on Prime.

Prime crouches down in front of her.

"You'll regret it if I call them," Prime murmurs, voice softer now. It's the first time she's said anything beyond *You don't really want that, you're panicking, it will be okay.* "It will go on your medical record. Lachlan's concern will increase. I won't be able to take your place anymore. But we have other options, Tamsin. We can take care of this. Come up here and lie down, please."

She pats the dining table.

Tamsin looks at it, then back at Prime. There are supplies jumbled on a nearby chair. Tamsin hadn't looked at them when Prime brought them, head empty of everything except a blaring, repeating, *this can't be happening.*

There are coils of rope on the chair. A glint of metal, smaller than a kitchen knife but just as sharp.

"I need my phone," she says.

"Come here, Tamsin."

She stands, but not to obey. Her phone—it's probably in the kitchen. She can get to it. Call 911, call Lachlan, call *anybody* else. Prime means well, but she doesn't understand—

Prime's hand closes on her shoulder. "Lie down," she says and steers Tamsin to the table. The force of being turned around makes her head spin. Prime's hands are firm as she helps Tamsin sit on the tabletop, then stretch out on her back.

The change in angle sends a fresh wave of searing pressure through her skull. Both eyes tear. Prime leaves her side, but not for long.

The first rope is cast over her chest.

"It will need to come out," Prime says and hauls tight. The rope pins Tamsin's upper arms to the table. Her hand drags away from her face, smearing blood and dropping the soaked gauze. The light bludgeons her optic nerve.

"No. No. We're not medically trained," Tamsin pleads, parroting in horror what Prime had told her on Friday.

"No, but I'm a quick study, and it's too risky to leave things as is. We can't manage an infection." Her smile is probably meant to be reassuring, but it only makes Tamsin whimper, thrash. Everything feels far away and too close all at once. Her body is heavy and numb and on fire. The Valium— was it Valium? She didn't read the label—widens the distance between impulse and action. She can't fight. She needs to fight.

"Let me go," she begs.

Prime reaches for another length of rope.

"Lachlan," Tamsin says. "Lachlan, we can trust her."

"That's not what you've told me before." The rope cinches. Tamsin can't see how Prime is tying the knots, but she is sure and certain and fast. Like she's practiced this before.

When could she have practiced it?

Why would she have practiced it?

"I'm a coward," she gasps. "*We're* cowards. It's easy not to trust. But if we tell Lachlan, Lachlan will keep the secret. She will do what needs to be done. It might mean changes, but—"

"I will not be dragged to a lab to be taken apart like a *thing*," Prime says curtly. "And you and I both know that's what would happen. You chose to lie to her, every time; you agree with me."

Tamsin remembers, wildly, sitting at this table and thinking about vivisection, about cutting Prime open to see what's inside, and if Prime only knew—

If Prime knew, perhaps she'd want to return the favor.

Maybe Prime does know.

Rope tightens across her ankles, and all she can do is thrash her head, but every attempt is agony. She's panting, gasping, hyperventilating, and why can't Lachlan be here? Why can't she intervene, unexpected and un- wanted (but oh god, she wants Lachlan here, needs her here, *please*. Every phone call—every phone call was wasted, and Prime had been there for all of them, hadn't she? Watching, waiting, and if Tamsin had just gotten up the courage, what would Prime have done then?)

Prime gets a last length of rope. It is rough against Tamsin's forehead. She's begging, babbling now, unsure of what she's saying.

And then the world grows quieter as Prime slides barely used foam yoga blocks under the rope on each side of her head. She pushes them toward one another, trapping Tamsin's skull, forcing her to stare straight up into her double's inverted face, backlit and shadowed.

"Don't do this," she whispers.

Prime offers a soft smile as reassurance. It doesn't touch her eyes. "This is for the best, Tamsin," Prime says. "Trust me. Our interests are the same; they always have been."

It rings true, cutting through the panic, but Tamsin doesn't understand, and it's impossible to trust. Impossible to cling to.

"Why don't I believe you?" she asks.

"Because you don't trust yourself," Prime answers.

The ropes ratchet tighter, tighter, until she thinks she might burst. She can't move, except to wiggle her fingertips. She can barely speak, her breathing has grown so erratic.

Beside Tamsin's head, Prime lays out supplies. Tamsin can't see what they are. She's can't see anything except for Prime's silhouette and the blinding light beyond.

Prime's hand settles gently on Tamsin's face, fingers tracing the orbit. Then they dig in, prying apart her eyelids.

"Now," Prime says, voice steady and even as she raises her other hand, metal gleaming between her fingers. "It's very important that you stay completely still. You can do that for me, can't you?"

The scalpel descends.

After, Prime moves her to the primary bedroom. The curtains are pulled tight and the lights are low. Prime has made a nest of pillows to keep her head elevated, to keep her from rolling over in the night, to *keep her.*

She doesn't want to be touched. Fuck, but she doesn't want to be touched ever again.

Her throat is hoarse. Her hands twitch on top of the comforter. She takes small sips from the meal replacement shake Prime holds to her lips, then shudders and thinks she might throw up.

Prime pets her hair, fingers scraping lightly when they pass over the bandages wound tight around Tamsin's skull. Tamsin wishes she could pull away, but doesn't.

"You did very well," Prime says. "So well. So good for me."

Tamsin answers with a low moan. Prime sets the bottle aside.

"Phone," Tamsin manages. "Lachlan."

Prime moves as if to stand, then hesitates. "Do you still intend to ask for her help?"

Yes. "No," she says. "But she'll call."

Prime chews at her lower lip, then nods. When she leaves the room, the door remains open.

Tamsin considers running.

This is not the first time she's been afraid since Prime arrived, but it is the first time that she's feared *Prime* this starkly. And yet—and yet—it was her own panic and mistake that led to her injury. The injury had to be dealt with. In the morning, she might even agree with Prime's decision.

In the morning, she's supposed to be at the press conference. In the morning, they're going to tell the whole city that it's sinking.

She can't think straight, thoughts careening into one another, borrowing intensity, fading out before their time. All she's certain of is that she can't leave the house.

Prime returns, holding out Tamsin's phone. Tamsin takes it with one shaking hand. It refuses to unlock for her face, and in the dark screen she can see the reflection of the white bandages.

She bites down another moan of fear and taps in her code instead, trying not to think about how the phone will now recognize Prime, but not her.

"Better not to call," Prime says softly. "She'll be able to hear the pain in your voice."

Not just the pain. Tamsin is certain she'll be able to hear the fibrous tearing of her optic nerve. The wet, almost insignificant plop of the eye hitting the table next to her head.

She pants, resisting the urge to scream. "I'll text," Tamsin manages weakly.

She pulls open the messenger app, taps on Lachlan's name. And then she stares at the too-bright screen, wondering what to say.

Ask for help, she tells herself.

"Here," Prime says, and Tamsin flinches, expecting her to reach for the phone. But she has a glass of water instead, and in her other hand, two tablets. The second Vicodin, and something she doesn't recognize.

"A sedative," Prime says when Tamsin doesn't take them. "Lachlan probably already knows it's been prescribed. You can tell her you've taken one and won't be available this evening."

"Why do you have that?" she rasps.

"I told the doctors about your sleepwalking."

Tamsin tries to frown, but it hurts too much. "I don't remember telling you about that." Each word tears at her throat.

Prime sets the glass of water down and strokes her hair. This time, Tamsin does pull away, despite the throb of pain that results.

"You did," Prime assures her. "In the hallway, after your panic attack. I was afraid you'd hurt yourself, do you remember?"

The knife. She'd had a knife. But she'd never meant to hurt herself. She'd gone . . . she'd gone to Prime's room . . . hadn't she? Or no, Lachlan had been there, had threatened her, and . . .

"You thought it was your only option," Prime murmurs, seeing her agony. "But it's not. You aren't well, Tamsin. You know you aren't well. You can't do this alone. Please, let me help you."

She needs help.

There are so few options available to her, and her mind cannot be relied on. Her judgment is skewed. Had she really intended to hurt Prime? She can't remember *why*. She can barely think at all, and half her thoughts are emotions, not logic. Raw, animal panic living beneath her civilized exterior.

She can trust Lachlan, or she can trust a version of herself that isn't compromised.

Slowly, she taps out a message.

From: Tamsin
Started medication. Hitting harder than expected. Will call tomorrow ahead of event.

Prime reads over her shoulder. "You'll take my place?" Tamsin asks, looking up at her perfect face, the face that looks how hers should. Her hair, lustrous and beautiful and cared for.

"Of course," Prime says, and Tamsin presses Send, then sets the phone on the nightstand with one trembling hand. She parts her lips. Prime feeds her the pills and water.

Tamsin swallows it all. They burn in her belly. Her missing eye screams in counterpoint.

The fog rises over her.

"Sleep," Prime murmurs, tucking her in. "You'll feel better in the morning. Everything will be easier."

Chapter Twenty-Nine

In the mirror, her face is drawn. Bandages wind around her head. Her hair is braided back from her face, but it is tangled, matted. She reaches out to touch the surface of the mirror, and it shudders beneath her fingertips.

She's dreaming. She's been dreaming for what feels like forever but might have only been a day. It depends on what she defines as *dream*. The hole in her head? Her reflection stepping out of this mirror?

The downward pull of the city?

It all makes sense, by the logic of dreams.

She doesn't recognize this bathroom. En suite? Guest? Downstairs powder room? Is it even hers, or is it institutional, a hint to her shattering mind that she's in a hospital somewhere? It could be any. All. The mirror ripples when she pushes against it, but it doesn't let her sink through.

In the mirror, the bandages are smooth and cold. Her features warp and shift in the low light, and she thinks she sees herself smile.

Tamsin jerks her hand away.

When she turns her head, there's only absence, until she turns far enough and her remaining eye catches up. The room is bigger than a hospital bathroom, she thinks. The tiles are vaguely familiar. But did she always have a showerhead like that?

Doesn't matter. Go back to bed.

Bed, or beneath the coffee table, or down into the basement. That's how all her dreams end.

But her slow rotation has brought her reflection back into view, and it catches her again. This time, she reaches up to touch herself.

She expects to find the mirror in place of flesh. Cold water. Shivering metal. Nothing at all.

Her fingers catch on the bandages. She finds the tape by how it pulls at her hair. It comes up in fits and starts, and then all at once. Cotton gauze falls, loose around her face, obscuring her remaining eye, and everything is gray and dark and whispering.

And then it's gone.

In her reflection, a yawning chasm of meat stares back at her where her eye should be. It's the first time she's seen it, though she knew all along that it was there. But *knowing* and *seeing* are different, and now she leans in. The flesh is slick in parts, dried and clotted in others, and all of it is swollen, swollen, swollen. There are stitches, in the depths. They are not even.

She stands there, transfixed, for as long again as she has been dreaming. This reflection isn't her, but when she reaches up, her fingers touch raw tissue. She flinches, even though it doesn't hurt as much as she thought it might.

She listens for the rasp of her own breathing.

Somewhere, her phone is ringing.

The sound draws her away from the mirror. She drifts through the doorway, into a hallway that stretches out forever. The lights are dim. She can't tell if it's day or night. Movement makes her head spin, her thoughts disjoint.

There are so many doors in this hall. Have they all always been there? Are they all *her* doors?

She doesn't know if this is her house, she reminds herself. She does know she's dreaming, and in dreams, don't proportions have a tendency to distort? University campuses covering hundreds of miles, science quads turning into meteor craters, her house into a labyrinth.

Her phone is still ringing; she follows the sound because she can't trust anything else.

She finds it sitting on a nightstand, by a bed that stinks of sweat and blood and fear. But by the time she grabs it, it has fallen silent. The phone tries to read her face. It can't, and it can't, and it locks up without showing her who called. If there are words at all on the screen, they are too bright and too small to make out.

But she can hear her breathing now. It is quick and pained, and her hand, where it grips her phone, is trembling and white. She's afraid. It washes over her, as if on a delay, and it is elemental. Writhing. She retreats from the nightstand, but she can't let go of the brick of metal and glass in her hand. The fear follows her back to the bathroom, back to the mirror, where she leans in once more.

And then, there, floating out of the darkness, is her face, her *true* face. Unmarred, familiar, vaguely concerned. It hovers just beside what she thought was her reflection. But when she shifts to line them up, the fake and the real, there is only her ruined face staring back at her again.

Tamsin can't help but cry.

It hurts as tears wick into the socket.

A soft sound, behind her, and then her true reflection is back, just behind her shoulder.

Prime. Prime, come to fetch her.

"Bad dreams?" Prime asks. She is beautiful. Immaculately made-up, with no bandages, no tangles or damage in her shining, unbound curls. She comes around Tamsin's side, holding out her hand. Entreating.

Tamsin looks down at the phone, still clutched to her chest.

"It was ringing," she says. She pulls it away from her body, tilts it up. The phone refuses to recognize her face. "I didn't see who it was."

Prime is close now, and Tamsin can smell her own perfume. It's comforting, a soporific, and what an odd detail for a dream to preserve, but all her dreams lately have been so striking. So enticing.

"Let me see," Prime says, voice gentle and soft.

She holds out a hand for the phone.

There's a reason Prime doesn't have the phone already, but it evades the grasping fingers of Tamsin's mind, a bit of trash bobbing in the water, pushed away by the act of reaching for it. *Do not give it to her,* she reminds herself, even though she can't summon the logic behind it. *It is not for her.*

Except it opens for Prime's face, not Tamsin's. It recognizes Prime only.

But whoever was calling wanted to speak to Tamsin. Didn't they?

Did she want to speak to them?

Is she supposed to be afraid right now? She thinks she is, but she can't tell if it's because of the missed call or because of Prime.

There is so much she doesn't remember. But this is only a dream; she can change the ending. Or she can let it bear her up and along, uncaring of the destination. She will wake up in her bed, and she'll recognize her surroundings, and the world will go on.

It always does. She's never been able to stop it.

Tamsin lets go. The phone tips into Prime's hand. She is rewarded with a glowing smile, warm and welcoming, and the lights around them dim. It's only the two of them, alone in all the world.

Prime slips the phone into a pocket. Her arms twine around Tamsin, and Tamsin lets herself fall. Her double cradles her, then lifts her up.

"Back to bed, I think," Prime murmurs against the crown of her head. Not a suggestion so much as a definition. *Sleep.* Tamsin will sleep. Her head lolls against Prime's shoulder. "I'll take care of everything."

The bathroom fades, transmutes to a hallway. It leads off into the darkness. From this angle, it looks different again, even though she knows she was just here. The bedroom isn't far. If she closes her eye, maybe she'll hear the phone ring again, and they'll be able to follow the sound home.

They turn. Tamsin's head spins. The ground slides away, and they are descending, step after careful step.

The motion rocks Tamsin to sleep.

Tamsin

Chapter Thirty

The air is cool and bright. The midmorning sun makes her head ache, the pain sharpest in her empty eye socket, even beneath the fresh bandages, but she's too focused on everything around her to take much note of it. The rosemary bush beside her is tall and fragrant. Cars drive by every so often on the road just beyond the yard. It's chilly, and she thinks that one of the garments by the door was for her to wear against the temperature, but she can bear it a few more minutes.

Maybe longer.

Because the world outside the house is expansive. Her mind is inundated with new stimuli with the slightest turn of her head. There is so much she doesn't know, so much she can *learn*.

She takes another step away from the house. She wonders what is down the road.

A noise behind her: the opening of the door to the house. She turns to the right to favor her eye.

Dr. Rivers stands on the doorstep, expression hard. "Nought," she cautions, voice low. "Come here."

"Have I done something wrong?" she asks warily, even as she obeys.

"It isn't safe for you out there," Dr. Rivers says, stepping away from the door so Nought can enter the building. "How did you get out?"

"The door was open. What do you mean, *not safe*?"

"There are people out there who might hurt you," Dr. Rivers says. The door clicks shut. Nought itches to open it again, then pushes the nonsensical impulse aside.

She's been having a lot of those.

"Why?" she asks. "Who?"

"There are not supposed to be two of me," Dr. Rivers says. She's said it before, though usually with good humor. There's no humor now. "And for as long as I am here with you, away from my lab, there's the risk of people getting—curious. The sooner I can trust you to remain here safely, the better for both of us. Do you understand?"

Nought's existence, as far as she knows it, began a few days ago. But Dr. Rivers sometimes acts like it's been longer than that, and Nought has found it's easier not to argue. There's so much she doesn't know about the world; questions about herself feel insignificant.

They are not insignificant to Dr. Rivers. Dr. Rivers insists on running test after test, personality inventories and psychological evaluations and physical exams. Many of these she leaves Nought to do by herself down in the basement, with its bare white walls and its soft lights. Dr. Rivers is a busy woman. Today, she's been on the phone or at her computer all morning.

It's engrossing and distracting, whatever she's working on. It must have held her so captive that she had forgotten to lock the basement door, Nought realizes. That she could explore the house was unintentional. No wonder Dr. Rivers is frustrated. Her disappointment makes more sense if Nought has just done something wrong again.

But nothing bad has come of it. That must count for something, right?

"I understand," Nought says, because she does understand Dr. Rivers's specific argument, even if she doesn't understand the full context. She glances at the frosted window beside the door warily, then retreats deeper into the house.

Dr. Rivers follows. "Besides," she says, "you need me to take care of your injury."

Nought does not remember losing her eye.

As far as she knows, she was born with a raw, gaping hole in its place, already securely bandaged. Somebody took care of her in the past. It's unclear if that has always been Dr. Rivers or not, but Dr. Rivers has two eyes, and there are no healing cuts on the skin of her face. And there are a few other physical differences between them, like how Dr. Rivers's hair is glossy and orderly, and Nought's is dull and matted. If Nought is patterned off of Dr. Rivers—

"Here," Dr. Rivers says. They are stopped not in front of the basement, but in front of a small room with porcelain fixtures inside. "Relieve yourself, and then I need to get back to work."

And Nought obeys.

Nought has a small cot, a tablet loaded with books, and a miniature fridge containing water and bottles of thick slurry that Dr. Rivers claims is food. The basement is very deep, and the steps are high. Compared to the staircase she saw leading to the upper floor of the house, and the dimensions of the hall and the dining room where Dr. Rivers works, this room is—odd.

It looks stretched, somehow.

The paint on the walls is fresh. There is limited ventilation in the basement, and the trapped fumes make her head hurt, when her injury isn't doing that on its own. The lights that ring the room remain on at all times, glowing down at her relentlessly, making it hard to sleep, but it's better than the alternative.

And then there is the door.

It looks like the other doors Nought has seen in the house, save for a few scrawled black marks on it and what looks like a patch of rust. It's made of wood, with a brass knob. She knows the names for these things intrinsically and wonders at it. But mostly, she avoids looking at the door.

She does not want to be *near* the door. It fills her with an instinctual dread, and she refuses to approach it to test if it gets worse or not. She doesn't need to. She's wary of what will happen if she does.

(Dr. Rivers has told her that she emerged from it, but Nought doesn't remember anything like that. One moment, she didn't exist. The next, she was—

Well. It's blurry. But she doesn't think she was in the basement. It's one of the few things she's kept from Dr. Rivers, unwilling to share it until she knows what it means.)

A day or so after Nought first arrived, or at least became aware, Dr. Rivers had come down to the basement to check on her. They'd gone over some of the tests Nought had filled out, but Dr. Rivers had seemed distracted the whole time. There are three cameras in the basement, and she'd fussed with them as they spoke. Then, just before she left, Dr. Rivers had paused at the top of the stairs. There had been a soft click.

The lamps had all gone out.

For a moment, there'd been a shaft of light from the door at the top of the stairs, and then the silhouette of Dr. Rivers, and then nothing.

Nothing but black.

She'd scrambled to her feet, crying out, shouting Dr. Rivers's name, but the towering ceiling had only thrown her own voice back at her. She staggered away from the cot, only to lose all orientation after the first step. Her body felt like it was tipping, and she'd gone to her knees, bone striking cement when she misjudged how far down it was.

Time stretched. She was reduced to the limits of her skin, and then beneath that, to the pulsing of her blood and the ache in her skull. The room felt colder without the light; she shivered uncontrollably. She tried speaking to herself to break the oppressive silence that made the walls seem just beside her and miles away, but she had so little to say back then. She knew almost nothing.

She'd repeated the inventory questions. Bits of the texts Dr. Rivers had allowed her to read. Things Dr. Rivers had said to her. At first, it was rote, but then she focused in on them, saying them again and again, sorting through the words for an answer.

Had she done something wrong? Tested poorly?

She must have. She couldn't find the misstep, but there was no other explanation for the dark, for the silence, for the lack of direction.

She'd been *abandoned*.

Across from her, where she knew the cameras were, and the door, came a soft sound: the faintest click of a latch being undone.

She'd recoiled, instinct seizing her limbs and dragging her back, back, away to the farthest wall she could find. She couldn't see the door, but she knew exactly where it was, could feel the weight of it. It wasn't open yet; there was no breath of air through its frame, and nothing in the basement changed, but it still pulled on her. A gravity well. An implacable, terrible call.

She'd turned to face the wall and pressed her face to the stinking paint.

Dr. Rivers had found her like that hours later, and she'd looked . . .

Disappointed.

* * *

Dr. Rivers still hasn't told her what she'd been testing that time.

Today, Dr. Rivers has left her with the lights on but no assessments to run through, so she sits curled up on her cot as far from the door as she can manage, reading. Several of the texts are not familiar, precisely, but she knows the content of them, if not the context. Books on physics, articles that bear Dr. Rivers's name. Dr. Rivers is brilliant. Nought can follow every thought and insight and design; does that make her brilliant, too?

It even gives her ideas. Raises new questions. There is a pen down here, forgotten some time ago, splattered lightly with paint. It writes on the walls very well.

Nought makes notes.

She is pondering the implications of set bundling on signal attenuation when the door at the top of the steps, the one she doesn't mind at all—and she isn't sure what that difference means—unlocks and opens. She turns, registering the faint cramping of her stomach that means hunger.

Dr. Rivers stands at the top of the stairs. She doesn't always come down, and doesn't now.

"Would you like to make dinner?" she asks with no lead-in.

On the surface, Dr. Rivers is asking for her preference, but Nought is certain that this is another unspoken test. There is a right answer and a wrong answer, and which is which has nothing to do with Dr. Rivers being hungry.

She considers the question from as many angles as she can manage and comes up with no hints one way or the other of what is expected of her. The only way to learn *that* is by introducing new data.

"Yes," she says, because the substance in the bottles is not food, and she is confident she can figure out how to feed them.

She watches Dr. Rivers closely for a reaction.

She sees delight. It echoes through Nought and makes her smile.

"Then come with me," Dr. Rivers says, beckoning Nought up the stairs and through the door she holds wide open. She leads Nought into the kitchen, where the blinds are tightly drawn. The room is spotless, the counters bare.

Dr. Rivers gives no more instruction.

Nought considers the cabinets, then turns to the fridge. It's larger than the small cube in the basement, but hums just the same; it's the best place to start.

There are four packages in the fridge alongside the ubiquitous bottles. (Nought notes with interest that Dr. Rivers must drink the stuff herself. She wonders if it tastes better to Dr. Rivers, or if she simply doesn't care.) There is also a faint, unpleasant odor that makes her queasy, as if something in the fridge has gone bad.

But each of the packages has a date stamped on it, and none is too far from the others; she guesses that means they're all still good. They also all bear the same logo, reading *SunHarvest, a Myrica Dynamics Product.* When she sorts through them, they are labeled with different titles: pumpkin chili with kidney beans and cashew crema; beet borscht with zucchini and white-bean fritters; sole with red pepper–caper sauce and lemon-garlic broccoli; quinoa-spinach grain bowls with fresh dill, feta, and fried eggs. The words tumble through her mind, many of them hooking up to concepts, none of them producing any feeling in her.

Why should they? She's never eaten any of them before. Still, she needs to choose between them, and she can't be sure this isn't another test. Her choice must have *a* reason behind it, even if it's not the right one.

The undersides of each container have instructions and cooking times. *Ah.* A quick meal, then, so that Dr. Rivers can get back to her work. She plucks the sole-and-broccoli box from the stack and puts the rest back.

(And she thinks, though she's not sure how she knows this, that fish goes bad more quickly than most things, and that *sole* is a type of fish. More indications of certain types of knowledge being preserved between her and Dr. Rivers. She makes a mental note.)

Dr. Rivers gives no indication of approval or disapproval as Nought looks for the tools the recipe calls for. Two frying pans, one larger, one small. A whisk, a spatula. Dishes for serving, based on the image on the front of the box. Pulling everything out of the cabinets and arranging them is unexpectedly difficult unless she goes slowly, using visual cues to judge distance. In the basement, she knows the landmarks well enough that her missing eye is rarely an issue. Here, though, even with a surprisingly intuitive knowledge of where things are, she fumbles occasionally.

Cooking is harder. The instructions are thorough and the ingredients are packaged separately and precisely labeled, but the actions need a great deal of attention. The broccoli is steaming in the pan when a trilling chime cuts through the air. Nought's head jerks up, a reflex she doesn't know the origin of, her hand already reaching out. But Dr. Rivers is pulling something from her pocket. Her phone.

She curses under her breath, then taps it and holds it to her ear.

"You're early," she says.

Nought can't hear the response, not with the pop of the pan, and not with Dr. Rivers leaving the room. Nought almost goes after her, then glances back at the stove clock. The recipe is quick; she can't let things burn.

And she can still hear Dr. Rivers's side of the conversation, wherever she's gone to.

"I'm keeping an eye on the news coverage. It's better than I'd expected, and Klein says Myrica is still polling favorably. . . . Yes, I'm feeling much better. You've read the diagnosis?"

The clock ticks over. Nought carefully slides the broccoli onto a plate, then wipes out the pan. Her finger brushes the metal. It burns, and she recoils, hissing.

"Yes, the antianxiety medicine is helping. As are the sleep aids. You were right."

Nought oils the pan, then sticks her burned finger in her mouth. Another reflex, something her body knows how to do. The oil heats, and she lays the fish against the metal. The flesh sizzles, almost drowning out the sound of Dr. Rivers's voice. Nought hurriedly gets the sauce into the smaller pan, then edges closer to the doorway.

Dr. Rivers stands near her laptop in the dining room. She does not see Nought lurking.

"Tomorrow? No, I'm busy." Another pause. Something like anger flickers over Dr. Rivers's face, twisting her elegant features, igniting the cold pools of her eyes. Nought watches, fascinated, then flinches as Dr. Rivers looks directly at her. The anger eases by degrees, replaced by a glimmer of interest. Nought relaxes. "The afternoon, then," Dr. Rivers says. "Yes," she says, "I'll be there. Of course. Good night, Mx. Woodfield."

Nought hasn't heard that name before. She wonders who it is. She wonders if it's one of the people Dr. Rivers fears might hurt her.

They consider each other across the space a moment longer before one of the pans gives a sharp *pop*, and Nought hurries over to the stove. She flips the fish. The skin tears slightly, perhaps more browned than the recipe called for.

Still, nothing about it strikes her as inedible. It smells wonderful. She takes the sauce off the heat as instructed; adds oil and whisks until it becomes smooth and lustrous. The fish is done not long after.

Dr. Rivers watches her work in silence, though it feels warmer this time. More relaxed.

She does not help Nought take the dishes to the dining room, but she also doesn't argue when Nought sets their dishes directly across the narrow width of the table from one another. That must be an acceptable configuration.

Nought goes back to the kitchen to get silverware and glasses of water. By the time she returns, Dr. Rivers is already seated, turning the plate from side to side, inspecting.

"Did I do well?" Nought asks.

"It looks good enough," Dr. Rivers replies, holding her hand out. Nought passes her a fork, then takes her own seat. She watches as Dr. Rivers cuts into the fish, then tastes it. "Perfectly fine," she declares once she's swallowed.

Pride is a new and warm feeling. Nought finds she rather likes it.

"Are you going out tomorrow?" she asks once she's eaten half of her meal.

"Eavesdropping is not polite," Dr. Rivers says. "But yes."

"Does that mean you trust me?" The alternative, Nought is certain, is a locked basement door for an unknown length of time. Not actually different from what she's used to, but she'd still rather avoid that, if at all possible.

"I haven't decided yet," Dr. Rivers says. "But it's better not to push Mx. Woodfield. I'm not sure how long I'll be gone for."

It's an uncomfortable thought, being trapped here alone. Though she supposes she won't know the difference; when the door is locked, she can hear nothing from the rest of the house. Dr. Rivers may have been gone all afternoon for all she knows.

The rest of her food seems less appetizing now.

"There's something I want to know about you," Dr. Rivers says, intruding into her thoughts.

Nought sets down her fork, looking up attentively. "What is it?"

"I have surgical pins in my ankle. From an old break." She cants her head to one side, burnished hair curling softly against her temple. It's so much more lustrous, more beautiful than Nought's. "We don't know if you have those pins as well; after all, your body is laid out differently from mine."

"Is it?"

Dr. Rivers's expression freezes.

"Yes," she says after some consideration. "You've . . . forgotten, but for a time we had an ultrasound machine."

For a time. A time when? Not in the last few days. Before that, then, in the more blurry space that she still isn't entirely sure is real and not a dream. The thought unmoors her. She knows she is sitting in a dining room, in a house, but she is also struggling to stay afloat in a dark and endless sea.

Dr. Rivers's voice calls her back. "Your internal organs are in the wrong orientation."

And then she is only in the dining room, looking down at herself, mind ablaze with a better mystery. The wrong orientation? What does that mean? She presses her hand to her abdomen, wondering what it looks like beneath her skin.

"This might be another way that we're different," Dr. Rivers continues. "I want to check."

Nought glances up and sees curiosity shining in Dr. Rivers's eyes. It must match her own. "How?" she asks, sitting forward, eager. "Can we get the machine again?"

Dr. Rivers shakes her head. "Not easily, no. I would need to cut you open. A minor surgery. Will you let me?"

That gives her pause. She doesn't remember the removal of her eye, but she knows the agony of its healing. The at-times relentless itching. The draining of fluid that crusts along her lash line. "It would hurt," Nought says warily.

"Some, yes," Dr. Rivers concedes. "And you won't be able to walk for a little while after. But there's no other way to check." Her fingers drum on the table. "Don't you want to know where I end and you begin?"

Yes. Yes, more than anything. She is desperate to know what she is. Dr. Rivers has made it abundantly clear that she is not human, but that leaves a wide gulf for the actual definition. Moreover, she doesn't want a repeat of the lights-out experiment; she doesn't want to fail at this, too. She wants to be *better*.

Pain is worth that. She can handle pain to know herself a little more, to please Dr. Rivers.

She licks her lips and flexes her cheek, just enough to feel a spike of sensation from her eye socket. A reminder to herself, and a promise.

"Yes," she says. "You can do it. But I want to watch."

Dr. Rivers smiles.

"Of course. I wouldn't have it any other way."

Chapter Thirty-One

In the morning, after Nought has made them both breakfast, Dr. Rivers carries a new light source down the basement stairs. Nought helps; it's unwieldy, and the steps are treacherous. When they have it all set up, it is brilliant, too brilliant to look anywhere near. Painfully sharp. The fresh white paint on the walls reflects it, banishing the few lingering shadows.

Next, Dr. Rivers brings down ropes and a small medical kit. She clears off the desk and makes sure it's positioned so that the light falls squarely on it. Then she dons a pair of gloves, checks Nought's eye socket, and changes out the bandages. The gloves and crusted gauze go into a small trash can, and Dr. Rivers turns away to make notes.

Nought fidgets with the ropes, thinking, as she has multiple times over the night, about Dr. Rivers's assurances that this will be worth it, despite the amount of pain it promises. One of the ropes has what looks like dried blood on it. Mostly flecks, as if the blood had sprayed against it, but in one or two places there's a darker stain, where it must have pooled.

She wonders if it has anything to do with her eye. It's the only wound she's seen. Nobody else comes to the house.

When Dr. Rivers turns back, Nought pulls away from the ropes, feeling guilty. Like she's been caught doing something that will make Dr. Rivers angry, though she has no specific reason to think that. There's only the memory of when Dr. Rivers locked her in the dark.

She stands ramrod straight as Dr. Rivers draws up beside her. There's no censure in her gaze or demeanor, no sign she's followed Nought's train of thought.

"Before we start," Dr. Rivers says, "I'd like for you to attempt to open the door."

The door. Her gaze snaps to it, and she half expects it to be closer now, somehow. It isn't. It stands where it always has, unaltered, watching. Nausea curls in her gut. Her pulse flutters.

With the lights on, she's not as terrified of it opening, but it's only a matter of degree, not type.

Nought pulls back and takes one hesitant step away from the door. "No," she says. "No, I don't want to do that."

Soft rustling behind her. "Why not?" Dr. Rivers murmurs close to her ear. Her hands settle onto Nought's hips, and she nudges forward. Together, they take a step. Two. Each one feels wrong, vibrating at a frequency inside Nought's sinews that demands she flee, flee, flee. "It's where you came from."

Nought swallows and gestures to her bandaged eye. "Where I came from doesn't seem like a place we should want to return to." *The ropes have blood on them,* her mind supplies; staying here might be worse. That wariness has little to do with the door, though, and isn't really why she's afraid of opening it.

She can't articulate *that* fear at all.

"But this door is not meant to be here," Dr. Rivers continues.

Her throat tightens. "And neither am I," she whispers.

"You're a matched set."

The words stroke down her spine, leaving ice in their wake. Nought clenches her hands into fists, voice trembling when she asks, "Do you want me gone?"

Dr. Rivers hums, her grip gentling. She draws back, allowing a little bit of space. But the door is close now, close enough to touch. Nought turns her head away, intentionally putting it into the oubliette of the missing left side of her vision, unwilling to look directly at it any longer. Her head swims.

"No," Dr. Rivers concedes. She doesn't sound certain, but Nought will take it. She latches onto that *no,* hangs on, because otherwise, she feels like she's about to fall. "However, I can't stop my curiosity. My concern."

"I'll do it later," she promises, desperate for the reprieve. "Not today, but soon."

"Your response to it is interesting enough," Dr. Rivers says. "What do you feel when you look at it?"

Nought edges away, back toward the desk. "Aversion," she says. "Sometimes—sometimes fear."

"Why?"

"I don't know."

Dr. Rivers hums thoughtfully, following Nought. "And the other day? When the lights were out? Were you aware of the door or only the dark? Were you afraid then?"

It opened, she almost says. *I heard it unlock.*

But if she says that, Dr. Rivers will turn out the lights again, won't she? Out of curiosity. She'll turn the lights off, and she'll make Nought open the door, and then—

"Just of the dark," she says.

Lying is easy.

Bearing up under the disappointment on Dr. Rivers's face is harder. She sighs as she pats the desk. "Up you go, then. Let's get to work. Maybe we can still make *some* progress today."

The desk is not meant to be sat on. It's barely wide enough, but Nought positions herself as best she can, hands clutching at the edge of the table-top. It's metal and cold. Dr. Rivers binds her legs down and slides foam blocks along each side of her knee, to stop it from moving side to side where the ropes have the most slack. Before she tightens the bindings, she folds Nought's pant leg up, baring her ankle.

It looks very exposed. Pale and narrow, almost featureless in the bright light.

"Here," Dr. Rivers says, handing her a notepad and a pen. "So that you can take dictation."

Nought clutches both, unsure if that will be possible, unwilling to complain. She's familiar with pain but not with what causes it, and she has no idea if this will be better or worse than the persistent aching in her head.

Dr. Rivers pulls a fresh pair of medical gloves on, then reaches for a scalpel. It is not in any sort of packaging, though it looks clean.

Nought holds her breath.

"Let's begin, then. First incision on the medial left ankle."

The scalpel cuts. Dr. Rivers is not tentative, and the metal bites deep, parting Nought's flesh easily. Blood spills over her skin onto the table. The pain is sharp and hot and building. Nought grits her teeth and clutches at the pen. She can't write. It's all she can do not to thrash and try to escape.

She expects Dr. Rivers to ask how she's doing, but the other woman is too focused, head bent, gloved fingertips prodding at the incision.

Nought can't see any metal aside from the scalpel. Can't see much of anything beyond the blood, even after Dr. Rivers blots gauze against it.

How much deeper does she need to cut?

Dr. Rivers talks, and Nought fumbles with the pen cap. It skitters away onto the floor. Dr. Rivers looks up with a displeased glance, and Nought begins to write. It's a messy scrawl, not fitted to the lines of the page, start-ing and stopping at each new incision, each fresh burst of pain as Dr. Riv-ers slides her finger into the cut and pushes flesh apart.

"Does it hurt?" Dr. Rivers asks after the third cut, sparing her another glance.

Nought nods, jaw clenched tight. She doesn't trust herself to speak.

"A human would be screaming," Dr. Rivers says. She returns her focus to where she's working, where the flesh is spread and Nought thinks she can see bone now, pale and solid through a thin scrim of flesh left intact. The only metal *is* the scalpel. "You must feel less pain than I do."

Nought wants to argue but can't find the words, the breath. If she screams now, how will either of them know if it's genuine? All Nought can do is dig her nails harder into the notepad and try not to pull away. The pressure of restraining herself makes her eye socket pound, pulse trapped by force of will.

Maybe Dr. Rivers is right. This may be excruciating to Nought, right up against the limits of her endurance, but perhaps a human couldn't even get this far. She would know better.

"Are the pins there?" she asks, breathless, even though she knows they're not. She'd be able to see them. Dr. Rivers would have mentioned them.

"No," Dr. Rivers concedes. She pulls back and reaches for a few slips of paper-wrapped butterfly closures. She opens one, then dabs at Nought's skin, making a clean-enough place to apply them.

Even that hurts, and Nought bites back a whine. She doesn't think those closures will be strong enough, with how deep the cut is, but she doesn't know why. So she doesn't argue.

"Are we done, then?" she asks instead, scribbling *no pins* haphazardly onto the page. They have to be done. She's gotten this far, but she's not sure how much more she can take.

"Mm. I couldn't find my old X-rays," Dr. Rivers says. She hasn't taken off her gloves. Everything is smeared with blood, red and sticky. She touches Nought's ankle and rotates it slightly, the rope scraping over her sensitized flesh.

Nought barely manages to stay silent.

"It's very possible the pins are only on one side," Dr. Rivers continues, heedless of how Nought pants for breath. "Don't you think we should be thorough?"

No. No. She tries to picture an ankle, how it works, how it might break. She can't. She knows many things she can't explain, but anatomy, it seems, is not one of them.

But Dr. Rivers has said that their knowledge base is the same. That their minds are the same, though Nought's is—docile. Biddable. Less rigorous than the original, and more malleable, Dr. Rivers had said that the first day. So if Nought doesn't know how an ankle works, then Dr. Rivers doesn't know either, and—

"Nought."

"Another day. We can look another day," she says, desperate.

"That will only prolong your recovery," Dr. Rivers chides. "A longer time where I'll need to help you up the stairs to the bathroom every day, or else a return to the bucket. I don't think either of us wants that."

And Nought will need to sit here and take this all over again.

No more, she screams inside her head. Instead, she whispers, "Alright."

She is rewarded with a smile and a bloody pat against her knee. "There's a small chance that we'll want to test the other ankle as well. Given the mirroring of your organs. It may be that the pins are in the opposite ankle from mine." Before Nought can protest, the scalpel meets flesh again, and Dr. Rivers intones, "First incision on the lateral left ankle."

The pain roars back, worse than before.

Dimly, Nought registers a sound from beyond the basement. The door at the top of the stairs must be open, because she hears—what? It sounds like a knock. Penrose, perhaps, making something topple from a shelf?

Dr. Rivers doesn't look up. She only deepens the incision.

It feels like it should be impossible to hear anything over the pounding of her heart, the whimpers that are leaking from her throat, and yet she heard the knock, and she hears, a moment later, *footsteps.*

Somebody else in the house?

She opens her mouth to alert Dr. Rivers, but then the scalpel bites deep, too deep, too fast, and there is a startlingly new type of pain. She screams instead.

The footsteps quicken, become pounding, and now, finally, Dr. Rivers stills, head jerking up, gaze fixed over Nought's shoulder, on the staircase. Slowly, she sets the scalpel down and pushes her chair back.

"Stay put," she warns. "Don't speak."

Blood soaks the table below Nought's foot. Even without the blade cutting into her, everything is still agony. She's beginning to shake.

She nods.

Dr. Rivers strips her gloves off and tosses them onto the table, and Nought twists at the waist to watch, even though that prompts another wave of pain. Dr. Rivers mounts the steps as quickly as is safe. But she's not quick enough. She'd left the door at the top of the stairs open wide, and in that doorway towers a dark figure. Dr. Rivers stops a few steps short of it.

"Get out of my house," she says.

"No," the figure says. The voice is low, vicious, and it plucks at something in Nought's spine, some half-remembered, half-imagined dream. "I've let you get away with more than enough already."

"Then let's talk upstairs," Dr. Rivers says.

"No. Step aside."

"Mx. Woodfield—"

Nought tenses all over and starts scrabbling at the ropes. Her fingers slip in her own blood.

"*Now,* Dr. Rivers. Or I will forcibly move you out of the way."

Dr. Rivers says nothing, but Nought can hear her retreating back down the stairs. She's breathing hard. Nought is breathing harder. The ropes are all tied below the table surface, and she tugs at the closest one to rotate it, abrading her skin, even as she remains twisted, unable to look away.

Woodfield is dressed in a knife-sharp tailored suit, all in black, with a black shirt beneath a black tie. Her dark hair is swept back from her face.

She has a broad but fine-boned jaw, a nose that has been broken more than once, and a piercing gaze.

She is terrifying. She is dangerous. Nought can't look away.

And neither can Mx. Woodfield. Her gaze lights on Nought's face, her tangled hair, the bloody wreck of her ankle. All color drains from Mx. Woodfield. Her expression goes from cold frustration, to confusion, to horror, to anger. She's stock-still on the stairs for a long, terrible moment, and then she turns once more to look at Dr. Rivers.

"Start explaining," Mx. Woodfield snaps.

Dr. Rivers breathes audibly through her mouth, teeth bared, and steps in between the stairs and Nought but makes no move to help her. "As you can see," she says, voice clipped, "there is a localized pocket of distortion in this room. I've been—"

"That's not what I meant, and you know it. Stop evading." Woodfield jerks her jaw in Nought's direction, and at her side, her hand curls into a fist. She descends the rest of the way to the basement floor, shoes clicking on the cement. "How long has . . . *this* been going on?"

"The specimen is a recent development," Dr. Rivers says curtly. "My main priority has been the distortion. As instructed."

Mx. Woodfield walks in a wide arc around Dr. Rivers, gaze flicking briefly to the lengthening walls, the stretched stairs. But it always comes back to Nought, who can't stop shaking. The pain in her ankle is distant; Woodfield is the bigger danger, prowling closer and closer. "Why did you conceal your," her lips curl back over her teeth, "*specimen*?"

Derision drips from that single word, and Nought flinches. Her hands flex on the ropes. She tugs them again and the knot slides up against her leg to where she can reach it.

"It was unclear whether it was related to the larger issue," Dr. Rivers says.

Mx. Woodfield snorts and turns to her. "Don't treat me like an idiot, Tamsin. We've known each other too long."

The first knot gives way. The rope slides to the floor with a dull thump. Dr. Rivers shoots her a warning look, but Nought ignores it; she needs to get away. She leans forward to work on the second, even though it makes her hips and calves burn, her ankle shriek as the skin tugs around the incisions.

Mx. Woodfield's gaze returns to her, piercing and direct. "What has she done to you?"

Nought freezes.

"You do not have to answer her," snaps Dr. Rivers. "This is my investigation, Woodfield. You speak to me, not it."

"*It*," Woodfield repeats with that same disgust. She steps around the table to better see Nought, her brown eyes flicking between her face and the blood that still oozes from the incisions in her ankle.

Nought shakes her head. *Don't look at me. Ignore me.* The weight of Woodfield's regard is crushing. She reaches out, reflexively, toward Dr. Rivers, as if the woman could protect her. Could resist Woodfield, could keep Nought safe the way she's tried to up until now.

"It's coming with me," Mx. Woodfield declares, reaching for the rope binding down Nought's knees.

"Lachlan, don't." Dr. Rivers's voice breaks, as if she's frightened, but Woodfield isn't looking at her. Nought is, and can see the gleam of the scalpel in her fist.

Please, she thinks. *Please, don't let Woodfield take me.* But that scalpel is still red with *her* blood, isn't it? And if Dr. Rivers makes Woodfield leave, she'll only tie Nought back down, cut into her again.

Which is worse?

The rope gives way, and Lachlan Woodfield reaches for her. Nought jerks back along the table, sliding in her own blood, looking between Lachlan and Dr. Rivers.

Lachlan pauses, gloved hand hovering over her right knee.

Dr. Rivers lunges.

The scalpel comes down, plunging into the meat of Lachlan's left arm. Nought covers her mouth with her hands and bites down a shriek, but Lachlan doesn't scream. She doesn't so much as flinch, instead rounding on Dr. Rivers in an instant and grabbing her wrist. The scalpel clatters to the ground as Lachlan shoves Dr. Rivers back into the nearest wall, her other arm braced below her jaw. There is no blood spattering onto the floor. No sign that Lachlan has been hurt at all.

But Nought saw the blow connect. Knows exactly how deep that blade can cut.

"Stop!" she cries.

Both of them look at her, and for a moment, it looks like Lachlan is distracted enough that Dr. Rivers will be able to get free. But then Lachlan delivers a blow to her belly, and Dr. Rivers goes limp, gasping for breath.

She needs me. Shaking, Nought swings her legs over the side of the table, but her head spins, and she has to clutch onto the edge to steady herself.

Lachlan twitches toward her, then seems to reconsider, dismissing her as a threat. She leans harder into Dr. Rivers instead, whose face is going red from the pressure. She tears at Lachlan's wrist.

"The specimen," Lachlan growls, "is property of Myrica Dynamics. What I've found here is unacceptable. I am going to take this *thing* into one of the secure labs, and then I am going to come back and deal with you. If you are not waiting here for me, ready to behave and explain, I will have you taken elsewhere for round-the-clock monitoring. Do you understand me?"

"You need me," Dr. Rivers rasps. "Can't—disappear me—"

"Don't confuse my personal affection for you with mercy," Lachlan says. "I will clean up your mess however it needs to be handled. *Do you understand me?*"

Nought is the mess. She bites down hard on her lip, hoping the pain will clear her head, and pushes up and off the table as silently as she can.

Dr. Rivers is aglow with fury. But she nods, the motion constrained by how firmly Lachlan's arm pins her to the wall. "I understand."

"I want all records you've kept on this room ready to be turned over when I get back. I will review them and decide when and how any additional information that may assist the team will be disclosed. This is no longer up to your judgment. Any of it."

"You can't take me off the team. Not so soon after the press conference. The city needs to see I'm still involved."

Lachlan cocks her head. "For now," she says.

The floor is cold beneath Nought's feet, and there's no weapon close at hand. But she can still be of use, if she can just get close. A distraction. She lurches forward, letting go of the table, but when her blood-slicked foot touches the floor, the pain lancing up her leg makes her knee buckle. She goes down hard, trying to swallow a scream of pain and failing utterly.

Dr. Rivers needs me, Nought thinks again, but Lachlan has dropped her, and there's nothing Nought can do to help. The scalpel is too far away. She can't stand.

Lachlan stands over her, the lines of her dark suit still immaculate. Her gaze flicks once more to Nought's ankle, and then, seemingly coming to a conclusion, she kneels and reaches for her.

Nought scrabbles back until she's pressed against the table leg.

It's not enough distance. Lachlan grabs Nought, hauling her into her arms. One of them is corded with muscle, tangible even through the wool of her jacket. The other is—something else, something hard and unyielding. Neither trembles as Lachlan rises to her feet, cradling Nought against her broad chest.

It doesn't hurt. When Dr. Rivers touches her, it always seems to hurt.

"Are you going to fight me, too?" Lachlan murmurs into her ear.

Nought should. She *should*.

Lachlan terrifies her, but her ankle hurts so much, and what will fighting get her aside from further injury?

Dr. Rivers only glares at the both of them, no trace of worry in her eyes. No gratitude, no fear for Nought's safety. She doesn't command *Don't touch her* a second time. She gives no orders to either of them.

And that *does* hurt. She's been abandoned all over. She's failed, somehow.

"No," Nought says, barely more than a whisper.

Lachlan inclines her head in what might be gratitude, and then begins the climb up the stairs.

Below them both, Dr. Rivers does not look away, rage seething in her eyes.

Chapter Thirty-Two

Nought sits in the back of a car. The interior is pristine dark leather, and she is handcuffed. She has been strapped in so that her legs stretch out the length of the seat, with the ankle Dr. Rivers cut into wrapped with Lachlan's tie and propped up on a rolled towel.

In the front seat, Lachlan is silent.

They've been driving for ten minutes, maybe more. The city scrolls by past the windows, and Nought doesn't care. Instead, she keeps her gaze fixed on the bit of Lachlan's head that she can see, convinced that the moment she looks away, that's when Lachlan will act.

She can still see, *hear*, Lachlan's fist connecting with Dr. Rivers's stomach. Her body is wracked with fine tremors, and her breathing has barely steadied since she left the house. Her ankle is still a blaze of pain, though the car moves smoothly enough not to jar it.

Lachlan hasn't hurt her, she reminds herself. Bandaged her wound, yes, and restrained her, but she hasn't hurt her. Maybe because Nought has cooperated, whereas Dr. Rivers didn't? But even if Lachlan hasn't hurt her yet, that doesn't mean pain isn't coming.

Property of Myrica Dynamics. Unacceptable. Secure lab.

Lachlan clears her throat.

Nought jerks as if struck, the seat belt hard against her chest. The car glides through an intersection. Lachlan doesn't glance back at her.

"What should I call you?" Lachlan asks. She sounds reluctant. Like speaking to Nought is a risk she doesn't want to take.

Nought can sympathize. She doesn't want to answer, even if she knows better than to disobey.

"Dr. Rivers named me Nought," she says after a strained delay. Her voice is unsteady. Weak. Lachlan's hands tense on the wheel, leather squeaking against leather.

"Did she explain why?" she asks after an extended silence.

"I'm a blank slate. No memories."

There's a small, horizontal mirror toward the front of the car, and if Nought moves her head just right, she can see Lachlan's eyes. Her brow is furrowed now. "None at all?"

"Not before a few days ago," she says.

That doesn't ease Lachlan's expression. If anything, it darkens further. Her hands flex again, and Nought recoils, looking away from the mirror.

"Is that when Dr. Rivers says you—arrived?"

Answering accurately and succinctly should end the conversation soonest. "Yes," she says, because that is what Dr. Rivers told her. It doesn't matter that she's still not entirely sure she believes it. The hazy certainty that she knows the upper floor of the house, when she's never actually seen it, remains in the back of her mind. "Before that, everything's . . . murky."

Lachlan hums, and it's a shockingly benign sound. Like she's only curious, isn't angry or disgusted. Nought looks up, wanting to see Lachlan's expression, and is met by Lachlan staring at her in the mirror.

"What happened to your eye?"

Nought opens her mouth, then shuts it, thinking back to the bloodstained ropes. "I don't know," she says finally. "Dr. Rivers said it was like that when she found me. I don't remember anything different."

"Does it hurt?"

"Sometimes. But it's healing well. No infection." She brushes one of the bandages with her knuckles, then jerks her hand away. Dr. Rivers was very clear that she shouldn't touch anything near the wound. Nought shifts uneasily in her seat at the memory, then decides to take a chance. "Where are we going?"

"Someplace safe," Lachlan replies. "What else has Dr. Rivers figured out about you?"

Someplace safe. Said so offhandedly, it might be a lie, or it might be simple truth. *Someplace safe,* and not *the lab,* and what if Lachlan really doesn't intend to hurt her?

What if Dr. Rivers was wrong?

(Wrong? Or lying?)

Abruptly, she wants the car to stop moving, but can't find the strength to demand it. The city outside the windows is too much now, too big, and her world has finally tilted too far off its axis.

"Nought?" Lachlan prompts, and Nought realizes she's pressed her face into the seat, hiding her good eye.

"Why were you at the house?" she asks. "She said you had a meeting this afternoon."

"We did. I didn't trust her to be as put together as she sounded. I decided to make a house call, to get a sense of where things stood before she could craft the narrative."

That makes no sense; Dr. Rivers has always been perfectly in control of herself. Nought wants to argue, but if Lachlan hadn't come when she did, Nought might still be on that table. Certainly still in the basement.

The silence stretches again. Lachlan sighs. "The more you can share with me, the better I can help you. Talk to me."

Help. Yes, Nought needs help.

Her voice shakes when she says, "She's determined that we're functionally identical in most ways."

"Most?"

"We differ on some personality indices, and she said that my anatomy is the reverse of what it should be. Like a mirror image." Nought takes a deep, shuddering breath and pulls away from the seat back. "But beyond that, I'm familiar with the same concepts she is, for her work. I have the same facility with mathematics. I have what she called *procedural memory*; I know how to cook, even though I've never been taught. I even know where things in the house are, most of the time." It gets easier, the more she says. Her breathing steadies. "We haven't run many tests, though. Some of these are just assumptions for now. Dr. Rivers was far more concerned with the subsidence question."

Lachlan grunts. "But you have no sense of personal history."

"Or cultural." She risks a glance out the window. This time, it's less overwhelming, though still difficult to understand. "Did you know grain bowls are considered more appropriate for breakfast than chili?" Dr. Rivers hadn't been amused at her choice this morning, and she flushes slightly with the confession.

"Depends on the person." The car slows, then pulls off onto a patch of ground covered in split asphalt. The plants here are very different from the ones in Dr. Rivers's manicured garden. They are scraggly and brown, crunching as the wheels come to rest on where they emerge from the crevices.

It's a strange, open space in the middle of a dense thicket of buildings. People walk by hurriedly on another part of the street, but not here. She doesn't know what that means.

Lachlan gets out of the car.

Nought stiffens and watches as she circles around, then gets something from the trunk. When she opens the door by Nought's feet, she's holding a small kit, which she sets in the footwell.

Nought pulls her good leg in reflexively. She tries to move the injured one, but it hurts too much.

"I'm going to stitch up these lacerations," Lachlan tells her, unrolling a fresh towel and placing it below Nought's ankle. Her touches are quick and practical, never lingering. She lays out a packaged, pre-threaded needle, a fresh roll of bandages. A small vial and syringe. A packet of wipes of some kind that stink with some sharp substance when she breaks the seal.

It's a more thorough setup than Dr. Rivers had, Nought thinks, gut twisting in delayed horror.

"You don't need to watch," Lachlan says. "I'm going to give you an anesthetic. You won't feel anything." She pauses a moment, then ventures, "I take it Dr. Rivers didn't do the same?"

"No." Her voice is barely audible, and she clears her throat, tries again. "We didn't have anything like that available."

"And she doesn't have the experience." Lachlan takes a deep breath, then leans in and across Nought, reaching for something in the front seat. Nought holds very still. "Here, I have something to keep you occupied." She sits back on her heels and pushes a tablet into Nought's hands. "While I handle this, I want you to log in to Dr. Rivers's work account, via this app." She gestures, but her glove doesn't interact with the capacitive touch screen. Nought taps it instead. It's awkward, with the cuffs on.

"I've never done this," she says quickly, and it's the same defensive impulse from before. Dr. Rivers was merely cold when she failed; she doesn't know how Lachlan will respond.

"I understand. Please try."

Nought's hands tighten on the tablet, but she nods and watches the app load. Maybe it will be like cooking. Like other procedural memories she possesses somewhere below the level of personal narration. There can't be cultural significance to her choices here, right?

There's a rustle from near her feet, and she peeks over the tablet to see Lachlan stripping off her leather gloves.

Her left hand is made of a hard, dark material Tamsin can't identify.

It moves with nearly identical dexterity to the other, made of flesh and blood, as Lachlan tugs purple surgical gloves on instead.

"Is that why she didn't hurt you?" Nought asks.

Lachlan glances up, then nods curtly. She unwraps the blood-stiffened tie from Nought's ankle, regarding the injuries with clear distaste.

"Reckless," she mutters, reaching for one of the wipes. "This is butchery, not exploration. Why didn't you try to stop her?"

Nought feels her cheeks heat, though she doesn't understand why she should feel as embarrassed as Lachlan's response implies. "Dr. Rivers said that she has pins in her ankle from a previous surgery. We wanted to see if I had them, too, or if we differ in that regard."

Lachlan frowns. "Tamsin Rivers has never had surgery on her ankle."

"But she said—"

"I have access to all of her medical files. Including the full-body scans done on her just last week. There are no medical implants of any sort in her body, and she knows that."

Nought winces as the wipe glides over the first incision, the one barely held shut by inadequate butterfly closures. It stings, and a concept wells up from below: antiseptic, isopropyl alcohol. Lachlan's jaw tightens into something adjacent to a snarl as she dabs around the cuts, but she's gentle as she eases Nought's ankle over to clean the other side. Angry at Dr. Rivers, not at Nought. "Almost through the painful part. Are you *certain* she did this just to—see what was inside?"

Of course she did; Dr. Rivers possesses a deep and terrible curiosity. Nought shares it, after all. And Lachlan must surely know that about Dr. Rivers already.

But then a thought occurs to her, seizes her in shredding jaws. Nought grips the tablet harder. "Yesterday, I went outside," she says, then stops.

Maybe she's wrong. Maybe she's overreacting. Lachlan seems primed to believe the worst of Dr. Rivers, but then there's how Dr. Rivers had so casually brought up checking the other ankle as well, and—

"She hobbled you," Lachlan says, voicing Nought's fear. "I have known her to be . . . heedless of ethics, when necessary," she continues, shifting where she crouches outside the car. "It's practically what we hired her for. But this is extreme, even for her."

"I could be wrong," she says, words rushed.

Lachlan reaches for the small glass vial and draws a measure of clear liquid into the syringe. "You're not," she says. "This is the anesthetic. It will hurt going in, but only for a moment."

Nought watches the needle pierce her skin, the way she watched Dr. Rivers cut into her, sickly fascinated and unable to look away in case something worse happens while she's not paying attention. Such a small sting against the throbbing pain of the incisions. Lachlan's hand moves on the plunger, and there is a bloom of cold that quickly heats to a burning itch.

The needle withdraws. Re-angles into a different bit of flesh. Again and again, and in its wake, a tingling numbness. Nought absently touches the bandage by her missing eye, wondering if it would help there, too.

It's so much kinder than what Dr. Rivers did to her. "Do you have medical training?" Nought asks, fascinated.

"In a fashion. More than Dr. Rivers." Lachlan sets the needle aside, then glances up. "The tablet, please."

It takes effort to look down at the screen. But when she does, she's seized by a ghostly familiarity. Her fingers fly across the glass. She knows the feeling of the codes she inputs. She knows the layout of the app, like she's done this a hundred times. The screen prompts *Confirm?* and she taps in one final, unasked-for sequence.

The app unfolds into a sprawling workspace. She's never seen it before, but she knows how to navigate it.

"It let me in," Nought says. She turns the tablet to face Lachlan, whose jaw clenches. Her hands cease stitching; she's halfway done with one side of Nought's ankle already, a line of neat sutures marching up the skin, hiding away the meat inside.

"Dr. Rivers hasn't logged in to this segment of her workstation for five days now," Lachlan says. That look is back on her face. Horror, perhaps, but—but something else, too. Resignation?

"What does that mean?" Nought asks.

Lachlan's grip on her ankle shifts, just a little, nitrile rubbing against swollen flesh.

"It means," she says, "that you're not the copy."

Chapter Thirty-Three

Lachlan refuses to elaborate as she finishes stitching Nought's ankle, then wraps it properly in fresh bandages. She's gone deep inside herself, to where Nought can't follow. Instead, Nought is left to stare at her hands, the numbness seeming to spread up her leg and into her chest, her heart, her head.

You're not the copy.

The thought is so impossible it almost makes her laugh. She barely notices Lachlan closing her door, or retaking the driver's seat, or pulling them out of the lot. She tries to imagine herself in Dr. Rivers's shoes, her fine clothes, with her effortless command of her environment. Her cruelty and her brilliance.

It's difficult, but not impossible.

Still, she can't conceive of what that might mean. If she's the original, if she used to be identical to Dr. Rivers, then what happened? What could have erased her so completely? Her delight in being in the yard the previous day, her wonder at the wide expanse of the world, was laughable. Pathetic. False, even, because it wasn't new. If she's the original, she's gone out into this world thousands of times.

But regardless of what she might have once done, it *was* new, wasn't it? Entirely real, and important, to herself in that moment. Past is not present. Certainly, most people have continuity. But she doesn't. It's that simple. She is who she is at this moment, and nothing more. What might have been can't matter, because she has no way of grasping it.

"Tamsin," Lachlan says. Nought's head jerks up, as if on a string. *Tamsin*, not *Nought*, and it fits. As if the world is finally beginning to make sense again. Her fingers splay in her lap, tracing out the letters. They have the feel of something long practiced, more than the cooking, more than differential equations.

Tamsin, she repeats to herself. *I'm Tamsin.* She can't be Dr. Rivers, but perhaps she can be Tamsin. It's as good a name as any.

"Yes?"

"You're under my direct care and supervision now. You're going to do as I ask, and in turn, I'm going to keep you safe. Do you understand?"

Safe. That word again. It's soft padding over the steel in Lachlan's voice. Her question is not for permission, only to ascertain if Tamsin is going to cooperate. "Yes," she says. She inspects the concept and finds it comforting, though the thought occurs—"You mean to keep me like a pet?"

Lachlan runs a hand over her hair. It barely moves for the product in it. "Care to elaborate?"

"Safety in return for a managed existence. Like Penrose."

"One of your cats," Lachlan translates.

"The cat," Tamsin corrects. "There's only one."

Lachlan returns her hand to the wheel, tapping at it. "Right," she says after a moment. "I suppose so, yes. Like a pet. Does that bother you?"

"Not really. Should it?" Penrose gets water, food, a safe place to live. He's comfortable and secure. Dr. Rivers doesn't pay him much attention, true, but does Tamsin actually *want* attention? Dr. Rivers's attention wasn't always pleasant, after all.

On the whole, it seems like a reasonable arrangement.

"I think that's a question for later." The car slows, and Lachlan turns into a discreet garage entrance beneath a building so tall that Tamsin can't see the top before they disappear into the earth. There's a gate blocking the driveway that raises as Lachlan nears; it must recognize the car. Inside, everything is sleek and well lit, and Lachlan navigates to a particular spot. The gate closes behind them.

The cars Tamsin saw parked along the sides of the streets on the way here were tucked in tight together, nose to tail. Here, the cars are arranged side by side, with wide gaps between them. Not nearly as efficient.

Lachlan parks. Once again, she goes for the trunk first, but this time, she comes back to the door by Tamsin's head, not her feet. When she opens the door, Tamsin can see a tightly packed nest of rods that, under Lachlan's practiced touch, opens into a small wheelchair.

"I keep it for emergencies," she explains, reaching in to unbuckle Tamsin. "More useful than crutches, at this point. I'm going to lift you again."

Tamsin nods, distracted by what Lachlan might mean by *at this point*, and allows herself to be shifted from the car into the chair. The air is cold, but the parking garage cuts the wind. She only shivers a little as Lachlan closes up the car.

"Here," Lachlan says and crouches down to undo her handcuffs.

"Is this the lab?" Tamsin asks, her throat finally unsticking.

Lachlan pockets the cuffs and circles around behind her. "I'm going to push the chair now. Just relax back into me. No, this isn't the lab." They make their way toward the nearby wall and door, Lachlan's hands curled around the top of the low chair back. There aren't any push handles, Tamsin notes belatedly. The user is meant to move the chair herself.

"Did I know you use a chair?" Tamsin asks, craning her head back.

"No. It's not something I disclose if I can help it. It's a potential liability in my line of work."

Tamsin purses her lips. "What is your line of work? Dr. Rivers only said that you were dangerous. But she talks to you every night, doesn't she?"

"I'm her handler, among other things." A pause, as they reach a metal door, and Lachlan presses a button on the wall. "Your handler, technically. You're employed by a large technology corporation called Myrica Dynamics. I help things run smoothly."

There's something going unsaid there, but Tamsin can't untangle it on her own. So she asks, "*Are* you dangerous?"

"Very," Lachlan says.

A small *ding* follows on the word, and the doors roll open. *Elevator,* her mind supplies from some dusty recess. Lachlan wheels her inside, then presses a fob to a reader. She hits the topmost button. The elevator doors slide shut and they begin to rise, the acceleration so smooth that Tamsin almost doesn't notice it.

When she does, she looks down reflexively. But of course Lachlan doesn't live *down*. Dr. Rivers didn't, either. Still, with each floor they climb past, she grows a little more antsy, a little more unsure of what to expect when the elevator finally opens again.

Lachlan doesn't seem to notice. "Myrica Dynamics operates in multiple spheres, not all of them official, and not all of them strictly legal," she says. "You were aware of that in general, though not the specifics. For you, I'm here to make sure you stay on task and to assist you in anything you need help with that may be unobtainable or risky to ask for through normal corporate channels."

"Do you handle other people?"

"Not to the same degree of intimacy."

The elevator glides to an elegant halt. The doors open not onto a hallway, which Tamsin vaguely expected, but into a foyer with recessed lighting, sleek cabinets, a bench, a door, and a wide hallway leading deeper into what she realizes is one large apartment. *Penthouse*, that same dusty corner supplies.

"Is this your home?" she asks.

Lachlan steps away from the chair. Her jaw works for a moment. "Yes."

"I've never been here before," Tamsin guesses.

"Nobody has."

Every line of Lachlan's body is wound tight, sharp and full of barely restrained violence. She paces back over to Tamsin, a predator down to the sinews.

Tamsin doesn't recoil. She wants to reach out and touch instead, curious what she'd feel like.

"Come on," Lachlan says. "Let's get you cleaned up. Then we can talk about what happens next."

The door off the foyer leads to a large bathroom. The shower stall is wide, with a plastic chair in the center of it, and the showerhead on a flexible metal hose mounted to the wall nearby. There's no tile, no grout to scrub blood out of, and there's a large cabinet that, as Lachlan opens it, Tamsin realizes is entirely dedicated to more medical supplies.

"How often do you come home injured?"

Lachlan throws her a look over her shoulder, a warning. "Enough," she says.

She retrieves a handful of things and fills a bowl with warm water. Then she shrugs out of her suit jacket and strips off her leather gloves to once more replace them with purple nitrile. She crouches in front of Tamsin, taking hold of her bandaged ankle.

"Is it hurting again?" she asks, wiping away the dried blood still staining her foot, then producing a plastic bag and securing it over her calf up above the top edge of the bandages.

"No," she says, "though it's not as numb as it was."

Lachlan stands and snags a plastic bottle off the counter. She tips a pill into Tamsin's hand, then fills a cup with water from the sink. "Painkiller," she says. "Better to take it now."

The little pill does not look like what Dr. Rivers has been giving her. She pinches it between her fingers, peering at it, then swallows it quickly, before she can second-guess.

Once she's swallowed half the cup of water, she says, "Dr. Rivers medicated me as well. She never said what the pills were, but they made me drowsy."

"I'd assume she was giving you the sleep aid and the anxiety meds that you—she—the doctors prescribed for *one* of you." Lachlan's voice is a frustrated mutter by the time she's done speaking. "Not that we're likely to ever know which it was."

"I doubt it was me. She didn't like me going outside, remember?"

Lachlan doesn't reply to that, but her gaze drops to Tamsin's ankle, then back up to her face.

"Let me see your eye."

Tamsin nods, then reaches for the bandages. Lachlan beats her there. She mostly uses her right hand to undo the fasteners, left hand held clear of Tamsin's hair. Tamsin peers at it, at the fine jointing mechanisms in the fingers still faintly visible through the nitrile. There's no skin equivalent covering those joints, and she realizes they would likely catch and pull at her hair even with the glove, if Lachlan used that hand for this.

The bandages slither loose. Lachlan, with a proprietary gentleness, eases the gauze pad away from Tamsin's eye socket. She takes a sharp breath when she can see the pit and the discharge Tamsin can feel crusted at the inside corner and along the lower lid.

"Fucker," Lachlan mutters.

"Is it bad?"

"Better than the work on your ankle, but only barely. A doctor—"

"No doctors," Tamsin says quickly.

Lachlan lets go of her face and leans back against the counter, careful not to touch anything with her hands. "Why no doctors?"

"If I'm on record as missing an eye, Dr. Rivers can't go out in public."

"Strategically, that could be to our advantage. It would establish you incontrovertibly as the real Tamsin Rivers." She goes back to the cabinet, fishing out a packaged single-use syringe with no needle and a bottle labeled *saline wound wash*. "And once she's in custody, she'll only be seen by Myrica-associated physicians under NDAs. People who know what she is."

Tamsin grimaces. "You can't lock her up. She has work to do. Work I can't do. Public appearances, for the city."

"You said your . . . procedural knowledge is as good as hers," Lachlan says, filling the syringe. "Even with the memory loss, you can resume your place. I have no doubt."

Tamsin shakes her head too violently. She hisses at the stab of pain and touches her temple. "There's too much to get me up to speed on. I know nothing, and she knows everything. She knows it well enough you barely knew the difference between us."

Lachlan's expression darkens. "I knew something was wrong," she says bitterly. "You'll forgive me if I didn't anticipate *this*."

"Could you say for sure when the change happened? When you stopped talking to me and started talking to her?" Tamsin presses. "Even in hindsight?"

Lachlan's jaw grinds from side to side. "Yes." She takes a deep breath, then concedes, "Probably. But only because you made a miraculous recovery after a few days of being too drugged up to talk to me outside of text messages. If anything, she's better at being the you I was familiar with than you were, in those last few days."

"And now? How good am I at being the me you knew?"

"Terrible." She scrubs a hand over her face, then seems to remember the gloves she's wearing. She changes them out for a fresh set, then reaches for Tamsin, cupping her jaw and angling her head as she aims the syringe. "But she can do the work from an isolated lab. She doesn't need to run loose."

Tamsin shakes her head again, jarring Lachlan's hold on her chin. "No. No, she's doing outreach. Political work. She has a meeting soon, with James . . . Dunford?"

Lachlan stiffens again, lip twitching toward a snarl. There's a small scar cutting into the left side of her mouth. "Who runs Myrica Dynamics's main competitor. Cara set that up, I take it?"

Tamsin doesn't know who that is. All she knows is that removing Dr. Rivers from play, unilaterally, won't end well.

"I should never have left her," Lachlan says. "Hold still."

The wash of saline is room temperature, but it feels cold, so cold Tamsin wants to flinch away. She doesn't, even as her heart races in her chest. The saline stings in places and runs down her cheek. Lachlan huffs and reaches, belatedly, for a gauze pad to mop it away.

Then she squeezes a pale paste onto one finger. "Antiseptic," she says and braces Tamsin's chin again. "This will probably feel strange."

And it does, skin-warmed nitrile swiping along the inside of the socket, into her skull, into what her brain screams is *her*. Tamsin bites back a gasp and trembles, holding onto the arms of the wheelchair tightly until Lachlan pulls away. It can't be more than thirty seconds, but it feels like a small eternity.

"There," Lachlan says, leaning back and letting go of her face. "That will have to do for now." She looks at the shower, then at Tamsin, then out to the foyer. Her mind is clearly on Dr. Rivers. On wanting to go after her, stick her in a little box, fix the problem.

But Lachlan doesn't leave.

"You're right, I can't lock her up," Lachlan concedes stiffly. Even without her suit jacket, her chest and shoulders are broad and imposing, and right now, they're tense. "I need to know more about the plans she has in progress before I can move." She groans and strips off her gloves, rubbing at her temple. "Let's—get you cleaned up and sorted first, and then I'll start making calls."

She goes back to the cabinet and withdraws a pair of gleaming scissors.

Tamsin recoils instinctively. Lachlan catches the movement and sets the shears down on the sink. "Your hair," she says. "It's only going to get more matted the longer it's left like that. Did she keep you from caring for yourself?"

Her pulse slowing again, Tamsin shrugs. "I suppose so," she admits after a moment's thought. "But I didn't know to ask. I just thought it was another difference between us. Like the eye."

Lachlan grimaces. "It started awhile back," she says. "I should have said something sooner. You never used to let yourself get this way."

Tamsin reaches up, tugs at the rough, thick tangle of a plait. "I'm sorry."

That makes Lachlan twitch, and she takes the scissors in hand again and moves around behind Tamsin. She takes the braid from Tamsin's fingers; Tamsin lets her. "Don't apologize," she says. "I can fix this, at least."

The scissors are loud as they slice through her hair. Her head feels lighter, and she closes her eye as Lachlan tosses the braid aside and runs her hand through the remaining length from scalp to ends. Her fingers catch in a few places, but the knots give quickly.

Another few snicks of the scissors, more passes of Lachlan's hand, and Tamsin's head drops back. It feels . . . good. Firm, but warm. She hasn't been touched like this before.

"There," Lachlan says, voice rougher than before. Tamsin peeks up at her and finds her eyes half-lidded, gaze heavy on Tamsin's face. "I'll send out for some hair products, but what I've got should be an okay start. Ready to get washed up?"

Tamsin nods and tugs the hem of her shirt, maneuvering it up and over her head. When Tamsin can see again, Lachlan is turned away, hand on the doorframe.

"Do you think you can get yourself between the chairs?" she asks. Her voice is tight.

Tamsin frowns.

"Does nudity bother you?" Tamsin asks. "I don't mind if you stay." She considers a moment, then rephrases. "I *want* you to stay."

Lachlan's hand twitches. But she does turn around and come to Tamsin's side once more. Tamsin strips out of her bra, and Lachlan helps with the rest, touch clinical, gaze averted. She looks undeniably embarrassed; Tamsin wonders why she didn't just say *yes* and leave. There's a faint reddening across her cheeks as she helps Tamsin into the shower chair.

"I'm going to get you more clothing," Lachlan says as soon as Tamsin is seated. She's gone before Tamsin can argue, taking the folding wheelchair with her.

Chapter Thirty-Four

Lachlan returns a minute or two after Tamsin shuts off the water. Tamsin assumes it's intentional; it's given her enough time to grab the nearest towel and rub herself dry with it, perched on the very edge of the shower chair to get at her lower back and thighs. As a courtesy, Tamsin holds the towel around herself as Lachlan enters, pushing a different wheelchair. It looks sturdier and like it's seen more use.

Once Tamsin is dressed in what must be Lachlan's loose shorts and oversized shirt, and seated in the new chair, Lachlan takes the time to comb out her hair. Tamsin tries to tell her not to bother, but Lachlan ignores her. It's not long enough to braid anymore, so she tucks it back behind Tamsin's ears, out of her face, then tapes a thick square of gauze over her eye. It's much more manageable than the bandage wrapping that Dr. Rivers had employed, and it's more *care* than Dr. Rivers ever extended to her. A bubble of what feels like grief rises up below her diaphragm. It's alien and overwhelming. She shuts her remaining eye against it.

"Tamsin?"

"I thought she had my best interests at heart," she says. Her voice is thick. "We're the same person after all. We have the same goals. The same interests."

"You may operate on the same rules, but your initial inputs are different. You're working from different knowledge bases. With different concerns. Who you are is . . . contextual." Lachlan shrugs. "Come on. Let's get you somewhere more comfortable."

Lachlan shows her how to steer the chair and move on her own. It's exhausting; she doesn't have the upper-body strength for it. But at Lachlan's instruction, she precedes her through the entryway and out into the apartment proper.

The room they emerge into is sprawling, with a kitchen tucked along one edge, a low, plush couch in front of a wide-screen TV, and an entire wall of plate glass, looking out at the city below. Where Dr. Rivers's home was colorless, glossy and manicured and barely lived in, Lachlan's apartment somehow manages to be cozy. It's still spotless and beautiful, but there's art on the wall, movie posters, an eclectic mix that feels organic. And the couch looks comfortably broken in.

But all of that fades as Tamsin realizes just how high up they are and pushes herself closer to the windows, transfixed.

It's impossible to see people from this far away. They're barely even specks. But she can track what she realizes must be cars, maneuvering through the streets below. She can see the tops of other buildings, crowned in pump houses and receiving towers, a patchwork of tile and white paint and the occasional riot of greenery. People keep gardens on their roofs?

Her eye hurts as she struggles to understand the distance, the *scale*, of everything she's seeing.

"Pretty different from the basement that thing was keeping you in," Lachlan says, softly, at her side. Her hands are in her pockets, sleeves folded up to her elbows. Her left forearm is made of the same material as her hand, and Tamsin can't see where it meets skin. "Unintended benefit, but hopefully it helps."

Tamsin nods, but she isn't sure. Beneath the wonder, she still feels uneasy, like she had in the elevator. There's just so much space, and it feels as if the building might tilt at any moment.

She wheels herself away from the window and over to the sitting area. Lachlan watches approvingly as she shifts herself out of the chair and onto the couch, then helps her prop up her ankle on a cushion.

"I'd offer you a drink," Lachlan says, going over to what turns out to be a liquor cabinet against one of the solid walls, "but it won't mix well with your meds. Do you mind?"

"No," Tamsin says, watching as she retrieves a glass and a bottle, uncaps the latter. For all of the danger etched into Lachlan's sinews, she has been shockingly careful and gentle with Tamsin, even when she hauled

Tamsin out of the basement. But since deciding that Tamsin must be the original, she's softened even further. Become more open, more . . . *doting*, almost. Perhaps it isn't that Dr. Rivers was not kind to Tamsin, but that Lachlan is far more kind than makes sense.

Who you are is contextual.

Tamsin watches her fill her glass, then says, "If I'm not aware of being the original, if I've changed so much, if she fits the definition better than I do—does it matter?"

Lachlan pauses, then tips more whiskey into her glass. "Yes," she says, capping the bottle and shoving it aside. "Yes, it matters."

"Why? Because I was technically here first?"

"Because your existence isn't tied to a physics-defying catastrophe. I find that much easier to trust. And because you've been harmed."

Tamsin shakes her head. "No. Not until today."

"And your eye? That's not harm?"

She reaches up to touch the gauze. "I don't know," she says. "And if I don't know, if I don't remember—"

"Don't ask me if it matters." Lachlan swallows half her drink in a single go. "Though I suppose I'm glad you don't remember whatever it was. Small mercies." She eyes the bottle as if considering refilling her glass, then comes over to a nearby chair instead, dropping into it heavily. Her movements are stiff, and she seems exhausted, though it's barely early afternoon. "*You* are my charge."

"Not my productivity?"

Lachlan grimaces and takes a sip. "Don't."

Tamsin leans forward. "If there weren't two of me, if I'd just had a—a medical event that left me amnesiac, would you still be tasked with watching over me? Or would your employer, my employer, cut me loose once I was of no more use to them?"

"But there are two of you." She throws back the rest of her glass. Tamsin thinks she's regretting not topping it up before. "And I've known you longer."

But she doesn't know Tamsin now.

"So what do you intend to do?" Tamsin pushes. "I think swapping us back is unlikely."

"Is it? It worked once, whatever happened." But Lachlan shakes her head, sitting back, sprawled with her legs wide, elbows braced on the chair arms. "No, for now I just start with observation. We let Dr. Rivers continue working on the subsidence project and keep an eye out for any-thing *else* she might be attempting in the meantime. You were right; if she can make progress on the subsidence, that's valuable."

"And what happens if she solves the problem? If she doesn't cause any other trouble?"

It's possible, even likely. Lachlan needs to face that, accept that. Tamsin has. Swapping them back seems fair on the surface, but it wouldn't be that simple.

It probably would be a disaster.

Lachlan frowns into her empty glass, then sets it aside. She drags her-self upright and goes over to the kitchen, a direction Tamsin cannot see from where she sits without twisting in place. Even then, she catches only glimpses. "We'll handle that when we get there," Lachlan says. "Now, what do you want to eat?"

There aren't many options, but the canned soup that Tamsin picks is bet-ter than a meal replacement. While Tamsin eats, Lachlan places a series of phone calls. She paces the apartment as she talks, and Tamsin only catches maybe a third of what is said. At a certain point, Lachlan shuts herself behind a door, and Tamsin hears nothing at all.

Outside, the day creeps onward. There are no shadows to lengthen as the sun passes overhead, but the color of the sky changes. The view down is still dizzying, and she can't look for long without fatigue, but it keeps drawing her back, over and over.

Eventually, the pain medication combines with her exhaustion, and she dozes. It's nearly evening when she wakes; Lachlan is sitting nearby, gaze fixed on her face. Tamsin stares back.

"She's behaving herself," Lachlan says. "And has asked to move back to working in her office. I've allowed it. Her assistant will be keeping close tabs on her; it seemed more appropriate to have her somewhere she could be watched."

"That's a good idea," Tamsin agrees, even as she wonders if that means

Dr. Rivers has given up on the basement. Her interest had always seemed perfunctory; she'd been much more concerned with Tamsin herself. Without Tamsin, the basement has lost its relevance.

She eases herself upright, head still foggy with sleep. Her ankle is starting to hurt again. Her head's constant ache returns, gentler than usual but still persistent.

She doesn't ask for another pill.

Lachlan gives her a brief tour. Bathroom, the door to her bedroom, the door to Tamsin's. She doesn't open either of the latter, says she's still tidying. Getting it fit for company.

For dinner, Lachlan orders out.

"I can cook," Tamsin says. The counters in the kitchen are lower than in Dr. Rivers's house, she's noticed; reachable from the chair.

Lachlan looks surprised but doesn't question her. "I don't have much that's cookable," she says instead. "I'll order groceries tomorrow." But she looks pleased at the idea of Tamsin cooking for her. A more genuine happiness than Dr. Rivers's curiosity. Tamsin's chest grows warm and loose.

After they eat, Lachlan insists on changing the bandage around her ankle and attending to the dressing on her eye. Tamsin protests that she can do it herself now, but Lachlan ignores her. Presses a pill into her hands and watches as she takes it.

"I take care of what's mine," she says once Tamsin swallows. Her gaze is strangely heavy, and Tamsin flushes faintly, remembering their discussion about Penrose. This isn't how Dr. Rivers looks at the cat.

Lachlan clears her throat, redirecting her gaze elsewhere. "Your room's ready. Are you tired?"

Getting it fit for company makes more sense when Tamsin opens the door and sees that Lachlan does not have a guest room, exactly. She doesn't entertain *guests*. What she does have is a room set up with a hospital bed. Lachlan assures her it's a nice model and doesn't explain why she has it beyond, "It comes in handy on occasion."

It's certainly more comfortable than Tamsin's cot in the basement, and it's easy to adjust its height to allow her to transfer from chair to bed without help. But to actually move, she does need Lachlan; she has trouble judging the exact position of the bed with only one eye while simultaneously bracing her ankle.

Lachlan helps without comment.

Once Tamsin is settled, though, she leaves, shutting the door behind her. Tamsin doesn't hear a lock click into place. She is alone, but not sealed away, and she can see the glittering lights of the city below through her window. If she wanted to, she could wheel herself back out to the kitchen.

She doesn't.

Instead, she leans back into her pillows and closes her eye.

When she opens it again, Dr. Rivers is sitting at the foot of her bed.

The room is dark around them. Dr. Rivers is only a silhouette with long, curling hair, the faintest glint of two eyes in the blackness.

"You're not supposed to be here," Tamsin says. Her voice is swallowed up immediately, and she's afraid Dr. Rivers won't hear her.

But she does. "I could say the same of you," she replies, and her voice is stronger. It fills the room. It isn't *loud*, exactly, but it is undeniable. Solid. Real. One of her hands slides beneath the blankets, circles around Tamsin's ankle.

Tamsin twitches, tries to jerk away. Dr. Rivers holds her firm and folds back the sheet with her other hand. She traces the lines of the bandages. "She trusts you," Dr. Rivers says as if surprised.

And she would be, wouldn't she? The last she saw, Lachlan had claimed she was taking Tamsin to a lab to be studied. Not home to be coddled and cared for.

"She thinks I'm the original," Tamsin says.

"She doesn't think you're dangerous. But you are, aren't you?" Her thumb presses unerringly into a line of stitches, even though she can't see them. They flex against her nail. The bandages begin to darken.

Tamsin feels the pain in her skull, not her ankle.

"No," Tamsin says.

"But I am," Dr. Rivers says. Her nail pushes harder. The bandages split and fall away, whisper-thin scraps, growing tick-thick with blood. "And we're the same." As the sutures split, images flake from her mind like scabs. A needle, driven into the skin of her double, just to see her flinch. Dreams of vivisection, standing over her own body split open on a lab table. In every scene, she is the viewer, not the tormented.

She has done this before.

They can't be separated. They can never be separated. They're the same, they're *linked*, but where Dr. Rivers distorts the world around her, Tamsin floats on top of it all, insubstantial, inconsequential.

Tamsin looks away, but there's nowhere else to look. What light filtered in through the windows is gone, velvety nothingness wrapping around her. Her eye is open, but no matter how hard she strains, she can no longer see the edge of the bed or the outline of Dr. Rivers. She can only feel her: fingernails digging into splitting flesh, breath on the side of her waist where her shirt has rucked up, the whispering trail of hair a moment later.

The mattress shifts. Dr. Rivers prowls above her. Her hands leave Tamsin's ankles but fall on her shoulders, shoving her deeper into the pillows. She's solid, *heavy*, and her relentless presence, the only tangible thing in a sea of emptiness, skewers Tamsin through the heart.

Tamsin can't move enough to fight her. She doesn't even have the strength to kick at the sheets.

"Come home," Dr. Rivers whispers in her ear. "Come back. She cannot give you purpose, but I know what you need."

The spike drives in deep, and all the world becomes nothing.

Chapter Thirty-Five

Tamsin wakes with a spasm, clutching at sweat-soaked sheets. Her breathing is so rapid it threatens to choke her, and she rolls onto her side, pushing against the bedding. Her feet dig into the mattress, and her ankle is awash in pain. But when she draws her knees up and reaches down, the bandages are dry and whole.

The room is not dark. There is sunlight spilling in through the window past a bank of clouds, leaving everything softly aglow. Dr. Rivers is not here. There is no weight pressing her down, no spike through her chest.

She doesn't understand.

Trembling, she drags herself from the bed into the wheelchair. Her hands are clumsy on it as she tries to steer herself from the room. The door is almost impossible to open; she needs to pull it back and out, difficult to do with her chair in the way. But she manages, and the exertion gives her heaving breaths some organizing force. By the time she's in the hallway, she isn't so close to tears, but the gauze over her eye socket is damp anyway, with discharge from the strain. Her remaining eye is dry.

She wheels herself toward the kitchen.

Lachlan is awake already; she leans against the living room side of the island. Instead of a suit, she's in a loose, sleeveless shirt and knee-length, baggy shorts. Her prosthetic arm is off, the limb ending just above the elbow. A metal post emerges from the rounded end of it, capped by a plastic cone.

The arm isn't her only prosthesis. Her right leg is mechanical, too, starting at the mid-thigh, attached by a similar metal stem into her leg. It moves naturally as her weight shifts and she reaches for the coffee maker.

Her shorts hang loose on her hips. There's a bit of exposed skin just above the waistband.

She looks uncomfortably human, dressed down like this. Vulnerable.

Dr. Rivers's voice echoes through her head. *She doesn't think you're dangerous.*

"Something happened," Tamsin manages weakly.

Lachlan's head jerks up. The vulnerability disappears, her body language shifting until, even without her suit, even without her arm, she looks like a weapon. She's strongly muscled, alert, and focused entirely on Tamsin.

"What?"

"I saw—I saw Dr. Rivers. Here. In my room. She undid the bandages, but they're fine now, and I don't—I'm not sure—"

Lachlan frowns, then crosses the wide expanse of room between them. She crouches down before her, gaze flicking across her body. Tamsin is wearing the same clothes as yesterday. They were soft enough to sleep in. The shorts hang down to her knees.

"A nightmare," Lachlan says finally, sitting back on her haunches. "You were dreaming."

"I was, but I wasn't. It was something else. It felt real."

"They do, sometimes. You'll get used to it," Lachlan says. She stands. "It's normal after traumatic events. The brain's way of recontextualizing new information."

"It felt *real*," Tamsin repeats, chafing under the dismissal. She may not have her memories, but she's dreamed before, and it wasn't like *that*. But she does have to admit that location doesn't shift in reality the way it did in her dream. And the pain wasn't so much a sensation as a memory of a sensation.

The fear was very real, though.

"She told me I was dangerous," Tamsin says, pushing her chair along and following Lachlan back to the kitchen. "And she—or my brain, I suppose—maybe has a point. We don't know what I am."

"I know what you are. You're Tamsin Rivers."

"I *was* Tamsin Rivers. Probably." She shakes her head. "I might be something else now. We can't be certain." And that lack of certainty tugs at her relentlessly. It's important. They need to keep it in mind, or else . . . or else . . .

She doesn't know what will happen, and that's half the problem.

Lachlan considers her silently. If she argues, it's only in the confines of her own skull. "We'll figure it out," she says eventually.

The coffee machine beeps, and she looks away at last, retrieving the mug. There's already one steaming on the counter. This one must be for Tamsin. Her movements are as confident with one hand as they were with two, but Tamsin still asks, "What happened to your arm?"

"Crush injury after an IED went off and took the leg," Lachlan says, glancing over as she adds sugar and milk to Tamsin's mug. She must see Tamsin's lack of comprehension, because she huffs a laugh. "Right. Not what you were asking. It's *off* because the arm took some damage yesterday to the shell, so I've got it running diagnostics. If everything comes back fine, I'm going to install some replacement casing once I have my coffee."

"If not?"

"Then I'll have to send it out and use an older model." She shrugs. "Won't be an issue. How are you feeling? A little steadier?" Lachlan pushes the coffee across the counter. Tamsin takes a sip.

It's perfect. That makes sense; Lachlan must know how she takes her coffee. Handy, since Tamsin doesn't. "A little," she says grudgingly.

"Good. I found something useful, last night after you went to bed. Did some digging." She ignores her own mug, stepping around Tamsin to retrieve a tablet from the coffee table. "You kept notes. On your phone, thankfully, or I may not have been able to access them. Dr. Rivers wiped them within a day of the file's creation, but the program I use keeps mirrored copies at intervals. If she'd deleted them any sooner, we'd have been out of luck." She taps at the tablet, then passes it over to Tamsin. "I haven't gone through them in detail yet, but they're not coded in any way. Read it and let me know if there's anything useful. I'll start looking for anything I can find on . . . what are we calling her? Your double? Not a clone."

"No, not a clone. Double, copy . . ." Some bit of disjointed knowledge squirms along her hippocampus. "Doppelgänger?"

"Doppelgänger," Lachlan agrees. "I have to head out around lunchtime, but I should be able to pull some files down before then." She circles back around and finally retrieves her coffee. She drinks it black. "You won't have access to the internet. Security measure. Is that going to be a problem?"

Dr. Rivers didn't let her have access, either. Tamsin considers. "I'll have to work only from the sources you find."

"I'm happy to chase down more, once you've defined the problem a little better."

"Why not let me look?"

"Control over the situation." Lachlan slides onto a barstool on the side of the island closest to Tamsin. "You're right. We don't know what you are. I don't think you're dangerous, not intentionally, but the fewer moving pieces, the more we can both be safe."

It makes sense. And it dampens the echo of Dr. Rivers's voice. Finally.

Tamsin moves to the couch with the tablet and her coffee. She's vaguely aware of Lachlan leaving the room and the sound of a door closing deeper in the apartment. But most of her attention is fixed now on the haphazard notes in front of her. They begin with a list of things she'd forgotten, things she can barely understand now for all the context she's lost.

But then there is a narrative.

She's read through it twice by the time Lachlan returns to the living room, now buttoned up in a fresh suit, arm back in place. She comes around the back of the couch, standing over Tamsin as she reads. Her gloved hand settles on the cushion behind her head.

"I called her *Prime*," Tamsin says.

Lachlan huffs. "Yeah, I don't get that one. *Prime* sounds like the base model. Or the best."

"*Tamsin Prime* and *Tamsin Nought*," she says, shaking her head. "Prime is the variant. Nought is the original, the definitional source. Interesting, that she didn't swap our names."

"She didn't need to. I assumed she just meant to name you nothing. You thought it was because you were a blank slate."

"But I might have figured it out." Tamsin twists to look up at Lachlan. "I probably would have. And she didn't count on anybody else ever meeting me." It doesn't fit, unless Dr. Rivers (*Prime*) has some inborn respect for their distinctions. She is Prime. Tamsin is Nought. That is immutable, no matter what else changes.

It's so out of keeping with the Dr. Rivers that Tamsin knows that it makes her head ache.

* * *

Before she leaves for the day, Lachlan pulls the notes that Prime dutifully turned over on the basement, as well as several sources on doppelgängers, though nothing so convenient as a comprehensive list. Instead, Tamsin has to comb through psychoanalytic monographs and literature reviews of the German Romantic tradition, plot summaries of video games and post hoc gatherings of old folklore that may be more than half fabricated.

In most cases, the double is just that: a copy, whose existence throws into sharp relief the failings of the original. The argument goes that people willfully ignore their weaknesses and cruelties, and the double's function is to make their venal natures obvious to all. They are a judgment, a reckoning, a manifestation of anxieties.

Doubles, in these stories, are prone to committing crimes, trapping the original with the blame or tipping them into destructive cycles. So many stories end with suicide, intentional or inadvertent. Desperate, the originals try to kill the reflection, only to take the mortal wound themselves. Sometimes the doppelgänger disappears at the same moment; other times, it is the last one standing. Winner take all.

The original always loses.

She has to take a break once she realizes that. Her head pounds and her eye is tired, the muscle sore, her vision slightly blurry. She lets the crush of resignation and dread press her into the couch. *The original always loses.* She's fairly certain she's lost already. The memory issues, the disorientation, the injury; she's already at the end of her story, isn't she?

But she's still alive.

And Tamsin *does* differ from the protagonists of all these stories. The memory loss alone is unique, and the apparent skewing in her nature. In these stories, the characters are all incapable of change. That's the exact reason they're pursued by their double. And very few stories show the original and the double in close contact. It's more of a haunting. Persistent, maddening, unyielding. Glimpses on the street, perhaps. Acquaintances recalling encounters the original has no memory of. Nothing so mundane as living in the same house, working on the same questions.

And none of the stories associate doubles or doppelgängers or even shadow selves with digging deep into the earth. That, it seems, is unique to Prime. To her.

She keeps working, keeps looking. Every break she needs to take to rest her eye leaves her a little more frustrated, a little less patient. The stories become more vague, more chaotic, less helpful the further afield she goes. Her attention catches on useless things. There's Capgras delusion, where the afflicted thinks that everybody *around* them has been replaced with an identical but non-original double. Strange-face illusion, where staring at your own reflection in a darkened room triggers hallucinations and a sense of unreality, unrecognizability. She lingers on a story: the devil teaches black magic to seven pupils in Salamanca, Spain. The last student to leave each night forfeits their soul. But one clever man argues that, when he leaves at sunrise, it will be his shadow that is last to leave the room.

The devil agrees and takes his shadow as payment. The man survives but lives out his days marked and miserable.

It's a variation on a final theme: doubles as the price of some bargain or trade. In this case, the double is less a concrete *being* and more a portion of the self, abstracted beyond even a reflection. But always, always, it's that abstraction that seems to make the price worth it. *Take this piece of me that I'm not using, and in return, make me successful beyond my wildest dreams.*

Prime would have done it, Tamsin is certain. She can only remember a few scant days with her double, but she knows that much; Prime is ambitious and callous, and willing to take risks. All those things were likely just as true of Tamsin, and so either one of them might have bargained the other away.

But that's not what happened. There's no abstraction, no shadow self. They are both living beings, and they exist alone together.

And yet she can't shake the feeling that the bargain is important. Maybe it's because of the door. A door, after all, is a choice. Step through, or leave it closed. Whatever is on the other side is forbidden knowledge, unobtainable. And once the choice is made, there's a chance the door will lock behind her for good.

What would it take, to open the door?

Chapter Thirty-Six

The rhythm of life in Lachlan's home is not so dissimilar to living with Prime. Lachlan has obligations that extend beyond Tamsin, taking her away for long stretches of the day. But Tamsin is not locked in a feature-less basement, and that matters; the apartment is undeniably designed, the walls a soothing gray, the furniture carefully matched, but it still looks lived in. Alive, in a way Prime's house (*her* house) never was.

Lachlan keeps her own bedroom locked, as well as a few other rooms. The clothes she brings home for Tamsin to wear are largely similar to what Prime wore, save for the inclusion of a few dresses with wider skirts and softer colors. Lachlan doesn't ask for her opinion, but Tamsin thinks, if it bothered her, if she asked, Lachlan would replace the unfamiliar clothing with something more comfortable.

She's not sure if it bothers her.

So she wears the clothing, and she goes over her notes again and again, and she considers turning on the television. Lachlan leaves her the remote that first day apart, after giving her a brief tour, but it seems too loud, too bright, too fast. She knows there was a television in Prime's house, but she never saw it on, never heard anything from the living room at all.

The second day, though, Lachlan leaves her with instructions to turn it on to a particular channel at a specific time. When she does, she sees Prime giving a public statement on the news, the Myrica Dynamics logo prominent behind her. The video is so high definition that Tamsin flinches away at first, then finds herself leaning in as far as she can, fixated on Prime's face. It's so familiar, so perfect, and so achingly far away.

Then she spots Lachlan standing a fair distance behind, barely in the shot. She's watching Prime, too.

"This is an evolving phenomenon," Prime says in response to a question from the audience. "We ruled out seismic activity early on in our investigation, which is why the team from San Francisco couldn't find any either—it wasn't there to be found. The microtremors that the university is reporting are new and highly localized to Rosewood and, we think, are a *response* to the subsidence process, not a cause. Now, that shouldn't take away from our recommendation to the city for a narrow-scope evacuation. Whether it's causative or not, there's a chance of older houses coming down, of sinkholes opening up. But we do think that Myrica Dynamics's new stabilization methods are a strong fit for the area, and we're thankful that San Siroco is partnering with us to help protect such a vibrant and storied neighborhood."

The news segment doesn't give a lot of background information, certainly not enough for Tamsin to catch up to Prime's work, but it does come with a lot of talking heads dissecting Prime's every utterance. By far, the largest amount of airtime goes to arguing against the subsidence evidence as a whole. Very few people seem willing to accept what they cannot see and what cannot be explained by normal physics. Instead, accusations fly, fast and furious, about a power grab by Myrica Dynamics, incompetence by city government, tax schemes and conspiracy theories that go over Tamsin's head. Prime's performance at an earlier press conference is compared with this one. Tamsin wonders how much time she's lost, exactly, because even in the original press conference footage, it's clear that it's not Tamsin on that stage.

She shuts off the television again.

Each evening, she cooks; her ability to judge position and depth quickly strengthens with the practice, and without fail, Lachlan eats with her and compliments what she's managed. They sit up into the night, talking about Tamsin's old life, about the world, about Prime's movements. Occasionally, Lachlan looks at her like she's in pain. Other times, she looks hungry. Most of the time, she looks professional, but warm.

When Tamsin asks about the press conference, Lachlan turns cold.

"Our hand was forced," Lachlan says, fussing with her glass of whiskey. "We always knew it would be difficult to get out in front of this. As terrible as it sounds, without a tragedy to explain, our announcement was always going to ring more than a little false. But we also didn't want to run the risk of having to sheepishly admit that we knew there was a problem the whole time."

"How was she?" Tamsin asks, because public relations doesn't interest her in the slightest.

"Enjoying the challenge," Lachlan says, grimacing, then gets up to refill her glass.

Three more days pass like that. She reads, and she watches the television. She cooks. She sleeps. Sometimes, it stops mattering if Tamsin is the copy or the original. They fall into an equilibrium, and the world spins on, and Tamsin thinks that maybe everything will work itself out. That Prime will find a way to fix the subsidence after all. That the horror of what happened in her house doesn't matter against the larger scheme of things. That, in her current context, there's been no harm done.

She doesn't know what will happen to her if that's the case; what space can there be for something like her, if Prime pulls through and saves the city? Does it look anything like Lachlan's apartment?

She wants it to.

But there are other options. Labs and prisons and elimination, if she proves useless except as a liability. Lachlan, *Myrica*, has no purpose for her. And if Prime saves the city, she'll be allowed to dictate terms. Or maybe she'll fail entirely, and the city will fall. Tamsin has access to her notes on the subsidence, or at least the notes she kept in ways Lachlan could find, and she can see no solution she hasn't already ruled out. She's exhausted the resources they could find on doppelgängers, and she's running out of avenues to explore. And sometimes, at night, she dreams of an expansive darkness, an absence of sound, the feel of a doorknob in her hand.

On the fourth day, she gives up on work. She takes a nap instead, once Lachlan has left for the morning. She wakes up sometime after noon and pulls herself into her chair, wheels herself out into the hall.

There is a door set in between her bedroom and the bathroom.

Tamsin stares.

It wasn't there this morning.

It matches the other two doors precisely, but there is nothing it can open onto; it straddles the wall between the two rooms. It is impossible, definitionally impossible, just like the door in her basement. But still, she goes into both rooms, tapping on the drywall, measuring crudely by arm length, desperate to prove herself wrong.

The answer remains the same.

There's no *space*.

She hunches forward in the wheelchair, pulse picking up speed until she can barely hear herself think above the pounding. The apartment seems to grow darker around the edges, shadows building, thickening. This can't be happening.

She needs to tell Lachlan.

But Lachlan won't be back for at least three hours. Maybe longer. Tamsin wheels herself back into the hall, staring at the door. It doesn't *look* like the door in Prime's basement, but then again, neither do any of the other doors in Lachlan's apartment. All of these doors are a deep slate blue with black hardware. She can't even be sure how long the door has been there, really, because she didn't actually count the doors that morning. She's just certain she would have noticed it before.

Tamsin watches the doorknob, heart in her throat. It's difficult to breathe around. This apartment can't be sinking; it's too high up in the air, and if it were distorting, surely somebody else in the building would have noticed. But are the ceilings higher? They're already lofted compared to those in Prime's home. She doesn't have a frame of reference.

She makes herself leave, retreating to the couch and seizing the tablet, pulling up her notes again. With the door out of eyeshot, she can breathe, just enough to think. When the first door appeared, that's when she began having strange dreams. Sleepwalking. It had, in hindsight, begun the cascade that ended with the loss of her memories, the change in her personality. The thought of it happening again, of having what little identity she's started to cobble together once more pulled out from under her, is enough to make her drop the tablet from shaking so hard. But then she realizes—

It's not your house. How is Lachlan sleeping?

Would she have woken up if Lachlan started sleepwalking?

Impossible to know; the penthouse is dead silent at night, and the walls are thick. But Lachlan doesn't know about the door, *that* she is sure of. If she knew, she would have broken it down by now. If she knew, she would have taken Tamsin somewhere else, somewhere safer.

Is it safe here now?

That depends on if the door opens.

What would it take, to open the door?

It's not long until she's in her chair again, in that hallway, staring at it. It conjures up the same gut-twisting aversion as the one in the basement, a demand to look away, to leave. She makes herself approach instead. Each rotation of her wheels takes a monumental effort, sweat beading her brow. She does not *want* to do this, can feel Prime pressed against her back, but she has to know. She has to confirm this is what she thinks it is. After all, it could just be that there is a linen closet, very small, the width of the door and a few inches deep.

(The math still wouldn't work out. But maybe—maybe—?)

The footplates of her wheelchair bump the door.

A shudder lances through her, white-electric, and she jerks back in her seat. She bears down and counts each inhale and exhale until she can move again. When she reaches out, her hand is shaking so hard she can barely grasp the doorknob.

But she needs to know.

The knob is less a knob than it is a lever, but it gives under her hand, the same way her notes described the knob turning in the basement. It acts as if it should open. No indication of a lock. No resistance. A smooth movement of the hardware.

When it comes time to push or pull, she can't do it.

She *tries*. She gives the order, but her body refuses to obey. Tears erupt from her eyes, both of them, empty socket and remaining organ both, burning hot, and she lets go of the knob and wheels back, hard, until she hits the far wall. She can't breathe, gasps and writhes and tears at her hair until she is curled up in the seat, panting into her knees.

If she can't see the door, she can pretend it isn't there. It's not hard, a magnet repelling its match; the dread fades when she isn't forced to think about it. It's the opposite of what the old Tamsin put in her notes, of the infiltrating fascination, the growing obsession. There is nothing for her here, *nothing*, and she doesn't understand her old self, the self so desperate to see inside that door, to know where it leads.

It shouldn't exist at all.

She flees.

* * *

By the time Lachlan returns, Tamsin has all but convinced herself it was a hallucination.

Her mind is not stable. That much is obvious from her notes. And while Lachlan hasn't pointed out any memory lapses, and she hasn't noticed any alterations in her perception or budding agoraphobia, it's been less than a week. The door provokes a panic response in her much like the concept of leaving the house once did. Something happened to her, something that destabilized everything inside of her, and she cannot be trusted. That much she's sure of.

So she doesn't tell Lachlan about the door.

She doesn't want Lachlan to think less of her or to pity her. The apartment isn't sinking, can't be sinking, and so there is no correlation between the basement and here. The door can't be real. She's simply—traumatized. *Harmed*, as Lachlan put it. It's like a nightmare, this hallucination. The mind trying to parse out the damage, an extinction burst, all tied to the pressure Prime had her under. Whatever happened to her eye. In the basement, she'd feared the door, just as Prime had before her. Now, here, there's nothing to fear, but her brain doesn't know that yet.

And even if something *is* wrong, even if the door is there, Lachlan had said that getting out ahead of something like this, before the tragedy, is a hard sell. She'll take the other tack. If something is wrong, Lachlan can discover it, like she did, and then they can find a solution.

But while Tamsin manages to pull herself together before Lachlan returns, she doesn't have dinner on the table like she usually does. She also has no explanation for the lack. Lachlan actually looks unbalanced by it, though she recovers quickly. She orders takeout for them. She laughs to herself as she pours them both a drink.

"It's not like you're a housewife," she says, passing one glass to Tamsin.

"I think we agreed I'm more of a pet," Tamsin replies.

Lachlan glances down at the dress Tamsin is wearing, one of the unfamiliar ones, with a curved neckline and soft green fabric. She doesn't say anything, but sips her whiskey.

"I'm out of materials," Tamsin says, mind returning to the issue of work. The door hovers at the edge of her thoughts, but she ignores it. She has enough to worry about with Prime and her own future. "I'm not any closer to an answer about the city. Or any closer to a theory of what Prime is."

Lachlan, settling in the nearby armchair, pulls off her gloves and reaches up to loosen her tie. "Do you know what else you want?"

"New data," Tamsin says. "How is she these days? Since my removal."

"Difficult. But behaving, as far as I can see."

"Did you see her? In person?"

"No. Not today." Lachlan tips her glass, watching the way the whiskey pools in the corner. "She might suspect that Cara is reporting on her, though. She's utilizing her more than she was, or you were, but there's something different about their exchanges. Cara is getting nervous. Doesn't know what's actually wrong, of course, but she knows something is off." She pauses, tips the glass the other way. "If you were her, if you were yourself again, and you were trying to slip my observation, what would you do? How would you lie to me?"

It takes all her effort not to look at the hallway.

"Distraction," she says after a moment. "Productivity. The more data there is, the harder it will be to find the discordant bit. How many hours is she logging in the lab?"

"She's slept there some nights," Lachlan says. She rises from the chair, strolling around the perimeter of the living room. "Which means I have her on camera at all times. I know where she is. I can see what she's doing, even hear what she's saying in most areas. She is rarely alone. As far as I can tell, she hasn't contacted FlexEast since the day I found you."

"But you can't watch her all the time, even with all of that coverage."

"No," Lachlan agrees. "And the longer she follows the letter of the law, the less leverage I'll have to insist on staying focused on her."

"What do you want to happen?" Tamsin asks. This time, she doesn't suggest anything.

She wonders if the passage of time has changed anything.

From Lachlan's hesitation, it has.

"I want her to make a mistake," Lachlan says at last. "I want her to give me an opportunity to take her in. To see what she is, what makes her tick. I want to take her apart."

She says nothing about Tamsin.

None of the reading Tamsin has done has presented them with an out.

In every story where the double is removed, the original goes with it. To kill a double is to commit suicide. And the only alternative is to sink deeper and deeper into madness, it seems.

She thinks she must be there already.

The click of Lachlan setting her glass down on the coffee table recaptures her attention. Lachlan braces one knee on the couch cushion and leans over Tamsin. Her nonmechanical hand cups Tamsin's jaw, tilts her head up.

"Bandage check?" Tamsin asks.

"There's something you're not telling me," Lachlan says. Her voice is low and soft, but there is an edge to it. Tamsin's spine straightens. She lifts her chin, feels the phantom handle of the door beneath her fingertips.

Come with me, I want to show you something, she could say. *Do you see anything strange here?*

But there is no door. There can't be. So there's nothing to tell.

"I could say the same of you," Tamsin says. "The dresses. The kindness. What do you want to happen?"

Lachlan's expression shutters for just a moment, a tightening of the skin around her eyes, a slight pursing of her mouth. And then she leans in and presses their lips together.

She tastes like whiskey. Her nearness is overwhelming, and for a moment, Tamsin thinks to pull back, to ask for an explanation. But her body knows this, even if it doesn't know Lachlan specifically. *Procedural memory.* Her lips part, and Lachlan's tongue slides into her mouth. She leans back against the cushions, slipping, falling, until she's stretched out on the couch and Lachlan is above her.

So much like the dream of Prime above her, holding her down, whispering into her ear.

Her back arches. Lachlan makes a low, rough sound against her mouth, and her hands drag up Tamsin's thighs, up beneath the hem of her dress. *Does nudity bother you?* Tamsin had asked, and now she thinks she understands. It had bothered Lachlan because she wanted to discover it on her own. Context is important after all.

Lachlan's mouth drops to her throat. Her teeth catch on Tamsin's skin, her tongue laving over the bite an instant later. The fabric of her suit pants is rough and thick between Tamsin's legs, Lachlan's thigh pressing firmly against her flesh. She tangles her hands in Lachlan's hair. The texture is crisp and unnatural, and it gives beneath her fingertips. And then there is the expanse of her back, and the barely there dip of her waist, and the muscles over all of it.

"Bedroom?" Lachlan murmurs against her sweat-slick skin. Her movements slow, her hands pushing hard on Tamsin's hips to restrain her.

Tamsin squirms. "Why?" she asks. The couch is perfectly fine, and she doesn't want to let go, not for anything.

Lachlan rears back.

It's so abrupt that Tamsin doesn't even try to follow, just stays splayed on the cushions, skirt rucked up around her waist. Horror sweeps over Lachlan's face, and she staggers away from the couch, running a hand through her hair, so mussed that it's falling into her eyes. Her lips are swollen.

"Lachlan?" Tamsin reaches for her.

"Don't," Lachlan snaps, stepping clear out of reach. "This was a mistake."

Tamsin aches, confused. "But you enjoyed it. You wanted it. You *have* wanted it."

"As a daydream. A fantasy. Not in reality," Lachlan says. She is angry, and it doesn't make any sense.

"I don't understand," Tamsin says, voice wavering.

Lachlan shows her teeth. "Exactly," she spits. "You don't understand enough to say *yes* to anything. You're . . . you're naive. Childlike. It's disgusting—"

A chime sounds from the entryway. The doorbell. Dinner. Lachlan walks away, and Tamsin stares after her, the pulsing heat of her body abruptly replaced by clammy stillness.

Disgusting.

Lachlan thinks what just happened was disgusting because Tamsin can't remember who she used to be. Because Tamsin doesn't behave the way she's supposed to. Because she's changed too much to be anything of worth.

She thinks that Tamsin's desires aren't worth responding to because they're the desires of a broken thing.

And for the first time, Tamsin is angry, *furious*, about what has been taken from her.

Chapter Thirty-Seven

They do not talk over dinner.

Lachlan barely looks at her. Tamsin returns the aversion. The food is flavorless on her tongue, and it accumulates in a noxious tangle in her stomach. There are no apologies or explanations or accusations.

When Lachlan goes to bed, she passes by the extra door without pausing. She can't see it, but Tamsin can. It sits there, silent, horrifying, and—

Familiar.

After Lachlan closes her bedroom door, Tamsin sits in the hall for as long as she can bear it, tracing the door frame's lines with her eye until that eye aches from being overstrained. She doesn't come close enough to touch. She doesn't need to. It reaches out to her, caressing her cheek. It feels like Lachlan, like Prime, like the weight of the self she can't remember anymore.

What would it take, to open the door? She's already sacrificed so much.

But maybe it's not a sacrifice if she didn't choose it.

Although she's read her own notes. She never once called for help. At every step, no matter her fears, she pushed onward, committed to something she didn't understand. The siren call of the subsidence, the distortion of her home and the accompanying distortion of her mind.

She retreats to her bed and sleeps, fitfully, and in the morning, she doesn't leave her room.

She can hear the sounds of Lachlan getting ready for the day. Shower. Coffee machine. Pacing footsteps. Tamsin lies in bed and feels at the edges of her anger, her pain, wondering if they map to the edges of herself.

Here, in this apartment, where does she end and Lachlan's control begin? The wheelchair beside the bed is useful, but it is also Lachlan's, and as long as Lachlan has not suggested she stop using it, Tamsin has not tried to. She hasn't had a desire to. Is she supposed to?

You don't understand.

And she hadn't. She hadn't known why Lachlan wanted to move to the bedroom (though she can guess now, if not see the necessity; privacy like that is an illusion at best). She didn't understand the meaning behind the clothing Lachlan picked for her. She doesn't understand a great many things about the world. But she does understand her work, and she understands Prime.

She understands herself.

Lachlan's argument is wrong.

So what, if she lacks the same cultural knowledge that Lachlan has? It doesn't render her incapable of desiring things, of making choices, of being independent. If anything, it's Lachlan's assumptions that soured last night. She was clearly following some script of a fantasy. Something to do with the dresses, with the concept of *home*, of pets and housewives. And then Tamsin, who didn't know the script, who reacted purely out of want and instinct, had responded in some way that had made Lachlan jump to the idea that Tamsin couldn't possibly know what she wanted.

And yes, Tamsin has changed. Somehow, some way, Prime reduced her to something approaching a blank slate. But her mind is as sharp as ever; it's only the context that has changed.

Tamsin levers herself out of bed and tests her ankle against the floor.

It's nearing noon, but Lachlan is still in the apartment. She paces, fully dressed save for her gloves, a phone pressed to her ear. Tamsin watches her from the hallway, standing on her own. She's wrapped her foot tightly in a supportive bandage. It's enough. It hurts, but the sutures aren't splitting. It hurts, but she can ignore it.

"Yes, of course. Thank you, sir," Lachlan says. She lowers her phone, mouth set in a firm line, tapping out commands on the screen.

"Bad news?" Tamsin asks. She's in clothing as close to what Prime wears as she could manage out of what's still clean. A sleek, knit dress, tight in the skirt, with a structured jacket on top. Her hair is freshly washed and set, thanks to muscle memory. Her hands had still expected longer curls, but they caught up soon enough.

When Lachlan looks up, it's clear that her appearance is having the intended effect. There is a simultaneous easing of tension and restoration of guard.

She doesn't comment on Tamsin standing.

"Prime has convinced the CEO of Myrica to reopen the deep node labs," Lachlan says, setting her phone onto the kitchen counter with a grimace. "She made what he described as a cogent argument in favor of their operational necessity to solving the subsidence issue."

Tamsin cocks her head to the side. She knows very little about the labs, only bits and pieces that she overheard Prime talking about. But where the specifics are lacking, her knowledge base assembles some basic suppositions: heavy particle and radiation shielding, something to do with communications, the necessity of digging deep. She's researched this in depth before. She can learn it again.

"And this is a problem," Tamsin says.

"It's a Hail Mary. If she can get this up and running, and if she can't stop the sinking, she at least has a world-changing innovation to bank the rest of her career on. But of all the arrogant, dangerous actions she could have taken—"

"Do you think there's a connection between the labs and the sinking?"

Lachlan scowls. "I couldn't tell you. You conveniently never proved it one way or the other. Couldn't locate a mechanism of action. You certainly had little incentive to, beyond the greater good. I cut the program because I didn't trust you to manage it effectively anymore." She retrieves her gloves from where they're discarded on the island, tugging them on roughly. "But if the media gets ahold of this, they could make assumptions. It could backfire spectacularly; it's unknown science coinciding with an unknown, imminent disaster, and *down* is *down*. Even at best, it will paint us as callous. Focused on profit over safety."

Which, Tamsin thinks, Myrica Dynamics *is*.

"I need to talk to her," Lachlan continues. "Convince her to act sensibly."

"At least she's nowhere near as erratic as I was," Tamsin says.

Lachlan pauses, halfway to the door. "Tamsin."

"She can be reasoned with. If she doesn't hate you, after what you've done."

Lachlan's upper lip curls back. Tamsin refuses to look away. Everything she's saying is true, after all. That it bothers Lachlan is not her problem.

"I'll be back when I can," Lachlan says.

And then she's gone.

There is, of course, an option Lachlan did not voice, but must have thought of:

Prime knows exactly what she's doing.

If Lachlan's initial fears of the communications experiments directly causing the subsidence were well founded, Prime may *intentionally* have opened the labs again, resumed the old experiments. Even, perhaps, accelerated them, in the service of hastening the disaster or some other outcome that isn't just fame and fortune; will Lachlan know to look for that?

For the better part of half an hour, Tamsin wonders if she should have said something. In the end, she lands on *maybe*; she doesn't trust Lachlan, right now, to respond thoughtfully to the threat. To understand and, moreover, believe her and take the right action. They both need to know more about the labs to discern the best way to stop whatever Prime has set in motion, and they need to know what Prime is after in order to anticipate her next move.

Tamsin needs more information, and she needs Lachlan to believe that she is who she always has been, that she can understand what she is advocating for. That she isn't just panicking or inventing stories. She needs a researched proposition instead of an idle theory.

(This, she suspects, was the crux of their original relationship: they have never been able to trust one another. Their interests have always been fundamentally opposed, even if their natures haven't been.)

More information means more research. Resources that Lachlan has taken from her. The tablet is not hardlocked out of the internet but does need a password that Tamsin can't begin to guess at. She knows, though, that there's a central object that organizes internet access for a home. She can't imagine where Lachlan would put it, but if she takes a step back, she can recall how that internet access *works*. From there, she can anticipate where it would be most advantageous to put the hardware.

Lachlan has not locked it away; it's simply tucked aside, near the television. There is no handy piece of paper with the password noted down on it, but after some inspection, Tamsin manages to reset the router to default. *That* password is on the original manufacturer's sticker along the bottom of the casing.

Certain apps won't engage with the reset Wi-Fi; it's missing some kind of key that flags the connection as approved. But general internet browsing works, and after some fiddling with both the router and the tablet, Lachlan's emails begin to populate. She filters for her own name and finds reports. Not everything loads; the tablet is missing necessary programs.

But there's enough to get her back up to speed. It's like rushing down a corridor, unlocking every door along the way, each one falling open with a light touch. It's all still there, simmering in the marrow of her. And it's enough to start theorizing about what, precisely, Prime might be up to.

Tamsin can't find paper, but she does find markers. Lachlan's walls are darker than the basement's, but they'll do. She retreats to her bedroom, then painstakingly maneuvers the hospital bed over against the wall. From atop it, she has a whole expanse she can easily reach, and the ability to raise and lower herself.

She gets to work.

Certain things are easier from her current vantage point.

The communications experiments are fascinating, but she has no personal investment, not like she once did, not like Prime might have now. It's unclear if she had been intentionally avoiding certain avenues of thought or if it had been a subconscious attempt to protect her pet project. Or perhaps, without a dominant intellectual milieu governing her thoughts, she's simply willing to move laterally more often. Whichever it is, she can feel new ideas clicking into place, settling in, filling in gaps.

She doesn't discard anything outright, not even the vague and spurious association she makes between the heavy darkness of her nightmares and the sensory isolation of the node chambers. Her old notes, too, mentioned dreams of creeping absence, of a void. Emotional links between ideas are not necessarily logical, but the fact that it has followed her across a major alteration to her cognition seems important.

More directly, while the pockets of distortion in the soil and stone below the city are not in any way related to a single plane, neither is the path of the particles that the nodes utilize for their long-distance, instantaneous transmission of data. That's the entire point of the labs; because they filter out so much of the noise of existence, what is left, even if it is erratic and intermittent, can be purposefully utilized. It is possible, therefore—likely?—that the particles Tamsin intended the node chambers to interact with are not the only things making contact.

But how does information become a door, become a copy of herself?

It's very personal. Of course, she suspects she's been inside the chambers more than most. But the other node-lab leaders, they must go in occasionally. And none of them have reported problems.

(They might be concealing their own disasters, but none of them are behaving erratically, at least as far as Lachlan has said.)

A door opens. Closes. Footsteps in the hall. *Lachlan*, Tamsin identifies, and pushes the input aside. There's never a knock on the doorframe, or Lachlan calling for her, so she must be fine to keep working.

Her double may not be a direct result of the subsidence; it could very well just be an accident, a side effect. The pockets of distortion, do they involve any sort of doubling? A mathematic increase of density. Or reduction. A copying of the inanimate, within a confined space, with no outlet.

Perhaps she's lucky that a house has more space to exist in than a hole in the ground.

But her basement didn't double in its dimensions, did it? Not all at once, certainly. But is it already larger than twice its original size? Smaller? If smaller, will it stop when it reaches the point of duplication, a perfect transformation?

And why did it only grow *down*?

More noises, soft but jarring, and Tamsin is at a standstill, so, at last, she looks over her shoulder to the hallway. She can't see anything from here, except that it can't have been more than an hour or two since Lachlan headed to work, by the quality of the light.

Lachlan shouldn't be home yet.

Lachlan hasn't come to ask about the Wi-Fi.

It's not Lachlan.

For a long moment, Tamsin doesn't move, her body heavy and buzzing with adrenaline. In Prime's house, she would have been expected to put herself back into the basement as quietly as she could—assuming she was even out of the basement at the time.

But this isn't Prime's house. There should be no intruders here at all. Is it somebody here to hurt Lachlan? Or worse, is it somebody who knows Tamsin exists?

Is it Prime?

Maybe she should hide beneath the bed. Take shelter, stay small, stay quiet. That's what Lachlan would tell her to do, she's fairly certain. But she can't. She can't sit by and allow this . . . this *intrusion*, this violation. She approaches the door silently, then edges through it. The impossible door beside her own is still there. She can't see any movement in the hall or in the other rooms.

There aren't any more sounds to follow, but she creeps toward the living room anyway. Her ankle protests. Her breathing sounds too loud, too jagged.

She has no weapon. Will she need one?

If it *is* Prime, will she . . . ?

But it's not Prime.

Lachlan stands in the middle of the living room, looking at the bank of windows. Her suit is immaculate, as always, but Tamsin has never seen this slope of her shoulders, the casual tuck of her hands into her pockets.

She's never seen that quiet wonder on her face.

"Lachlan?" she asks. "What are you doing home already?"

Lachlan turns to her, mouth curving into a sweet smile. "Hello," she says. It's her voice. Her mix of gravel and honey. It's not the timbre but the openness, the soft space at the end of her words, that's all wrong. "Do you live here?"

It's not Lachlan, but Tamsin already knew.

She draws closer, looking for some flaw. Some alteration, besides in manner. There is none. She's certain that if she could see below the suit, this thing would still have a mechanical leg, based solely on the way it balances its weight, physics guiding stance, rather than personality or preference. Every similarity she catalogs only nauseates her more.

"I do," she says when not-Lachlan's expression begins to turn confused and hurt at the silence. "You don't."

The double frowns. "Oh," she says. It's such a wrong sound, from that mouth. Allowing. Sweet. Empty-headed and trusting and . . . and . . . *flattened.*

Like me, Tamsin thinks, even as she recoils with disgust. This is how Lachlan sees her. How Prime sees her.

Pathetically childlike. Empty. A blank slate.

And the worst of it is, she understands it now. She feels it down to her core. She can't endure this reflection of what she's become, and having it written onto *Lachlan's* face, of all faces, is—is—

She can't stay here.

But when she staggers back, her ankle twists, and the incision sites burn, as if they're ripping back open. She gasps with pain, and her knee buckles, unwilling to allow her to keep hurting herself.

And the double surges forward and catches her.

"You're hurt," the double says. Its grip on her is like iron, unrelenting, precisely the way Lachlan had taken hold of her in Prime's basement, but its expression is alien. There's no cold remove there, only empathetic pain and worry. The only recognizable traces of *Lachlan* are its features and the possessive light in its eyes.

It moves to scoop her up into its arms.

"Let go," Tamsin protests, trying to pull away.

But the double's grip just tightens. "You need care. Let me help you."

If this was Lachlan, she'd give in. But it's not. This thing is just mimicking Lachlan at her basest level. Tamsin's disgust and panic turn to rage, to rejection.

"I said let go!"

She throws her weight to her left side. The double overbalances, surprised and refusing to release her. Something in its leg gives a high, metallic whine and buckles. The double spills onto the floor and Tamsin along with it.

The double's head hits the coffee table on the way down.

Tamsin stares. She hadn't even known it was there. Now the corner of the table is slick with hair and blood and bits of flesh. The floor is smooth; more blood spreads across it, inexorably, until it reaches her skin.

And beneath her, Lachlan's body is motionless.

Chapter Thirty-Eight

It takes fifteen minutes for the double to die.

It doesn't open its eyes in that entire span, but it moans occasionally. Once or twice, a finger twitches. Tamsin stands vigil over it all, half out of a sense of obligation and half out of frozen horror. Blood drips from the table edge, and what she thinks might be bits of brain, pinkish grayish globs of tissue that can't quite hold together.

At fourteen minutes, the double's eyelids flicker.

Tamsin kneels and smashes its head into the floor, again and again, until the last tremors are gone.

It's the safer option. There's no chance of the double getting up again. No chance of it stealing everything from Lachlan, the way Prime has taken everything from her.

But it's also no longer an accident.

She stares at the body, her hands still gripping the sides of its head. In its face, she now sees only Lachlan. Lachlan, trapping her in this gilded cage. Lachlan, who thinks she's some helpless, childlike thing to be coddled and shielded. Lachlan, whose form she has murdered.

It's too close to the real thing. Her breathing is coming too rapidly. Her head is starting to spin. She lets go and pushes herself away, knowing she needs to not look, unable to do anything but.

Lachlan, murdered.

Bits of quantum-entanglement theory drift through her mind. Bodies as particles, lives as equivalent exchange. And those stories she'd read, scrounging for any hint as to Prime's nature, they'd all said that killing the double had meant killing the self. Murder became suicide. The knife wound in the reflection became a knife wound in the flesh.

What if—

What if—

Her entire body tenses, and she twists to the side at last, hand clasped over her mouth as she tries not to vomit.

She stays there, huddled over and shaking, now as unable to look as she was to turn away. The body is just Lachlan's. Her one ally, the only fixed point aside from Prime. Now meat, just meat, and here she is, alone, no obvious road ahead of her.

She can't do this. There's too much she doesn't know, doesn't understand, and she wants to scream at the thought.

But she doesn't. She forces herself to breathe. To think.

There must be options.

There always are.

If Lachlan is dead—and she can't assume that's true, not until the sun sets and Lachlan isn't home—*if* she's dead, then Tamsin is on her own. There is nobody left to stop Prime, or to solve the mystery of the doors, or to look out for other doubles. If Lachlan is dead, she needs every advantage she can get, every scrap of data.

She makes herself look at the double again. Her hands ache with the echo of each slam of skull against floor. She can still hear the crunch and squish of bone and brain. Except it is not Lachlan; it is something very like Prime. The thought doesn't give her comfort, but it fights back the nausea, the tears, and her hand almost doesn't shake as she reaches out to touch it.

It's still warm, but not warm enough to feel right.

She scoots closer until her hip is pressed to the double's leg. Blood soaks into her dress. She touches the double's face, tilts it this way and that, until she is sure there is nothing to be gained from it.

Then she moves on to the rest.

Tamsin tugs at the double's clothing, trying to get it off, but its limbs are heavy and unresponsive, fighting her as she goes. She manages, finally, to drag the jacket off, the blood that has soaked into the wool smearing onto her hands. She searches it for flaws in the suit's construction, not knowing what she's looking for but desperately hoping she'll know it when she sees it. The fabric is heavy and smooth enough to be expensive. The label is recognizable along the same axis. Except—

Except she can't actually read the label.

She squints at it. Blood obscures some of the text, but not all. She should be able to read it. She *thinks* she can read it. But when she tries to sound out the word, she can't. There's a block.

She blinks, and the words resolve.

Momentary lapse, or something else? She wants to grab the tablet, go through her old notes again, because the door had behaved similarly, hadn't it? That had been damage, yes, but between one blink and the next, the door had been able to change. (Perhaps. Maybe. Or she's still panicking. The simulacrum of Lachlan's body is unmoving and too soft beneath her hands, no longer reflexively tensing, not resisting anything she does to it. Its blood is warm but cooling fast. She hates it.)

She doesn't get the tablet. She needs to minimize the cleaning that comes next. Instead, she tugs loose the tie, unbuttons the shirt. It tears as she maneuvers it off the body's shoulder, but beneath, the prosthetic limb looks exactly as Tamsin remembers it, though it's been a few days since she's had an unobstructed view. Except the flesh on the residual limb is smooth; where the scars from multiple surgeries should be, there are only faint indentations.

A blink, and the scars are there.

It's as if the double is still constructing itself, even in death, based on observation. Tamsin, when she saw Prime for the first time, already knew herself in depth; the physical mimicry was perfect from the start. But Tamsin is only just beginning to know Lachlan, to see her. It takes longer for whatever is happening to pull the details from her.

She doesn't reach for the fly of the trousers, even though she's desperate to see if the leg behaves the same way. She needs to contain the effect, in case the remaining differences are keeping the real Lachlan safe. She forces herself upright, ankle protesting, other foot slipping in the blood. Towels. She'll need towels. Cleaning fluid. But first, she needs to move the body. It needs to go *away*.

Tamsin retrieves the wheelchair from her bedroom. Blood smears from her hands onto the metal, sticking, tacky between flesh and chair.

From the hallway, the body looks almost as if it's sleeping. But she has left it in shambles, shirt torn half off and flesh exposed. The blood, now that it's drying, looks less oceanic than it had felt beneath her legs, but it still turns her stomach.

There is a blanket along the back of the couch. One of those lived-in details. She tugs it free and spreads it out over the mess, fighting it as it balls up and drags through the puddles. With a desperate pull, she hauls it over the double's face and the wreckage of its skull and uses the corner to wipe down the edge of the table, knocking brain matter and hair loose. Then she wipes the rest of the blood off her hands, a faint scrim remaining only in the creases of her knuckles, along her cuticles, beneath her nails.

It helps.

From there, she tries to lift the body, but it's so heavy. Not stiff at all, and still not cold, either. The distribution of weight is unpredictable without muscle tension to hold limbs and organs firmly in place. Her arms tremble. Her body protests, and the press of what is almost Lachlan against her is unbearably intimate. An arm slides loose of the blanket and drapes over her shoulders, and it is so very close to an embrace.

She stands. Her knees quake, and her ankle screams, but she stands.

With a cry, Tamsin heaves the body into the wheelchair. Without consciousness, it can't hold itself upright; it slumps, begins to slide down. Tamsin catches it, bracing it chest to chest, and shoves the unresponsive limbs into place. The head hangs forward, heavy, onto her shoulder.

Dead. Dead. Lachlan, dead.

She pushes the thought aside. If it's not Lachlan, then the body itself doesn't matter. It's just a thing to be gotten rid of. Put out of the way, so she can work.

She hides it in the front bathroom, the one with all the medical supplies. The shower stall is large enough. She shoves it inside, then goes through the cabinets, looking for things she might need. Painkillers for her ankle, which is throbbing sharply, even when she has no weight on it. Saline wash and antiseptic ointment and fresh gauze for her eye socket. She has to assume she'll need to care for her own wounds from here on out, while she . . .

What?

The future is still a gray fog. Impenetrable, unsettling.

She needs to clean everything as best she can, she decides, to give herself more room to think. Her clothing is stained through, and her hands are growing stiff, even wiped down. She scrubs at them in the sink, then staggers out of the room.

With a door between her and the corpse, she already feels more capable. In the foyer cabinets, she finds cleaning fluid and rags along with a bag she can shove it all in when she's done. She carries everything back to the living room, gets down on her hands and knees, and scrubs.

The blood is stubborn, but the material the floors are made of is slick and nonporous. It doesn't stain. When she's done, she tosses the rags into the bag and strips out of her own ruined clothes and stuffs them in after. The bag is at capacity.

Naked, Tamsin limps to her own bathroom. Her legs are still covered in blood, and she can't tell if she's popped a suture or if her ankle has just been too sorely used. She hopes it's the latter, because she needs to get washed up and changed before she can leave.

And she's going to have to leave.

The sooner, the better. Lachlan's double means things are accelerating somehow; *somebody* needs to know. And if Lachlan is still alive, Tamsin doesn't want to be here when she returns and sees what Tamsin has done.

But a few steps from the bathroom, she stops.

The impossible door is still there.

She's not sure why she expected it to be gone. The double's body is still, for lack of a better word, active. It is adjusting under observation. It's not alive, not the way she is, but it exists. The door, as well, remains.

If she could reach out and take the knob, would it open for her?

She almost tries, but the dread and terror is stronger than ever. She ducks into the bathroom instead.

Her ankle is swollen, but the lines of neat sutures remain intact. Now, washed clean and dried off, she perches on the edge of the tub and bandages it the way Lachlan did. Then she gets one of the pain pills and cracks it in half with her thumbnail. She swallows it dry as she pads to the bedroom. Her equations and notes stare down at her from beside the rearranged bed as she slips into the last dress, one of the delicate things Lachlan had purchased for the version of Tamsin that is little more than a pet. It fits her perfectly.

There are no shoes in the closet. Nothing, not even slippers. It will look strange, being outside without shoes, but what other option does she have now? Lachlan's bedroom is always locked.

She leaves her own room and all her notes behind.

Out through the living room, now free of blood, but wrong, all wrong. Its lived-in comfort has been tainted immutably. And from there to the foyer, where she thinks she can smell blood even through the closed bathroom door.

She has to go, and she has to go now. Tamsin reaches out and hits the call button for the elevator.

The indicator doesn't light up. There is no sound from the elevator shaft.

"No," Tamsin says. "*No*," she repeats, finally recalling the fob Lachlan had used to clear them to come to this floor. The pieces slot into place. It's a key, just as much as the keypad on the door to her basement.

Security, Tamsin thinks. Lachlan doesn't compromise on security, or on privacy. But there must be some other option, a way out in case of an emergency. Lachlan would have insisted, just as much as she would have insisted on a strong lock to her front door.

There aren't any signs pointing the way, and she doesn't know how to tell a stairwell door from an interior door, not really. But she finds it. It's the one door that locks from this side. It's the one door with more than one lock.

It's the one door with a keypad and a metal box bolted securely to it, tamperproof and inaccessible.

She's trapped.

She retreats, a hunted beast, to her bedroom, grabbing the tablet and curling up atop the hospital bed. The tablet wakes up when she taps it, but the battery is running low, and she's not sure where the charger is.

She'll have to move quickly. Think quickly. Her lack of understanding about the outside world will be a hindrance, but there must be something she can utilize from the scraps Lachlan has given her and the bits and pieces she's gathered from the television.

First, she pulls up a map and locates everywhere she thinks might be relevant. This building's address. A visual of where her house's address puts it in the city. The main Myrica Dynamics building. The deep node labs.

Then she pulls up everything she can find on electronic locks. She couldn't find a maker's mark on the box, so she can't pull up a manual, but everything she does find states that guessing the code is likely not an option.

But everything also says that, except in extreme cases where the risk of death to those inside the locked structure is judged less important than whatever the lock protects, the lock will disengage if she cuts the power.

The problem will be in getting inside. Specialized tools are cited more than once. She jots down everything that might be helpful and then moves on to Lachlan's contact list.

Even if she can get out of the building, she has no shoes and no idea how to obtain a ride. Her best option for actual rescue is to utilize the internet connection to call for help; as long as she has Wi-Fi, there's an app that claims it will work. She's not entirely sure who she's going to call. Cara, perhaps—Prime's assistant. But Cara will know something is wrong if a second Dr. Rivers pings her while the first is standing right there. The same goes for everybody who works in Dr. Rivers's lab.

The CEO of Myrica Dynamics? He'd know something about her sounded off. He'd try to call Lachlan, surely. And if he couldn't reach her, what then?

None of the other names on the list are recognizable. For all she knows, any one of them could be happy to help her and willing to not ask questions. She looks at all of them, one by one, willing some memory to spark.

Nothing.

She finds herself, in the end, staring at the entry for Dr. Tamsin Rivers. She calls Prime.

Chapter Thirty-Nine

Prime answers her phone on the third ring.

It's a long enough delay that Tamsin's resolve has begun to waver. Unable to pace, she chews at her fingernails. She stares at the battery, down to four percent now.

And then, "This is Dr. Rivers speaking."

Tamsin nearly hangs up.

The sound of Prime's voice makes her ankle flare in pain, her missing eye ache along the walls of the socket. *Don't go back,* her mind hisses. *Don't go back, she'll hurt you again.*

"Mx. Woodfield?"

"It's me," Tamsin whispers, mastering her fear as best she can, shoving it down. She needs to see Prime again, no matter her terror. They are bound together. Something is at work between them. If she can figure out what it is, how it functions . . .

Her eyes drift to the wall.

Something new leaps out at her. A base premise even she hadn't thought to question, though she's had no way of proving its validity:

All her node labs, she's assumed, have been *here.*

But there's another option, isn't there, if she's already been forced to accept that Prime exists, that the door appeared, that the world is shifting below her feet? What if Prime didn't come from nowhere? What if Tamsin's actions didn't make her? What if, like Tamsin's naive state, Prime's was induced? Consider two iterations of the world, side-by-side, very similar, and two iterations of Tamsin working on the same project. Consider two node labs communicating across that divide, making contact.

What is a door, besides a point of transition? Of connection?

"Nought?"

She swallows down her fear. "I need your help."

Silence.

"I'm at Lachlan Woodfield's apartment," she says, and if her voice still trembles, it's an effective appeal to Prime's superiority. She stammers out the address. "I can't speak for long. But she's not here, and I can't leave on my own. The elevator is keyed to a token she has. The stairs have an electronic lock of some kind."

"I'll come by the stairs," Prime says at last. "I'll find a way to get the door open. And then you'll come home with me."

No.

"Yes," she says. "Please."

It is better if she's sweet and biddable. It's better if Prime doesn't know what she's capable of. Killing Prime may not be an option, but there must be some answer, some way to exploit the link between them or to finally, *finally* open the door.

What would it take, to open the door?

"I'll be there in twenty minutes," Prime says. "Be ready. We won't have much time."

She almost tells Prime not to worry. That Lachlan probably isn't coming back. But that, at least, she keeps for herself.

In the hallway, Tamsin crouches down in front of the locked stairwell door. Beside her is the small bag she's filled with medical supplies and what tools she could find in the few unlocked cabinets in the foyer and stashed in kitchen drawers. The metal housing of the electronic lock is smooth. The keypad is wiped down.

Lachlan did not design this apartment as a prison, but as a fortress. There must be a quick disarm code, something to allow Lachlan to escape in case of an emergency. She wishes she knew Lachlan well enough to guess it. Wishes she knew enough about the broader world to know what the average person might choose.

She'll need brute force instead.

None of the tools she's found fit the tiny screws in the casing, and they and the surrounding metal are hard, harder than she was prepared for. There are seams, but she can't get anything into them. She fights it for the better part of twenty minutes, all the time she has, while her brain works over the implications of her new theory. If Prime came from somewhere else, she can go *back* to somewhere else. If Prime is not just a distorted reflection of Tamsin, then her goals may be more complicated, less predictable. If the node labs are back on, then they could be talking to Prime's origin, and who knows where that could lead?

The minutes tick by, and nothing is working. There's not even a scratch on the housing. Tamsin gets up, swaying on her feet, and lurches toward the living room. She grabs the heaviest object she can find, Lachlan's espresso machine, and carries it back. She eyes the casing, bites her lip.

If she smashes it hard enough, it might disrupt the power.

It's inelegant, but the first collision leaves a mark at last. The metal dents. Her arms vibrate with the referred force, and she thinks of the double's head in her hands again. The wet snap, the eventual give. How different that felt from this, and yet the fear and anger driving her is the same.

She brings the espresso machine down again, and this time, there's a crunch and a spark. Panting, bent double, she sets the machine aside and reaches for the doorknob.

There's a series of clicks, and it twists under her hand. She doesn't need Prime after all. She can do this. She can—

Behind the open door, Prime stands on the landing. There's a sleek black case in her hand.

She's beautiful. Her makeup is perfect. Panic flares in Tamsin's chest, uncontrollable, overwhelming, but she clamps down on it. *Nought* feared Prime. Tamsin, by contrast, is beginning to know her.

They know each other.

"How?" she asks, not entirely conscious of shaping the word.

"EMP," Prime says. She takes in Tamsin's shorter hair, her delicate dress, then peers around her, into the hall. She looks intrigued, not cautious.

"I'm ready," Tamsin says.

But Prime ignores her, stepping past her into the apartment. Tamsin's hand tightens on the door. The animal urge to run away (hobble away) wars with her ability to be patient, to keep Prime close until they get back to the house. It's the best option she has in a sea of terrible ones. Maybe, if she knew Lachlan was still alive (*don't think about it*), she could try to delay Prime long enough to summon Lachlan here to deal with her, but she's still operating under the assumption that she's on her own.

Which means either finding someplace, impossibly, to hide and care for herself and try to fix everything without getting close to Prime, or staying close and going back to where it all started.

It's abundantly clear which is the better move.

"Hm," Prime says, unerringly approaching the door that shouldn't be there.

Tamsin wedges her little bag in between the door and the frame and eases the door almost shut. Then she limps up behind Prime. "How could you tell?" she asks.

"Poor placement," Prime says. "But I wasn't sure. Have you tried to open it?"

"I can't even move the lever," she confesses.

"Has anything else?"

Any*thing* else. But of course; it's an obvious leap. *Not yet*, she needs to say. *It only just appeared.*

Prime looks away from the door, at last, and back to her. She takes Tamsin's measure, then makes a small, thoughtful sound and walks deeper into the apartment.

Tamsin follows, mouth going dry.

"Bleach," Prime murmurs, moving inexorably toward the living area, the coffee table. It's clean, all clean. Too clean? Prime is looking around the room, gaze never settling, taking everything in. Trying to reconstruct Tamsin's actions or taking the opportunity to learn about Lachlan? Either way, she's in the territory of an adversary.

There is a slight discoloration on the floor where the double's body had been, Tamsin realizes, heart sinking. Not a stain, but a lightening. She should have diluted the bleach, she thinks too late.

Prime kneels. Fingers the table corner. Her nail catches in a depression. Was that there before?

"Where is it now?" Prime asks.

"It was an accident," Tamsin says, helpless.

Prime rises smoothly and turns to face her, her expression all concern and sympathy. "I understand," Prime says, using the same patronizing tone of voice she'd used on Nought over and over again. Tamsin does her best not to glare or show any hint of how much it bothers her. "I don't blame you. But I need to see it."

"Why?"

"It's a data point," Prime says. "It's like you. We don't even know if you'd stay dead if you were killed; for all we know, you'd re-form. Or re-emerge from the door. Can you take me to it?"

(*This is good*, Tamsin tells herself. *She doesn't know I've figured out I'm the original*. But it makes her sinews tighten, her breath quicken.)

Tamsin shivers and hugs herself around the middle. "We should go," she says.

"As soon as I've seen it. Don't make me look for myself, please. That will only delay us."

Tamsin grimaces, but nods, and leads the way out to the foyer. She waves a hand at the bathroom door. "In there," she says. "I couldn't—I didn't want to look at it anymore."

"Understandably." Prime hesitates a moment, as if considering laying a reassuring hand on Tamsin's shoulder, but moves away without any contact. She opens the door.

Prime stands motionless for a long time, gazing at the body of Lachlan's double.

Tamsin can't see it, but she can smell the blood. Feel again the unresisting, too-heavy weight of the body, the slide of its insensate arm around her shoulders, the loll of its head. Flecks of brain and clumps of hair on the table edge.

Dizzy, Tamsin sinks onto the bench, putting her head in her hands.

Eventually, the door snicks shut, footsteps approach her, and a hand settles onto the crown of her head.

"Well, that explains why the scalpel didn't do anything. Why did you remove her shirt?"

Tamsin sucks in an uneven breath. "To see where she differed from the original. To prove she *was* different from the original."

"Did you find anything?"

It would be very easy to lie. The double's arm is identical, now that she's inspected it. Prime probably didn't strip her down the rest of the way. She wonders if she should conceal what she's figured out. If Prime would prefer her still naive and oblivious to what's happening to the both of them.

Maybe Prime doesn't even know this part. Maybe Prime is asking for herself. Because even if she walked in through a door from a world just like this one, something happened to her, just like something happened to Lachlan's double. That period of reconciliation. Adjustment. Correction. Something about the transition leaving details unfinished. But come through the door, and the adjustments begin. Maybe *that* is the source of Prime's blank slate when she first appeared.

Not actual recent birth, but a loading state. Then, with time, with exposure to Tamsin, Prime didn't so much become Tamsin as become herself again.

It's only a theory, and it doesn't explain what's happened to *her*, but it's the strongest explanation Tamsin has. It coils in Tamsin's belly, enticing, intoxicating. Giving it to Prime is a risk. But Tamsin can still explain her actions, even if she holds the conclusions tight to her chest.

The basics only, then. For now. "Yes. The duplication was—incomplete, until observed. Until *I* observed her. The scars on her arm were barely there, and then I blinked, and they were the way I'd seen them before."

"Like the door," Prime says. An olive branch, a bit of information Tamsin shouldn't have, except that she's read her own notes.

Tamsin lifts her head. Prime's hand slides down to cup her jaw.

"How much do you know about what we are?" Tamsin asks, testing out the waters of what Prime has discovered on her own.

Any response is liable to be incomplete or an outright lie. Regardless, whatever Prime tells her will always have meaning. Either accuracy, or insight into what she might be concealing and why.

Tamsin just has to hope she can discern the difference.

Prime's hand drops away. "I know that we are physically identical, save for the surgical pins." *At least one lie.* "And those did not appear as I searched for them." She looks toward the elevator door, though her eyes aren't focused. "I know that we have the same knowledge base. Slightly different personalities. And nobody would ever mistake us for one another if they heard us speak."

"We haven't been near each other for very long," Tamsin says. She hopes she sounds guileless. "If it's an active patterning, perhaps exposure is required."

With more time, maybe whatever process stripped Tamsin of herself will begin to reverse. Maybe she'll regain what she once had.

Or maybe she'll have to step through the door first.

Her hands begin to tremble.

"Perhaps," Prime says, eyeing her carefully. "You've been thinking, then, in your captivity?"

Tamsin's laugh is weak and gasping. "You could say that." She hugs herself tightly, then relaxes and makes herself stand. "I've been doing research. At Lachlan's behest." Her gaze drifts to the closed bathroom door. "In maybe half the stories about doubles and doppelgängers, when the original tries to kill their double, the original dies with it."

Prime tilts her head. To all appearances, she looks thoughtful, as if she's never considered this before. "A sympathetic resonance, of a sort. Like the patterning you observed. Bringing mirror images into agreement. But when I cut into your ankle," she adds, "mine remained unharmed."

True enough. And Tamsin's eye is gone, but Prime's remains. Prime's hair is still long. If she blinks, the wounds on her body don't ramify onto Prime's.

(She's not sure whether she's glad for that or not. On the one hand, it means Lachlan might still be alive. On the other, it would have been a direct line to harming Prime, should it become necessary.)

Though—

"Perhaps it doesn't go both ways," she says before she can filter the thought.

Prime's gaze sharpens. "What do you mean?"

The blood drains from her face, and she turns away, fusses with a cabinet door. "I don't know."

"No, you have a theory." Prime's hand closes over her shoulder. "Tell me. In which direction *would* it go?"

"From the original to the double," Tamsin stammers. "The source of the pattern to the recipient." It sounds good. It sounds better, really, than her actual leap, that the original can't influence the double, but the double can harm the original. Her only evidence for that is how Tamsin's memories and mind had begun to fail after Prime appeared, but temporal correlation doesn't mean causation.

Prime circles around her, looking at her intently. "You called because you thought Lachlan, the original, was dead. Because of those stories."

She swallows against a tightening throat. "Yes," she says softly.

"That doesn't match your hypothesis. But there's more to it, isn't there? You're afraid she's not dead at all. You're afraid of what will happen if she returns. If she sees what you've done."

Tamsin flinches. "And the door. The door is still here. I need to know what it means."

Prime's jaw works as she runs her tongue over her teeth. She parts her lips with an audible pop. "Well then," she says and pats Tamsin's shoulder. Then she turns and walks back into the main room.

Tamsin follows. They're almost to the hallway when she hears the rumble. The crash. The floor beneath her shudders, then stills again, and the faintest threads of sirens follow in the quiet after.

She sways on her feet, unsteady and stunned. She stares at the bank of windows.

There used to be a building off to the right of the view. Almost as tall as this one but of a different design, with less glass, more stone. Not *close*, but not far, either; the blocks between them were almost countable.

It's gone now, replaced with a plume of smoke.

"Come on," Prime says, voice flat and resigned behind her. "It's time to go."

Chapter Forty

Prime's phone rings constantly as they near the ground floor, but Prime ignores it, too busy urging Tamsin down ahead of her. Tamsin's ankle is bleeding again. She can feel it, hot and slick against her bandages, and there is a trail behind her. She has to clutch hard to the railing, and it's only the consistent rhythm of each step down that keeps her from tripping, the world swimming around her, her depth perception strained.

Forty-seven floors is too many. Prime couldn't have come up this way. Maybe she took the elevator to the highest non-secured floor, climbed the rest of the way, but if that's an option, Prime hasn't suggested it now.

Too great a risk of being seen together, Tamsin thinks. And Tamsin is anything but forgettable.

They emerge, finally, into the same garage Lachlan had brought her in through. Her head is spinning, and she sags on Prime's arm. "Just a moment," she whispers.

"Not much farther now," Prime says. She sounds winded, too, at least.

There's activity all around them. Cars pulling out, leaving. Nobody coming in. Nobody sparing them a second glance. "Is this building going to go down, too?"

Prime doesn't respond. Instead, she pushes against Tamsin's back, making her stumble forward a few steps. They don't go far at all, just a few parking spaces over, and—

It's Lachlan's car.

Lachlan's car sits in the spot where Lachlan had parked it days ago, when she brought Tamsin home. Lachlan is not inside it or leaning against the door. It's empty. It unlocks when Prime pulls keys from her pocket.

Her heart gives an unwelcome pang. *Dead. Lachlan is probably dead. This isn't her car anymore.*

"Wait," Tamsin whispers, but Prime is already pulling open the door.

"Get in," Prime says. Her hand closes on Tamsin's shoulder, and Tamsin recoils. Prime doesn't let her get far. Tamsin looks around the garage, frantic, and there are people, people she could call out to, but she needs to cooperate. She needs Prime to keep trusting her.

Tamsin crawls into the back seat.

"Now, stay down until I tell you otherwise. No need to draw attention." And she covers Tamsin with a blanket.

It's not one Lachlan would have picked, Tamsin thinks, the realization incongruous and useless and achingly painful. While Prime closes the door and circles around to get in the driver's seat, Tamsin pets the fabric. It's brightly colored. Extremely soft, but synthetic. Not something Prime would've chosen either. Something from the lab, then?

But not Lachlan's. This is Lachlan's car, but there's no trace of her, and if Prime has it, then that suggests—

The car pulls into motion. Slow, and they stop and start as Prime navigates them out of the garage, through the scrum of panicked people. Tamsin wishes she could look. Could see anything beyond her own hands. She already feared Lachlan might be dead, so why is she responding so strongly to what feels like proof? It should be a relief. The answering of a question, the closing of a boundless anxiety.

Confirmation, too, that killing Prime is not an option, but she doesn't care about that.

She can't breathe. Tamsin throws the blanket off, gasping for air. The car runs as silently as ever through the din of sirens now around them. She can't see the emergency vehicles from here, but they're close. A few streets over, maybe. There's too much dust to be sure, the sky darkened as if dusk is approaching. Through the haze, the sun is a small pink circle.

"*Nought,*" Prime snaps, but Tamsin can't bear to cover herself up again. She's too busy staring out the window.

"I'll keep my head down," she whispers.

The colors are all wrong. Yellow and gray and gritty, and all around them is screaming. People on phones, tearing at their hair. People running toward the disaster. People running away. People not moving at all.

The road they're on is nearly gridlocked, but traffic is creeping forward. There's a man at the intersection waving people through. The traffic lights are out.

"It's not just that one building, is it?"

Prime fusses with the touch screen in the center console, ignoring the chaos all around them, the pain, the terror. "No," she says distractedly. "There have been major water-main breaks in at least four different locations across the city. A few apartment buildings went down up north about an hour ago. We appear to have hit an inflection point; I assume further collapses will happen throughout the day."

"It's accelerating," Tamsin says, looking at the back of Prime's head. "Our—your projections said we had weeks left still."

"You can sit up now. Put your seat belt on," Prime says. Tamsin straightens up and fumbles with the buckle. The car passes through another intersection only for Prime to veer off at the last second, making a severe turn that leaves other drivers honking furiously. But the street she takes them onto is a little emptier, the other cars moving faster, and they pick up speed. The sirens don't fade, but the voices do. The air grows clearer with every block.

"What have you done?" Tamsin asks.

Prime flexes her fingers on the steering wheel. "What Myrica Dynamics has asked of me," she says. "Nothing more, and nothing less."

She must mean the node labs, the communication project, and yet Tamsin isn't certain. Prime is in Lachlan's car. She is confident and easy and powerful in the driver's seat, steering them through the city as if she knows it, navigating like Lachlan navigated. Maybe the reciprocal damage of double to original isn't via resonance, wounds appearing as if by magic. Maybe her murder of the double coincided with *Prime* hurting Lachlan.

Two pairs of doubles, intertwined, bleeding into one another. *Dangerous.*

"Prime," she says, and her voice trembles. "Do you know if Lachlan—"

Before she can finish the question, Prime's phone rings again. She glances down at it, the car slowing slightly until she touches something on the dash, and the car takes over its own steering. She hits Accept on the call, then thumbs it to speakerphone.

"What have you done?"

Lachlan's voice fills the car, and Tamsin chokes. Her eyes close as relief floods her. Lachlan is alive.

Lachlan is alive and is going to learn exactly how dangerous Tamsin is. The relief curdles, rises into her throat, and she gags on it.

(*Isn't this what you wanted? Now she'll never treat you like a helpless child again.*)

"Your vehicle is company property, Mx. Woodfield," Prime says, voice smooth and even. "It can be requisitioned by employees of sufficient rank during an emergency, which I am and this is. Apologies for not being able to tell you I was taking it. Are you able to get to safety?"

"I'm standing in my apartment right now," Lachlan snaps. "I want to know why it smells like bleach and blood, and where you've taken Dr. Rivers."

Prime's eyes are reflected in the rearview mirror. She looks directly at Tamsin as she speaks. "What an interesting choice of nomenclature," she says, voice chilly. "And just now, the double called me *Prime*. What did you fill her head with, I wonder? I don't think I have to point out that you didn't take her to a lab, do I? That I found her dressed up like a doll?"

"Don't," Tamsin pleads. This isn't relevant. How had she slipped, called Prime *Prime* instead of Dr. Rivers?

She feels the shreds of power she had grasped in the foyer slipping away.

"Is that her? Is she there with you?" Lachlan demands. "Tamsin?"

"I'm here," she says. Her voice is still shaking.

"You called *me*, Mx. Woodfield. And so did she, for that matter. She asked me to come retrieve her. She's frightened of you."

"Tamsin, tell me where she's taking you."

Tamsin opens her mouth. Nothing comes out. She's caught, pinned between two truths: that she doesn't trust Prime not to hurt her, and she doesn't trust Lachlan to be able to help.

"You asked about the blood. Have you checked your front bathroom yet?" Prime asks, smiling.

Tamsin lurches forward. "No, Lachlan, don't—"

But she can hear Lachlan's footsteps, loud and purposeful enough to transfer over the phone, and then a door slamming open, and—

"What?"

All the anger has left her, and she sounds . . . deflated. Empty. Tamsin closes her eyes, wincing as she pictures it: Lachlan standing in the bathroom doorway, staring at the slack, disheveled image of herself, dead and long cold now.

"It was an accident," Tamsin whispers. She doesn't know if Lachlan can hear her.

"I am glad to hear you're still alive," Prime says. "Our mutual charge was concerned that murdering your double would harm you. It seems you've dodged a bullet, Mx. Woodfield."

"What does this mean?" Lachlan demands.

"It means you may not want to stay in the building for very long," Prime says curtly. "You never know when things might begin to distort."

"*Wait—*" Tamsin says, louder this time, but the sound cuts out. The line is closed. Prime slips the phone into a pocket.

Tamsin's face couldn't unlock the screen anyway; the gauze square and the wreckage below make sure of that. *She hobbled you,* Lachlan's voice echoes.

"Well, we've disproven the stories," Prime says. The car beeps, screen showing an alert for closed roads ahead, and she takes over steering again, moving them through another shorted traffic light, around a sinkhole the length of a truck. "Killing the double didn't kill the original. As for the other direction . . . you think that you're the original?"

The interior of the car is warm, warmer than the chill radiating through the windows, but not enough to explain why the air feels like it's starting to boil.

"If I do," Tamsin says warily, "if I am, does it even matter? Nobody but Lachlan can tell."

"I'm curious as to how you arrived at your conclusion." She pauses, car slowing as she catches sight of a knot of ambulances and fire trucks ahead of her, then makes a tight turn to send their car back the way it came. "It never occurred to me, when I was in your position."

Tamsin claws one hand into the seat to stop herself from scrambling forward or reaching for Prime. She never expected such an easy admission that Prime is the double, let alone honesty about what came before. "What do you mean?"

"When I came to with no memories in your basement. When you imprisoned me, treated me like a thing to be studied. I never once thought

I might be the original. And yet you not only conceived of the possibility, but seem wedded to it. Is it just because Lachlan told you to think that way?" Her lips tighten into a sneer. "I didn't think you were that malleable."

"That's not it," Tamsin says. "She noticed first, but—there were tests."

"Of what kind?"

"Procedural memory that you didn't know to implement," she says, because there's no reason to lie at this point. "And Lachlan had a copy of my notes. The phone isn't secure."

Prime grimaces, then taps out a few commands. The car once more takes over, no more alerts on the screen popping up to warn Prime of road closures. They must be past the worst of it. "I cleared it."

"Not before she saved a copy."

Prime leans back against her seat, staring forward. Her fingers drum on the wheel, which moves without her input, twisting back and forth, avoiding small buckles in the asphalt that its sensors pick up. Tamsin watches, pinned in the back seat by the belt across her chest.

"What happens now?" she asks when she can take the silence no more.

"We're going home," Prime says. The car makes another turn.

"Don't you need to—to help? With the subsidence recovery efforts? You'll be expected."

Prime twists in her seat to smile at Tamsin. "You're more important," she says. "I'm making the time. The city will still be here in the morning. Mostly."

Tamsin squeezes her eye shut. "How much do you know?" she asks only slightly above a whisper. "About what you are? About what's happening to us?"

Prime hums thoughtfully, but doesn't answer. Instead, she says, "I'm not going to hurt you, if that's what you're afraid of."

Tamsin tries not to flinch. Her ankle throbs. "You've done it before."

"Yes. But I don't need to now. Do I?"

Prime reaches between the seats to touch Tamsin's knee. It is gentle. Light.

"We're the same person, Tamsin. I'm sure we can come to an understanding."

An understanding. Prime wants something from her, but it isn't her death. Strange, because if Tamsin is dead, and Prime survives her, Prime becomes Dr. Rivers with no way it can be taken from her. She *should* want it.

Tamsin makes herself look again. Prime's eyes are bright. She does not look angry. More curious. Engaged. Just like Tamsin, when she's bearing down on an answer.

"How much do you know?" Tamsin asks again.

"Enough," Prime says.

The car makes a soft chiming sound, and Prime pulls away, turning her attention fully back to the road. She takes over steering the car as it glides onto a street Tamsin recognizes. Her house sits three blocks ahead of them.

Two.

One.

Hurting Prime will not, necessarily, hurt *her*; if it does, it will only be because of the car spinning out of control or Prime fighting back. But it also can't help her. Lachlan's double is dead, and the door still sits in Lachlan's hallway. There's some last piece she's still missing, and there's only one place she can find it.

Prime parks just in front of the house. She steps out of the car, then circles around to hand Tamsin out onto the sidewalk.

The cement is cold against her bare feet. The garden has begun to die back for the winter into manicured ranks of bare stems, the exact forms of the plants unrecognizable now, stripped to their cores.

She walks up the path. Prime doesn't let go of her hand and leans across her to unlock the front door. She does not unlatch it.

"After you," Prime says, and Tamsin pushes it open.

Chapter Forty-One

The house is exactly as she remembers it. Penrose sits on the stairs, watching the both of them, his tail flicking idly. She is acutely aware of Prime just behind her, trapping her in this place where she has been cut apart, rearranged, repurposed.

"Is something wrong?" Prime asks, stepping around her.

Tamsin recoils, and it's only her swollen feet that keep her rooted to the spot. *Yes*, she wants to shout, but she can't give Prime that. "Just wondering," she stammers instead, "how much of my familiarity is because of how long I lived here before I forgot everything."

"Some, I'm sure," Prime says, depositing her phone on the nearby console table. "A base level of emotional comfort. Reflexive navigation. Particularly if you don't pay attention to it, you should be able to get around just fine."

"My notes said that there were times I didn't understand the layout of the house," Tamsin says, letting the door fall closed and moving a little deeper into the space. Her notes say that there was a knife, once. She'd had a knife but couldn't remember why, or what had happened to it.

She thinks she has an idea now. Some part of her had figured out there was something very wrong, and she'd almost fixed it.

"Panic attacks and nightmares. Part of the degradation of your consciousness, I think. You didn't always remember, afterward. It was an early sign."

Tamsin swallows hard. "An early sign of what?"

Prime touches her elbow, guiding her into the hall. Toward the basement. "That you were losing hold of yourself."

Tamsin limps forward, against the screaming in her ankle and her head. "You say that as if it wasn't inevitable. That you weren't taking myself from me."

"Is that what I was doing?" Prime asks, sounding, just briefly, unsure.

Tamsin thinks back over all her notes, all her justifications for why she wasn't seeking help. Why she wasn't telling Lachlan the truth of what was happening to her. She'd been so afraid, *more* afraid, of what Lachlan would do. What Lachlan might take from her. The woman in those notes had been paranoid, misanthropic, and reflexively cruel to herself.

Maybe, if she hadn't been, or maybe, if she'd panicked and killed Prime the way she killed Lachlan's double . . . maybe she'd still remember herself. Maybe she would never have changed.

Does that make Prime blameless?

They reach the locked basement door. Prime takes Tamsin's hand again and positions it over the keypad.

"I don't know the code," Tamsin says, but her fingers are already twitching into motion, just like with the tablet.

The lock disengages.

Prime smiles.

Tamsin latches onto that smile, that brief flare of approval, because she isn't ready to look down, not even as the door swings open. The basement has a smell to it, familiar-unfamiliar, her own sweat and bodily fluids and privation, layered over with cleaning products and a subtle staleness. Prime hasn't been down here, she thinks, not since she cleaned up after the surgery.

"Go ahead," Prime says, tilting her head toward the doorway. "Look."

And Tamsin does as she's asked.

It's her empty eye socket that's closest. She sees nothing, at first, until she turns far enough that she can see the frame, then the space beyond. Her heart twitches in her chest in a rhythm she can't translate. Fear? Yes, there's fear, but there's also longing, and revulsion, and need, and a bone-deep feeling of *coming home*. Coming home feels the worst of all of them.

Behind the door, the stairs have stretched so far that they have gone beyond treacherous to nearly impossible to traverse safely. Each riser must be at least two feet from the one below. The high-powered light that Prime had brought down for the surgery and the other floor lamps are all absent, and the ceiling lights are too dim to reach the floor.

Tamsin stands rigid at the threshold.

"It's only been six days," she says.

Prime leans against the jamb. "Everything has accelerated," she agrees, sounding vaguely satisfied. Not worried, certainly not worried.

"Because of the nodes." Tamsin turns away from the stairs, though it makes her feel as if she's about to tip backward, tumble into the shadowed depths. She clutches at the rail behind her. "What have we done?"

We, not *you*. Tamsin is sure, now, that they've both been working toward this all along. That they both existed before the door appeared. It slips out of her, but she doesn't mind now. It feels important, here at the end of the world.

If Prime notices, she gives no conclusive sign. "We thought that the absence of noise meant an absence of everything," she says after a moment, and she could be just referring to taking over Tamsin's work, but Tamsin knows she isn't. Knows, deep down, that Prime worked on the same thing, on the other side of the door. "But that's not entirely true. If you speak in an empty room, nothing is there to hear you. But if you speak in a *silent* room . . ."

"Then you're the only thing left to notice," Tamsin finishes. She looks back at the stairs. The faint shadow of the table below. She can almost make out her cot in the corner.

She can see the lintel of the door on the far wall.

Slowly, she sits down on the top step and eases her legs over the edge. Her toes find the next step, and she guides herself down. Step by step, in a controlled falling, she slides down into the dimness. Prime closes the door to the hallway and follows behind. She does not push. She does not even urge on now.

Tamsin descends because there is nowhere left to go.

The deeper she descends, the less the darkness consumes. From down here, the light seems to reach a little farther. Her eye adjusts, pupil dilating, revealing the room that is as she's always known it. The ceiling lights are tiny suns, far above. But where shadows gather, they are impenetrable. Beneath her legs are inky smears eating away at the steps.

The next one jars her ankle. It hurts, sharp and pure.

She is not dreaming.

At last, she reaches the floor. The polished cement is a different texture from the stairs, the only way she can be certain that she will not step out into an abyss if she walks forward. Rising to her feet leaves her swaying with pain. The bandages feel too tight.

She limps toward the door.

Tamsin can see it now. It is white, marked with a smear of dried blood and a few lines of ink. It gathers what little light remains and reflects it back, the only landmark in the gloom. It is so small compared to the towering walls around it but perfectly proportional to Tamsin.

"What do you feel when you look at it?" Prime asks from behind her. Her voice is hushed, almost reverent. Nowhere near the demanding, imperious Dr. Rivers of the day she cut into Tamsin's ankle.

Tamsin takes another step closer. Her hands have begun to shake. Her heart pounds. Her head swims, and the world narrows, until it is only her and the door. But there is an exhilaration, too, a brighter note on the adrenaline surge, breaking through the scrum of fear, and she is drowning in it.

Is this what it was like, when the door first appeared? Her notes recorded fascination. Obsession. Eventually, the inability to leave it, even to feed herself. She sacrificed everything to be close to the door, even knowing she couldn't open it.

"I don't know," Tamsin whispers.

Her hand flattens against it. The painted wood is smooth and cool, almost as cold as the cement beneath her feet. She slides her fingers toward the knob, but doesn't touch it yet. Just being this close makes her tremble.

I'm afraid, she tells herself, because she must be. But it doesn't feel like fear, even if the physiological reality is nearly identical to what she has felt every other time she's come this close.

"This is how you lost your eye," Prime murmurs. She is close behind Tamsin, so close Tamsin can feel the warmth radiating from her. Her body is as real as Tamsin's, as human, as fragile. "Trying to open the door. You were so desperate. I couldn't stop you. You couldn't stop yourself. I put you back together again, after."

"Is that when it happened?" Tamsin asks. She rubs at the wood, as if she can learn something from it. "When I forgot?"

"Close. Surrender is a longer process. But it marked the point of no return."

Her hand itches. Her breathing is coming rapidly now, panic and desire intertwined. She takes the knob in hand, and it begins to warm to her touch.

"What's beyond the door?" Tamsin asks.

Prime does not answer.

"You want me to open it. To go through it." She almost glances back, curious as to what Prime's face will show, but the metal of the strike plate catches a fragment of light, even with her shadow covering the wood around it. She can't look away.

"Yes."

"But I didn't come from there. You did."

"I'm no longer governed by what lies beyond it."

The confession cuts through the fixation. Tamsin turns, her hand remaining on the knob. "You know. You remember?"

"Bits and pieces. Fragments of another life." Prime strokes the backs of her knuckles along the curve of Tamsin's cheek. "They come to me in dreams. Childhood memories, failed relationships, flashes of another corporation that wrote my paycheck, another city. But they aren't mine anymore. What is real is moving to San Siroco. Being recruited by Myrica Dynamics. Years of partnership with Lachlan Woodfield. It pains me that she no longer trusts me, just like it once would have pained you."

"It does. It still does."

"Not the same way. Yours is the pain of desperation; you have nobody else, no anchor to orient from. Mine is . . ." She trails off, and Tamsin looks past her to where there is still blood on the desk. The bit of wall that Lachlan had thrown Prime into. Their interactions—Tamsin saw no pain in them. Just fury. "Mine is disappointment," Prime finishes. "She should know better than to doubt me."

Is that what Tamsin would have felt in Prime's place? It sounds hollow, thin, insubstantial. *Disappointed?* No, no, there would have been something more. Pain, as Prime said, but not out of desperation.

Out of longing. She remembers her notes, her narrative. A part of her had wanted Lachlan to see through her lies. A part of her had wanted to be rescued.

And she had been. For a time.

"Why did you resume the experiments if you knew it would damage the city?" she asks. "The program is untenable. It can't be used the way we'd planned. If it comes out that it's the cause of all this destruction, you'll never work again. You'll lose everything."

Prime sighs. "I wanted you to come home," she says. "Can you imagine what it's like to have a piece of yourself walking out in the world, never knowing where it is, never knowing what harm has come to it? If Lachlan hadn't kept you for herself, they would have cut you open. Destroyed you and learned nothing from it. I couldn't let you go to waste."

A shiver wracks her, and she leans into Prime then, her ankle no longer willing to bear her weight. Prime catches her, arm around her waist. Her hand loosens on the knob, but not entirely. She cannot bear the separation.

"You're not made for this world anymore," Prime murmurs. Her thumb brushes across Tamsin's cheekbone, just below the gauze pad covering her eye socket. "And you never will be again. But it's okay; there are other worlds for you."

Other worlds. Worlds she can ruin? Or somewhere Prime has already destroyed?

She ducks her head against Prime's shoulder. "What happens when the door opens?" Tamsin's lips graze Prime's collarbone. Her pulse is high, though not as high as Tamsin's.

"You walk through it. You'll find yourself somewhere else. Maybe my lab. Maybe my home."

"And you?"

"I'll remain here. The door will shut forever. There will be no more door." She smiles against the crown of Tamsin's head. "I'll shut down the labs again, and you'll shut them down in that other world. Chaos will go back into its box, and the exchange will be complete. But until it's complete, the city will keep sinking. It's an unstable state of affairs. There aren't supposed to be two of us."

Tamsin makes herself pull away to see if Prime is still smiling. And she is. Steady and calm. No desperation, as if she's already sure of what Tamsin will choose. "And if I don't go? What happens to the other door? Doors? How many—?"

"They'll keep appearing. More exchanges will be made."

"What was the exchange?" She cups Prime's face the way Prime is cupping hers. "What does it take, to open the door?"

302 ··· CAITLIN STARLING

"I wanted a different life," Prime says. "To know *more* of what was out there. I wanted knowledge, unrestricted. And when I walked into the abyss of the node chamber, when I found a door that had never been built, I didn't hesitate."

Tamsin thinks of a cave, of seven students, of the devil lecturing. The last to leave the room owes their soul.

The last to leave the room is a shadow, when the door opens onto brilliant light.

"If you'd found the door first, you'd have done exactly what I did."

She can still hear the soft unlocking of the door the night that Prime had left her in darkness. Slowly, she turns back to face it. Beyond that door is a room, somewhere else. And when she walks through, Prime's shadow, she'll take her place.

"The lights need to be out," she says. "To recreate the effect."

Prime pulls something from her pocket, a small remote. She taps it, and every lamp extinguishes. The walls and floor and ceiling all fall away, and it's only the two of them, twined together, the only reminder of where she starts and where she ends.

Her heart kicks up, the old panic, the instinctual fear of not being ready to leave, not being ready to leap. The lurching drop of losing track of herself, her edges unspooling into the dark. Prime had been ready when the door had appeared. Tamsin hadn't been, not after she'd lost all hold on herself.

Is she ready now?

"I'm afraid," she says.

Prime's arm around her waist retreats. She feels the loss like an erased definition. "Are you?" she asks. "Or are you excited? This is only stage fright, Dr. Rivers. Activation of the sympathetic nervous system in anticipation of a crucial performance. You chose this. You called to me, and I answered. And now we have to finish our work. Are you ready?"

Tamsin thumbs the knob and, with a shuddering breath, closes her eyes. She lets herself *feel* the pull of the doorway, buried underneath the reflexive revulsion. Another world. Another life. Something to separate her from Prime with irreversible finality. She wishes she could look at Prime one last time. One last moment of connection, of reflection; is her eagerness the same as Tamsin's anxiety? It must be. They are the same. They have always been the same.

They cannot continue to exist together.

"Yes," she says.

She turns the knob, and the latch gives way. The door opens. Not far, she doesn't think, but it's so hard to tell without any reference point. An inch? Two? Its hinges are well-oiled and make no sound. There is an abyss on the other side, the swallowing nothing of a half-remembered dream of falling, and Tamsin almost balks. Almost turns to run.

She reaches back and seizes Prime's hand. She finds it unerringly.

Prime doesn't recoil. Instead, her breath shifts over Tamsin's cheek. She's there, just beside Tamsin. Tamsin, just beside her.

"Don't hesitate," Prime says. It's not a demand; it's advice, learned and freely offered. "It will be harder if you hesitate."

And Tamsin nods, pulling the door wide. The void calls to her, and her only anchors to clutch to are the door and Prime.

She lets go of the door.

She lets go of Prime, but only for a moment. Then Prime's hand is on her shoulder, and hers is on Prime's. Mirror images, moving in synchrony, and their breathing is the same, too, their heartbeats, because the reflection and the original can only ever move together. A shadow can distort in dimension but never in action.

They both push.

And then there is nothing, nothing but the abyss around them and their screams, until her hand catches on the doorframe. Her nail tears, a bright pinpoint of pain, and she stops falling. She stumbles back into the room. Ahead of her, she sees a faint red light kindle in the darkness. She sees her own silhouette, the barest of impressions. Hair, arms, legs, unable to reach the frame in time, unable to hold on to anything at all.

The door falls shut, as if gently weighted. The latch clicks into place. She half expects frantic knocking from the other side or for the knob to turn again.

But there's nothing.

Dr. Rivers reaches out, and there is only a wall under her hand.

Trembling, she falls to her knees, hard enough to bruise. She pitches forward, breathing hard, scrabbling for some trace of sensation outside of herself, some proof that she's in her basement still. The floor is cold. The wall is solid. Sound eases back into the world, the white noise of the void replaced by the natural quiet. She can no longer hear her pulse.

Her sobs are soft at first, but grow louder as she shakes apart. The door is gone. The door is gone, and she will never step through it. She doesn't know if she shakes with relief or devastation.

Both, she thinks.

They're inseparable.

Chapter Forty-Two

From: Lachlan
We need to talk. Your house, 6 pm?
From: Tamsin
Come over.

It's been five weeks since the door disappeared. Since she turned on the lights and found her basement returned to its previous proportions. Since she repainted everything for the last time, hauled out the table, scrubbed everything clean. The railing is the only lingering change, so at home it might have always been there.

Now, with her house purged of every scrap of Prime, it's easier. Her nails are done, and her hair has been touched up professionally. She's had her ankle and her face looked at. Two eyes sit in her skull. She's stable.

Stable.

Stable, like the city is stable. No more subsidence, but the damage is ongoing. What hasn't collapsed yet may still crumble; materials and civil engineers are working overtime to evaluate every building and every inch of infrastructure still nominally intact, prioritizing what must be fixed now and what can be left another month, another year.

She has kept herself busy, these last five weeks. She goes out most days, but not to Myrica's campus and not with anybody who knows her from before. She catches up on research. She sits up late with Penrose, watching movies she's missed. Officially, she's on medical leave. Officially, she was injured in the chaos of the subsidence. Only Lachlan knows the full truth.

About a lot of things.

Lachlan's double remains the last known occurrence, though *known* is a misnomer, as only she and Lachlan are aware of the doors and their consequences at all. There's a small grave in the backyard big enough for one missing cat, Prime is gone without a trace, and Lachlan . . .

Lachlan has experience handling bodies and has promised her that she doesn't need to worry about it.

(She worries anyway, late at night. Worries that it's not actually over. Worries that Lachlan is lying when she says the door in her hallway is gone.)

They haven't seen each other since before she killed Lachlan's double, but they text. They speak on the phone. That Lachlan wants to see her is . . .

She isn't sure what it is, but she cleans up the house. She checks her liquor cabinet. She showers and dresses neatly.

It's exactly six when Lachlan knocks. Tamsin answers almost immediately, too close to the door from pacing to preserve any type of dignity. (Dignity has turned out to be both shockingly easy and stubbornly difficult to properly learn; she is not always ashamed of what she should be, but once experienced, it's almost impossible to get rid of.)

Lachlan is not in her suit. She wears her gloves along with her coat and her sweater and her slacks, but the overall effect is softer. Still guarded, but informal.

"Can I come in?" she asks.

Tamsin wasn't expecting the request. "Of course," she says and moves out of the way. Lachlan keeps space between them as she steps inside and sheds her coat.

"You look—good," Lachlan says after a moment's awkward silence. Her gaze lingers a moment too long on Tamsin's face. Her eyes.

Tamsin smiles. "Like myself again?"

Lachlan grimaces briefly, but reins herself back in. "Yes," she settles on. "And—healthier. The surgeons did a good job, I guess. I'm glad."

"You look tired," Tamsin says, holding out a hand for her coat. Lachlan hesitates, then pulls her gloves off and tucks them into the pockets before passing it over.

"Myrica is keeping me busy," Lachlan says. "I keep telling Mr. Thomas that just because I've been in war zones doesn't mean I know how to organize help, but apparently the city's disaster-response teams are managed by desk jockeys who have the wrong priorities."

"And you're volunteering."

Lachlan shrugs.

"Come on through," Tamsin says and leads Lachlan back to the living room. It's strange, remembering that for a time, Lachlan knew this house better than she did. She goes over to the liquor cabinet to get them both some bourbon, then pauses.

There's a little vial of bitters set out. A covered dish of sugar. A small container of dried blood-orange slices. She hasn't put them away, unsure of when she might need them.

Lachlan catches her looking. "Those are ours," she says, then clears her throat. "Or—yours, that you used when I visited. They go into an old-fashioned. You'll need ice, too."

Tamsin glances at her and smiles. "Do you want one, then?"

"It'd be . . ." Lachlan stuffs her hands into her pockets and sits down in an armchair, knees splayed, shoulders slightly hunched. "Nice," she settles on.

Tamsin nods and disappears into the kitchen to fetch ice (and look up the recipe quickly on her phone). When she returns and begins to build the drinks, muscle memory takes over; she adjusts proportions based on nothing but impulse, allowing herself to obey the reflex. It's usually easier that way.

Lachlan takes the glass from her and holds it to her nose. She takes a small sip, then a larger one.

"Well?"

"Just like last time," Lachlan says. Her smile's a little easier when she lowers her glass, cradling it in her lap.

Tamsin settles onto the couch across from her. The cushion is stiff, but beginning to yield, to sink beneath her weight. The sterility of the house is finally beginning to give way the more that she lives in it, interacts with it. There are fragments of her reassembling life on the coffee table, the side tables. The books have been moved around on their shelves, and the ones she wants to get to soonest have been pulled out of their orderly rows and stacked by the couch. Penrose sleeps on the windowsill on a cushion she liberated from the upstairs guest room. The blinds are up now, and beyond the window her backyard is beginning to grow wild, just so she can see what it will do.

Lachlan takes it all in.

"You said we needed to talk?" Tamsin asks when she's idly drunk enough of her cocktail to feel the alcohol buzz spreading, warm and tingling, through her limbs.

Lachlan grunts in reply but does, at last, look back at Tamsin. Her polymer fingers tap lightly against the glass. "The node labs are formally decommissioned," she says. "They're under round-the-clock surveillance until such time as we're able to get them broken down and filled back in. Understandably, it's not so high a priority that we can visibly pull resources away from the stabilization and reconstruction efforts."

"Of course not," Tamsin agrees.

"The official position is that the communications experiments never happened. Mr. Thomas's position is that you are still an employee of Myrica Dynamics." Lachlan rolls her glass in her hands. "Your team has been put under tight NDAs and reassigned to separate projects across the country, but your lab is yours again. If you want it." Her jaw is tight as she speaks, and when she finishes, she knocks back half the cocktail in one swallow.

"You think I shouldn't," Tamsin says.

"I think you're not the person you once were."

There's more to it than that. Tamsin can see it. Lachlan has her best interests at heart, most of the time, but Lachlan also knows that Tamsin's nature is responsible, directly, for the subsidence. She doesn't know the full extent, though. Tamsin has kept that part to herself.

Just like the muscle memory, she's found convenient elisions to be . . . easier.

So all Lachlan really knows is that the node labs were involved, and that Prime is gone for good. Tamsin texted Lachlan a photo of the basement wall without its door, the only proof she could give. Proof that there's no more risk.

That's not enough for Tamsin to be pulled before a court. And if Mr. Thomas wants her back in the lab, that erases all other chance of consequences.

Lachlan lives in a gray area and is fond of Tamsin, but that gives even her some pause, clearly.

Tamsin draws her legs up onto the couch, tucked up neatly. Lachlan pointedly does not glance at the movement. "Do you think I couldn't continue to do my job?" Tamsin asks.

At first, Lachlan says nothing. She looks instead at her glass, rolling the ice from side to side. Is it discomfort, or is it guilt?

Tamsin had been so afraid, before, that Lachlan would disappear her in order to fix the problem of the subsidence. Maybe she should be afraid again.

Or maybe a photo of a wall wasn't enough. Maybe Lachlan is evaluating her not in terms of safety, but of identity. Evaluating this old-fashioned against past ones.

"That's—yes, you could do your job," Lachlan says finally. She gazes at her glass, then sets it aside. "I think you *shouldn't*. I think . . ."

She trails off. She rubs at her temple.

I think I can't trust you, Tamsin fills in silently. *I think you're more dangerous when you're encouraged by Myrica. I think if you go back, you'll become more like your old self again, no matter who walked through that door. I think I never knew you at all.*

Going back is certainly a possibility. She's considered it. Exposure to her previous life doesn't spark anything in her, exactly; it doesn't bring on fragments of memory or lost behavioral tics. She is not absorbing her nature from its echoes. But Myrica Dynamics is a particular type of environment, one she was well suited for, and if she goes back, it would be simple to make herself into what she once was.

Through that door is power, and wealth, and work. She has all of her notes still. From before the basement began to sink and even after, photos of the scribblings on the basement wall before it was repainted. A decent proportion are useless, but almost half contain the kernels of . . . *something*. And pursuing that *something* would be so much easier with Myrica's backing.

Another door leads to a great blankness, indefinite, unknowable. She might never see Lachlan again if their relationship is contingent on her employment, or at least on her lack of employment with a competitor.

But Lachlan may hang around, regardless, if she's really so worried about what Tamsin might do. Who Tamsin might become. Does she want that?

Tamsin has enough savings that, from her growing understanding of finance and the larger world, she thinks she could live quite comfortably for some time, particularly if she moves to a smaller house. But it could only ever be temporary. She does not want to be a kept woman, even if she herself is doing the keeping. She has seen where that leads: the unhappiness, the disgust. Her mind needs the engagement. Needs the outlet. Eventually, if she lives a quiet life, that need will consume her.

So she'll go out into the world and find some new way to be, some new place to be in. It's overwhelming, that route. She doesn't know enough, not yet. Learning will be painful.

But she's willing to exchange pain for knowledge. She's done it before.

Both doors sit side by side. Both options stretch out before her, enticing in their own ways. The choice would be impossible if not for one thing: going through one doesn't necessarily mean never opening the other.

From across the table, Lachlan gazes at her steadily. Her glass sweats, not quite finished, not quite ready for a refill.

Tamsin smiles.

"I'll think about it," she says. "Now. Are you hungry?"

Acknowledgments

In many ways, *Last to Leave the Room* is the Book of James: my son was conceived shortly before I wrote the first draft and born (unexpectedly) a few days after I turned in the last substantial edits. As of the writing of this page, he's an incredibly funny seven-month-old, and he'll be forever inseparable from this book for me. I can't exactly say you helped, little man, but you sure did hold my feet to the fire, and I'm proud of what I managed with you along for the ride.

Speaking of the wild ride that was the last two or so years—David, thank you for being the best husband and friend through COVID, miscarriages, book drama, and two cross-country moves. I love you so much. You helped keep me sane and the city sinking, with slightly more coherent technobabble than before. This is not the Chuck Starling book you've been pushing for, but it's a step in the right direction. (And congratulations on that master's degree you got during it all!)

I wrote much of this book while living with my incredible great-aunt, Lynn Narasimhan. Thank you for taking us in during our Chicago pandemic experience; for all the jigsaw puzzles where I talked through my plotting issues; for the use of your living room floor while I desperately tried to draft this thing and your guest bed when James was sapping the life right out of me; and just for being the best aunt and friend I can imagine.

Integra and Alex: I'm not sure I can finish a single project at this point without coming crying to your digital doorsteps. Your power at helping me unfuck my manuscripts is unmatched. The relentless cheerleading all the while just feels over-the-top indulgent. Thank you, so much, for being my friends and rubber ducklings.

To the entire Murder Basement: thank you for the support, the writing sprints, and the brainstorming sessions where I ripped out my hair over exactly how to pull off that doctor scene. I hope you all enjoy the particular screwy flavor of this book.

To Florian and Dan, with whom I first created the character who would one day become Dr. Tamsin Rivers—she's a little different from the Sileust you knew back in the days of Gaia Online, but she wouldn't exist at all without you.

Lachlan's prosthetic limbs are based on current technology, but accelerated a decade or so, as befits a woman working for a shady cutting-edge tech company. A big thank-you to Chelsea, who listened to what I'd researched on my own, helped me adjust to something feasible, and otherwise was a fantastically generous resource for figuring out what Lachlan's at-home life might look like. All remaining mistakes are absolutely my own.

The team at St. Martin's Press has truly been a joy to work with, and I'm so glad I've gotten to do a second project with you all! Sylvan Creekmore, thank you for helping me turn a seed of an idea into a novel, and giving invaluable feedback on the first draft. Sallie Lotz, your new perspective gained Tamsin an entire integral hair arc, among other fantastic edits. Michael Homler and Cassidy Graham, thank you for joining for the home stretch and getting things over the finish line—I can't wait to see what we do together next.

Rivka Holler, in marketing, is a genius and a champion. Kirsten Aldrich, thank you for wrangling my wildly variable styles into a coherently copyedited whole. Olga Grlic, the cover of this hardcover edition is beyond beautiful and entirely spooky. The devil teaches her pupils in a basement in San Siroco . . .

To my agent, Caitlin McDonald—we pulled off another one! I'm so glad to still be working with you. You help shape and find the best homes for my twisted little stories. Here's to many more!

And to all my readers who have followed me from exoplanet caves to pseudo-Victorian mansions to this relentlessly expanding basement, thank you for all your support, and I hope you've enjoyed the journey.